A JOURNEYMAN SERIES

JOURNEY
TO THE LAND OF
INTEGRITY

BRUCE BECK

CLAY BRIDGES
PRESS

To my grandsons Elijah, Noah, Micah, Jesiah, and Andrew.
You fill my heart with joy as I watch you grow and become young
men of faith and character. There is a wonderful, beautiful world to
explore, but it needs men and women of integrity. Walk with a clearly
defined path, set your heart on daily hearing from God, and be men of
integrity. Those who walk in this way will change the world.

TABLE OF CONTENTS

SPECIAL THANKS

Special thanks to Rachel Boulos, who coached me through understanding fiction writing. Your hours of helping me define plot and characters were invaluable. You challenged me to get to know my characters, which took me to such a deeper relationship with each of them.

Also, special thanks to the Lucid Team and all their help in putting this book together. Your professionalism, teamwork, and process were exceptional.

PREFACE

A few years ago, my son-in-law asked me to participate in a project with his eldest son, my grandson, Elijah. He was turning 13 years old and beginning a whole new phase of life as a teenager. His father asked me and four other men to invest a year in mentoring Elijah on specific topics. The topic he gave me was integrity.

The idea of integrity is not new. However, this launched me on a personal journey of reflection and introspection. How do I not only explain what integrity is but rather help him understand that integrity is birthed from character, and character comes from clearly defined values, and values are developed through faith and family. As a Christian, I found that listening carefully to the call of God through the power of the Holy Spirit and scripture provides clarity and direction. Ultimately, obedience is required to heed the call.

We live in a complex, rapidly changing world that can be confusing. We are tempted to compromise, cut corners, shade the truth, and sometimes simply walk past the needs surrounding us. Walking with integrity means we must be open to hearing the call to action, doing the right thing despite the cost.

I spent time with Elijah over the year, just having fun as grandfather and grandson, but we also used the opportunity to talk about integrity. Through our one-on-one time, I came to realize how much he loved reading fantasy books, and an idea was birthed to write a short story where integrity was the main theme. I started writing, and it grew and grew. A book was birthed. It became a labor of love for not just Elijah but all my grandsons. Perhaps someday they may pull down a dusty old book from their bookshelf and hand it to their grandson.

In *Journey to the Land of Integrity,* we follow Isaiah, a young teenager who struggles to fit in at school and deals with intimidation and bullying by upperclassmen. He makes a bad choice and finds himself struggling with a dark secret. A secret that is robbing his joy, creating depression, and impacting his relationships with his family and friends. As he struggles to simply get through each day, a kind, wise old woman tells him about a mystical land called the Land of Integrity.

Isaiah is ultimately led on a journey to this mystical land that not only exposes his weaknesses and fears but also shows him how to walk as a man of integrity. Isaiah's journey is filled with intrigue and danger, and many new relationships that have their own secrets as well as enemies who are bent on destroying him.

It is my hope that this story will be both entertaining and thought-provoking for the reader. That each reader simply ask, *Am I walking as a man or woman of integrity? Am I listening to the Voice? What lie is the enemy trying to tell me? Where do I need to take a stand in my own life as a man or woman of integrity?*

CHAPTER 1
RIGHT THING

Isaiah ran across the brick alley and hid behind some crates filled with trash. His eyes darted back and forth down the alley, and his heart pounded in his chest. He wanted to get far away from this place. People were running out of their homes and down the main street, yelling. He couldn't quite make out what they were saying, but he knew one thing: he wanted to get as far away as possible from this alley...right now!

It was as if the entire town had erupted into chaos. He peered out from behind the crate and saw three men run by on the main street carrying something in their arms. It happened so fast that he couldn't tell what they were carrying. They were soon followed by others, and then a couple of men stopped at the alley entrance and turned and started to run down it. Isaiah forced himself as far behind the crate as he could, so he was wedged between the crate and a building wall. As they ran by, he tucked his head even further behind the crate. They ran past and kept going, oblivious to Isaiah's presence in the alley.

Isaiah stuck his head out and realized his hiding place would only last so long. More men started to come down the alley and run past him; it was simply a matter of time until someone saw him. He knew he had to take a chance and get out of this alley as quickly as possible. He looked across the street and saw Sawyer's Grist Mill. A place where local farmers brought their grain to be ground into flour. He was very familiar with the mill since he and his friends often hung out behind it on the banks of the river. He waited until more people ran by him on the main street and then darted across the street to the front steps of the porch that wrapped around the grist mill. He sprinted up the steps and lay flat on the porch in the shadows and prayed that nobody saw him. He was breathing hard and felt exposed, and he knew it was only a matter of time until someone saw him. He crawled down the porch and found a window left partially open. He nervously looked around and quickly pushed the window up and slid through the open window into the grist mill and closed it behind him.

For the moment, he could catch his breath and gather his thoughts in the blackness of the mill. *What had just happened,* he thought to himself. What started out as a night of excitement and hanging out with older classmates had suddenly turned into a nightmare. Thoughts raced through his mind: *Why did Jason and Brian leave him? I thought we were friends. It all seemed so stupid.* He still heard shouts outside and saw a strange glow. He crept over to the window while making sure he stayed in the shadows and peered out the window toward the cookie shop. He stepped back from the window and made an audible gasp. Granny Rose's store was on fire with men running around dumping buckets of water. He plopped on the floor and began to shake uncontrollably. *What has he gotten himself into?* Suddenly, Isaiah heard a noise outside and slid back to the window just in time to see four men walking directly toward the grist mill.

The entire mill was in darkness except for the yellow glow coming through the windows from across the street. Isaiah didn't make a sound but leaned back against the wall and stayed in the shadows.

He could feel his heart pounding and his breathing increasing. Sweat appeared on his brow and ran down his face. He was scared and afraid that his beating heart and breathing would give him away. The men reached the front door and rattled the locked door. He could hear one of them say, "I am sure I saw someone come in here. Let's try another door."

Isaiah could hear the repeated thud of men as they walked around the wooden porch to another door and tried the handle, which was also locked. He breathed a sigh of relief and thought they would simply turn away, but unexpectedly, he heard the sound of keys rattling.

"Here, I've got a key to this building somewhere," stated one of the men. This was followed by the sound of a door opening.

Isaiah's heart was pounding so hard that he wanted to just jump up and run out the door, but he had no idea where the men were in the building. He looked around the room for somewhere to hide, when suddenly he heard footsteps getting nearer to his hiding place. He looked frantically at the door to the room and waited for a shadowy figure to appear any moment, when he saw out of the corner of his eye a large grain chest with a lid. Without any other options, he slid over to the bin and cracked the lid open – it was empty. He jumped up, lifted the lid, and slid his young frame down into the bin while he tried not to make a sound. Just as he closed the lid, he saw through a crack in the bin two shadowy figures appear at the doorway.

Isaiah did his best to calm down and not breathe too hard, but the floor creaked as the men walked around the floor looking in the dark for any sign of anyone. One of the men leaned against the bin and started talking to the other, "It doesn't look like we'll be able to save much of that shop. Too bad. Granny Rose is such a good lady. I don't see anyone in here, let's head on back."

Isaiah peered through the crack in the bin and caught the shiny glint of sheriff's badges on each man. *These men are sheriff deputies. I am going to jail.*

Isaiah stayed in the bin for quite a while until he was sure they were gone, and then he slowly opened the lid and climbed out. He stood in the darkness of the room and continued to shake as he began to grasp the seriousness of the situation and how close he had come to being caught, but then it hit him ... *I need to get home ... right now!*

Isaiah was very familiar with the old grist mill and riverbanks behind it. He knew there was a small trail that led along the river and through the woods back toward his home. If he could get to that trail, he could slip away and get home undetected. He swiftly slipped out a back door into the cool night air and headed across the mill yard in the direction of the path. The sweat on his face and arms now made him feel chilly as the cool night air hit him. To his left was the river with the L-shaped mill building behind him and on his right. Halfway across the yard, he heard voices from just around the corner of the building. "I forgot to check back here. Let's just swing through and make sure nobody's back here."

Isaiah swung his head around in the direction of the voices and realized a couple of the deputies were headed his way. He started to panic but then saw an old stone well in the middle of the yard. It was his only chance to hide. He and his buddies had played around that old well and actually crawled down into it to explore. He knew it was a shallow dry well, and six to eight feet down was filled with dirt and grasses at the bottom. He ran to it and climbed over the stone wall and dropped into it just as the deputies rounded the corner.

The deputies started checking the windows and rattling doorknobs. Isaiah listened and began to worry if he had closed and locked the back door. He soon heard one of the deputies call to the other, "Hey, this door is not locked." The other deputy joined him and examined the door.

Isaiah held his breath and trembled as sweat ran down his face. The deputies locked the door and began to cross the yard to look around. Isaiah pressed his body as flat as possible into the shadows of the well. He simply had to wait for the deputies to leave and hope they didn't look down into the well. It gave him time to review the events of the evening.

Three hours earlier

Isaiah had no idea his life was about to change, but he knew one thing: if he didn't show up tonight, he would never live it down. They would find a way to make his life miserable ... and he was no coward.

"Come on, Dad. I'm just helping a friend." Isaiah shoved food around on his plate and looked up to see his father raise an eyebrow.

Charles Owens's eyes showed fatigue as he listened to his son, Isaiah. His sweat-stained plaid shirt was typical for a hard day's work in the mill or the fields. One day blended into another as he worked to support his family. Charles rubbed his chin with a calloused hand as he considered Isaiah's request. He reached for his glass, clanging it against his plate as he lifted it to take a drink.

"No, it's too late to be out."

Isaiah grimaced. When Jason had pulled him aside earlier at school and told him to be downtown at 9 p.m., Isaiah was shocked. He knew he'd have to do some fast talking if he was going to convince his parents to let him come.

"It's a school night, Isaiah, and that's simply too late," added his mother, Ester. She spooned more soup from the stove and placed it before Charles, wiping her hands on her apron.

Isaiah took a deep breath and looked at her with wide eyes as if pleading for some help with his father's decision. "Yes, but I have already completed all my homework, and tomorrow is an easy day at school. There are no tests."

A lump formed in his throat along with a sense of panic as he realized that his father had said, "No." The panic raced through his mind. *He would be embarrassed, and Jason and Brian would destroy him. He was going to become a laughingstock at school. He could hear them now, "Little boy couldn't come out because it was too late."*

As Ester sat back down at the family table and looked at Charles, Isaiah saw a potential crack in their parental alliance. She cocked her head, raised an eyebrow at Charles, and spooned mashed potatoes onto her plate.

Charles gave her a slight smile back and asked Isaiah, "Who exactly are the boys you want to meet downtown?"

Isaiah felt a rush of hope flood through his spirit, and for the first time, he felt there was a real chance of changing his father's mind. He quickly responded, "Jason, whose dad you know, Mr. Hunter. He owns the general store. You and Mom shop there all the time. Oh yeah, and Brian, another kid at school."

"Brian and Jason? I thought they were the ones..." asked his brother, Caleb,

"...that need help moving boxes out of the store." Isaiah abruptly finished as he gave his brother Caleb a piercing stare. Caleb's eyes narrowed in disapproval as he realized his older brother was shutting him down. He looked over at his younger brother Zac and gave a small shake of his head, showing his disapproval.

"Wait..." chimed in Zac, "isn't Brian the one who always asks Peter..."

"No, I'm sure it's not the same, Brian."

Zac looked back at Caleb and shrugged as he realized his older brother was also not going to let him speak. Isaiah saw Zac and Caleb exchange glances across the table, but neither said anything more. It seemed like they were going along with it... for now. Isaiah knew the rumors circulating at school, but he didn't believe them. He just hoped his brothers wouldn't repeat them as soon as he left the table.

"Jason's dad, Bill Hunter, is a family friend," said Ester. "And he has been so good to our family. He always gives me a discount on goods at his store. Maybe it's not such a bad idea to let Isaiah help him."

Ester passed a plate of potatoes to Caleb and gave an encouraging nod toward Charles. Isaiah's heart leaped as he suddenly realized that his mom had become his advocate.

Charles leaned back in his chair. "How long will it take?"

"No more than an hour."

Charles took a deep breath and glanced at Ester, and then there was a long pause. "Isaiah, I just don't feel right about you going down there tonight. So, the answer is still, 'No.'"

Ester recognized Isaiah's disappointment and put a hand on his shoulder as she began removing plates from the table. She knew, as a mother, this was a big deal for her oldest son, and it was part of growing up, a rite of passage. She understood his disappointment but also knew it was important for him to respect his father's decision. Isaiah looked at his glass of water and took a big gulp and then asked to be excused. He got up from the table, went to his room, and shut the door.

Isaiah lay on his bed and stared at the ceiling. *Why did his dad not let him go? How could he do this to him? He was treating him like a baby. He was growing up, and all his friends were often out much later. His dad just didn't care about him. Jason and Brian are going to destroy him.* He pounded his fist into a pillow, and the longer he lay there, the angrier he became. He looked at the clock, and it was now 8:20. He was supposed to meet Jason and Brian at 9:00. His dad went to bed early because he often got to the lumber mill around 5:30 in the morning. Isaiah looked at the clock and his bedroom window. He took a deep breath and said to himself, "Why not?" and climbed off his bed and grabbed some blankets and extra pillows and began stuffing them under his covers. He pulled the cover up and, with his hands, shaped the outline of a body under it. He stepped back and said, "Not bad, looks pretty real."

At 8:30 p.m., Isaiah put on his jacket, turned off the lights, and headed over to his bedroom window and slid it open. He had climbed out this window many times and slid across the attached porch to a nearby tree limb. He quietly climbed onto the tree and worked his way to the ground without anybody hearing him.

He walked taller and felt independent...grown up. He was on a mission tonight to hang out with the in-crowd. Jason and Brian were a couple of years older than he was, and he wanted them to think he was cool and mature. He had not known them well until a couple of weeks earlier, when they had just started to talk and hang out during lunch periods.

Everyone in the school knew Brian and Jason. They were two of the school's best athletes and were very popular. The school year had just started a few weeks previously, and already the pecking order had been established. Initially, Isaiah felt out of place, unsure of where he fit in. The upperclassmen were physically bigger, stronger, and seemed more confident in every way. Isaiah felt fortunate that both Brian and Jason had befriended him despite him being several years younger. He wanted to keep it that way, which was why it was so important to show up when Jason asked for his help.

Isaiah thought about his new friendship with Jason and Brian. When they started talking to him a few weeks ago at school, he was shocked they even knew he existed. He usually spent time with a couple of friends in his class but recently started to spend more time with Jason and Brian. He started to eat lunch at their table, and after school, he often hung out with them behind the old grist mill where they shot their slingshots at bottles across the small river. He found out that Jason and Brian were normal guys, and he had to admit that it felt good being seen as one of the in-crowd. He seemed to have found his place at school, and it allowed him to walk a little taller and feel more confident.

The Owens' family lived on a small farm outside the little town of Providence. It was late summer, and the sun was setting earlier each night. As it disappeared, the temperatures dropped, and a slight chill filled the air. It would not be long before summer would be history and give way to changing leaves and brisk nights of autumn. Isaiah pulled his jacket closer around his neck as a breeze hit him in the face, and he shuddered.

As he came to the edge of town, he could see lights still on at Doc Mahoney's office. He was obviously working late tonight. He was the town's only doctor and had practiced for nearly 30 years out of this same house. He had delivered nearly every kid in the town and even a few of their parents. His office was on the first floor of his two-story house. A large, covered porch ran across the front of the house with two rocking chairs and a porch swing.

Several other small shops lined the simple downtown area, including a barber shop where men of the town gathered every day to discuss and debate the issues of the day. The shop's purpose was denoted by a large barber pole hung outside the shop. The shop itself was small with only two barber chairs and a row of chairs opposite the barber chairs where customers waited, while others often just sat and visited with no intent of getting a haircut.

He continued to walk toward the center of town but couldn't help but notice the most impressive building in the town, a limestone bank building with several large columns across the front. Broad steps ran up to a portico, and massive, heavy doors created an image of security and wealth. A clock tower jutted above the roof line with a clock that tolled every hour.

Next up was a town favorite, Granny Rose's Cookie and Candy Shop. This was a two-story shop that sold the best cookies and candies in the entire region. People would come from miles around to buy cookies and candy from the long glass counters that ran the length of the store. Granny Rose, who owned the shop, was a treat in herself. She was loved by everyone and seen as a grandma figure. She had a way of making every person who came into her shop feel special and very loved. Isaiah's family had known Granny Rose for years. She had even babysat him when he was younger. She was family.

Across the street was Sawyer Grist Mill. Farmers would bring their grain here and have it ground into flour by the water-driven grinding stone. A large water wheel hung on the back of the building, which was turned by flowing water from the river that ran behind the building. The building was three stories with a covered porch that ran across the front and down one side.

And finally, across from the grist mill was the large building that housed Hunter's General Store, which sold everything from vegetables and dry goods to tools and clothing. If you needed it, Hunter's was a good place to go. His parents shopped there often for everything from food to clothing to parts and tools for the farm and mill. A large sign hung over the covered porch with their name and slogan, "*Hunter's General Store: If we don't have it, we can get it.*"

Isaiah stopped and looked around for Jason and Brian, but then remembered that Jason had told him to meet them in the alley behind the store. He rounded the building and saw an old truck in the alley with Jason and Brian standing beside it.

"Hey, Jason and Brian, I'm here," called out Isaiah.

Jason turned with a frown on his face as he looked a little perturbed by Isaiah's greeting. "Shh, shh, we don't need to make a lot of noise."

"Ah, yeah... don't want to wake the neighbors," added Brian.

The response seemed a bit strange to Isaiah since it wasn't that late, but he thought, *Oh well, whatever, Jason's in charge.*

Jason unlocked the door, and they began removing boxes from the back of the store into the old pickup truck. About a half hour passed, and they had removed a number of boxes, and Jason looked at Brian and said, "That'll do." And then he pulled a tarp over the bed of the truck and secured it tightly so no one could see what was in the bed.

Brian looked at Jason and said, "I'm hungry, how about some of Granny Rose's cookies?" Jason smiled and said, "Sure," and headed down the alley toward Granny Rose's cookie store. Granny was a legend in Providence and had run the store for as long as anyone could remember. She made the best candies and cookies in the entire region, and people who came into town to shop always made sure they stopped at her store.

Isaiah trailed behind Jason and Brian, a bit confused, as it was heading toward 10:00 and Granny's store had been closed for hours. Jason got to the back of her store and turned to Isaiah and said, "I need you to go to the end of the alley and keep a lookout for us. If anyone comes toward this alley, knock on this door three times."

Isaiah was stunned. *What exactly was he being asked to do?* His heart raced and sweat began to appear on his forehead.

"What, what are you doing?" he asked.

"Why, we're getting some cookies, you'll love'em. She bakes them fresh before she leaves each evening, so when she opens, she has fresh cookies," stated Brian very matter-of-factly.

"But she's closed, ...are you, ...are you going to break into her store?"

"Well, I don't look at it quite like that. Granny is always giving out free cookies. She won't mind. We will be in and out, and she will never know we were even here. She won't mind; we've done this plenty of times."

Isaiah's stomach was turning. He wondered, *What did I get myself into?* But he stayed quiet and simply nodded at Jason and Brian and turned and walked down the alley to the corner in a daze. Everything had suddenly turned from feeling like a part of the "in-crowd" to feeling guilty and fearful. He didn't know what to do; he didn't want to just run away. He'd never live that down, and these guys would make his life miserable.

Isaiah reluctantly took his position and glanced back down the alley. He could see Jason hoist Brian up on a low roof section. Brian rapidly went to a window, slid it open, and climbed in, entering the second floor of the dark store. Seconds later, the back door opened, and Jason entered the cookie store.

Isaiah's focus was suddenly interrupted as he heard a sound coming from down the street. He peered around the corner and saw a deputy sheriff going door to door of shops, checking to make sure they were locked. Isaiah froze in fear. *What should he do?* The deputy moved from door to door, and finally, Isaiah bolted toward the back door of the cookie shop and knocked rapidly three times on the door. His heart was pounding so fast he thought it was going to explode out of his chest. It seemed like forever, but finally Jason opened the door and Isaiah stammered out, "Dep… dep… deputy coming!" Jason looked down the alley and could see the deputy walking toward the shop. He spun and, with a loud whisper, said to Brian, "We have to go…now!"

Isaiah heard a loud crash sound from inside the store, which was followed by both Jason and Brian running right by him, pushing him to the ground. They ran down the alley and turned the corner, where they jumped onto the truck and began driving it immediately out of town.

Isaiah sat on the cobblestone alley in the dark, dazed and terrified. The deputy had heard the noise and gone to the front door of the store. In the meantime, Isaiah stumbled to his feet, looked around, and thought: *What do I do?* Finally, he ran down the alley in the same direction taken by Jason and Brian, but they were nowhere to be seen, having left in the truck. In the meantime, he heard yelling coming from the front of the store and realized he needed to get away as fast as he could.

* * *

The deputies finally left, and Isaiah crawled out of the well and found the trail along the river. He worked his way back to the house, climbed the tree, tiptoed across the porch roof, slid open his bedroom window, and climbed back into his room.

In the darkness, he plopped on his bed and stared at the ceiling. Tears began to stream down his face. He thought to himself: *What have I done? What just happened, and why didn't he do anything to stop it? Why did he not listen to his dad?*

CHAPTER 2
GRANNY ROSE

The next morning, Isaiah woke from a deep sleep and realized he needed to hurry, or he would be late for school. He jumped out of bed, shook his head to clear away the sleep, and looked down at his wrinkled clothes that he had slept in. He quickly pulled off his dirty, wrinkled plaid shirt and stuck his arms through the sleeves of a fresh one from his closet. He bounded down the stairs, grabbed a biscuit and the lunch his mom had packed, and was out the door and on his way to school.

Before school, everyone was talking about the fire at Granny Rose's the night before. The firefighters had managed to put the fire out, but not before extensive damage was done to the shop. Granny would be out of business for quite some time...maybe forever. People speculated on how the fire happened with various theories that included that it started in the kitchen, that a kerosine lantern was left burning, or some even suggested...arson. Isaiah stayed quiet in the hallway during conversations and prayed that no one would ask him for his thoughts. He was grateful when the school bell finally rang to start classes.

By lunch, Isaiah just wanted to get away from everyone to avoid any questions or comments about the previous evening. He walked to an old shed behind the school and sat on a log to eat the sandwich his mom had prepared for him. He took a bite and felt a hard thud against the wall of the shed, followed by angry voices. He looked around the corner and saw Jason and Brian shoving a blond-haired kid back and forth between them. Isaiah recognized the much smaller kid as Peter, a very nice and smart kid who was in the same grade as Jason and Brian.

Jason grabbed the collar of Peter's shirt and pulled him close. "I told you, Peter, cough up your math homework from last night. I was kind of busy and need to copy it!" Jason demanded.

Peter stammered back, "I...I can't do that. It would be cheating. It's...it's not fair."

"Shut up, Peter," growled Jason with a deep, menacing whisper, "Just give me your homework." He slammed Peter to the ground and kicked him in the stomach.

Brian reached into Peter's bag, found what he was looking for, and tore it out of his notebook. "Here it is, we got it, now let's go."

Isaiah stood frozen at the corner of the shed, trying to process the scene he had just witnessed. The sandwich he was holding fell out of his hand and hit the ground. Both Jason and Brian looked up and saw Isaiah standing there frozen with a stunned look on his face. He had watched it all.

"Hey, Isaiah, you keep your mouth shut, you hear? Nothing about this or what happened last night. Nothing...and I mean nothing if you know what's good for you," snarled Jason. "Remember, we know your brothers."

Jason and Brian took off around the building, and a stunned Isaiah slowly walked out into the open, watching them as they disappeared. Isaiah now stood over Peter, who was still gasping for air from being kicked in the stomach. Peter, now covered in dirt with a torn shirt, slowly got to his feet and began to gather his remaining materials from his bag. Isaiah didn't know what to say; he was speechless at the violence he had just witnessed. Peter stared into Isaiah's eyes, bewildered and angry with a look that said, *Why didn't you do anything?*

Isaiah felt exposed, and an overwhelming guilt swept over him. "What is wrong with me?" he said out loud, "I just stood there and did nothing."

* * *

Over the next several days, cleanup had begun at Granny's cookie shop, and school returned to its normal pace, but Isaiah saw very little of Jason and Brian. They no longer seemed interested in associating with Isaiah, which was just fine to him. However, Isaiah internally struggled to process everything that had taken place. He felt guilty for being involved in any way with the break-in and fire.

A week later, at a town council meeting, the investigation by the local fire chief determined that a small kerosene lantern had apparently been left burning in the store office and caused the fire. In reality, Brian had lit the lantern and set it on the floor. When Jason had yelled that they should go, he had kicked it over in his haste to get out the door. Kerosine spilled out and the flame lit it as it spread across the wooden office floor.

Granny Rose quietly listened to the explanation by the fire chief but knew she had not lit the lantern and that something more sinister was going on.

Since the fire, Charles and Ester had noticed that Isaiah had been quieter than normal. He had little to say at dinner and often retreated to his room right after dinner. They talked about it but decided to give it some time.

Several days after the fire chief's report to the town council, Isaiah walked home from school alone, and his path took him right past Granny Rose's damaged store. A pit formed in his stomach, and he looked down to avoid seeing the store. He quickened his pace to get by it when a voice halted him.

"Hello, Isaiah. How are you?" Isaiah turned to see Granny Rose sitting on a bench under a big oak tree directly across from her store. The pit in his stomach grew bigger.

"Oh…hello, Granny. F…fine…I guess."

"Well, come here and sit with me a bit." Granny patted the wooden bench with an old, leathery hand. "We haven't talked in forever."

Isaiah's eyes darted back and forth as he tried not to make eye contact with Granny. "I'm in a bit of a hurry, Granny,"

"Oh, nonsense. You can sit with me for a few minutes," replied Granny as she grabbed her bag off the bench to make room for him and pointed to the empty bench seat beside her. He realized there would be no further discussion.

Granny Rose was not an easy person to say no to. She was a seventy-five-year-old woman with striking gray hair distinguished by its gentle waves and curls. Her wrinkles told a story of a fulfilled, adventuresome life. She usually walked at the pace of a person half her age and always had boundless energy. Isaiah loved her like a grandmother and had known her his whole life. She had babysat for him and his brothers when he was younger, and she attended the same church as his family. She was a remarkable woman with incredible wisdom who lived out the Good Book in words and deeds. She had the ability to look right into your heart. Yes, Granny Rose was very tuned into the Owens family.

This scared him. *Would she see right into Isaiah's soul and see the terrible secret he held?* Part of him wanted to jump up and run, and yet, another part of him wanted to just open up and tell her everything that happened and get it all off his chest. To cleanse his soul once and for all of the weight of his dark secret.

"Ok," said Isaiah somewhat reluctantly. He strode over to the bench and slid into the seat next to her. Seeing the charred remains across the street seared his heart. "Ah... Granny...I am so sorry about your store...and you know...the fire."

"Oh, that old store? That's nothing. We'll rebuild and make it better. I've been through so much worse, and the good Lord has always provided and taken care of me."

Isaiah was amazed at her resilience and positive attitude.

"No, this will be no problem." She waved her hand in the air and pointed toward the charred building. As she talked, she pointed to specific areas of the building as if painting a picture. "I already have put some plans together for the rebuild. A new display cabinet in the front, and we'll have more space in the back for people to sit and visit, and a surprise...I am adding pies to the menu," she giggled.

Isaiah was jealous of her joy, considering the heaviness he felt. He looked at her, and she stopped giggling and looked deep into his eyes. "What's troubling you, young Isaiah?"

Isaiah was taken aback by the question and didn't know how to answer it. Tears began to well up inside his eyes, and he turned his head, blinking several times to fight them back. She peered deeply into his eyes, and time seemed to freeze. Then a gentle, peaceful smile appeared across her face as if it said, *It's okay, you're safe here.*

"Granny, how do you know what the right thing is to do?"

There was silence for a moment, and a gentle breeze rustled the oak leaves above them. Her eyes grew distant as if focused on a memory from long ago. Isaiah waited, knowing whatever she was about to say would be full of love, compassion, and wisdom. Granny tilted her head back and closed her eyes while taking a deep breath as the breeze grew stronger and flowed through her gray curls. A gentle smile crossed her face before she spoke. "It's interesting what you asked me: how do you know what the right thing is to do? That implies that there is a right thing to do, and that you want to do it... that is good, yes...very good." She smiled at him and pulled Isaiah into a side embrace.

Granny spoke softly, "Isaiah, every man and woman must wrestle with understanding and acting with integrity. They must choose their path, and it ultimately defines their character. Some are even called to make a special journey to the Land of Integrity."

Isaiah looked up at her, perplexed. *What is she talking about? Land of Integrity? Nobody talks like that these days.* Integrity was rarely used in conversations, and Isaiah wasn't even sure if he could define it. In fact, many people, especially those of Isaiah's age, didn't understand what it meant. He stared directly at Granny Rose and asked, "What do you mean by the Land of Integrity?"

Granny gently patted Isaiah's arm and smiled. "The Land of Integrity is the name some of us have come to call it."

Isaiah leaned back with a puzzled look. "You mean it's an actual place, not just some expression or folklore?"

Granny smiled and said, "Of course it exists, but few have traveled there. It is a very special place...many lessons to be learned in the Land of Integrity, many treasures to be found."

Isaiah had now become deeply focused on every word that came out of Granny. "Have you...have you ever been there?" stammered Isaiah.

Granny smiled and said, "Why of course, but that's a discussion for another day."

"Where, I mean...how do you find it?" asked a wide-eyed Isaiah.

Granny paused as if contemplating what she was about to say. She pulled Isaiah closer. Her voice dropped, and her smile disappeared. Her words became more deliberate as she peered deeply into his eyes and very soul. Finally, she spoke, "You don't find it, it finds you. But when it does find you, your life will be changed forever." She then let go of Isaiah and smiled. "Perhaps it will call for you someday. Keep your ears and heart open. Yes…I think you will be on a journey soon, very soon."

With that said, Granny stood up. "Well, that's enough of that. I must be off to fix dinner. Perhaps we will talk again in the future of some glorious adventure." She started to walk away, but suddenly stopped, spun around, and called back to Isaiah. "You know, I won't miss the store because we'll make it even better. But strangely…a box I had in my safe with some very personal items turned up missing. It was strange, yes, very strange…that box…that I will surely miss." She then winked at Isaiah and strode off down the street with the pace of a much younger woman.

Isaiah stood there now in the early twilight and tried to process all he had just heard: Land of Integrity, Journey…and a box…a special box. Suddenly, an image flashed through his mind of Brian bolting out of the cookie shop that night while carrying something under one arm. *Was it a box?* Isaiah wondered. *It could have been. It was just so dark, and things were happening so quickly. Did Brian and Jason break into Granny's safe to steal her box? Possibly, but why?*

Isaiah went home, hastily ate supper and headed up to his room as he had been doing. He continued to struggle with the events with Jason, Brian, and his involvement. Lying on his bed, Isaiah replayed it all in his head. *I knew what they were doing was wrong, but why didn't I try to stop them? Was I just afraid? Was I intimidated by them? Why didn't I try to stop them from attacking Peter? Why have I not gone to my mom and dad? Would Jason and Brian really hurt my brothers?*

The longer he thought about the situation, the angrier he became. He was, of course, angry at Jason and Brian for their deception and intimidation. They weren't trying to be his friend. They simply wanted to use him. But Isaiah was also angry at himself for not stepping up to do anything. *Maybe I am a coward,* he thought to himself.

Suddenly, there was a knock on his door, and a voice from the other side interrupted his thoughts.

"Hello…Can I come in?" It was his father, Charles.

Isaiah quickly wiped the tears that had begun to flow down his cheeks.

"Ah…of course, Dad. I …I just wanted to get some rest. Been a long week at school."

Charles opened the door and stepped into the low-lit room, which Isaiah was thankful for since it hid his red eyes. Charles held up an apple and asked, "Would you like an apple, son? You didn't eat much at dinner."

"Ah… no thanks, Dad, not hungry."

Charles leaned against the bedroom wall and took a bite out of the apple, chewing it slowly as if contemplating his next words.

"Are you okay, son?" asked Charles.

"Oh, yeah, Dad…just fine," Isaiah lied. Nothing was fine. He felt lost with a heavy weight in his chest.

"Well, your mother and I have been concerned about you. Over the last week or so, we have noticed you've been very quiet at dinner and just come up to your room and spend the evenings by yourself. What's going on? Do you want to talk about it?"

Isaiah looked up and responded, "Oh no, I'm okay, just got a lot on my mind. School's harder this year and we just started… you know."

"Well, school does get more and more challenging as you get older. Is there anything else you'd like to talk about?" asked Charles as he studied his son.

Isaiah started to deflect once again, but stopped and blurted out, "Have you ever talked to Granny Rose about the Land of Integrity?"

Charles swallowed his last bite of apple. He stood straight up as his facial expression became very serious. There was no smile now, but through tired eyes from a hard day of work, he stared directly at his oldest son and listened intently. A silence hung in the room as he considered how to respond to him.

At first, Isaiah thought he may have asked a forbidden question, but after a few awkward seconds of silence, Charles' posture relaxed slowly as he moved closer to Isaiah and sat on the corner of the bed. His gaze was still penetrating as if searching for something.

"What exactly did Granny say to you today?" Charles asked.

"Ah…she said, the Land of Integrity is what some people call it, but it has other names," Isaiah said, hoping this would satisfy his father.

"And what prompted this conversation?"

Isaiah felt nervous and sat up in his bed, adjusting his covers while trying not to make direct eye contact. He searched for words to describe why this subject had come up. "Oh, I asked her about how people know the right thing to do and stuff like that," he responded while hoping this would end his father's questions.

"And her answer?" asked Charles, clearly waiting for a response.

"Well…she said it's interesting what I asked her. That my question implies that there is a right thing to do and that I want to do it."

Charles leaned forward and didn't take his eyes off Isaiah's eyes as he listened intently.

"Oh yeah, and then she said…that is good, yes…very good."

Isaiah felt a bit more confident as he blurted out, "And she said perhaps I can go on a journey to the Land of Integrity or whatever… but…but she then said something very strange, almost like a riddle. She said, 'You don't find it, it finds you. But when it does find you, your life will be changed forever…' and perhaps it will come looking for me someday. She told me to keep my ears and heart open to hear the call because I would be going on a journey soon…very soon."

A small smile crept across Charles's face, "Of course she did."

Charles started to leave the room but stopped at the door and turned around to face Isaiah.

"Tomorrow is Friday, and we haven't camped overnight in a long time. Get your backpack ready. I'll pick you up early from school."

Isaiah knew the look on his father's face and the tone of his voice. It wasn't a question or issue for debate. He would be ready.

Isaiah dozed off to sleep from emotional exhaustion, but around 4 a.m., he awoke, staring at the ceiling of his room. Granny's words replayed over and over in his mind: *lessons to be learned, treasures to be found. Going on a journey soon...very soon.* He couldn't block it out. He knew he needed to talk to his dad about the fire, as well as about Jason and Brian. Perhaps he would have a chance and the necessary courage to tell his dad on the overnight camping trip. He wrestled back and forth in his mind about how to bring it up with his dad as he tried to get back to sleep. It was useless. Finally, as the first rays of dawn began to push back the darkness, Isaiah decided to get up and get ready for the day.

That afternoon, Charles and Isaiah headed out with backpacks into the woods to begin their overnight camping trip. Little did Isaiah realize that it would be far from a normal trip, nor only overnight.

Charles and Isaiah hiked hard all afternoon and into the setting sun before they stopped to make camp. They had climbed a mountain, crossed streams, and ventured deeper into the forest than Isaiah had ever gone. Most of the trip, they simply bantered back and forth and enjoyed the beauty of God's creation but avoided any deeper discussions.

They finally spread their sleeping bags out on the ground and built a small fire to give them warmth and heat for cooking the food that Esther had packed for them. Charles quietly sat under the stars for a while, and Isaiah wondered if he should say anything about the fire and Jason and Brian.

Just when he was about to conclude that he should not bring it up, Charles said, "Isaiah, you are now at an age where you will be exposed to some very adult things. With age comes a burden and a responsibility to handle situations with integrity."

Isaiah couldn't help but notice how integrity had appeared again in a conversation, his mind flashing back to his conversation with Granny Rose. However, he was exhausted and welcomed the chance to rest under a star-filled mountain sky. He lay in his sleeping bag and pondered the words of his father and Granny Rose. Finally, in the still of the night, he asked, "Father, have you ever heard of the Land of Integrity?"

Only crickets and a few owls echoed his question under the stars. After a few minutes, Charles said, "Tell me more of what Granny Rose told you about the Land of Integrity."

"She said it was a very special place with many lessons to be learned there and many treasures to be found. She said that she has been there but didn't tell me anymore. She went on to say that you don't find it, it finds you, and I should keep my ears and heart open to hear its calling."

Charles shifted in his sleeping bag and put both his hands behind his head to prop his head up to take in the star-filled sky. After a few minutes, he spoke, "Granny Rose speaks the truth and is very wise. The Land of Integrity is a very real place. It finds you only when you open your heart to hear its Voice. When you do that, your life can be changed forever. Knowing and doing the right thing becomes clearer. Perhaps we can discuss this more tomorrow. Let's get some sleep."

Isaiah returned to gazing at the stars, and a large meteor streaked across the star-filled sky, leaving a long glowing trail. It disappeared over a mountain peak, triggering a sudden bright glow in the distance. Isaiah thought to himself, *Granny Rose said there are great lessons and treasures to be found in the Land of Integrity. Perhaps there are answers there for me to know the right thing to do and the courage to do it.* The sound of crickets with an occasional owl hoot mixed with the crackling sounds of the campfire to lull him to sleep under a beautiful star-filled sky.

* * *

Isaiah jolted awake in the middle of the night to a noise and sat up. He looked over at his dad, who was on his side, facing away from him, apparently sound asleep. He smiled. Perhaps it was just his dad snoring. He settled back down into his own sleeping bag when suddenly he heard the sound again. This time, he definitely knew it was not his father's snoring.

Isaiah threw the sleeping bag back and stood straight up. His eyes squinted to see through the darkness to find the source of the sound. A distant, inaudible sound like a low buzz came from behind two large oak trees to his left. *Was it an animal or someone else in the woods?* He turned his head and cupped his hand behind his right ear to better capture the sound. For a moment, he heard nothing but the crickets and owls he had heard all night. Then he heard the sound again, but this time, as a gentle breeze blew, it sounded like a voice—a whisper—now more audible. He looked around and saw no one, but he definitely heard a voice in the wind, though he couldn't make out what it was saying. Isaiah instinctively reached down and picked up his backpack as he walked slowly toward the oak trees while continuing to cup his hand behind his ear to hopefully understand what the voice was saying. The breeze picked up and blew through his hair as he approached the trees.

"Isa…iah."

Isaiah froze in his tracks. *Did I hear that correctly?* he thought.

Barely audible, he heard it again. "Isa…iah." Was it his name, or had he just imagined that he had heard his name?

Isaiah crept closer to the large oak trees and realized there was a small opening between two of the largest trees. Branches had intertwined and formed a natural tunnel entrance to a nearly hidden trail. He stopped at the entrance and took a deep breath to calm his emotions. He felt fear, mystery, and intrigue all at the same time. The trail ascended to what should have been complete darkness, but it was somehow lit by a green mist suspended low over the trail. Despite the strong breeze, the mist seemed to remain in place unmoved.

Isaiah paused and turned back toward his dad, who was still asleep and facing away from him. He felt a pull, a yearning to follow the trail and find the source of this voice that called out his name, but he was also nervous and apprehensive. Questions raced through his mind. *What will my dad do if he wakes up and I am not here? Is it safe to go down this trail? Who out here knows my name? What is this green mist, and where did it come from?*

Finally, he thought, *perhaps I should just go back to bed. This may be just a dream.* Isaiah sighed and convinced himself this was the logical, safe thing to do. He started to turn and head back to his sleeping bag when he heard the voice call out.

"Isa…iah, this is where you begin."

Isaiah spun around, fully awake. He wondered if he had heard that right. But if so, what did it mean? It couldn't be that he was dreaming. He was too awake and heard the voice. It wasn't quite clear, but Isaiah was now completely transfixed on the Voice and followed it deeper and deeper into the woods.

Charles lay on his side in his sleeping bag, his eyes wide open as he listened to Isaiah get up and respond to the voice and head off down the trail. He prayed, "Lord, protect him on his journey and lead him to lessons and treasure that will change his life."

Isaiah worked his way down the trail and strained to hear the voice clearly and discern its source. With each step, the voice grew more intense in his spirit; it continued to call out, "Isa…iah, this is where you begin." Finally, he reached a clearing, and the early morning glow of a coming sunrise was just appearing over the mountains in a golden hue that was spectacular. He stopped and took in the glorious morning that had arrived. It was breathtaking.

Suddenly, the breeze picked up, and he heard the Voice say, "Follow the trail…follow my voice."

CHAPTER 3
THE RIVER

And so, the journey began. Isaiah walked down the trail under a canopy of large oak and maple trees as he watched the first rays of the morning splinter through the branches in beams of light that awakened the forest. The trees were so large they created a cathedral effect, almost sacred in appearance, as if the sun's rays were coming through stained glass windows of a cathedral. The birds awakened and chirped to one another while a hawk occasionally flew high overhead looking for its breakfast.

The farther Isaiah walked, the steeper the terrain. He began to huff and puff as he now had to climb up and over rocks. Finally, he reached a plateau where the trail gradually began to descend. From this height, he could see a heavily pine-wooded valley with a winding river surrounded by other large mountains that he had never seen before. Isaiah stopped and took a deep breath of the fresh, cool mountain air. He slowly turned around to take in the magnificent scene. It felt hallowed and unspoiled by human hands. It felt like a long, long way from home.

The trail descended and became narrower, and he stopped for a drink of water from his canteen. After hiking for hours, Isaiah sat on a log and rested for a moment. A distant sound like a roaring wind, non-stop and unvaried, reached his ears. He listened carefully but could not quite make out what it was. *Perhaps it was the Land of Integrity, and he was there.* He quickly gathered his backpack and canteen and continued down the trail to find the source.

Isaiah steadily descended the trail, carefully stepping over logs and sliding down large boulders while trying to keep track of the trail he had been following. The sound became louder and louder until finally he stood on a rock outcropping overlooking a hundred-foot falls with water roaring over the top. The torrent of water fell onto rocks below and droplets of water sprayed into the air, creating a constant white mist. The now afternoon sunlight danced through the mist and created a rainbow that arched over the pool below the falls. Tree-covered mountains rose above the falls on both sides of the river, creating a lush blanket of green foliage sliced by a white ribbon of frothing rapids that wound through the forest. The mist from the falls cooled the air and produced a very comfortable estuary at the bottom of the falls.

Isaiah worked his way down the side of the bedrock to the pool at the bottom of the falls and dipped his canteen into the water to refill it. The cool water was refreshing, but he had to hold on tight to the canteen with both hands. The current was so swift that there was no obvious way to get across the river. Water cascaded swiftly and slammed into rocks. The twisting rapids and swirling whirlpools could easily drag someone under. It became clear that it was not safe to dive into the water and try to swim across. He must find another way.

Isaiah headed down river and looked for a quieter place to cross, but the high waters and fast current presented no opportunity. The roar of the rapids was deafening. He worked his way along the river for an hour or more before the afternoon shadows grew long, and the sun began to set. The river widened and slowed at one point but was still too swift to swim across. Isaiah sat on a boulder, exhausted from the day's hike, and pulled out his canteen. *Perhaps there is no way to cross, perhaps I should turn back. Perhaps this was a huge mistake on my part, perhaps it was all in my mind, there was no Voice,* he thought to himself.

He spun his head at the howl of a wolf in the woods from behind him, and the hair on the back of his neck stood straight up. The howl was long and drawn out as male wolves do when they are calling to their pack. A few seconds later, another wolf called in response. Then another. And they seemed to be headed toward him and the river.

Isaiah's heart raced. He had grown up in the woods and knew that the wolf packs were dangerous. They rarely traveled alone and hunted in packs, circling and attacking from all directions. He needed to cross the river — now. There was no going back. Isaiah knew he had to get away from the wolves while they were on his side of the river.

Isaiah quickened his pace and scanned the riverbank for any opportunity to cross. The sun had set, and only a golden glow on the horizon remained. His mind began to see movement in the trees as his imagination convinced him that wolves were stalking him in the shadows. He worked hard to convince himself that there were no wolves nearby when suddenly, another howl penetrated the early twilight and the sound of the rushing river. Another chorus of howls echoed all around him, now much closer.

They were clearly hunting, and he appeared to be the prey.

Isaiah spun his head around and tried to fight sheer panic. He knew he must stay calm and think through his options. Isaiah searched the ground for a large stick and spotted a perfectly sized piece of driftwood. He hurriedly tore the small branches from it to make it into a club. He stood on the bank, weighing his chances of diving into the swiftly moving river, when he caught a glimpse of something in the last bit of light.

A large tree had fallen across the river and formed a makeshift, if not hazardous, bridge. This was his chance. If only he could get to it in time. He must try; he must hurry.

Isaiah bolted toward the downed tree, followed by a chorus of howls closing in fast. He reached the tree and discovered it was not as large as it looked from a distance, but it still looked usable for crossing the river. The tree narrowed across the river and rested on a large rock on the other shore. The last bit would be especially treacherous, but there was little choice. The water below the tree roared through a violent rapid.

Isaiah stepped onto the tree trunk with one foot to test its strength and determined that it supported his weight. He stepped with the other foot on the trunk and nearly fell off. The tree was covered with green moss. This, combined with the spray from the rushing river, had made the tree trunk very slippery, almost like ice. He would have to be very careful and edge across the trunk.

Isaiah took a short step to test his footing and the support of the tree trunk, when out of the corner of his eye, he saw movement. He turned and caught the gleam of snarling white teeth. A wolf with the most penetrating yellow eyes stood growling at him, along with at least five other wolves pacing and snarling. Nearby, on the rock, at the base of the fallen tree, was the alpha male—the largest wolf Isaiah had ever seen.

Isaiah took a couple more careful steps down the tree to separate himself from the monster. He was now over rushing water, and there was no turning back.

The large male wolf howled in defiance and snarled at Isaiah. He took a step onto the moss-covered tree and slid off onto the rock. Undaunted, the wolf climbed back onto the trunk again. This time, though, he used his razor-like claws to tightly grip the tree trunk, edging ever closer to Isaiah.

Isaiah knew the time to go was now. He could not be cautious. He gathered his courage and began to move hastily across the slippery fallen tree toward the other side of the river. The alpha male howled, snarled, and clawed his way behind him, though Isaiah had created some distance. Still on the shore, the other wolves paced back and forth in a frenzy. They howled nonstop and lunged at the fallen tree as they encouraged their leader to continue the pursuit.

Isaiah's heart raced as he edged himself closer to the other shore. However, he realized he had a new problem. The alpha wolf was on his heels and would soon join Isaiah on his side of the river.

Fifteen feet from the shore, Isaiah suddenly heard a loud crack followed by a sudden jerk of the tree trunk. Isaiah's balance was thrown off, and he began waving his arms and wobbling back and forth. Suddenly, the trunk cracked again and snapped completely, throwing Isaiah and the alpha wolf toward the raging river.

Isaiah hit the cold water, which stunned him and immediately took his breath away. He managed to grasp his backpack straps and hold on tightly. The river tossed him about like a rag doll bouncing off rocks, but fortunately, they were only glancing blows. He flailed in the water to gain some control, but to no avail. The rushing water continued to bounce him off rocks and dunk him under, and it took everything he had to keep his head above the water and grab breaths of air.

As cold water and exhaustion overtook his adrenaline, Isaiah found his last strength leaving his body. He wondered, *Is this it? Am I going to die?* He coughed up water and made a final gasp for air. His body was now powerless to fight the rushing water, and his arms and legs were nearly frozen stiff from the cold. He was carried wherever the current took him. He was at its mercy.

Isaiah drifted in and out of consciousness. He was about to totally yield to the river when a hand grabbed his jacket and lifted him out of the water.

CHAPTER 4

JOURNEYMAN

Isaiah opened his eyes and found himself lying on a blanket in front of a roaring fire in a simple but cozy cabin. The warmth of the fire had dried out his clothes, and he had no idea where he was or how long he had been there. The smell of warm vegetable soup and fresh hot bread filled the room. His stomach rumbled, and he propped himself up on an elbow and turned to survey the cabin and his surroundings. It was then that he saw an old man seated in a rocking chair with the Good Book across his lap.

The man gazed into the roaring fire as if mesmerized and deep in thought, quiet and reflective. After a moment, the gray-haired man with a salt-and-pepper beard turned slowly and said, "Hello, Isaiah. I've been expecting you."

Isaiah was surprised to hear his name since he didn't recognize the old man.

Isaiah sat up fully, rubbed his tender forehead, and felt a large knot where he had hit a rock. "Who...I mean, where...where am I?"

"In my cabin. Actually...on the floor of my cabin, to be exact," said the old man with a sly smile. "You have had an adventuresome day. Been chased through the woods, which ended with a swim in the river after running into those wolves."

Isaiah listened and realized this stranger was well aware of what he had gone through. *Had he watched the whole thing? Do I know him somehow? How does he know my name?*

"I was fortunate to grab your jacket and lift you out of the river. Not sure how much longer you could go being tossed around against the rocks."

"Oh, it was you...Thank you for pulling me out, Mr....."

"Iswa, is the name. Just Iswa." Iswa turned and pointed toward the table. "There's some vegetable soup and fresh hot bread on the table. You need to eat."

Isaiah nodded and sat down at the table, devouring the soup and hot bread. He quickly dispatched a bowl, and Iswa spooned out another helping. After eating, Isaiah's eyes grew heavy, and he slipped back asleep in front of the fireplace.

Isaiah awoke the next morning refreshed, though still feeling sore. He walked outside and sat by a fire pit near the porch. He listened to the crickets and the birds in the late summer morning and took in his surroundings. The cabin was a simple log cabin with a long, covered porch. A couple of rocking chairs were on the porch along with a storage bin for firewood. The porch provided a beautiful view of a large, deep blue lake surrounded by mountains. Occasionally, an eagle would swoop down majestically to the lake and grab a fish and effortlessly soar off with its next meal. Isaiah had discovered that the man who owned the cabin and had rescued him was named Iswa, but he knew nothing else about him.

Iswa sat for long periods on the porch of his cabin. In quiet solitude, he would just gaze out over the large lake or sit reading the Good Book. The deep blue water extended right up to the trees on the shore, and the thick forest ascended the mountain range from the lake shore. Above the tree line were rocks and patches of snow highlighted by the deep blue sky above.

Isaiah was unsure how to approach Iswa and his quiet personality. In the late afternoon, while sitting on the porch next to Iswa, Isaiah worked up the courage to ask, "Mr. Iswa...is...is this the Land of Integrity?"

"Humph," replied Iswa gruffly. He slowly shook his head. "You mean Endemar. That's what we call it. And no, this is not Endemar. This is Tiree. And it's Iswa, not Mister Iswa."

"Oh, sorry," Isaiah said, "But do you know how to get to ah... Endemar? I am on a journey there."

Iswa paused and looked over the top of his reading glasses at him. "Young man, what would make you want to go to Endemar?"

"I'm...I'm on a journey...to the Land of Integrity, or rather Endemar...to learn lessons and find treasure."

"On a journey, you say. Who told you to go on this journey and about Endemar?" sighed Iswa as he closed the Good Book and set it down while impatiently tapping his fingers on the arm of his chair.

"Granny Rose told me about the Land of Integrity...or Endemar as you call it. And she said that she has been there, but, of course, you may have never heard of her, or met her, so that would make sense since this is not Endemar that you may not know her, and of course..." Isaiah talked faster and faster as he blurted out the details of the conversation with Granny.

Isaiah finished and waited for a response from Iswa. There was a long, awkward silence, so much so that Isaiah began to think he had said something wrong. Finally, Iswa took a deep breath while looking out toward the lake. "Rose told you this. Interesting...yes, very interesting."

Iswa stood up, walked off the porch, and down a path toward the lake. Isaiah didn't know whether he should follow or stay on the porch. Iswa turned, looked at him, and said, "Well, are you coming?"

Isaiah joined Iswa, and they walked a distance before Iswa began to speak. "I am well acquainted with Rose, though I haven't seen her for a few years. Is she well?"

"Yes, quite well," said Isaiah. "She lives in Providence and runs a candy and cookie shop…or did …until it recently caught on fire. Everyone in town knows and loves Granny Rose."

A smile spread across Iswa's face. "Of course they do. Rose has a certain effect on people. Now, about this journey that she supposedly sent you on. Tell me a bit more. What led to this so-called journey discussion?"

Isaiah suddenly felt a bit exposed and avoided eye contact with Iswa. He had never shared the true reason for his discussion with Granny, and he wasn't ready to share it now with Iswa. At least not yet.

"I…I asked her a question. I asked her how you know what the right thing is to do…and then how to do it."

"And her answer?" asked Iswa. This strangely reminded Isaiah of a similar question his father had asked him while they sat around the campfire just two nights previously.

"Well…she said my question implies that there is a right thing to do and that I want to do it."

Iswa stopped walking and looked into Isaiah's eyes.

"Oh yeah, and then she said…that is good. Yes…very good."

"Intriguing," contemplated Iswa, "and did she say anything else to you about this so-called journey?"

Isaiah now felt a bit more confident and responded by going through the conversation he had with Granny Rose on the Village green across from her burnt-out store. This entire conversation with Iswa seemed so strange to Isaiah since it so mimicked the conversation he had started with his father. Iswa listened intently and had asked similar questions, but when they walked a bit further, Iswa stopped and asked, "How did you end up at the river the other night?"

Isaiah gulped and felt a lump in his throat. *How would he explain the green mist and the Voice that spoke to him?* He stammered a bit but finally said, "I know this may sound crazy, but I…I heard a Voice calling me…and oh yeah, there was also a green mist."

To Isaiah's complete surprise, Iswa did not respond as if he were crazy but instead listened intently and asked, "What did the Voice tell you to do?"

Isaiah somewhat hesitantly answered, "The Voice said this is where you begin…follow the trail…follow my voice." He watched Iswa carefully as he spoke and expected some kind of response. Iswa's expression was unchanged as he listened carefully to every word from Isaiah.

After several quiet minutes, Iswa said, "The Good Book tells men of integrity to carefully listen for the Voice. The Voice never goes against the Good Book but provides insight, guidance, and teaching. The Voice has called you, Isaiah, to a journey…to be a Journeyman."

Isaiah listened intently but was a bit confused. *Journeyman – what does that mean exactly?* he thought to himself. He finally asked Iswa, "Excuse me, but what exactly does that mean to be a … Journeyman?"

Iswa's eyes narrowed and became fixed on Isaiah's eyes, and his face grew even more serious as he said, "A Journeyman is a man or woman called by the Voice to complete a very specific mission. It is not trivial, and it is often very dangerous. Success is not guaranteed, and failure will occur if the Journeyman is unprepared or does not listen or follow the Voice. It depends on the Journeyman's willingness to listen, follow, and act. In essence, they must listen carefully to know the right thing to do and then be willing to do what it takes. It requires great discipline and courage."

Isaiah was taken aback by how serious Iswa had become. There was silence as they continued to walk. Finally, he asked, "You said success is not guaranteed and failure will occur if not prepared. What happens if a Journeyman is not prepared and fails?"

"Several things can happen, including great pain to many people, personal loss…and even death." The words hung in the air for Isaiah to contemplate. These were serious words, adult words, life-changing words. Iswa continued, "The Journeyman must accept or reject his mission. If he rejects it, then he simply returns home to continue life as it is. However, if he accepts the mission, he begins a process of preparation and life-changing experiences."

Iswa stopped, turned, and put both his hands on Isaiah's shoulders and peered directly at him. Iswa's dark blue eyes seemed to pierce right into Isaiah's heart. Isaiah felt very vulnerable and overwhelmed.

"Now you must choose which path to take."

The tension in the air was electric, and Isaiah started to stammer a response when Iswa held up a hand and interrupted him. "Don't decide now. Take some time, but not too much time. There is an urgency in the air. I sense it clearly." With that, Iswa turned and headed back down the path toward his cabin in the woods. He left Isaiah to his thoughts on the shore overlooking the deep blue lake with the snowcapped mountain range in the distance.

Isaiah couldn't help but feel overwhelmed and walked out onto a small dock to just think and clear his head.

"So, you think you're a Journeyman," came a voice from behind him.

Isaiah whirled to see the largest gray and black wolf he had ever seen standing near the shoreline, right at the other end of the dock. Yellow eyes stared straight at him as the wolf flashed a set of long, white teeth. Isaiah jumped back, startled, and immediately looked around for a means to escape. The events and terror of the last few days were still very fresh in his mind. With an eye on the wolf, he looked around to see where the voice had come from.

"Who are you looking for?" asked the wolf. "I'm talking to you."

Isaiah couldn't believe what he was seeing and hearing. The wolf talked. *I must be going mad*, he thought.

The wolf chuckled and said, "Oh, don't be startled, Isa…iah. I believe that's your name, correct?"

Isaiah shook so hard he could only nod his head in response to the wolf's question. He edged further out onto the dock to the very end as the wolf walked toward him.

"Oh, let me introduce myself. My name is Temp, and as you can see, things on this side of the river are quite different than on your side."

Isaiah looked around for some kind of escape route, but water was on three sides. The largest wolf he had ever seen continued to move toward him.

"Don't be afraid. I want to be your friend. I overheard your and Iswa's conversation. Why Iswa and I have been old friends for many years. We go way back."

"Friends?" Isaiah stammered. He relaxed slightly but still felt very exposed and in danger.

"Did he tell you that old folk story about Journeymen?" Temp asked. "Why, you're no Journeyman. You're just a kid, and way too young. Journeymen are much older, much stronger. You don't have the strength and courage to be a Journeyman. Temp scoffed, scanning Isaiah from head to toe. Look at yourself, you're shaking like a leaf. No, in no manner are you a Journeyman. No, that would not be good at all for you, I'm afraid. There are very dark forces that come against Journeymen." He was now so close that Isaiah could feel his hot breath, which smelled like sulfur. Temp dropped his voice low and slowly emphasized his words, "Very dark and very powerful forces. Forces that destroy and even kill."

Temp practically towered over Isaiah at the very end of the dock, and Isaiah had nowhere to go. Isaiah's heart pounded and his breathing quickened. He was about to totally panic when he heard a voice say, "Trust me, Isaiah, trust me."

Isaiah recognized the Voice and glanced over his shoulder to see a green mist suspended over the water.

"Jump, Isaiah, jump." It was now completely dark outside, and the water looked like black ink with only the green mist providing any light source. "Remember, Isaiah, you want to know the right thing to do and then do it…trust me, Isaiah…jump!"

Isaiah glanced backward, took a deep breath, and leaped into the water.

The cold water momentarily shocked him as his muscles immediately tightened. It was pitch black, and Isaiah sank deep into the water. He had trouble knowing up from down. Suddenly, something grabbed him, pulling him down deeper into the water and away from the dock. He started to fight the downward pull, but then clearly heard the Voice again. "Trust me, Isaiah."

A peace came over Isaiah, and he swam with the force that pulled him deeper into the water. Unexpectedly, the direction of the force changed upward, and without warning, Isaiah burst from the water. He found himself inside a cave, bathed in a glow from the green mist that covered the entire cave floor as well as the water.

Isaiah crawled out of the water onto a sand-covered beach inside the cave. The green mist enveloped him as he sat on the sand. He gathered his wits about him and took in deep breaths of air. A cool evening breeze accompanied the fresh air coming down through the cave. It was clear that the cave led to the outside.

The mist began to swirl and glow, building into a churning, green column. The Voice spoke from within the column. "Isaiah, I have called you. Trust me, follow me. Don't believe the lie that you're too young. Don't give in to fear. Be strong and courageous because men of integrity are called to stand and act. I will teach you;

I will guide you; I will help you know the right thing to do and give you the courage to act. Remember, there are lessons to be learned and treasure to be found." The column of mist rapidly rose and flew down the cave and out the exit.

Isaiah slowly stood up on the sandy beach, took in a deep breath, and considered what he had just heard and experienced. With each breath of fresh air, peace and clarity came over him, and he headed down the tunnel toward the outside of the cave. He knew what he must do.

CHAPTER 5

TRAINING

Isaiah stepped out of the shadows of the cabin onto the porch. He blinked several times and rubbed his eyes as they adjusted to the bright morning sunrise. The morning air was crisp, and he adjusted his coat collar around him to block the wind. The sky was a brilliant blue with not a single cloud in the sky. He found Iswa sitting by the fire pit, reading the Good Book as was his custom. Isaiah approached and asked, "Can we talk?"

Iswa didn't look up from the Good Book but motioned with his hand for Isaiah to sit. Isaiah sat nervously, tapping his fingers on the arm of the chair as he waited for Iswa to finish and look up. Iswa's eyes finally raised and met Isaiah's.

"I'm in...I mean...I'll do it...ah, I mean...I want to be a Journeyman."

There was no look of shock on Iswa's face. Instead, he simply smiled and said, "Very good...yes, very good indeed. Gather your things. I want you to meet some friends of mine."

Isaiah gathered his daypack and looked ready to hike. Iswa, on the other hand, always looked the same, sporting his gray hair and salt-and-pepper beard, a long black coat, and a walking stick.

They began down a wide trail next to Iswa's cabin. As they walked, the path became noticeably narrower and went past the lake and up into some foothills where the terrain changed to a more rolling meadow. After hiking across the meadow, Iswa stopped and said, "We are here."

Isaiah had no idea where "here" was. They stood in a small rolling meadow encircled by tall trees that allowed enough light to penetrate to grow grasses and berries. Suddenly, from behind them, they heard a voice, "Good day, fine gentlemen."

Isaiah turned to see a brown three-foot rabbit standing next to him who had on a Bowler hat and a red vest. Isaiah jumped back, startled at the sight. The rabbit spoke again, "Forgive me for surprising you, good man. I had no intention of frightening you."

Isaiah stumbled backward and tried to process the fact that he was talking to a three-foot rabbit. "You're...you're a rabbit?"

The rabbit looked around, picked up his foot, felt his tail, and then reached up and grabbed his ears and gasped, "Oh my, I'm a rabbit!" The rabbit giggled. "Master Isaiah, things are quite different on this side of the river."

Isaiah glanced at Iswa, who was thoroughly amused and trying hard not to burst out laughing, but he finally could not hold it any longer. "Hon is one of my oldest friends. Say hello to him formally, Isaiah," smiled Iswa as he put his arm around Hon.

Isaiah stuck out his hand, took Hon's paw and gently shook it, and introduced himself. The idea of actually having a conversation with a rabbit wearing a Bowler hat and red vest with a decidedly English accent had not completely registered yet.

Hon invited them to his small hut that was on the edge of the meadow. It was so well hidden that it was not easily seen. The hut was part tree, part stone, and part mud. Inside, it was masterfully shaped into a warm, cozy room with a fireplace in the corner, along with a table and chairs. A staircase led to a bed in the loft.

They sat down to have some hot dandelion tea when there was a sudden knock on the door. Hon jumped up. "Oh my, they're here," he said and hopped to the door to greet his new visitors.

In walked a groundhog, who had on a plaid jacket and wire-rimmed glasses. He was followed close behind by a squirrel with a woolen sweater and a small pocket watch. Isaiah rubbed his eyes. "Why not?" he shrugged. "I have spent the last hour talking to a rabbit wearing a Bowler hat and a red vest."

They all sat down, and it became quite noisy as the old friends told stories and laughed while they caught up on life and current adventures. Isaiah sat back and enjoyed the scene as he watched Iswa laugh until tears rolled down onto his salt-and-pepper beard. Isaiah discovered that the groundhog, Esty, lived across the meadow and over a small hill. He raised chickens and sold eggs but also turned out to be a master storyteller. He kept everyone entertained as he used strange sounds and voices to recount tales and adventures.

Hon was uniquely British in his speech, and every time he spoke, you sensed a kindness and gentleness. As Isaiah got to know him, he came to appreciate Hon's patience and kindness with everyone, and behind it all was a deep, deep joy. A joy that seemed to say, I know who I am, and I know where I'm going, and it's all good. Hon joined Esty in the retelling of stories with an infectious laugh, and at one point, he laughed so hard that he fell off his chair and onto the floor.

Riddle was much quieter but chuckled and smiled continuously. He appeared to simply relish the time with his dear friends. As Isaiah watched, he came to appreciate how deep the bonds of friendship and brotherhood ran among these four friends. As Isaiah listened, it became very clear that each member had learned much on their own journeys. He realized there was much wisdom here regarding the Land of Integrity.

After much laughter and storytelling, Iswa chuckled and leaned forward in his chair and held up his hand as if he was stopping traffic. "Okay, okay, that's enough reminiscing…for now at least. We have a serious matter to attend to, my friends. Young Isaiah has decided to accept the call to be a Journeyman."

The room fell silent as each one turned and looked directly at Isaiah. He suddenly felt very conspicuous. The look on their faces was serious and penetrating, but also supportive as one by one they nodded toward Isaiah. The only sound was the crackling of the fire and clinking of Riddle's spoon stirring a cup of tea.

"My friends, I am here today to ask you to take on the responsibility of training young Isaiah."

Hon immediately spoke up, "Of course, we will help you, my friend. It shall be our honor." The others nodded in affirmation, and Esty even grunted in support.

Iswa paused with a sense of sadness in his eyes. He spoke slowly, "My friends, my time has passed for training Journeymen. I need you to take this on yourselves. I believe young Isaiah would be in better hands if you took the responsibility."

Riddle, the sweater-wearing squirrel who had been mostly quiet, slammed the palm of his paw on the table. "Nonsense, my friend, pure nonsense. Every man makes his own decisions to follow or not follow the Voice. That is not yours to decide, but rather it is your responsibility to instruct, train, and obey. We will help you, but you will lead the training, and that is the end of the matter, period."

Isaiah's eyes darted back and forth between Iswa and Riddle as an awkward silence hung in the room. He was confused by Iswa's reluctance to train him and Riddle's adamant response. Iswa silently stared at Riddle, who set his jaw and had a determined look in his eye. The kind of look that said, *there will be nothing to debate here.*

Isaiah wondered if Iswa simply did not want to train him or possibly did not think he would succeed. Nobody spoke a word. The only sound was an occasional crack and pop from the fireplace. Iswa and Riddle continued to stare at one another for some time as if engaged in a silent battle of wills, but finally, Isaiah was relieved when a gentle smile crept across Iswa's face.

Iswa sighed. "So it will be, my friends. I shall train him, but only with your help." They all nodded and promptly returned to laughing, drinking, and eating. Isaiah made a mental note to pursue this issue with Riddle in due time.

As the sun was about to set, Isaiah and Iswa returned to the cabin, and Iswa announced, "We begin tomorrow...be ready."

* * *

"Get up. Time to begin."

Iswa's loud voice jolted Isaiah awake from a deep sleep. Disoriented, he rubbed his eyes and blinked several times to adjust to the light that came from the open cabin door.

Iswa stood in the cabin doorway, silhouetted by the early morning sunrise. He was fully dressed and ready for the day. "Five minutes. Out front with your day pack and dressed ready to hike."

Five minutes later, Isaiah found himself outside the cabin in the early dawn hours. He continued to blink and rub his eyes, wiping the sleep away. He yawned loudly and shook his head to try to clear away his urge to go back to bed. Iswa stood with his gaze fixed on the mountains across the lake. His own day pack hung over his shoulders. He looked like a soldier on a mission and did not turn to acknowledge Isaiah. "Try to keep up," he said abruptly. And with that, he took off in a fast trot down a trail.

They hiked hard for an hour through the forest and small meadows. As the sun began to rise, rays pierced the forest, casting beams of bright sunlight onto green foliage, making it glow against still dark shadows, and dew-covered ground sparkled like diamonds. The entire forest slowly awakened from sleep, and birds began to chirp, announcing a new day. Isaiah thought to himself, *This feels…spiritual.*

After another hour of hiking at a fast pace, they came to a small waterfall that gently fell into a pond that reflected like a mirror the trees and blue morning sky. Iswa called for a rest break, pulled some food from his pack, and handed it to Isaiah. He also reached into his pack and pulled out his copy of the Good Book. He instructed Isaiah to sit on a boulder, handed him the Good Book, and asked him to read a specific section. As Isaiah began to read, the now familiar green mist appeared from the waterfall and spread across the entire pond. It spread up onto the shore and swirled around the boulders that Iswa and Isaiah sat upon, and Isaiah felt a soft breeze flow through his hair accompanied by a quiet stillness. Iswa stopped Isaiah at various sections and asked him to put in his own words what the Good Book had said. They discussed it, and Iswa interjected questions and thoughts to add to Isaiah's views. This became the daily pattern for several weeks: rise early, hike fast, and read and discuss the Good Book.

Each morning, at the conclusion of their time at the waterfalls, Iswa took Isaiah on a completely new cross-country route. Each route included one or more challenges for Isaiah to figure out a solution. It often required him to overcome some type of obstacle with creative solutions that often included activities such as rappelling off cliffs, canoeing through rapids, or crossing gorges on ropes. With each new experience, Isaiah grew more confident in his ability to analyze and come up with solutions. In addition, his muscles and endurance grew stronger, and before long, he was out in front of Iswa on trails.

They had finished their time at the waterfall one morning, and Isaiah asked Iswa, "Can you tell me about Endemar? Why do people call it the Land of Integrity?"

Iswa leaned back and fixed his eyes on the waterfall and the still pond. There was silence with only the sound of falling water and an occasional loon call. It was as if he were reaching far back into memories that had been hidden away and kept in the dark for a very long time. He took a deep breath and slowly began to speak.

"The kingdom of Endemar has been in place for centuries and has been the center of governance, protection, and rule for seven regions. For generations, people have come to live, work, and trade in the city and kingdom. There have been times of peace and plenty, but also times of great challenges, including war, disease, and famine.

Through good times and bad times, Endemar has been led by kings of very high integrity. Kings who listened carefully to the Voice. These kings cared for the people and led with wisdom, bravery, and justice. They sought to know and do the right thing. Their legacy of such high integrity became so legendary that people would travel great distances to seek out the current king's wisdom and insight regarding the right thing to do. As a result, people would often refer to Endemar as the Land of Integrity."

Isaiah leaned forward and listened intently to Iswa's explanation and interjected, "So, Endemar is ruled by one of these kings of integrity."

"Not exactly, Endemar has been without a king for many years, and a darkness, a great darkness has invaded. I fear for Endemar."

Iswa abruptly stood up, gathered his day pack, and took off hiking with Isaiah scrambling behind him. This discussion was clearly over, for at least now.

Several days later, Iswa led Isaiah to a high ridge on a mountain. The view across the valley was spectacular, but on this day, Iswa had a long bag over his shoulder. He stopped on a plateau and pulled from his bag two wooden training swords. He handed one to Isaiah and said, "Today, we focus on swordsmanship. It is important, as a Journeyman, that you understand how to use a sword." He raised the sword and pointed it at Isaiah's chest and firmly said, "On guard."

Isaiah struggled to lift the wooden sword. It felt awkward and clumsy in his hands, and Iswa began to gently tap each side of Isiah's extended sword in a steady back-and-forth rhythmic fashion. After several taps, he repeatedly landed the blunt tip of the training sword on Isaiah's chest and said, "You're dead. Now, again."

Iswa gradually increased the force of the taps until Isaiah's sword flew out of his hand and bounced across the gray rock plateau. "Pick it up. Now, again. On guard," came the command from Iswa. This time, he took a step toward Isaiah as he repeated the rhythmic tapping back and forth. Isiah back peddled and stumbled, turning his body. Iswa quickly stepped forward and put the tip of his sword on Isiah's back and declared, "You're dead. Now, again. On guard."

Isaiah spun around and squinted at Iswa and set his jaw. He wasn't about to let Iswa beat him again. This time, he lunged toward Iswa with the point of his wooden sword aimed at Iswa's chest. Iswa, however, stepped aside and swatted the sword away and delivered a clean whack to Isaiah's backside as he went by, causing him to land face-first sprawled out on the plateau.

Isaiah rolled over and looked up at Iswa, who had a smile on his face. "Now, let's begin."

The plateau came alive with the slow rhythmic clunking sound of wooden swords repeatedly tapped against one another. Iswa continually emphasized the proper position of the arms and feet for balance as they sparred across the plateau. Isaiah felt awkward at first, and yet they repeated this day after day until he began to feel more comfortable and competent. The morning sword training went from slow rhythmic clunking sounds to faster taps and clicks as they moved quicker and quicker each day. Iswa would continually give words of instruction and encouragement as they repeated this routine morning after morning across the plateau. Over time, their mock battles became more intense as Isaiah moved from simple competence to true skill with a sword. Iswa was forced to work harder and harder to stay ahead of him.

One morning, after their time at the waterfall, Iswa looked at Isaiah and asked, "Why do you think we come to the waterfall to start each day?"

Isaiah thought for a moment and said, "Well, it gets our day started and we get into a rhythm."

"Yes, it does," responded Iswa, "but we also read the Good Book because the Voice always speaks in agreement with the Good Book. So, if we know the Good Book, we have tuned our heart and mind to hear the Voice. We can recognize the Voice from all other voices because it always agrees with the Good Book. It never is in conflict, but rather provides understanding, clarity, and direction in applying the Good Book."

"So, by starting our day with the Good Book, we get our heart and mind ready to hear the Voice. Is that correct?" interjected Isaiah.

"Exactly, Journeymen must work continuously to hear and follow the Voice."

Iswa took the wooden sword from Isaiah's hand and said, "No sword training today, you go on ahead, and I will catch up later." He went on to explain where he would meet up with Isaiah but gave no further details on the challenge for the day. Isaiah was familiar with the trail but had never gone off it onto a separate trail that Iswa described. It was strange that Iswa was not with him, but he felt comfortable enough with the area that he grabbed his day pack and headed out on the several-mile hike. He came to a branch in the trail and paused to make sure he selected the correct path. As he stood there, an uneasiness came over him: *"Be cautious, something was amiss here, something is not right."* He wondered if this was the Voice or if he was just being overly cautious since Iswa was not with him. Isaiah proceeded down the trail that descended into a valley with rolling meadows when he froze. He smelled something. With each breath, his lungs burned...it was smoke.

Isaiah looked back and forth to identify the source of the smoke, as fire and forest were not a good mix. He looked around and saw dark smoke rising above the trees ahead of him. He hurried down the trail and heard voices shouting. He got to the edge of a meadow and stopped dead in his tracks. Across the meadow were men with torches. They were outside a farmhouse and barn with nearby hay bales and grass on fire. The men were doing nothing to put out the fire, but rather one of the men walked over to another nearby hay bale pile and set it on fire. The reality of the situation hit Isaiah; *These men intended to burn the farm to the ground.* Outside of the houses were families of women and children screaming as they saw their houses and barns about to be burned to the ground. Two men had pushed a farmer dressed in overalls to the ground and were taking turns kicking him. He was curled up in a ball and took blow after blow from their kicks. Isaiah's heart began to race, and he looked around frantically for some way to stop them. Unexpectedly, from around the barn, several large wolves walked. The men and the wolves were together. Fear gripped Isaiah, and his breathing became rapid, and his heart raced. His first thought was to hide; after all, what could he do? He wanted to run but finally dove behind a fallen log and peered over it at the destruction and violence. He began to shake all over.

He took a deep breath and said a prayer and then noticed a water tower next to the house. He saw an opportunity; it would be risky, but if he could get to the tower and throw open the water gate. It would flood the entire barn area. That is … only if the tower was full of water. But these men are still beating this poor farmer. *How can I stop them?* His only option was to directly attack them and beat them off; however, with the wolves nearby, this option did not look promising. Still, he could not sit by and do nothing. He grabbed a large branch and quickly made it into a club. He rose up from behind the log and began to jump over it when a large hand grabbed his shoulder and planted him down in the dirt. He started to protest, but he was spun around to see that it was Iswa who had him. Iswa put his finger to his lips for silence and motioned that Isaiah should go for the tower, and he would go for the attackers. Isaiah nodded that he understood, and they jumped over the log, and Isaiah raced toward the tower while Iswa headed directly toward the men who continued to kick and pummel the farmer.

The attackers had their backs to Iswa as he approached, and what Isaiah saw next was nothing but astonishing. Iswa slid to the ground on one knee behind the man, kicking the farmer, and did a leg sweep to completely take the attacker off his feet. He then popped up so fast that the other man had no time to respond to a powerful fist to the stomach, which caused him to double over. By this time, Iswa was behind the man and came down with a heavy blow to the back of the man's head, which knocked him completely out. The first man tried to get to his feet, and Iswa delivered a snap kick to his head that sent him backward, where he landed with a thud, also unconscious. Iswa turned to the farmer, reached down, and helped him up, and told him to get his family and flee into the woods in the direction he had just come from.

In the meantime, Isaiah ran as hard as he could for the water tower and the ladder that led up the side to the large valve. The two wolves saw Isaiah and were now in full pursuit as they growled and ran across the barn yard in a full sprint directly at him. They were rapidly gaining ground, and Isaiah knew he could not outrun them, but in a last-ditch effort, he lunged for the ladder rung and caught it with both hands, which allowed him to swing up on the ladder just ahead of their sharp white teeth. He climbed the ladder to get to the valve but then realized the rope to open the valve was hanging straight down from the valve on the bottom of the tank, and he could not reach it. The wolves went crazy and leaped up the ladder and were just inches below his feet. The fire had spread, and he knew they were just about out of time if they were to have any chance of saving the barn and house. There was only one option. He steadied himself and measured how far he needed to leap to catch the rope and hang on long enough to pull the valve open. The new problem was that he would clearly be within range of the wolf's teeth. There was no other choice. He took a deep breath and leaped.

Isaiah caught the rope with both hands and held on tight. His weight and momentum caused him to swing at first, but then gravity took over, and he was hanging in the air, holding on to the rope the best he could. The valve creaked and moaned from his weight and then suddenly gave way, opening the valve to the water tower. Water began to gush out everywhere in a flood. However, with the valve opened, the rope dropped a couple of feet, and he was no longer above the wolves.

He let go of the rope and fell to the ground just as the two enraged wolves arrived. The growls and snarls were terrifying enough, but the drool that dripped from their sharp white teeth and the fire in their eyes said one thing: they were here to kill. He raised his hands to defend himself when, out of nowhere, a sword blade landed on the neck of the closest wolf, killing it instantly. Isaiah looked up with astonishment to see Iswa in his long black coat with his wild gray hair and salt-and-pepper beard brandishing his sword over his head, not the wooden training sword, but his real sword that normally hung over the mantle in his cabin. The second wolf quickly backed off when it saw its fellow wolf dispatched so easily. It then circled Iswa and Isaiah to measure them and finally decided to lung at Iswa, who abruptly ran the blade in its side. The wolf yelped and stumbled off into the brush to die.

The water did the job and completely extinguished the grass fire, which was about to consume the buildings. Isaiah looked at Iswa, and a smile came across Iswa's face, "Well done, yes, well done, young Journeyman."

Both Iswa and Isaiah returned their attention to the farmer and his family, and they found them hidden in the woods. Iswa asked, "Why were these men beating you and trying to burn down your farm?"

The farmer groaned as he rubbed his stomach, which still hurt from the repeated kicks, but finally responded, "They were looking for someone, and they thought we knew where to find them."

"Why did they think that?"

The farmer paused and looked at his wife, who nodded and encouraged him to speak. "They found a shirt with blood on it in our barn. A few nights ago, a young man, who had been wounded, came to us in the middle of the night. We gave him food and bandaged his wounds, but he left suddenly before dawn.

"Did you know his name?"

"No, I had never seen him before, but he was fairly young, probably a couple of years older than your friend," and he nodded toward Isaiah.

Iswa and Isaiah made sure the farmer and his family would be safe with friends and headed toward home since it was quite late in the afternoon. They had hiked for quite a while when Isaiah asked Iswa, "Who were those men who attacked that farmer?"

"They were thugs or even mercenaries from Endemar. Hired to hunt someone down...bounty hunters. Who and why, I'm not sure. We have a mystery to solve," replied Iswa.

"And ah… what about the wolves," continued Isaiah, "I've never seen wolves quite like them." He had not told Iswa about his run-in with Temp.

"The wolves are from the darkness. They can look like wolves today, but they can take on many shapes, including the appearance of men. They are shapeshifters. They embody evil and take their direction from the dark one, the Prince of Darkness. They lie, tempt, manipulate, and destroy all that is good whenever possible. I try to send them back to the pit anytime we cross paths." Iswa glanced at Isaiah as he described the wolves, to see his reaction. Isaiah's eyes were wide open, and the look on his face showed he was a bit stunned. "Yes, Isaiah, things are quite different on this side of the river. Never trust a wolf."

They got home after dark and soon retired from exhaustion. Isaiah lay in his bunk and stared at the ceiling, replaying the intense events of the day. He thought about the lightning actions of Iswa and his words about darkness, wolves, and shapeshifting. Yes, things are quite different on this side of the river. He wondered, *Will I ever be a true Journeyman?*

CHAPTER 6
THE CHICKEN COUP

The next morning Isaiah awoke and found a note from Iswa. The note instructed him that starting today, he would work with Hon, Esty, and Riddle. He explained that each day would present a new challenge. Today, he would be with Esty.

With no further instruction, Isaiah headed over to Esty's cabin, which was down the trail toward the edge of the meadow. Esty lived just over a hill from Hon, and once there, he traveled through a gate and found a small home with a broad porch across the front of the house. In a rocking chair, on the front porch, sat Esty, who looked at his pocket watch and simply let out an audible, "Humph." He then turned to Isaiah and said, "Ok, you see that chicken coop down the hill?"

Down the steep hill, some distance away, was a small building with a fence above and around the coup. The gate was open, and chickens were everywhere picking at feed on the ground for their morning breakfast. There were over 100 chickens, and no more than ten were in the coop at the time.

Esty continued, "I need your help. Can you watch after my chickens and get them all back in their coop by noon? I need to go over to Hon's Hut this morning. Can you commit to doing that? It's important."

Isaiah looked at him to make sure he was serious and then responded, "Yes, sir, I'll do my best."

Esty looked him up and down and let out a loud, "Humph," and mumbled, "We can only hope that's good enough."

Isaiah proceeded down the hill and began to size up how he would get the chickens back in the coop. He was a bit perplexed by Esty's sense of urgency and his importance to simply watch over his chickens. It all seemed very trivial. Oh well, he would make the best of it. This looked like it was going to be a very quiet day compared to the previous day.

He decided he must trick the chickens to get them back into the coop. With that strategy, he decided to herd them casually toward the gate, so he spread his arms wide and began to call the chickens like they were dogs, "Here chickee, chickee, here chickee, chickee." The chickens simply scattered wildly and did not follow Isaiah's lead at all. Next, Isaiah decided to rush them and push them into the coup. This was completely futile as the chicken quickly and easily outmaneuvered him and scattered. He next tried to catch individual chickens and place them in the coop. From a distance, it looked like a humorous dance of Isaiah with a chicken. Chickens ran between his legs and dodged him until he fell in the dirt and dust of the coup, completely exhausted. In utter frustration, Isaiah screamed, "This is crazy, I've had enough!"

"So, you're done playing with chickens," came a voice with a devilish chuckle from behind the coup.

Isaiah picked himself up and dusted himself off. He crept over and peered around the coup. He immediately jerked back, stumbled backward, and fell on the ground. From around the corner walked a tall, thin man with long black hair streaked with gray down to his shoulders. The man's eyes were very dark, a grayish tone. His nose was slightly crooked as if it had been broken at some time in the past. The smile on his face looked strange, not normal, but instead more of a smirk. Isaiah's heart immediately raced as he quickly regained his balance and retreated.

"Oh, excuse me for frightening you, young man," said the stranger. "I'm a good friend of Esty's. I live just down the trail." He gestured toward a narrow trail leading off down the hill.

Isaiah was shocked to suddenly see this peculiar-looking man standing next to the coup. He felt an uneasiness about the man but couldn't quite define what made him feel this way. "Oh, oh hello, can I help you?" stammered Isaiah.

"I just came by to say hello to an old friend, Esty. I usually come by two or three times a week to sit on his porch and ah… just chew the fat, so to speak," he replied with a strange chuckle." He continued, "I hope we can become friends." He looked right at Isaiah with a grin that looked more like a snarl.

"Has old Esty got you chasing chickens?" chuckled the man. "He pulls that prank on every new Journeyman. Some have been out here for hours, wallowing in the dust, chasing chickens. They all get a great laugh out of it."

He continued, "Well, now that the prank is up and you know, you can go on down to the lake and take a swim and wash the dust off. I'll watch the chickens. Done it many times."

Isaiah stammered, "I… I don't know about that."

"Ol'Esty has already had a good laugh as he watched you wallow in the dust, and he will understand – go ahead." The man's voice dropped lower and was very deliberate on the last two words.

Isaiah thought for a moment of how good the cool water of the lake would feel, and he did want to wash the dust away. He smelled like chickens and had dust in his hair, on his clothes, and all over his arms and hands. He thought to himself, *Well, Esty had his laugh, and everything would be ok. It won't hurt anyone for him to wash off. The chickens will be fine.*

He was just about to agree to take up the man's offer when a big red hen began to peck at seed right at his feet, and she looked up at him. Her eyes were big and looked distressed, she was shaking, and suddenly she spoke, "What did you promise Esty?"

Isaiah stepped back, stunned. She burst out, "What's wrong, you haven't ever talked to a chicken? But you have talked to a three-foot rabbit who wears a bowler hat, a red vest, and has a British accent, as well as a groundhog who wears wire-rimmed glasses. Why not talk to a chicken?" He found it hard to argue with her; the last several days had been filled with new experiences.

She repeated herself, "What did you promise Esty?"

"Well, Esty asked me to get you all into the coup."

"Is that all he asked?" replied the hen with a firm, almost chastising tone.

"Well, um, I guess not, he also asked me to look after all of you."

"Exactly," she exclaimed with a firm voice.

The man had overheard this exchange and interrupted, "You're not going to listen to a stupid chicken, are you, and let her spoil all your fun. That water is really refreshing."

Isaiah felt a twinge of intimidation from the man's words. They felt like heavy weights placed on his back. They implied that if he listened to the chicken, he would be stupid.

The man's chastisement drew his attention back to the cool water of the lake. It would feel so good, but he looked once more at the hen and she looked up at him with her big eyes and simply said in a soft voice, "What did you promise Esty?"

Softly, almost with a mumble, Isaiah said, "No, I think I'll stay with the chickens." Then, as if he had gained some form of new strength from his own words, he turned to face the man and firmly said it again, "No, I think I'll stay with the chickens."

His newfound courage seemed to take the man by surprise and caused him to take a step back. He wasn't quite prepared for Isaiah's firmness and resolve.

The man muttered under his breath, "You fool," and stepped backward.

The hen watched the conflict between the man and Isaiah unfold and urgently asked Isaiah, "What do you need from us?"

Isaiah looked around and said, "I need all the chickens to get in the coop."

"No problem," said the hen, "get chicken feed out of the drum and throw it into the feed trough." Isaiah quickly threw open the drum, grabbed a scope, pulled out an overflowing amount of feed, and poured it rapidly into the feed trough as the hen had instructed. The sound of the pouring feed caused every chicken to stop and perk up its head. Then suddenly there was a mad dash, a chicken stampede, into the coup by every single chicken. Isaiah had to jump out of the way as chickens ran by him.

Isaiah swiftly closed the gate, locked it, and turned around to tell the man he would not be needed to watch the chickens. He was nowhere to be seen.

Isaiah stayed the rest of the morning to keep an eye on the chickens. He did not see the strange man again. At noon, he saw that Esty had returned, and he climbed back up the hill to find Esty back in his rocking chair, quietly rocking. Isaiah sat down in the chair next to him and sat in silence for a few minutes until he found the courage to ask Esty a question.

"Esty, why did you want me to watch the chickens this morning while you went to Hon's?"

Esty responded, "Oh, of course, that's a good question. I guess I didn't mention this morning that we heard that an old wolf had been seen prowling around the area. The wolves love to eat our chickens, and we must protect them."

"Oh, I see, that makes sense, and by the way, your neighbor came by to see you."

Etsy looked at him with a puzzled look and asked, "Which neighbor?"

"Oh, I'm sorry I didn't get his name, a tall thin man with black hair down to his shoulders, said he was coming by as he usually does to just sit on the porch and a…chew the fat."

Esty turned and looked carefully at Isaiah. "I don't have any neighbors who fit that description."

When Isaiah heard these words, it created a lump in his throat. He knew how close he had come to not only abandoning the chickens but turning them over to this man. The situation sobered him and caused him to rethink the whole episode when suddenly, he remembered the words of the man, "He pulls that prank on every new Journeyman." *How did he know he was a Journeyman?*

It had been a strange morning for Isaiah on many fronts, which included a strange talk with a chicken. That afternoon, as Isaiah walked back to Hon's hut, he came across Iswa.

"How did your morning go with Esty?" asked Iswa.

"Interesting, very interesting."

"How so? What did you learn?"

"Well, for one thing, chickens are hard to herd and get to go in one direction," replied Isaiah.

Iswa laughed and said, "Yes, my old friend Esty's chickens have been teaching journeymen for years, but what is the deeper meaning of the chickens?"

"Promises are promises," replied Isaiah.

Iswa nodded.

They walked a bit further, and Isaiah went on, "I came to realize that when you make a promise to do something, it's very important that you follow through and do what you said you would do."

Iswa nodded again and said, "Yes, promises should never be treated lightly."

Isaiah went on, "I never had any idea how what seemed like a simple, somewhat trivial promise could ultimately be so serious, even life and death."

They walked a bit further, and Iswa went on, "A man of integrity treats his word as very important. He does what he says he will do. You made a promise to Esty to watch after his chickens. It may have seemed trivial at the time, but you did exactly that – your words and your actions aligned."

Iswa's last words sank deep into Isaiah's heart. He knew that he had almost turned the chickens over to what was possibly a shapeshifter wolf. It sent a chill up his spine.

Isaiah thought about his encounter with the man and Iswa's description the day before of wolves and shapeshifters. *Could the man have been... Temp?* He just didn't know how to approach it with Iswa. It now appeared that he had come very close to turning the chickens over to the man ... who may have been Temp. At the time, it seemed logical, an acceptable thing to do, but now, as he thought back, he knew that he had been driven by his desire for the cool water of the lake and frustration with the chickens. He had come so close to failing. He realized he still had a ways to go to becoming a Journeyman.

CHAPTER 7

THE GOOD SAMARITAN

Hon had just removed the last weeds from his garden when Isaiah and Iswa walked back up the trail from Esty's home. "Hello there, master Isaiah, how has your morning been?" called out Hon in his rich British accent. He had a twinkle in his eyes as if he already knew about the events of the morning.

"Interesting, very interesting," replied Isaiah.

Hon just chuckled and then asked, "I have a task I need some help with, Master Isaiah. Can you help?"

Isaiah is always amused by Hon's very proper English speech that referred to him as "Master Isaiah." In fact, he had grown quite fond of the title and smiled every time Hon used it.

"Of course, what can I do to help?" replied Isaiah.

"Well, wonderful, good man. Just wonderful. This will be such a help. I have a wagon of goods to take to Mrs. Endis. She makes a huge order every year at this time. It's always one of my biggest of the year and quite profitable. Could you take them to her, Master Isaiah?"

Isaiah responded affirmatively, but then paused and asked, "One thing though, who is Mrs. Endis and where does she live?"

Hon explained that she lived down the trail behind his house. He would know he had arrived when he came to the beautiful cottage built inside a tree and covered in beautiful marigold flowers. Well, it wasn't precise directions, but from Hon's description, Isaiah supposed he could find it without too much trouble. Isaiah smiled because he had come to learn that everything in this magical land seemed to be just down the trail.

Hon showed him to a small wagon filled with goods that included flour, corn, carrots, beans, and plenty of fruits and honey. It was quite a load.

"Now, this is Cletus," Hon pointed to the donkey that pulled the wagon. "He knows the way." Cletus turned and gave a loud "Hee Haw" and then turned his head and said clearly, "Hello, Master Isaiah."

Isaiah responded with a smile and thought, *Cletus must be British also.*

Isaiah climbed up into the wagon and released the brake, and off they went. Fortunately, he had driven a wagon back on his father's farm and was quite comfortable.

The trip was going quite smoothly as Cletus set an even, steady pace. Occasionally, Isaiah and Cletus would talk, which was both entertaining and informative to Isaiah. Cletus pointed out various landmarks along the way and described previous adventures he had been on with prior journeymen. Cletus' life was far from dull as he told stories of midnight rescues and victories won over bandits and thieves. It was quite interesting and exciting.

The sun had begun to dip low in the sky as they plodded along the trail, and Isaiah realized this was much farther than "just down the trail." Suddenly, they stopped.

Cletus turned and cocked his head to listen, "Did you hear that, Master Isaiah?"

Isaiah had not heard a thing but realized Cletus's hearing might be a bit more sensitive than his own. He asked, "No, what did you hear?"

"I'm just not sure."

They slowly progressed forward, and Cletus kept his head cocked while Isaiah cupped his hand around an ear to carefully listen for the sound. Without warning, in the distance, ever so faint, it sounded like crying.

"Do you hear it?"

"Yes, yes, I do, very faint, but I definitely do hear it this time."

They edged ahead cautiously and listened carefully to identify the source of the sound. Then they heard it again, but much louder, and it came from their right side. Both Cletus and Isaiah turned their heads to follow the sound and saw a small bridge over a creek. At the foot of the bridge lay a small wagon turned over on its side.

Isaiah jumped from the seat of his wagon and raced through the woods to the spot of the wagon. When he arrived at the bridge, he paused to take in the sight. The wagon was nearly destroyed, and a raccoon dressed in a topcoat lay next to it. The raccoon appeared to have a serious head wound as blood ran down the side of its face. Another raccoon dressed in a dress was crying hysterically and trying to stop the bleeding from the head wound.

The female raccoon cried out, "Help us, please help us." Isaiah jumped down from the bridge and came alongside her. "Please, help us," she said, "my husband has been injured, and I need to stop the bleeding!" Isaiah froze for a second; he simply did not know what to do, and then he remembered something Hon had said just as they were leaving, "Oh, by the way, there's a medicine kit under the driver's seat."

Isaiah turned and said as calmly as he could, "I'll be back in a minute. I need to get something from my wagon." He leaped up and ran up the embankment back to the wagon. When he got to Cletus, he was nearly out of breath but managed to tell him about the wounded raccoon. He opened the lid to the driver's seat and plunged his hand into the well under the seat and felt around for anything that might be a medicine box. His fingers ran over oily rags and the cold steel of tools used to repair wheels on the wagon, but nothing felt like a medicine kit. "Where is it?" he said out loud, "Certainly, Hon had not been mistaken." Suddenly, his hand bumped against a flat surface with what felt like hinges deep within the seat well. He grabbed it firmly and pulled it out. In his hands was a small wooden box with the words Medicine Kit painted across the top. He quickly opened the box and found gauze and cotton, but then his hand bumped up against a bottle. He pulled it out and read the contents. Scribbled on the bottle were the words Licorice Root. He knew from his time on the farm that this root could create clotting and stop bleeding. His father had used it on both the boys and the animals.

Isaiah jumped up and ran back to the destroyed wagon and plopped to his knees beside the injured raccoon. He opened the bottle and began to sprinkle the ground licorice root on the raccoon's wound. The raccoon's anxious wife looked on and tried through tears to compose herself enough to help. She collected herself and continued to dab the wound with a blood-soaked handkerchief. Isaiah put his arm around her in an effort to console her as they both sat silently and waited to see if the medicine worked. After several anxious minutes had passed, it became clear that the bleeding was subsiding. Isaiah took a deep breath, and the wife continued to dab at small amounts of blood that still trickled from the wound, but the situation had greatly improved.

They heard a low guttery moan come from the husband. He slowly opened his eyes and blinked several times. His wife began to cry again, but now out of relief. She leaned over and they embraced. Isaiah leaned back, satisfied that they had stabilized the situation.

The husband looked up and stammered out, "Who, who are you?"

"A friend," responded Isaiah.

His wife turned to Isaiah with tears running down her face and said, "Thank you."

At just that moment, three young raccoons scampered out of the tall grass and embraced their mother; all were crying and needed reassurance. The scene nearly brought Isaiah to tears.

As things began to calm down, the wife wrapped her husband's head in bandages, and she and Isaiah began to talk. He found out the husband's name was Liam. And her name was Sovi, and they have three children. They live in a small den some distance from here.

"That was quite an accident," said Isaiah.

"Accident, this was no accident," responded Sovi.

Isaiah sat back and looked at her with a puzzled look, "What do you mean?"

She went on but became more agitated as she talked, "We were attacked by coyote bandits and thieves. We had a full wagon of goods. Our entire supply for the upcoming winter. They just jumped us at the bridge and threw Liam off the wagon. They took our supplies and smashed our wagon to bits; they left us here to die."

Isaiah was shocked by the story. He had no idea what had occurred and felt very sorry for this small family. It was just then that a thought hit him… a terrorizing thought. *Cletus was up on the trail by himself, still hitched to the wagon, which was full of goods.*

Isaiah jumped to his feet and said, "Uh, uh, Sovi, please forgive me, but I must get back to my wagon and check on Cletus. Please trust me. I'll be back shortly." With that, he bound up the bank and headed into the woods to where he had left Cletus and the wagon. His mind raced with fear as he wondered what he would find. *Would the wagon be ravaged, and all the goods gone? Would Cletus be injured or…even dead?* He tried not to think about it but instead ran as fast as his legs would carry him. As he got near the main trail, his muscles were screaming with pain from running so hard. He burst through the trees, and to his great relief, there stood Cletus still hitched to the wagon with everything in order.

He took a deep breath, and his heart began to calm. He smiled and slowed to a jog as he came up to Cletus. He bent over to catch his breath and, with his hands on his knees, asked, "Are you ok, my friend?"

"Why, yes of course," replied Cletus, somewhat startled by the sudden appearance of Isaiah and the urgency of the question. "Shouldn't I be?"

Isaiah stroked Cletus' neck and let out a sigh of relief, "It is good to see you, my friend." He then filled him in on what he had learned from Sovi about the coyote bandits.

"We must load the family and get them to safety as quickly as possible!"

Just as the words left his mouth, he heard the high-pitched howl of a coyote. He spun his head and looked in the direction of the sound and saw a large, slender coyote standing on a rock above them. The coyote threw his head back and let out another howl. It was threatening and intimidating to watch. The sound sent shivers through Isaiah.

The howl was followed by another coyote howl, and soon other coyotes began to appear on rocks above the wagon. They began to spread out to completely surround Cletus and Isaiah. They growled, snarled, and looked down menacingly at Cletus and Isaiah.

Isaiah estimated twelve in all and knew they were in for a fight. He quickly ran behind Cletus and unhooked him from the wagon, which allowed him to spin around and face the coyotes face-on with Isaiah. The coyotes didn't attack but processed the fact that big Cletus was no longer bound by a harness and now stood beside Isaiah shoulder-to-shoulder. Perhaps their courage had been a bit dented by the change in odds.

The coyotes began to spread out not unlike the wolves Isaiah had faced days before. They looked for a weakness, a moment when they could pounce, but this time not simply to injure and steal but rather to kill and ravage.

Cletus turned his back to the coyotes and looked over his shoulder. Isaiah was confused at first, but then saw a wink from Cletus that said, I'm ready. Isaiah turned his back to Cletus and, with his eyes fixed on the coyotes, stuck his hand deep into his pouch, and felt around for his slingshot. Ever since the wolf experience at the river, Isaiah had been carving a new slingshot in every spare moment. On the other side of the river, in his world, he was known as the best slingshot shooter in the village. He could hit a bullseye from twenty yards away, time and time again. Today, he needed to be that accurate, if not even better.

The coyotes began to yelp and growl louder and louder until they worked themselves into a frenzy. Finally, one of the coyotes charged Cletus from behind when he thought he had an advantage, since Cletus faced the other direction. Cletus spun his head quickly and bucked and kicked as the coyote charged. The kick landed with a thunderous thud on the chest of the coyote and launched him in the air thirty feet. The coyote let out a loud yelp of pain as the kick made solid contact. At the very least, the kick had knocked the wind out of the coyote, but it appeared to have actually broken several ribs. When he landed with a loud thud, he lay on the ground gasping for air and for the time was out of the fray.

Next, another coyote assumed he could avoid Cletus' powerful hind legs and charged from the front, but just as he was about to leap, Isaiah let loose his slingshot, and a piece of granite shot through the air and buried itself in the head of the charging coyote. The impact brought him to a complete stop in his tracks, and he lay unconscious in the dust of the road.

The coyotes became outraged, and now several at once charged in an attempt to outnumber Isaiah and Cletus. As they charged, Cletus caught two coyotes at the same time, one with each hind leg, and launched them backward, and each crashed against a large rock where they lay motionless. On Isaiah's side, two more charged him, and as they launched themselves through the air to attack him, he deftly dived under them and spun and delivered perfectly aimed rocks into the chest of each coyote. They hit the ground stunned and gasping for air.

Isaiah knew that this needed to end, and end now. The only way was to take down the leader, who was a large coyote that stood on a large rock that overlooked the battle. The leader continually gave out orders to the pack. As Cletus continued to buck wildly, Isaiah dropped to a knee and took careful aim at the large alpha male coyote on top of the rock. He drew back his slingshot, slowed his breathing, and did everything he could to slow his heartbeat. It would be a long shot, longer than any he had ever made before. He aimed between the eyes of the coyote that stood on the rock some thirty yards away. He paused, and suddenly an arrow pierced the chest of the alpha male. It lurched backward for a moment and seemed to hang in the air and then went completely limp and fell dead from the rock.

The remaining coyotes stopped in their tracks and turned toward the rocks and their fallen leader. They seemed confused and suddenly alone and vulnerable. Another arrow flew and caught another coyote squarely in the chest, killing it instantly. The coyotes that were left hastily turned and ran off into the woods while Isaiah and Cletus' heads spun from side to side, prepared for the next attack. Their adrenaline made them hyper vigilant, but slowly they came to realize it was over; they had won.

Cletus turned to Isaiah, and a big grin appeared, "What an adventure," he cried, and then he began a huge donkey hee-haw laugh. Isaiah smiled and embraced his new friend around the neck. Isaiah, though, now turned his attention to the woods. The question was, "Who shot those arrows?"

There was no obvious answer to his question. He couldn't see anyone in the thick cover, and tension started to return as he started to look around anxiously. Who was out there?

Out of the corner of his eye, he caught movement and spun his head to catch a glimpse of someone in the trees some thirty yards away. Isaiah called out, "Hello, thank you for helping us."

For what seemed like an eternity, there was no response and only the sounds of birds and crickets. But then a figure appeared and stepped out of the shadows toward them. It was a young man, a few years older than Isaiah. He carried a bow in one hand and had a quiver full of arrows slung over his shoulder. He was thin and taller than Isaiah and had brown hair that came down to just short of his shoulders. He had dark brown eyes. The boy had dirt smudges on his face and all over his clothes, and it was apparent that he had been out in the forest for some time. His eyes darted back and forth, and he moved cautiously toward them. All of this seemed normal except for the obvious blood stain on his lower left shirt. He had obviously been wounded at some time. Isaiah immediately thought back to his and Iswa's conversation with the farmer and his wife. They had provided bandages to a wounded young man.

He approached Isaiah with his bow in one hand and an arrow strung in the bow and pulled back with his other hand. Isaiah spoke up, "We're friendlies, no need for the bow here."

The young man was clearly in a heightened state of alert and continued to look from side to side and slowly turned to check behind him as he walked. He came up to Isaiah and abruptly asked, "Who are you? What are you doing here?"

Isaiah responded, "My...my name is Isaiah, and this is Cletus," as he pointed to his donkey friend. He went on to explain who they were and the purpose of their trip to deliver supplies to Mrs. Endis. The young man seemed unfazed by Isaiah's explanation, but he finally did relax a bit as he deemed them to be no threat.

He turned to Isaiah and said, "You need to get out of here quickly before they return, and believe me, they will return." Isaiah understood and rapidly re-hitched Cletus to the wagon and turned to the young man and said, "Why don't you travel with us? There is safety in numbers."

The young man started to decline but thought about it and agreed to travel to the house since the wagon would move quickly and save him energy. He climbed up in the wagon and stood behind the driver's bench as a sentinel with his bow in hand. Isaiah said, "Wait a minute," and jumped off the wagon. "I need to get Sovi's family."

"What...we don't have time," protested the young man. "They are only raccoons!" and he climbed into the driver's seat and tried to get Cletus to move. Isaiah jumped in front of the wagon and yelled, "We're not going anywhere without them." Cletus saw Isaiah's reaction and dug his donkey's hooves into the soil deeply. He made sure they didn't go anywhere until Isaiah's say-so. The young man threw his hands in the air in frustration and yelled, "Fools," and sat back in the seat.

Isaiah ran as hard as he could down the hill into the ravine. The raccoon family was still down at the destroyed wagon but had hidden when they had heard the battle up the hill. Slowly, Sovi peeked her head out to see if it was all clear and saw Isaiah coming rapidly down the hill. He called out, "Sovi, we must move quickly and get all of you into our wagon. We have defeated them for now, but who knows when they will return."

When she heard this news, Sovi was relieved and anxious as she knew all too well the persistence of coyotes. She shouted to the children, "Children! Gather your things, we must go now!" With that, the children poured out of the tall grass and began to run toward Isaiah.

Isaiah proceeded next to Liam and stooped down, gently lifting the male raccoon in his arms. Liam moaned but was conscious, a good sign. Sovi and the children trailed behind as Isaiah made his way back up the hill to the wagon. He gave a quick introduction to Cletus and turned toward the young man who was now standing in the wagon with an arrow drawn in his bow and rapidly turning from side to side, looking toward the trees. "This is a... new friend, acquaintance...who helped us." The young man simply nodded at Sovi. The children clung to their mother at the sight of the dead coyotes around them. They all got in the wagon, and Isaiah laid Liam down and did his best to make him comfortable. He jumped in the driver's seat and wasted no time as he released the brake, and they headed rapidly down the road. The sun was just about to set, and they had no intention of still being here after dark.

As they travelled down the road, the rhythm of the wagon and the long shadow from a setting sun rocked the children to sleep in the back of the wagon. Isaiah broke the silence and asked Sovi, "What will you do now?"

Sovi sighed, "I don't know, Liam is badly injured and will need time to heal." She paused and then continued, "The bandits took all of the supplies." She paused again as if to compose herself, but tears began to trickle down her face, and she tried to wipe them away with her sleeve. "All of our winter supplies were in that wagon. We had gone down into the valley to buy everything we needed for the winter." The words seemed to break the dam of her emotions, and she began to cry harder into her blood-soaked handkerchief. Isaiah felt very sorry for the family and fought back his own tears. *What can he do to help this poor family*? He thought to himself.

The sun had set, and they had rounded a bend on the trail when both Isaiah and Cletus saw a light in the distance. "Ah, perhaps that's Mrs. Endis' home," called out Isaiah, but as they drew closer, it didn't match the description given by Hon... This was a two-story stand-alone house, no tree, no marigolds; however, there were lights on, which was a good sign.

Isaiah jumped down from the wagon and went to the door and knocked with the large, heavy metal knocker. The young man who had joined them stood in the wagon with his bow in one hand, with an arrow ready to be drawn back by the other. He turned quickly in a circle and kept an eye on the surroundings. There was no response at the door, so Isaiah knocked again and waited. Finally, after what seemed like minutes, they heard the sound of the door handle being turned from the inside. The door cracked open, and a portly groundhog with wire-rimmed glasses and a mustache peered out at them. "Heh, hem," he cleared his throat, "Hello, may I help you?" he said somewhat formally.

Isaiah introduced himself, pointed to the wagon, and explained that they had a very injured friend in the wagon. The groundhog threw the door open and said, "Why didn't you say so first? Quick, bring him in here." Isaiah went to the wagon and lifted Liam down and helped him into the house as Sovi and the children trailed behind. The groundhog cleared his dining table with a push of everything to the floor, and Isaiah laid Liam on top of the table. The groundhog gave a brief glance around Isaiah to the shaken, wide-eyed children and gave a loud, "Grumf," and then returned his attention to Liam.

"Humm, this was a bad blow he took. Did he have a fall?"

Isaiah looked at Sovi and then said, "Well, sort of, with some help from some bandit coyotes."

"Blasted coyotes," erupted the groundhog, "ahem...excuse my language, ma'am." He nodded toward Sovi and the children. Liam saw a smile come across Sovi's face for the first time as she seemed to agree with the sentiment.

"Well, it looks like you did the right thing to stop the bleeding and bandaged it properly. He needs some stitches, though. I'll get my kit," said the groundhog matter-of-factly.

Isaiah looked at Sovi somewhat quizzically as the groundhog went into another room and reappeared with a small black bag. When the groundhog returned, he sensed their confusion. He looked over his wire-rimmed glasses and mustache and said, "Oh, excuse me, I didn't properly introduce myself, my name is Doctor Nesta. I am the Doctor in these here parts."

Isaiah looked at Sovi, and they both burst into laughter. They had come to the exact person they needed to see, Dr. Nesta.

The Doctor proceeded to stitch Liam's wounds and make him comfortable in one of his beds. He turned to both Isaiah and Sovi and said, "he shouldn't move for a few days. He needs his rest. He and you and the children can stay here."

The young stranger had come into the doctor's house but stayed near the window and looked out constantly as if he expected someone or something to arrive any minute. He was clearly still in a high alert mode with his bow in his left hand and a quiver of arrows slung over his shoulder.

Doctor Nesta walked back into the front room and took one look at the young man's blood-stained shirt and said, "Now it's your turn, better let me take a look at that wound."

The young man began to protest, but the doctor insisted, "Listen, let me at least look at it and make sure it hasn't gotten infected." The young man reluctantly consented, and the doctor pulled his shirt up and removed a blood-stained bandage that revealed a nasty, deep wound that was still seeping blood and yellow fluid. "No, no, no, that's not good," murmured Doctor Nesta. "Some infection has started to set in, and we must clean the wound and treat that right away or it will only get worse and could...kill you." He looked directly in the eyes of the young man as he said these words, and for the first time, some response came from the young man as he flinched in pain as the doctor began to clean the wound. "Son, what's your name?"

The young man's eyes darted around and assessed whether he should answer, and finally said softly, "Luc."

"Well, Luc, you're going to be alright, thanks to your friends who brought you here."

* * *

Isaiah was just about to climb into the wagon when he paused with one foot on the wagon step. He froze as if something was on his mind. He turned and looked at Sovi who had just come out of the house. He then turned and walked to the back of the wagon and began to unload goods onto the ground. Sovi, who was there to see him off, asked, "What are you doing?"

Isaiah came up to her and looked her in the eyes and said, "There is a long, cold winter coming, and you will need these." Sovi began to protest, "But, but I have no way to pay you."

Isaiah smiled and said, "Let's just not worry about that. You just take care of Liam and the kids." She began to cry and, through tears, said, "Thank you, thank you – God Bless you."

Isaiah turned to Luc and said, "We have a bit further to go tonight, you're welcome to join us." Luc nodded affirmatively and climbed up onto the wagon, and with that, Isaiah, Luc, and Cletus continued down the road toward Mrs. Endis' house. Cletus looked around at Isaiah and smiled while Isaiah thought about how he was going to tell Mrs. Endis that she only got half her goods.

It was late, but they finally arrived at Mrs. Endis' house, and she had waited up for them. She came out of the house with amazing energy for the lateness of the hour.

"Welcome, welcome, welcome, I'm so glad you made it. I had begun to get worried," called an energetic female groundhog who was obviously Mrs. Endis.

Isaiah and Cletus explained what happened to Mrs. Endis, and she was quite understanding of the entire situation: "You poor boys, you must be exhausted."

"Well, now that you mention it, I am pretty tired," said Isaiah. By now, Cletus had wandered off to a feeding trough and bucket of water. She invited Isaiah into the house and asked, "By the way, how is the ol'buzzard?" Isaiah obviously looked perplexed, and she abruptly added, "You know old Doc Nesta, or Nasty as I like to call him." She winked at Isaiah and giggled with her last words. It was clear that she and the Doc had a history together.

Isaiah unloaded the goods, and Mrs. Endis indicated she would make do with what she had until more provisions could come. Suddenly, Isaiah could hide it no longer; he gave out a huge yawn as the fatigue hit him.

"Oh, my poor dear, you must get some rest. You can use one of my rooms upstairs."

"If it's all the same to you, I 'd like to sleep in the barn with Cletus tonight; we've been through a lot together today." She simply smiled and said, "Of course, that would be fine."

That night, Isaiah lay on a pile of hay and fell into a deep sleep next to Cletus with his arm wrapped around his new friend's neck. The adventure they had today would be with them forever.

Luc sat in the hay loft on a bale of hay with his bow clutched in one hand, and he peered out the window. His weary eyes continually scanned the field and woods beyond.

CHAPTER 8

LESSONS

Early in the morning, just as the first rays of sunlight rose into the sky, Isaiah rolled over on the pile of hay and blinked his eyes several times. Cletus lay next to him, still sound asleep, and was snoring loudly. Isaiah smiled, propped himself up, and looked around the barn. It was a well-organized barn with several horse stalls lining each side. Bridles hung from hooks between each stall. He stood up and remembered that Luc had been in the hay loft, so he worked his way around to see up into the loft and saw Luc sound asleep against some bales with his bow still in his hand. He smiled and headed outside to get some water from the well in the center of the barnyard.

He lowered the bucket into the well and began winding the handle to raise it when he heard a voice. "I see you had some trouble coming up here." Isaiah froze as he recognized the voice of the strange man with the long black and gray hair, the crooked nose, and the strange smile.

"I came across several dead coyotes. They can be a mean bunch. Nasty business dealing with that pack. I've seen their work before." Isaiah didn't know how to respond. He felt very uneasy, so he just nodded and continued raising the bucket.

"I noticed that a couple of those coyotes had been killed by arrows. It took some real skill to shoot them; the arrows went clean through the heart. Didn't realize you had that kind of skill with a bow. Congratulations, nice shooting." Isaiah lifted the bucket and set it down on the ground and didn't respond. There was a pause as the strange man stared at Isaiah but finally continued. "Well, Journeyman. I guess you've completed your mission."

Isaiah spun his head. "What...what do you mean?"

"Well, you saved that raccoon family, didn't you. A very noble thing to do. Yes, indeed, a very noble thing. So, you can return home. You accomplished your mission."

Isaiah was confused and stammered, "Well...well...I don't know about that."

"Of course you do, journeymen are called to do noble things and accomplish certain missions. What could be more important than saving that raccoon family with those little children?"

Isaiah knew he was correct, but was this his calling to save Liam and Sovi and their children? Was he done?

"In fact, I can assure you that you can go home right now!"

Isaiah looked intently at the strange man and asked, "What do you mean?"

"Look into the well that you just drew water from."

Isaiah was confused, but the man continued, "Go ahead, step up and look down into it, get a good look. Tell me what you see."

Isaiah edged over and peered down into the blackness. The blackness of the well and water at the bottom began to give way to a swirl of light and colors, which transformed into an image that got clearer with every swirl. Isaiah suddenly realized he was looking at his family's cabin with smoke trailing from the chimney. It was a bright, clear morning, and the front door opened and out stepped his mother, who walked toward the chicken coop with a basket. He knew her routine, and she was on her way to gather eggs for family breakfast. He smiled and peered lovingly at his mother.

She stopped outside the chicken coop, leaned against a tree, reached inside her apron, pulled out a handkerchief, and wiped her eyes as she began to cry. Isaiah pressed closer to the well and asked, "Why is she crying?"

"She misses you; she longs for you to come home...she is very afraid that something very bad has happened to you."

"Mother, I am here, I am fine. Mother, don't worry," shouted Isaiah down the well.

"She can't hear you, Isaiah. She comes out here day after day and cries for you. She is deeply troubled and has become very depressed, but you could go home right now and take all the pain away. You've done your duty, completed your mission. It's time to go home."

"What do you mean...right now? How...how could I go home... right...right...now?" asked Isaiah with tears now flowing down his face.

"Why, that's easy, just follow that path between those two oak trees across the barn yard. That path will take you home in just a few minutes. Remember, things are quite different on this side of the river."

Isaiah was now looking at the path between the two oak trees that the strange, long-haired man was now pointing to with a crooked finger. He took several steps toward the path to see down it when the Voice began to speak to him. "Trust me, Isaiah. I define the mission of the Journeyman; no one else." Isaiah stopped and looked back at the well and then back at the man and took a deep breath. "No, I am not done yet; there is still more for me to do here. I haven't made it to Endemar yet."

"Humph, suit yourself, I guess you want to make your family suffer even more, especially your mother. I would have thought you loved them too much to make them endure so much grief. Sounds very selfish, yes, very selfish."

"Enough," shouted Isaiah. "I am a Journeyman, and I will follow the Voice. Leave me alone."

"Alright, I am leaving, but don't say I didn't warn you. I'm not responsible for what happens next. Not at all, it's all on you. I pity your family, especially your poor mother."

"Get away, I said, leave me alone!" With that, the man turned and walked down a pathway that led deep into the woods. "Oh, by the way, I'd be very careful heading home to Hon's place. Those coyotes have friends, lots of friends." As the man got to the opening of the path, he stopped and asked, "By the way, one more question, have you happened to see a young man a bit older and taller than you running around these woods?"

Isaiah was incensed and just stared at the man and said nothing.

Isaiah ran into the barn and shouted at Cletus and Luc up in the loft, "Time to go, we must get out of here – now!" Cletus immediately sprang to his feet, sending hay flying in all directions, and Luc stumbled down the stairs from the loft, wiping sleep from his eyes. "What's up?" asked Luc.

"I'll explain later, but we need to get out of here now. Those coyotes we dealt with last night have friends, and I have reason to believe they are on their way here...right now."

Cletus ran out to the wagon and got in position to be hitched to the wagon, which Isaiah did without delay. Luc grabbed his backpack and bow and climbed up on the wagon and stood behind the driver's seat as Isaiah began to lead Cletus and the wagon out of the barnyard.

Luc suddenly shouted, "Stop!" Isaiah brought Cletus and the wagon to a stop, and both he and Cletus turned and looked at Luc. "I know another way back home. It is a bit out of the way, but it should be safer. Those coyotes will be lying in wait for us to come back the same way we came, but this time they will have many more with them. More than the three of us can handle."

Isaiah looked at Cletus and then back at Luc and said, "Ok, lead on."

For the first hour, they were quiet and just listened to the sounds of the forest as it came awake for a new day, along with the steady clip-clop sound of Cletus's hooves. The sunrise cast rays through the trees that created an early morning cathedral of light that looked like search lights through the last shadows of night. Finally, Isaiah broke the silence and told Luc about the farmer that he and Iswa had rescued. He turned to Luc and asked, "Why were those men and wolves chasing you?"

Luc was initially flustered by the direct question and stammered back, "What makes you think I had anything to do with that?"

"Well…the farmer and his wife described a young man who was a couple of years older than me with brown hair down to just above his shoulders and had a wound in his side that they bandaged."

Luc looked at him and didn't protest but sat in silence for a minute to gather his response. A small smile came across Luc's face. "I guess that does fit me. Let's just say we had a disagreement over some property."

"It must have been some property that they were willing to kill you over it."

"Well, it didn't belong to me, but it didn't belong to them either. I just wanted to return it to its rightful owner."

"And what exactly was it that you intended to return?" asked Isaiah.

"I'm not exactly sure what it was. It was in a wooden box. I never could get it open. The interesting part is, I don't have it now, but they think I do, I got rid of it…er, rather hid it. They have been after me for weeks to get it back, but I don't have it."

"Really, you don't have it. What did you do with it?" asked Isaiah with a shocked look on his face.

"It never left the city of Endemar. I dumped it."

When Isaiah heard the name Endemar, he spun and looked at Luc and asked, "Luc, are you from Endemar? That's where I am headed."

"No, I am from Gebil, on the coast," replied Luc. "Why are you going to Endemar?"

This was a very interesting question for Isaiah that he wasn't quite sure how to answer. The Voice had beckoned him to go, but it was unclear why or what his mission would be there. He hesitated in quiet, and all you could hear was the steady pace of Cletus' hooves and the birds still singing.

"I am called to go there. I am not sure what my mission is yet, but it will become clearer when I get there."

Luc looked back at him and raised an eyebrow, and asked, "Are you a Journeyman?"

It was the first time Isaiah had been asked that question, but he paused and then answered, "I hope to be, I'm still in training."

Luc's eyes widened, and he leaned back in his seat and said, "I have never met a Journeyman, heard about them throughout my life, but mostly legend and myth. So…who's your mentor?"

"The watchman, Iswa, is my mentor," replied Isaiah. "In fact, I'm sure Iswa could help you get home."

Luc became quiet and didn't ask another question about his being a Journeyman, but finally asked, "How close were they to Hon's hut?" Isaiah responded, "About 20 minutes away." Luc suddenly said emphatically, "Stop the wagon."

Isaiah stopped the wagon, and Luc gathered his bow and quiver of arrows along with his small backpack and jumped off. "Time for me to leave. If you're ever in Gebil, look me up," and he turned and headed off the trail into the deep woods.

And just like that, Luc was gone as he disappeared instantly into the underbrush.

It was late morning when Isaiah and Cletus brought the wagon to a stop in front of Hon's hut. Isaiah had spent much time the night before considering how to tell Hon that he had given away half his goods.

"Good day, gentlemen," came Hon's voice across the meadow as they pulled the wagon onto his property. "How was your trip, delightful, I hope?

Cletus glanced at Isaiah and winked. "Well, quite eventful," replied Isaiah. There was a slight chuckle that came from Cletus that he quickly disguised as a whiney.

"Oh, do tell me about it, I'm so anxious to hear all about it," responded Hon.

Isaiah responded and went through the whole story of the coyote bandits and the fight, injured Liam and his wife, Sovi, and the children, and ol' Doc Nesta. As he retold the story, Isaiah began to realize not only the magnitude of the events but also how many ways they could have been killed. It was truly a miracle. When he came to the end, though, he had to give Hon the bad news. Isaiah paused and then continued, "Hon, I have to give you some bad news, though. I gave half of the goods to Sovi and Liam to get them through the winter. I'll find some way to make it up to you, but I felt it was the right thing to do." There was an awkward silence between them for what seemed like minutes, and then Hon finally smiled and spoke in a calm, almost quiet tone, "Outstanding, excellent decision, Master Isaiah. The absolute right thing to do, and you did it. Yes, excellent."

Hon turned and said, "Ok, let's begin to gather replacement goods for Mrs. Endis," and that seemed to be the end of it. Isaiah was a bit stunned as he had prepared for a long-drawn-out discussion about the decision he had made, but none of that occurred. Hon just moved on, and Isaiah jumped in with Hon to fill crates and barrels with carrots, beets, and berries.

Isaiah had worked hard for a couple of hours when he stopped for a break and took out a rag to wipe the sweat from his face. From behind him, he heard Iswa's voice, "It sounds like you had quite the adventure yesterday."

Isaiah looked up at him and smiled, "Yes, we did," and laughed. He then turned serious and said, "I was scared and wasn't sure what to do. When I found Liam unconscious and saw all the blood, I felt helpless, and then a voice spoke to me and said, 'Remember what Hon said, there's a medicine kit under the seat.' I hadn't thought about that at all since we left Hon's."

Iswa listened quietly but intently as they walked together in silence, but then finally spoke, "But you heard the Voice, and you obeyed...and Liam lives." He let the last words sink in and then went on, "Men of integrity must learn to hear and understand the Voice. The Good Book tells us that the Voice will guide us and direct our paths. Our job is to listen and obey."

They walked a bit further, and Isaiah finally responded, "Sometimes it's hard to hear and know that it's the Voice speaking."

Iswa responded, "Yes, it does take time, but that is why this is a journey and not necessarily a destination. Throughout your life, you will continue to learn how to listen and obey. The important thing is to continue to strive to listen and hear his Voice."

"I think I understand. When I went to get on the wagon to leave the doctor's house, I just couldn't leave with the feeling that I must do something to help Liam and Sovi and those small children. It had a grip on me." Isaiah continued, "I looked at those supplies and thought this family needs help. They won't last the winter without supplies. Then I looked at the supplies in the wagon, and a Voice inside me said, 'Give them half.' So, I did."

Iswa smiled as he listened to Isaiah describe the events of the previous day.

Suddenly, Isaiah stopped and turned toward Iswa and looked him in the eye, "You know what was really amazing, when I told Hon, he didn't bat an eye. In fact, he said, 'Outstanding, excellent decision,' and then immediately started to collect more goods for Mrs. Endis."

Iswa nodded, smiled, and asked quietly, "What was your first impression of Hon when you met him?"

Isaiah thought for a second and then said, "I noticed how gentle and patient he was." Iswa listened intently and just nodded again, "and... and there was this incredible peace about him."

"Hon wasn't always this way. No, not at all." Iswa paused to collect his thoughts and then continued, "When I first met him, he was always very stressed, always running about, nervous, and trying to succeed in his business. He was very proud. The stress became so big that it nearly broke him. It was when he started slowing down and trusting the words of the Good Book and listening to the Voice that he began to change dramatically. Isaiah listened intently and took it all in carefully.

Iswa went on, "Men of integrity must learn to hear and trust the Voice; they must let it teach and guide them and develop their character. Hon has learned that lesson well, and that's why he responded the way he did. He recognized the Voice's direction and work in everything you went through yesterday. Who was he to challenge that or chastise you for giving away half the goods? Hon knows that carrots, flour, beets, and honey are all replaceable, but to hear and act on the guidance of the Voice – that is...very special."

Iswa paused, turned, and looked straight into Isaiah's eyes, "The challenge the last two days was to learn to listen carefully to the Voice when under stress and to make decisions with integrity. "Well done, yes, very well done, Isaiah."

Isaiah returned to his work in Hon's garden, where he filled crates and barrels. As the day began to draw to a close and the sun began to set, they finished the last of the replacement crates. Hon let out a giggle and pronounced, "There, that will do it! We have all the replacement goods needed to fill Mrs. Endis' order. Let's call it a day and head in for some supper." Isaiah looked at the filled crates and barrels and felt a sense of fulfilment, gratitude, and a deep sense of accomplishment. It had truly been a good day of hard work.

As they walked up to the hut, Isaiah heard a voice call out, "Mr. Isaiah, Mr. Isaiah." He stopped and turned around to see Riddle walking toward him rather swiftly. Riddle was a red-tailed squirrel that Isaiah met on his first night at Hon's. He was a unique individual, and Isaiah remembered his quiet demeanor at Hon's hut. He laughed with the others and only occasionally told a story or interjected some fine detail into someone else's story. Very nice fellow, but somewhat reserved. Despite his quiet manner, Isaiah also remembered well his confrontation with Iswa. He had seen him only a few times since his arrival, but each time he appeared as he did now - walking fast with a sense of purpose.

As Riddle came close, he stopped and asked, "Mr. Isaiah, could I possibly impose upon you to help me with some work tomorrow?" Isaiah looked at Hon, who smiled and nodded. He did not want to leave Hon hanging without help, but they had caught up today, and Hon's nod gave his approval.

"Sure, what can I do to help?" said Isaiah as he thought to himself, "...and now the third challenge begins."

"Wonderful, several of my workers need to be out of town, and you would be a great help. Thank you so much. I will see you tomorrow," and with that, Riddle began to bounce off on another mission. Isaiah, a bit surprised at the abruptness, called out, "But where shall we meet?"

Riddle stopped, turned, and giggled, "Oh, forgive me, I sometimes get in a bit of a hurry. Meet me across the meadow near those large pecan trees. At sunrise, if you will, please." And with that, he was off on another mission. Isaiah smiled at the nature of the conversation as Riddle seemed to always be scurrying about – on another mission. Isaiah thought to himself, *I have no idea what he wants me to do, but it will undoubtedly be some new challenge.* And with that, he headed into the hut to clean up and have Hon's incredible carrot and beet stew.

CHAPTER 9

PURPOSEVILLE

Isaiah was up bright and early and walked across the meadow toward the large pecan trees. The sun rays had just tipped over the treetops, and there was a fog that hung low over the meadow from the previous cool evening. It was quite surreal, and he walked through the fog that was up to his waist. Very beautiful and peaceful, but suddenly he heard Riddle's voice call out, "Good morning, Mr. Isaiah."

"Where are you?" called Isaiah.

Riddle giggled and said, "To your right, lad, and then come straight ahead." Isaiah followed his directions and voice until he stood directly in front of Riddle. "Well, thank you for your help today, Mr. Isaiah. Please follow me and we can get started." With that simple greeting, Riddle bound off into the trees and weaved back and forth around roots and branches and over rocks and through leaves. Isaiah stumbled to keep up as he tripped over roots and rocks and landed face-first in the dirt. He got up and stumbled forward with toppled trees in front of him. He put his foot on a moss-covered tree trunk and climbed over it while he tried to keep an eye on Riddle. Next, large pine trees with very low branches blocked any recognizable path, but Riddle simply scampered under with ease. The low branches presented a unique problem for Isaiah in that he had to find a way around or duck and crawl under as Riddle hurried ahead. Despite the difficulty, they soon reached a clearing in the trees where the fog had begun to burn off. Isaiah blinked several times to adjust to the bright sunlight, which was in sharp contrast to the darker shadows of the woods he had just come through.

His eyes adjusted, and he realized they were surrounded by pecan, walnut, and persimmon trees; all filled with nuts. Riddle called out, "We're here, what do you think?"

This question confused Isaiah for a moment as he didn't quite know what to say. "Well…" he said in a drawn-out manner, "there sure are a lot of nuts in those trees."

"Exactly! Just as there should be, for now," exclaimed Riddle, and Isaiah looked at Riddle quizzically.

"Follow me," said Riddle emphatically, and with that, he bound over to a nearby group of trees. At the base of the trees were large tarps and piles of burlap bags. He quickly spread out a tarp on the ground under one of the trees and then ran up the trunk into the branches. This all happened with the typical Riddle boundless energy. Before Isaiah had a chance to say anything, Riddle began to shake the tree violently, and a rainstorm of nuts came falling from the tree.

"Ouch, ouch, augh, ouch," yelled Isaiah as falling nuts hit his head, arms, and legs. He instantly jumped to avoid the hailstorm of nuts.

From his perch up in the tree, Riddle leaned around the tree trunk and giggled, "So sorry, forgot to warn you, Mr. Isaiah. You need to take a step back to avoid the falling nuts." By this time, Isaiah had figured this out on his own and moved a distance away.

After he had shaken the tree for some time, a large pile of nuts had collected on the tarp on the ground. Riddle bounded back down the tree and asked Isaiah to hand him a burlap bag. A shovel was at the base of the tree, and Riddle immediately began to shovel the nuts into the bag until it was full. He then grabbed another bag and continued to fill bags until all the nuts had been collected off the tarp. Riddle stopped, threw up his hands, and said matter-of-factly, "And that's how it's done."

Isaiah was nearly out of breath as he watched Riddle. It was an absolute whirlwind of constant movement and action. Isaiah stammered out, "Exactly, how what is done?"

"Collecting nuts, of course," responded Riddle with a broad smile. "We must harvest these nuts and get them to market. It is time." This straightforward, matter-of-fact response by Riddle was direct and to the point. He went on to explain that they, which meant he and Isaiah, must harvest the nuts from all these trees as quickly as possible.

Isaiah looked at the trees all around and wondered what he had gotten himself into, but this is what Riddle needed, and he had said he would help., So, off they went and for the entire morning went from tree to tree, shaking out nuts, collecting them, and bagging them in the burlap bags. Riddle flew from the ground up each tree and then back down to the ground over and over again while Isaiah became dizzy as his eyes went from the trees to the ground over and over again. The nonstop action with showers of nuts was continuous until the bags were filled beneath each tree. Riddle would then move to the next tree and repeat the whole process. Isaiah followed from tree to tree and filled bags.

After a short break for lunch and water, they continued until mid-afternoon when Riddle abruptly announced, "I have to leave for a while, but you keep on going," and with that short declaration, he turned and scampered away through the woods at his typical frenetic pace. Isaiah could not respond to Riddle quickly enough, and he was gone, leaving him standing there alone in the forest among the nut trees with his own thoughts. *Where did he go? Why did he have to leave so quickly?*

Isaiah was puzzled by the sudden departure but continued to work and assumed that Riddle would return at some point. He continued to fill bags and put them in piles around the meadow. When Riddle finally did return later in the day, he shouted, "Wonderful, very good, you have made excellent progress. Tomorrow we will move to the next orchard!"

Isaiah's head snapped around as this was news to him that there was more than one orchard, but he had committed to help, so back he would go tomorrow. They gathered all the bags from around the meadow and loaded the wagon, and Riddle went off to the market to deliver them to customers.

The next day was a repeat of the first day that included Riddle announcing mid-way through the afternoon that he had to leave and would return later. The work was not difficult for Isaiah, but it took time to shake trees and fill bags one after another. Sweat ran down Isaiah's face and drenched his shirt. He stopped for water and leaned up against a tree when he heard a voice. "Ol' Riddle's got you doing his work for him, huh?"

Isaiah recognized the voice immediately. It was the tall, dark-haired stranger who had claimed to be Esty's neighbor. An immediate uneasiness hit him, and his senses went on high alert. The man glared at Isaiah with a strange, crooked smirk on his face. His dark gray eyes had a thin yellow color around each pupil.

The stranger walked toward Isaiah, and he instinctively took a step back. "What, what are you doing here?" said Isaiah.

"Oh, I was in the area and thought I'd check up on you, old friend," responded the stranger with a low chuckle on the words, "old friend." "So, where's Riddle, that mangy little rodent. He always tries to skip out of work. This is an old trick of his that he's done before. Get some poor Journeyman to do all his hard work while he goes off and plays. Disgusting, I'd be mad if I were you.

Working so hard and sweating in this heat. What for, what do you get out of all this?"

The question hung in the air for a moment, and Isaiah thought, *he does have a point,* but he quickly dismissed that thought as he remembered who stood before him. "Get away from me, I know who you really are…Temp," he shouted. "I don't want you around here, so go… now!"

The stranger took a step back and said, "So you think you know who I am? Well, let's just get real with each other," and the stranger's hair began to grow out all over his body. His face contorted grotesquely into the snout of a wolf, and his body and arms twisted while his spine also contorted. Long claws appeared on what had been hands, and a long bushy tail appeared and menacingly whipped back and forth. His ears became wolf ears, and long, sharp fangs grew out of his mouth, and drool dripped from them. Finally, his once dark gray eyes changed into piercing, yellow eyes with pupils that looked like spears, long and narrow. He slipped down onto all fours and before Isaiah was Temp… the wolf.

"There, do you like me better this way, old friend?" Temp slinked away but continued to talk. "Ok, ok, I'll go, but you just remember what I told you. You'll see, he's using you. You fool!"

Isaiah picked up a rock and threw it in the direction of Temp, who had already disappeared into the woods as he yelled, "Get out here and don't come back!" Sweat was running down his face, and he tried to wipe it with his shirt, but it was already sopping wet from sweat. He began to shake and collapsed onto the dusty ground, breathing hard, and finally pulled his shirt off to cool down. Temp was nothing but trouble, deep trouble, and he certainly didn't give him any credence, but he did have a point. *Where did Riddle go each afternoon?*

The rest of the day went as the previous days, and Riddle returned enthusiastically to collect the bags and take them to market. On the third day, things went pretty much the same, but as Isaiah worked, he couldn't help but think about Riddle's daily exit. *Where had he gone? I thought this was very important. Was there some logical reason he would leave?* However, he continued to shake trees and collect nuts along with Riddle all morning long.

After lunch, they returned to work, and once again, as before, Riddle stopped and announced he had to leave and would be back later. This time, as Riddle left, Isaiah stopped and watched him leave and bound into the woods. *Where is he going?* thought Isaiah. *Perhaps, I could just follow a bit behind and see what he's up to. I could look out for him, protect him, especially since Temp has been in the woods recently. Yes, yes, that's what I'll do.* With that, Isaiah dropped the burlap bag he had in his hand and raced off to find where Riddle was headed.

Isaiah climbed over logs and jumped over streams and did his best to keep up, but eventually he lost sight of Riddle and found himself lost in the woods. He continued for a while, but finally, the heat of the day got to him, and he had to sit down, so he plopped down on a large fallen tree to rest and regroup. While he sat there, he heard a noise coming from straight ahead. Someone was out there ahead of him, laughing. He bent down low and crawled from tree to tree to stay hidden.

Finally, he came to a large rock on the edge of the meadow, and as he looked over the rock, his jaw dropped in disbelief. There in this quiet meadow surrounded by lush forest was a beautiful, quaint village with shops, small houses, barns, and a school building right in the center with a lush green manicured lawn in front. The houses had grass roofs with flower boxes on each window, with lush red, yellow, and blue flowers cascading out of each box. The whole village looked alive with people who apparently lived in the houses and worked in the shops. But then his eyes caught sight of Riddle on the green lawn surrounded by children, some sat on the grass while others stood and played together, while yet others ran up and gave Riddle a hug. It mesmerized Isaiah as he watched the entire scene. There seemed to be such joy, happiness, and harmony in the entire village. Isaiah watched for a while and then realized he must get back to the orchard, so he quietly slipped away and worked his way back to the meadow with the nut trees.

The rest of the afternoon, as Isaiah worked, he thought about the scene he had witnessed in the village and tried to understand the story. *Why was this village in such a remote, hidden part of the woods? Why were there so many children? Why were the children so happy to see Riddle?* All of this ran around in his mind. *Perhaps Riddle made business deals in the village, or did he just go there to kill time and not work?* None of his explanations seemed to make sense, and then he heard the voice he had come to detest.

"So, did you see him? Wasting time, he lets you do all the work while he plays. I told you so! It's wrong, I tell you it's wrong. He has abused your generosity!" Isaiah turned to see Temp, back again, and standing under a pecan tree he had just shaken.

"Go away, Temp, I don't want to hear it. Whatever Riddle is doing, I'm sure there is a good explanation."

"If it were me, I'd quit right now, that'll teach him a lesson to abuse your generosity. Yes, that's exactly what I would do. Teach him a lesson," snarled Temp.

Isaiah snapped back, "I told you to leave, now get out of here!" and Isaiah took a step toward Temp to emphasize his point.

Temp stood his ground, and the hair on the back of his neck stood up, and his eyes got narrower and even more yellow in hue while his teeth formed into a snarl. "So...you want to challenge me?" snarled Temp with a low, slow growl. "Perhaps not today... but soon, very soon." And with that, Temp turned and bound off into the woods.

Isaiah was left there alone with his thoughts. His heart raced like it had been in the fight with the coyotes. Temp's words made him so angry.

He slowly got back to work and worked hard to catch up when Riddle returned late in the afternoon. They finished the day's work and headed home. That night, Isaiah lay in his bunk and contemplated what to do about Riddle. *Should he confront Riddle and address his concerns?* He tossed and turned and weighed the pros and cons when he remembered a verse he read once in the Good Book: *"Don't worry about anything; instead, pray about everything."* Isaiah closed his eyes and began to pray. He then fell into a deep sleep.

The next morning, Isaiah awoke refreshed with a deep peace in his spirit. Before he crawled out of bed, he took a deep breath and said a thank you for the rest and his newfound peace. The anxiety he had wrestled with the night before was gone and replaced with a confidence that everything would be alright.

A short time later, he made his way through the meadow to the orchards to begin the day's work, when he came upon Riddle. They greeted and started the same pattern as before. They worked until lunch, and then in mid-afternoon, Riddle excused himself and left.

Isaiah continued to work and fill burlap bags throughout the morning, but he felt an urge to go back to the village once again. This time, though, the urge wasn't to catch Riddle but rather to understand this beautiful village in the woods and the people who lived there. He wanted to experience the peace he felt in this place once again.

Since he had been there already, he knew the way and quietly and deliberately moved through the woods. He found a safe place to hide behind a large rock and watched carefully as events played out. Today, Riddle had a wagon with burlap bags filled with the nuts they had collected. He handed them out to townsfolk as they came onto the green lawn. People thanked him and then carried the bags back to the cottages.

Unexpectantly, from behind him, he heard Iswa's voice, "It's pretty amazing, isn't it?"

Surprised by Iswa, Isaiah responded somewhat confused by the question, "Yes, I guess so."

Iswa sensed his confusion and went on, "Do you understand what's going on here and what this is all about, Isaiah?"

Isaiah looked back at Iswa and finally asked, "To be honest, I'm confused. What is this place, and what is going on exactly?

"This is Purposeville, and everything you see was started, built, and funded by Riddle."

"Really, that's...that's incredible," responded Isaiah. "All by Riddle? Was it a business venture he started?"

"Oh no, nothing like that at all," replied Iswa, "This is a very unique place with a very special purpose for very special people. Many years ago, Riddle would harvest nuts in this forest, and he was quite a successful businessman. Everyone in the valley came to him to buy their nuts. One day, while he worked in a new section of the forest, he came across three orphaned children. Their parents had been killed, and they had nowhere to turn, so he brought them home and cared for them. He fell in love with them and treated them as his own, but slowly he began to find others. Children, lost in the woods without parents, and he knew he had to do something. The Voice spoke to him and told him to build them a home, so that is exactly what he did. He built a home for orphans, and they continued to come, and he added on and on to meet the needs. He built a school to educate them, and as they grew older, some stayed on to help take care of the new orphans."

Iswa went on, "This place became Riddle's purpose. God had given Riddle a purpose for his life that went beyond just harvesting nuts for money, and as a result, we have *"Purposeville: a place where you can find love, peace, and purpose."* He pointed to the sign above the school entrance with those words inscribed on it.

Isaiah stood there frozen and took in the entire scene. He slowly shook his head and gave out a whistle, "Wow, he … he built all this? But what about the nuts? He still harvests the nuts. That's what we have been doing all week."

Iswa smiled and nodded, "Oh yes, he still harvests the nuts. Those nuts that you have worked so hard to collect and bag all week go to fund Purposeville. The fall harvest of the nuts is vital for this work to continue, and you might have noticed, Riddle has been a bit intense this week."

Isaiah smiled and chuckled, "You could say that!"

Iswa turned toward Isaiah and said, "Come with me," and he left the shelter of their hiding place and struck out across the meadow toward Riddle and the townspeople. Isaiah followed close behind him.

"Hello," shouted Iswa.

Riddle turned, and a big grin appeared on his face. "Hello, my friends, please come join me!"

Isaiah followed Iswa to the green lawn where Riddle stood surrounded by townspeople and children. Riddle introduced him as his close colleague and friend who had been so vital to this year's harvest. The small children flocked around Isaiah and wanted to shake his hand or give him a hug to thank him. They were followed by adults who introduced themselves and thanked Isaiah over and over for his hard work. The look of appreciation and love on people's faces warmed Isaiah's heart, but also made him, uneasy and embarrassed for any negative thoughts he had considered toward Riddle.

Isaiah walked back to the Orchard and weighed the events of the day. *How could he have even entertained the thought that this kind squirrel had somehow taken advantage of him?* Riddle was kind and caring and sacrificed for others. He acted with purpose to benefit others, and he was not just happy but filled with joy as he followed his purpose in life. Isaiah determined that he had much to think about and still learn, but one thing was for sure… he could never trust Temp.

Isaiah finished his work at the orchard that day, and two days later, he and Riddle had completed the fall harvest. The experience at Purposeville was impactful and would stay with him forever. This red-tailed squirrel had made such a huge difference in so many lives with nuts by simply listening and following the Voice.

On the last day, Isaiah got the courage to ask Riddle a question that had plagued him from the first time they met in Hon's hut. "Riddle, can you explain to me why Iswa initially didn't want to train me to be a Journeyman?"

There was a long silence, and Isaiah began to worry that he had asked some forbidden question and offended Riddle, but finally Riddle answered. "Over thirty years ago, Iswa washed up on the shore as the only survivor from a shipwreck. He had been a very fierce soldier, feared and respected by his enemies, but here in Tiree, he began to change, and he opened himself up to the words of the Good Book and the Voice. He came to realize that the Voice speaks truth, encouragement, insight, and wisdom. As a result, he became a different man. The Voice led him to become a watchman over the region of Tiree. His mission was to protect against the dark forces, to confront evil, and to help those in need. He also became the mentor for numerous Journeyman who were led here by the Voice."

"So, he trained many journeymen over the years? Then why did he not want to train me?"

Riddle continued, "It's been a long time since a Journeyman has come through here and been trained by Iswa. The last two that came through were two young men whom he trained together.

One of the young men successfully completed his mission and returned to the other side of the river to live his life as a man of integrity. However, the other turned to the darkness. He stayed here and gave himself to evil, to greed, to pursue his desires and the promotion of darkness. It deeply hurt Iswa, and it still grieves him deeply. He has questioned his own abilities to effectively mentor. When you came along, his first reaction was to step away and let Hon, Esty, and me train you. He had lost his confidence. We all knew that was not the right answer and simply needed to challenge his thinking...and... also encourage him. Fortunately, he listened, and here we are today."

Isaiah leaned in and listened carefully to Riddle's explanation. It not only brought clarity and understanding about Iswa's background and history, but also about the past journeymen that he had trained. The idea that a Journeyman had actually given in to the dark forces had never crossed his mind. This revelation was sobering and sent a shudder through him. He wondered, *would he be strong enough?*

CHAPTER 10

BOUNTY

The next morning, Isaiah returned to Hon's garden, where Hon was already busy filling new orders. Hon looked up and cheerfully said, "Top of the morning to you, Master Isaiah."

Isaiah smiled at Hon's typical British greeting and replied, "Good morning to you also, Hon."

"Oh, by the way, Iswa was here earlier and asked if I saw you, to have you join him down at the bay by the dock. He also said, 'Make sure he has his backpack.'"

Isaiah thought the request was uniquely specific and wondered where they might be off to and what challenge he would face today. The certain rhythm of daily adventures had settled into expectation and a norm for his training as a Journeyman.

Isaiah disappeared back into the hut and hurriedly gathered his things, which included his backpack and pouch that he carried around his head and shoulder. He opened the pouch to make sure that his slingshot was still inside. It was, and he went off toward the bay and dock.

As Isaiah approached the dock, Iswa stood on the dock and stared straight out at the ocean. He looked as if his eyes were fixed on some far-distant object, focused and mesmerized. His long black coat flowed in the morning breeze. The image was surreal, and he looked like a watchman on the lookout for potential dangers. Isaiah smiled and thought, "Ah, for once I'll surprise him, but then he heard Iswa speak, "What did you learn from your time with Riddle the last several days?"

The question and the fact that once again, Iswa seemed to always have the upper hand in the conversation made Isaiah stammer for an answer. "Ah, ah, where do I begin? He's an incredible man, or rather, squirrel."

"Yes, he is at that," Iswa responded slowly while continuing to stare out at the ocean.

"But what did you learn about yourself?"

Isaiah turned red in the face as he had an instant lump in his throat and struggled to find words. *How does he respond to such a question? Does he know about meeting Temp in the orchard? Does Iswa somehow know that he had begun to question Riddle's motives?*

"Ah...ah, quite a bit," said Isaiah, as he tried to be vague while his mind and heart raced for an adequate answer.

"You know, Riddle is a great example of integrity. He opened himself up to learn about his own strengths and weaknesses. He sought out brothers to come alongside him in his journey. They supported one another, and they were honest with each other about their weaknesses, their struggles, their needs, and their dreams. This close group grew together, and when Riddle had the vision to build Purposeville, all his brothers were there to support him on this remarkable journey. He was not alone."

Isaiah stood there quietly and intently listened as Iswa went on, "And with Riddle's remarkable energy and gift for business, he put action to his vision. He saw a need, he had a vision, and he acted, and this is a key characteristic of men of integrity. Their words and actions align."

In a soft voice, Isaiah asked, "Were you one of his brothers?"

Iswa turned and looked him in the eyes and said, "Yes, and so was Hon and Esty. We are brothers. We have supported one another for many years through good times and bad. You need to find these kinds of men in your life, Isaiah. Men who will build you up, be honest, and support you."

Finally, as tears filled his eyes, Isaiah could hold it no longer, and he blurted out, "I talked to Temp in the orchard! He told me Riddle simply used and abused me to do his work."

Iswa turned and, with no emotion, looked Isaiah in the eyes and said, "I know."

Isaiah was completely shocked, and the color drained from his face at this revelation from Iswa. "You...you knew, but how?"

Iswa replied, "I have fought with Temp for many years in these woods and seen his tactics with many journeymen. I know how he works, and I know his lies and deception. He twists words and distorts truth to spin ugly tales and draw people into his schemes, like into a spider's web."

Tears ran down Isaiah's face as each word Iswa spoke penetrated his heart and brought sadness, regret, and sorrow. It was all so true.

Isaiah finally blurted out through tears, "Yes, but I nearly gave in to him three times. Once at the chicken coop, then in Mrs. Endis' barnyard, and finally in the orchard. I nearly gave in to his lies and deception."

Iswa calmly asked, "But did you?"

Isaiah, now somewhat composed, responded, "Well, no. No, I guess not. But I feel so bad that I almost gave in to his lies."

"Well, good, that is a very good sign. You will fight Temp and his type, your whole life. They are practitioners of deceit, lies, schemes, and destruction. As a man of integrity, you must recognize evil when you see it. You ultimately recognized that Temp was trying to deceive you at the chicken coop, the barnyard, and in the orchard. You didn't give in to his schemes, and that is good."

Iswa continued, "Isaiah, your training here is complete. You have successfully faced numerous challenges. These challenges have taught you the simple impact of keeping promises, the value of going out of your way to help those in need, and the power of truth over lies."

Isaiah felt refreshed, as if some deep, dark secret was no longer hidden and the light of day had given new perspective and somehow renewed strength. Iswa abruptly said, "Come with me, Isaiah," as he turned and walked out on the dock.

They walked in silence, and Iswa turned and looked Isaiah directly in the eyes. Iswa's dark blue eyes seemed to penetrate deep into Isaiah's soul. There was a depth, sincerity, and gentleness in his look, but also a strong intentionality in his words: "Isaiah, your time with us has now come to a close, and you must move on in your journey."

Isaiah listened intently and wanted to protest, but he knew it was time.

Iswa continued, "I cannot go any further with you. You must make the next step on your journey alone, but you have a choice: you can return home to your world now or go on to the forest of Endemar down the coast. Before you decide, you should know that Endemar is a very different place from here. It is filled with wonders and challenges. There are very dark dangers present in that place. You, though, must choose."

Isaiah did not hesitate but quickly responded, "I came here on a journey to the Land of Integrity, and that is where I shall go."

"Very well, then it shall be," responded Iswa with a half-smile.

"My young Journeyman, listen carefully to me, there is one thing you lack, but you must find upon your arrival in Endemar. You must find the Sword of Integrity. This is why I taught you swordsmanship.

It is a very special sword, a sword not only for defense but also a powerful offensive weapon for dealing with enemies. Find it, obtain it, and use it."

Iswa turned, and together they walked out onto the dock to a sloop with rigging for a head sail and an aft sail. The sloop could hold a small crew plus a number of crates and barrels. Iswa introduced Isaiah to the owner and captain of the boat, a fox named Kwidley, and told him that Kwidley would take him down the coast through the inner passage to where he could enter the forest of Endemar.

"Very well," said Isaiah, and he started to climb into the boat, but Iswa stopped him and spun him around and, in an uncharacteristic show of emotion, pulled Isaiah close to him and held him tight.

Iswa whispered in his ear, "God be with you…my brother."

With that, Isaiah climbed into the boat, and Kwidley cast off from the dock and unfurled the sail. As the sail filled with the morning breeze, the boat began to move swiftly through the water and away from the shore. Isaiah looked back and saw the gray-haired Iswa still on the dock with his hair and long black coat flowing like a flag in the wind. A watchman still watching.

Isaiah sat in silence for a bit and thought about his experiences with Iswa, Hon, Esty, and Riddle. He didn't know if he'd ever see them again, but there was a deep assurance in his spirit that this was not a goodbye but rather until we meet again.

Kwidley was an adept sailor and set the sails to catch the breeze at just the right angle to propel the boat swiftly forward. Isaiah asked Kwidley, "Do you make this journey often to Endemar?"

Kwidley responded, "Only once a month or so to drop off supplies." He nodded toward the crates and barrels tied down in the center of the boat and went on, "Don't like going there, not a safe place." He did not go any further to explain his statement, and Isaiah just nodded back at him. Kwidley stood behind the wheel of the boat and continued to steer the boat and catch the breeze in the sails. He stayed pretty much silent but continually scanned around the horizon with a concerned look as if he expected someone or something. It would take several hours to sail up the coast past numerous small islands that, for the most part, looked uninhabited.

They weaved between the islands with a relatively calm ocean lapping against the boat and the rocks on each island. The sky was cloudless with a bright blue color that matched the ocean, and Isaiah began to relax and take in all the beauty around him. He leaned back on a tarp that covered some crates and suddenly heard, "Ouch, get off me." He leaped forward and spun around as he pulled the tarp back. Underneath the tarp sat Luc, who looked up and smiled.

"Luc, what are you doing here?"

"I needed a ride to Endemar and Kwidley agreed to give me one… ah…for a small price," chuckled Luc, while he looked back at Kwidley, who just smirked.

"I see you both know each other."

Luc and Isaiah looked at each other and smiled, and Isaiah spoke. "Well, let's just say we've been through a few things together." They continued to talk and helped Kwidley adjust the sails properly to catch the ocean breeze as it shifted. Isaiah turned to Luc and asked, "You told me that the people looking for you wanted some sort of box that you had at one time but don't have now, but hid somewhere…correct?"

Luc paused and then responded, "Yes, I know it sounds confusing, but it's a long story."

"Well, it's a long trip and we have time, explain it to me," responded Isaiah, with a bit of surprise at his directness with Luc.

There was another pause, and then Luc began, "I started to run with some people in Endemar who, shall we say, were not always the most…legal in their actions. They were a gang that would do anything to make a buck. Steal, intimidate, deceive, sell stolen property, run illegal items… You know… if it could be turned into money, they did it. My specialty was getting things others couldn't get."

"What do you mean, getting things?" asked Isaiah.

"You know, I was capable of getting into certain places and removing specific things."

"You're a thief," responded Isaiah.

"Ah, yes, I guess…but a very skilled thief. I can get in and out without being detected. I have a special skill."

Suddenly, they heard Kwidley let out a very loud, "No, no, no." They both turned to see that a large three-masted schooner had just come around the island behind them. It was big and moving very fast with full sails. They were on a mission, and the mission appeared to be Kwidley and his sloop.

"Who is that?" yelled Luc.

"I am not sure," yelled Kwidley from behind the helm wheel, "… mercenaries, or possibly pirates. There is no way we outrun them, and I don't know whether they are after one or both of you."

"Listen," yelled Kwidley, "since I can't outrun them, I need to hide you, but not on the boat. They will board me when they catch me. I am about to round this island on our starboard side. When I do, I will get as close as I can and have you jump off and swim to the island and hide. I will sail on, and when they catch me, they will board me and find nothing but me and a few crates of goods and supplies. They'll move on."

Isaiah snapped his head around to keep an eye on the schooner that trailed behind them, but when he heard Kwidley's plan, he immediately turned and focused his attention on the small island that they were about to go around on their starboard side. He yelled back at Kwidley, "What are you talking about? We will be stuck on an island here in the ocean."

"No, you won't, I'll double back and pick you up after they leave. Might be a couple of hours, but hold tight."

The ocean winds had picked up significantly, and the schooner was rapidly gaining on them. Isaiah looked at Luc, who stood at the railing with his bow in one hand and a quiver of arrows over his shoulder. They were worthless in this situation but brought some comfort to Luc as his head swung back and forth from the schooner to the island like an animal trapped in a cage. "We have no other choice. We can't outrun them; we'll swim to shore together and hide in the trees and underbrush."

Luc looked at him with fear in his eyes and simply nodded affirmatively.

Kwidley brought the boat around the island, catching the ocean breeze perfectly in his sails. He then spun the wheel hard to starboard and dived toward the island coast that was mostly jagged rocks. He knew that he must be very careful not to get too close, or he could gash the boat on the rocks. The chasing schooner was now out of sight, being hidden by the island as it pursued them. Kwidley steered the boat as close as he dared to the rocks and yelled, "Now, jump! Jump now!"

Isaiah looked at Luc, and they jumped together into the surf. The water was cold and initially stunned them both as they fought to the surface. The waves were higher than expected, but they both got their bearings and began to swim as fast as possible toward the shore. Isaiah knew that they must get out of the water and hide before the schooner rounded the island. Isaiah made it first to shore and climbed up on a large boulder to look for Luc. As he got on top of the boulder, he could not see Luc anywhere. He finally saw him to his left, pinned against another large boulder and unable to get to shore. He was bobbing, like a cork, in the water but being pummeled by the waves against the bolder. Isaiah ran over to the large boulder to see if he could help. Just as he arrived, out of the corner of his eye, he saw the foremast of the schooner come around the island. He had no time to spare, so he lay down on the boulder and at the next swell he stretched and grabbed Luc's shirt collar and yanked hard to get him up on the rock. Luc was beat up and exhausted, but Isaiah managed to force him to his feet long enough to dive into the underbrush and lie perfectly still as the large schooner passed by within yards of their position.

Kwidley had continued to expertly catch the wind and keep ahead of the schooner, but it was simply a matter of time until they would catch him. As the schooner sailed away in pursuit, Isaiah peered up to get a good look at it. He saw that there were wolves on the ship with the men. This was clearly the group that had been after Luc.

Isaiah and Luc lay in the underbrush where they caught their breath and dried off. Luc looked at Isaiah and said, "Thank you." Isaiah simply nodded and smiled and then stood up to assess where they were exactly.

The island was rocky but covered with trees and dense brush that made it a challenge to move around, but before long, Isaiah had found a pathway that they could climb through to a greater elevation. Isaiah and Luc used the path to climb up to a plateau that allowed them to look out toward the direction that Kwidley and the schooner had sailed. It would be some time, but hopefully they would see Kwidley return without the schooner. He was their only hope to get off this island.

Isaiah turned to Luc and said, "You keep a lookout, I will explore a bit to get our bearings around the island." Luc nodded and was more than happy to sit a bit and rest after the pounding he took against the rocks. Isaiah climbed further up the rock face and found a path that led into the interior of the island. He battled his way through low-hanging branches and thick brush that caused him to trip and stumble. As he moved to the interior of the island, the forest became a jungle that blocked out much of the sun. Tall royal palm trees rose up, creating a thick jungle canopy, while large, glossy, blue-grey elephant leaves rose from the jungle floor, reaching toward the sky. Tropical birds flew from branch to branch and called to one another in a non-stop chorus of singing along with the call of an occasional tree monkey. He stood in the shadows on level ground with the lush vegetation all around him. He finally stepped back and viewed the whole scene and decided on a direction to take to pick his way through the dense foliage. He proceeded cautiously and was surprised to find himself up to his ankles in a stream of water. He stooped down and took a handful and tasted it. It was fresh water which excited him because he knew they would need fresh water if they were to be here for any length of time, so he decided to follow the stream to find its source.

Isaiah climbed a bit further and found the source. It came from a small waterfall that fell from a rock face some twenty feet above him. There was obviously a source at an even higher level, so he climbed the rock face hand over hand as he tried not to slip on the wet rocks. Finally, he climbed over the ledge and rolled on his back to catch his breath. He took deep breaths and finally stood up to find himself next to a beautiful pool of water surrounded by what looked like man-made columns with a table that looked like an altar on the opposite side of the pool. Vines grew over the columns and table, which blended them in harmony with the surrounding jungle. But what really caught his attention was a green mist that hung over the entire pool and altar area.

A peace settled over Isaiah and embraced him like arms wrapped around his heart. It reminded him of the night in the woods with his father and the cave after his first encounter with Temp. It felt holy, sacred, and he proceeded carefully and respectfully. He walked to the altar, and the Voice began to talk, "Your mission is to save the kingdom, and while doing that, save Luc."

Isaiah was overwhelmed, "Save the kingdom, what does that mean? And save Luc while I'm doing it? Save him from what?"

The Voice continued, "Your mission will become clearer as you go. Proceed to Endemar, and it will become clearer with each step you take. There will be trials and tests, but trust and obey, and it will go well."

With that, the mist swirled around him and rose to the sky and disappeared. Isaiah found himself alone by the pool and dropped his head and said, "Thank you."

Isaiah headed back down to where he had left Luc, but when he got close to the spot, he heard voices. Neither voice belonged to Luc, but they were angry and loud. He ducked behind a rock and decided to crawl out on the rock ledge to peer over toward the spot where he had left Luc.

There were two men who stood over someone on the ground. Isaiah became sick to his stomach as he realized they were looking down on Luc. Luc's hands were tied behind his back, and one of the men reared back and kicked him in the stomach. Luc gave out a loud moan. One of the men cursed at Luc and said, "You little thief, where's the box?" Luc just moaned in agony. The other man let out a laugh and said, "This is our lucky day, we were just minding our own business fishing, when those blokes in the schooner came by and offered us a bounty if we found you and turned you into them. All we have to do is wait for them to pass back by and row out to them, and we're a whole lot richer. They even said that they would give us a bonus if you had a box with you, so where's the box... Sonny?" He reared back and kicked Luc again, but this time in the head.

Isaiah knew he had to do something. At this rate, they just might kill Luc before the thugs on the schooner showed back up.

He then noticed that a fishing boat was tied up below them. This boat obviously belonged to these men, and Isaiah had an idea. They could take their boat and row out away from the island and hopefully meet Kwidley on his way back to pick them up, as long as it was before the schooner came back this way. It was risky, but there was no other option. The question was, how would he get both of them on that boat?

He watched and listened for a while to the men's banter and realized that they had no idea that he was on the island. They thought Luc had come to the island alone. That worked to his advantage. They weren't looking for him or expecting him. He had the element of surprise on his side. He also realized that they could not see their boat from their vantage point. He could see it from above, but they couldn't – another advantage.

From his vantage point, he also could see an alternate path down to the gravelly beach the fishman had pulled their boat upon. If he could get down there undetected, he could push the boat out into open water and row away, but what about Luc? There was no way he would leave this island without Luc.

An idea came to Isaiah. *What if he created a distraction with the boat to draw both of the fishermen down to the shore? That would leave Luc unguarded, and he could sneak up and untie him while they were desperate to deal with the boat.* Timing would be critical, but he determined that he could sneak down, untie the boat, set it adrift, and then quickly get back up above the two fishermen and Luc. He would have to do all this without being caught, but it would solve one problem, freeing Luc.

His second step would be to have Luc act as a distraction to draw the fishermen back up the rocks to chase and recapture him while Isaiah snuck back down and stole the boat and rowed it out to deeper water. While the fishermen chased Luc, he would row to a cove around the corner where Luc could jump from cliffs to the water and be pulled on board. Timing was paramount, but he needed to tip Luc off so he could distract the fishermen's attention away from their boat.

One fisherman watched over the sea in hope that the schooner would show up soon, while the other paid little attention to Luc and sat back, closing his eyes. Luc had become very quiet, and they figured that they had either beaten him so hard that he was unconscious or was simply unable to speak.

Isaiah took a deep breath and slowly climbed down from his perch some twenty feet above them. He slid carefully down the slope and made sure he didn't disturb any rocks or snap any branches. He got within five feet of Luc and had hidden in some brush when the fishman spun around and stormed at Luc. "Did you say something, thief?" Luc just moaned, and the fishman gave him another kick in his side. Isaiah wanted to jump up and defend Luc but knew he needed to stay completely concealed. The fishman turned back toward the edge of the cliff and continued to look over the ocean while he rambled incessantly with his fellow fisherman, who still had his eyes closed and just mumbled in agreement. Isaiah saw his opportunity and crept closer to Luc and whispered, "Luc, Luc!"

Blood ran out of Luc's nose as well as the corner of his mouth, and he slowly opened his puffy, swollen eyes and smiled at the sight of Isaiah. Isaiah whispered again, "Luc, I will get you out of here, but I need you to draw both fishermen over here in ten minutes. Make sure they both get over here. Can you do that?" Luc nodded affirmatively, and Isaiah slinked back into the underbrush. Isaiah knew that he could not waste time, and he needed to work his way down to the boat as fast as possible. He prayed that Luc could distract the fishermen long enough for him to get the boat back in the water without being seen.

Ten minutes passed, and Luc began to moan and blabber loudly. At first, the fishman by the edge of the cliff yelled, "Shut up, thief," but the one who had his eyes closed opened them wide and came closer to Luc, "Did he say he'd tell us where the box is?" Luc started to spin a yarn about the box being hidden on the island and full of gold, a lot of gold.

"I'll...I'll tell you where to find the box. Just don't hurt me anymore. I can take you to it if you just let me go. It's full of gold coins worth far more than what those thugs in the schooner will pay you. It holds a lot of gold. You will be far richer if you just let me show you the box and you leave with it. Far more than the meager sum they promised you."

One of the fishermen stood straight up and stroked his straggly beard with his hand and squinted as he thought about what Luc had said to them. "Gold, you say, hum...he makes an interesting point, why not keep the box."

"You'll lead us to it, right thief!"

"Yes, I will, just let me go."

The two fishermen began to weigh their options and consider Luc's proposal.

In the meantime, Isaiah had silently gotten down to the beach and pushed the boat out into the water. He noticed a long rope inside the boat and rapidly tied it through an eyebolt on the boat, laid it over the side, and let the boat drift farther out into the ocean. He didn't want it to drift too far away, or nobody could get it. He took the rope and found an underwater rock some five yards offshore that he secured it to so the boat could not drift any further than twenty to thirty yards from shore. He slipped out of the water and swiftly and silently returned to his perch above the fisherman and Luc. Step one was successful. Luc reared up on his elbows and noticed the boat out in the water, and he smiled and collapsed like he had fainted once again.

The fishermen became enraged because he had not completed telling them where the box and treasure were hidden. One of the fishermen began to kick Luc again, but the other screamed, "Stop, you idiot. We don't want to kill him yet. We need him to finish telling us where to find the box." He spun around to look at the ocean and immediately began to scream, "The boat, the boat...It's drifting away. Hurry, help me get it before it's gone."

They both took off, but the second one stopped and yelled, "What about him?" pointing at Luc. "He's unconscious and tied up. Leave him. We must not lose the boat... hurry, now, hurry!" They both took off down the rocks toward the shore, and Isaiah saw his chance.

Luc was on his side when Isaiah slid up behind him and began to untie the ropes that held Luc's arms and feet. Isaiah began to panic. It was simply taking too long, and he feared the fishermen would return before he had freed Luc. He could hear the fishermen yelling and splashing in the water to get to the boat. He worked furiously to untie the ropes while listening to the fishmen now bringing the boat back to shore. He looked up and caught sight of a knife left on a rock by one of the fishermen. He jumped over Luc, grabbed the knife, and quickly sliced Luc's ropes.

He whispered to Luc, "Can you get on your feet? We must get out of here." Luc nodded affirmatively and staggered to his feet with Isaiah's help. Isaiah practically dragged Luc up the rocky path to his elevated hiding place. Once again, he turned to Luc, grabbed him by his shoulders, and asked, "Can you keep these guys busy while I steal the boat?" Luc was in bad shape but nodded affirmatively. "Now, listen carefully, I need you to follow this path higher and lead them up to the higher cliff. Make sure they follow you. Do you understand?" Again, Luc nodded.

When you get to a large cliff overhang above a cove, look for me below." Luc's eyes got wide as he began to realize what Isaiah was about to ask him to do. "When you see me below in the boat, you will have to jump. Don't hesitate, just jump."

Luc stumbled higher up the rocky hill, and Isaiah began to descend back down to the shore and boat. The fishermen had retrieved their boat and had it back on the shore. Luc found a hiding place above to observe the fishermen as they proceeded to climb back up to the plateau where they had left him.

"No," yelled the first fisherman. "He's gone; we have to find him."

The second fisherman yelled back, "He had to have gone higher because we didn't see him as we came up." The two fishermen began to scramble up the rocky slope to a higher elevation.

Isaiah now saw his chance and slipped down the rocky slope to the shore and ran directly to the boat to push it back into the water, but suddenly he stopped dead in his tracks. They had used the heavy rope to tie the boat securely to a large boulder. It would take a long time to untie the heavy, taught rope, but then he realized, in all the excitement, he still had the knife in his hand that he used to free Luc. He immediately began to work on the rope. It was a thick rope, but the knife was sharp, and the rope finally fell away. Isaiah put his shoulder into the boat and pushed with all his might to slide it into the water, where it began to float freely. He walked it out into deeper water while he kept watch over his shoulder for the fishermen, but Luc had forced the fishmen to climb higher and higher after him. They became more frustrated with each step and cursed Luc as they climbed.

Isaiah climbed into the boat, grabbed the oars, and began to row the boat rapidly out and around a rocky outcrop from the island. On the other side was the cove that he told Luc about. As he turned the corner into the cove, he began to scan the cliff tops looking for any sign of Luc. He became anxious, "Come on, Luc, hurry up, just get to the cliff and jump."

Suddenly, Luc appeared on the cliff, and he looked over to see if Isaiah and the boat were in the cove. He waved at Isaiah, and Isaiah waved back and shouted, "Jump, Luc, jump." Just then, one of the fishermen stuck his head over the edge of the cliff and was about to climb up with Luc. Luc reached down and grabbed a large piece of granite and held it over his head. He was about to smash the head of the fisherman just below him. It was the very fisherman who had beaten him so badly.

Isaiah yelled, "No, Luc, let it go, just let it go." Luc held the large rock above his head, frozen. Everything in him said, take your revenge. Kill this man for what he did to you, but he paused and looked back at Isaiah, who calmly said once again, "Let it go, Luc, let's get you home." Luc's eyes met Isaiah's, and he let the rock slip through his hands and fall to the ground, and then he turned and leaped.

Luc hit the cold water, which was refreshing for his many cuts and bruises from the beatings. He bobbed to the surface, and Isaiah quickly pulled him into the boat and, together with each at an oar, began to rapidly row out into the open channel between islands. All they could do was hope Kwidley found them before the schooner came back.

An hour passed, and they were now well away from the island when Isaiah jumped up, pointed, and let out a shout, "A sail!" As they got closer, they recognized the distinct sails of a sloop. It was Kwidley. He had returned to get them, and they were soon back on the boat with a story to tell, but both were too exhausted and could barely talk.

Isaiah finally broke a long silence and said, "So you were saying, you were a thief but with special skills."

He looked at Luc and smiled, who also broke into a wide grin, "Yes, very special skills." And they both broke into laughter.

CHAPTER 11

DAGGER HAWK

They sailed onward throughout the afternoon with no more threats or interruptions from mercenaries or pirates. After some time, Isaiah asked, "So, what did you do with the box? Where is it?"

Luc smiled and said, "To be honest, I'm not sure. I had stolen the box and was just about to turn it over to the people who hired me to steal it. I then found out that the people who hired me weren't who I thought they were. They were people that I would never work for under any circumstances. They were sworn enemies of my family, and I had no idea that I had actually stolen the box for them."

"So, what did you do?"

"Well, I took off with it," said Luc very directly.

Isaiah laughed at the audacity and straightforward manner in which Luc responded. Luc saw this as completely logical and the right thing to do. "Ok, so you took it, but what happened to it?"

"Interesting that you ask," responded Luc with a smile. "As you can imagine, people were more than a little upset, and everyone went crazy. They put out a bounty on me, and I was hunted by everyone. That's how I ended up in Tiree, which is about as far as you can get away and still be in the Kingdom. I have been on the run for weeks."

"But where is the box?"

"I'm not sure, I was being chased, and it was too cumbersome to haul all around, so I dumped it."

"What do you mean you dumped it?" asked Isaiah in astonishment.

"One night, it was raining very hard, and I was being chased through the city streets. It was very dark, and I was disoriented from turning down one street and then another. I came to a plaza and saw a well, so I ran toward it and climbed down into it to get away from the people who were after me. I was down in the well for quite a while until I thought it was safe to climb out. While down there, I realized there was a ledge that went into a small cave well above the water table. I sat in there and waited for my pursuers to give up. While hiding in there, I looked around and thought, *"This would be a good place to hide the box.* So, I left it in that cave and climbed out."

"So, you do know where it's at?"

"Ah... not exactly. As I said, it was a rainy night and very dark, and I was in some plaza that I had never been to before. I climbed out and got out of there as quickly as I could. I simply don't remember which well or which plaza, but it should still be there, right in the heart of the city."

Isaiah was amazed at the story and wondered what was so valuable in this box. He remembered the words of Granny Rose, "In the Land of Integrity, there are lessons to be learned and treasures to be found." He wondered if this was one of the treasures that Granny had talked about.

"Perhaps, you can help me find it when you get to the city, Isaiah. I fully intend to retrieve it. There has been too much fuss made of it. It must be very valuable. Yes, I will find it."

Isaiah simply smiled and continued to think about the words of Granny Rose, *lessons to be learned and treasures to be found.*

As they got closer to the shore, Isaiah could now see the land, which they called the Forest of Endemar. The shore was filled with inlets and coves that each appeared to hide a unique secret and mystery. The shore was rocky with very little area for a smooth beaching of a boat. There were no docks in sight, and large rocks dominated the shore with intermittent areas of small, crushed stone that led into the water. It was these areas that would provide the best place for a landing.

The shore was not large because, in a short distance, the shore gave way to trees, enormous dark trees, bigger than any tree he had ever seen. As the trees rose up from the ground, their dark, dense foliage created a dense canopy over the forest floor. Above the trees lay a dense bluish mist that covered the treetops

Kwidley called out, "we're about here, get ready to land and get off quickly. I have no intention of staying in this place long."

It was clear that Kwidley was very uneasy about this trip, and he abruptly turned the boat and nudged it into a rare sandy-gravely soft section of the shore. Kwidley jumped out of the boat with a splash into the shallow water, pulled a rope up to shore, and tied it off on a rock. He then, with Isaiah and Luc's help, quickly began to unload the crates and barrels. They stacked the crates and barrels neatly together on the shore, and to Isaiah's surprise, Kwidley abruptly said, "I must go," untied the rope from the rock, and began to push his boat back into the water.

Isaiah, stunned at the abruptness of Kwidley's departure, called out, "What about the supplies?"

"Someone will come for them, but I wouldn't wait around to meet them."

Isaiah, now even more concerned, called out, "But which way should I go?"

"Depends on where you want to go. I'd head along the shore, but don't stay there long, not safe, too open," Kwidley responded and pointed to the north. "There is a trail I have seen up in that direction. God be with you."

And with that, Kwidley and his boat were gone, and Isaiah was left on the shore beside the supplies and a bruised and battered Luc.

The afternoon breeze off the sea was cool, and Isaiah gathered his jacket around him, picked up his backpack, and headed north along the shore with Luc. He heard the typical sounds of gulls squawking offshore as they fished and the occasional sound of a loon's call across the water. It was quite peaceful, and he found the hike to be refreshing as he was able to stretch his legs, but suddenly, he saw a large shadow appear on the ground that covered him completely. He turned just in time to see an enormous hawk diving right at them with its talons flexed like daggers ready for a kill.

Isaiah screamed, "Look out," and grabbed Luc and pulled them both to the ground just in time to avoid what could have been a lethal blow from one of the talons. The hawk rose up toward the sky, squawked in a defiant manner, and lined up for another attack. Luc hit the ground hard, which added more bruises and cuts to his already bruised and cut-up body. He lay there a second, confused and startled by Isaiah's tackle. He rolled over to see the cause of Isaiah's tackle and yelled, "Dagger hawk," and grabbed his bow. Isaiah immediately looked for some cover and again grabbed Luc and pulled him across the rocky shore to a large boulder and dived behind it just as the hawk completed another dive that just barely scraped Isaiah's back.

Isaiah had never seen anything like this from a hawk. Back home, on the farm, he often would see them dive on small rodents but never on people. However, he did have to admit that he had never seen a hawk this big; it could easily carry away a full-grown man.

The hawk circled again, and Isaiah watched it line up for yet another attack. He remembered his slingshot in his pouch and reached in and grabbed it. He had plenty of rocks around him, so he grabbed one, loaded it, and drew back his sling. Just as he was about to let the stone loose, the hawk broke off his attack and flew away.

Isaiah looked around and knew that they were very exposed on the shore and needed to get under cover quickly before the hawk decided to return. The edge of the woods was roughly thirty yards away, so he grabbed his bag and took off in a dead sprint with Luc behind him. They reached the edge of the woods and dived headfirst through a thicket of branches and tall grass. They tumbled down an embankment into a dried-up creek bed. Isaiah was bruised from the landing but otherwise fine. Luc was a bit behind, and the dried creek bed simply compounded the bruises and cuts he had already experienced. Luc lay in the creek bed moaning as everything seemed to catch up at once with him. Isaiah stood up and tried to focus his eyes from the bright sunlight to the dark shadows under the tree canopy. As his adrenaline level went down, he suddenly felt a very sharp pain in his back just behind his right shoulder. He reached over his shoulder to rub the pain away and felt a tear in his jacket, and when he pulled his hand back, it was covered in blood. A thought raced through his mind. *Something is not right.*

Isaiah knew they needed to move and get as far as they could under the cover of the trees. The dagger hawk could not execute a dive through the very thick tree canopy. He looked up as he stumbled through the dry creek bed to where Luc lay motionless and saw the hawk high above circling them. Isaiah's vision still had not adjusted, and he stumbled continuously over roots and rocks. Strangely, his balance also seemed off, and he fell face-first in the mud. He picked himself up and tried to move, but the surroundings seemed to be spinning, and he could not focus on anything. He felt very strange, disoriented, and fell again. Luc crawled over to him and yelled, "Isaiah, Isaiah, what's wrong?" but Isaiah couldn't even form the words to respond. The dagger hawk let out a loud screech and circled above the trees.

Luc helped Isaiah get to his feet, and they stumbled together, now about a quarter mile from the shore. Isaiah fell again and became more and more disoriented when they both heard a noise. A noise that sent a chill down Isaiah's back and caused Luc to grab his bow tightly. It was the long howl of a wolf, followed by another and then another. Isaiah's heart quickened, and he tried as hard as he could to focus, but something was wrong. He finally formulated words and stammered out, "Wol...wol...ves. We need to... to get out...of ...here!"

Luc scanned around for some escape route and finally saw what looked like a fairly wide trail in front of him that ran across the dry creek bed on a crudely made bridge and turned into the deep forest. He turned to Isaiah and said, "We can move faster on the trail and get away from any wolves."

Isaiah had just started to climb up the embankment to follow Luc when a hand or paw, he wasn't sure which, went over his mouth and whispered in his ear, "Come with me, if you want to live." The hand over his mouth kept him from protesting as it clamped down tightly, and with the other hand, this mysterious individual grabbed around his chest and dragged him back down to the creek bed. There was another being present, but he just couldn't focus his eyes. He was now completely disoriented and unable to stand if he wanted to. The two dark figures grabbed him and dragged him down the creek bank and threw him into a deep crevasse between two giant tree roots. They quickly began to throw leaves, branches, and mud over top of Isaiah to cover him from head to toe. Finally, the mysterious stranger leaned over and whispered again, "Don't make a sound or you die," and with that, the mysterious duo vanished.

CHAPTER 12

SMUGGLERS

Isaiah smelled pine needles and maple leaves as he lay perfectly still under the heavy layer of branches and leaves. He felt paralyzed and couldn't move his arms or legs. He had no choice but to lie still and not make a sound. There was just enough of an opening that he could see some light with one eye, but then he heard it, the heavy breathing and growling of wolves. He tried to control his own breathing and heartbeat, but everything in him wanted to jump up and run.

He heard a wolf growl to a companion, "I'll check the creek bed and make sure he's not down there," and with that the wolf leaped down into the creek bed and Isaiah could hear his massive paws and claws breaking twigs and his sniffing back and forth, as he tried to pick up Isaiah's scent. The massive wolf was nearly right on top of Isaiah. He was so close that Isaiah could feel his breath. Isaiah wanted to scream and jump up, but something inside him kept him very still. He prayed silently, "Oh, God, protect me, please protect me."

The wolf turned and called to his companions, "I may have something here," but just as the word came out of his mouth, there was a loud crash on the other side of the trail up the hill. The wolf jerked his head in response to the sound and heard a voice yell, "Hey, mangy fleabags, are you looking for us?" The wolf took off up the hill and was joined by the other wolves, who all climbed the hill in pursuit of the noise and voices. They all howled in a frenzy, and Isaiah soon found himself in silence with only an occasional distant howl. He faded from consciousness as the little light he could see grew dimmer and dimmer.

* * *

His eyes opened slowly, and he blinked several times to regain his vision. The room was dimly lit by the light of a crackling fire in a fireplace. He had no idea where he was or who had taken him here. He was on a bunk in some kind of dimly lit cabin with a table and chairs in front of a stone fireplace. A rocking chair was positioned across the room directly in front of the fireplace, and the smell of corn biscuits and vegetable soup filled the room. He started to get up from his bunk, and a sharp pain shot through his shoulder. He let out a moan in response. "Careful there, lad, don't be in such a hurry to get up. That's a nasty wound you have, yes, very nasty," came a voice from somewhere in the room.

Isaiah lay back down to gather his senses and thoughts. Finally, he stammered out, "Where...where am I?"

"You are safe, in my den with my family. Rest, regain your strength."

Isaiah turned on his side and saw a gray fox who wore a dark sweater. The fox went on, "My name is Dwiddle. I believe you've met my cousin Kwidley, who brought you here on his boat." Isaiah gave a slight smile and nodded affirmatively. "We looked for you after we saw Kwidley's boat leave the cove, but unfortunately, the wolves were on patrol in the area. It was unfortunate that you had that run-in with that dagger hawk. The wolves use them to do reconnaissance out ahead of their patrols. They usually don't attack, but this one had a serious attitude for you. These types of hawks have a powerful toxin on their talons that immobilizes their prey. When his talon caught your back, the toxin took its effect. That's why you were so unstable on your feet and could not focus or think straight. Fortunately, it has mostly worn off by now. You're lucky, their prey rarely gets a chance for the toxin to wear off."

Isaiah lay there a minute longer, collected his thoughts, and then sat up and swung his legs off the bunk. "Careful now, take time to get your sea legs," cautioned Dwiddle. Isaiah's head was a bit woozy, and he sat there a moment and took Dwiddle's advice.

Suddenly, Isaiah realized he hadn't seen Luc. "Where's my colleague who was with me? Is he ok?"

"He's fine, he evaded the wolves, and we caught up with him and brought him here also. He went outside to help my son gather some wood for the fire."

"My name is Isaiah, and I'd like to thank you for saving my life."

Dwiddle smiled and nodded and then abruptly said, "Oh yes, by the way, this is my wife, Sarta, and my daughters – Selde, Ion, and here comes my son Eldamo, who by the way helped me hide you in the creek bed and lead the wolves away."

Isaiah smiled and looked at Eldamo and said, "Thank you for saving me." Eldamo simply smiled and nodded. Selde brought Isaiah a bowl of soup, and for the first time, he realized just how hungry he was as he sat down at a table to eat it with some warm, fresh bread.

Luc came through the cabin door with an arm full of wood, and they visited the rest of evening with the family in the safety of the den. They learned about the clever design of the den that the family lived in. Dwiddle had built the den under a very large tree that had died and rotted out in the middle. This allowed smoke from the fire to rise all the way up until it dispersed into the ever-present mist that hung over the forest. When Isaiah later went outside, he found the entrance to the den literally undetectable.

Dwiddle leaned back in his chair, took a deep breath, and asked, "What brings you to Endemar forest, young man?"

Isaiah looked around at Sarta and the children and said, "I'm on a mission to get to the city of Endemar. I'm...I'm a Journeyman." The words almost sounded like an apology, but they got both Dwiddle and Sarta's attention, and Dwiddle leaned in, "So say you, a Journeyman. Very interesting, haven't seen one of those in quite some time. Yes, that's very interesting."

They continued to talk, and Isaiah found out that a large population of wolves had recently come to the forest and created havoc across the countryside. Residents such as Dwiddle's family had either fled into hiding or been killed. However, the wolves had still failed to take complete control. The wolves and their allies, the coyotes, dagger hawks, and hired mercenaries, continually terrorized the countryside, and killed anyone who resisted. They stole supplies and burned homes if people did not cooperate. Fortunately, the city of Endemar remained a safe haven with no reports of wolves or mercenaries inside the walls. Isaiah also found out that some residents in the forest were without food, and starvation was very prevalent. This revelation suddenly made Isaiah feel guilty for the soup and bread he had just eaten.

Dwiddle added, "We have formed a resistance group that moves in the shadows to make sure supplies are shared and spread around to the neediest." Isaiah was impressed and saddened by their stories of avoiding, tricking, and sometimes simply outrunning the wolves, coyotes, and mercenaries.

Isaiah thought, *Is there anyone who can help them*, but stopped short and instead said out loud, "How can I help?"

Early the next morning, just as the first rays of light penetrated the darkness, Dwiddle awakened Isaiah and whispered to him that he and his son and several others were about to leave to smuggle some supplies to starving families. The wolves had cut them off, and they had gotten word that they were literally starving.

"I want to go; I want to help."

Dwiddle responded, "No, Isaiah, you don't have your full strength back yet; you need to rest."

Isaiah quickly replied, "I have enough strength, and I want to help. Please let me come. Besides, I can carry more supplies."

Dwiddle looked at him intently and said, "Very well, gather your things and come with me, but we must hurry."

They slipped out of the den and gathered in a small clearing where there were several backpacks filled with food. Isaiah, along with Diddle and his son Eldamo, was joined by two other foxes. There were short greetings, and each of them grabbed a backpack from the pile and slung it over their shoulders. Isaiah did likewise and was immediately impressed with the heavy weight of the pack. They certainly had used every corner of each backpack. He was also amazed at how much weight each fox could carry. When Isaiah threw his pack over his shoulder, there was instant pain as he was reminded that he had not yet healed completely from the dagger hawk attack.

The door to the den opened, and Luc stepped outside into the early morning air. He stretched and wiped his eyes to remove the sleep and then looked up to see Isaiah with a backpack on and surrounded by foxes. He came toward Isaiah and grabbed his arm and pulled him aside.

"What are you doing? This is not your fight, Isaiah. Let it go. They can take care of it. "

"These people saved my life, and I can help. I need to help. It's the right thing to do."

"They don't need you, and if you're not careful, you'll get yourself killed. So much for your so-called mission. You'll be just another dead Journeyman."

"I am here, and I can help, so that's what I am going to do."

Luc shook his head, looked directly in Isaiah's eyes, and said, "Well, don't count on me. It's not my fight. I'm out of here. If you're ever in Gebil, look me up," and with those words, he turned and went back into the den.

In the early morning hours, the group headed off in a single file. They moved quietly and swiftly through dried creek beds, over hills, and navigated over and under fallen trees. Isaiah noticed that they had a definite plan and purpose for the path they took. He noticed that every time they came to a trail, they deliberately did not take it but rather crossed over and made sure they left no tracks behind.

They had traveled for nearly an hour when one of the foxes out front raised his paw, and everyone stopped and got down as low as possible to the ground. Isaiah did likewise, but felt very conspicuous since he was so much bigger than the foxes. He began to worry that his presence presented an unnecessary risk.

Dwiddle turned to Isaiah, who was bringing up the rear, and whispered, "Patrol," and he pointed ahead. They lay silently on their faces for what seemed like hours, but it was only ten minutes until the patrol had passed. The point fox signaled that all was clear, and they all stood and quietly continued their journey in the opposite direction of the patrol.

They traveled another half-hour and came to a small meadow in the middle of the forest. The point fox made a high-pitched whistle, and it was returned by three short whistles. He stood up and slowly around the meadow other foxes, otters, raccoons, and squirrels raised up out of the tall grasses, as well as from behind trees. The band of five who carried the backpacks all stood up and joined them in the meadow. There were quiet greetings of handshakes and hugs. They were very grateful for the supplies but could not stay in the open of the meadow long. There were wolf patrols in the area.

They quickly and quietly said goodbye and then slipped back into the forest where they once again blended into shadows, foliage, and crevasses to avoid detection. Isaiah brought up the rear with Dwiddle immediately in front of him and Eldamo directly in front of his father. The other two foxes took the lead positions and navigated carefully through the terrain to avoid detection by patrols.

They had traveled for about an hour when the slope changed and forced them to ascend a ridge line. All of a sudden, the ground under Eldamo gave way, and despite his efforts to grab for roots, tree branches, and grasses, he tumbled and rolled down the side of the slope, where he crashed into some fallen branches and dead trees.

Dwiddle yelled, "Eldamo," and tried to grab him, but it was to no avail, and he went down the slope.

The group all froze in shock. Dwiddle yelled again, somewhat softer, "Eldamo…are you alright?"

There was a moan from below, and they heard Eldamo say, out of breath, "I…I think so. I think I just got the wind knocked out of me."

"Can you climb back up?" called his father. The other foxes were quite concerned and looked around nervously. They knew that noise of any kind would expose them and their position, but they also knew they had to rescue Eldamo.

Eldamo called up to his father, "My foot is caught under a log, and I can't get it free." The situation had gone from bad to worse in that Eldamo was now trapped and unable to get his leg free.

I'm on my way down," and with that, Dwiddle slid himself down the slope while he held on to roots and branches to control his slide. He reached the bottom and saw his son on a pile of brush with his leg twisted under a log. He immediately went to him and began to remove branches and logs to free his leg when he heard a voice.

"This is interesting, it looks like I have found two of the scumbag smugglers everyone's been looking for. I should get quite the reward for bringing you two in."

Dwiddle turned around rapidly to see a large coyote with sharp fangs and drool dripping out of its mouth. Dwiddle jumped back and instinctively hissed back at the coyote. His reaction was to let the coyote know he wasn't going without a fight. It worked, and the coyote stopped and crouched as if about to pounce. Then it leaned his head back and gave a long-drawn-out howl that called his colleagues to join him. There were almost immediate replies in the distance. He turned and grinned at both Dwiddle and Eldamo. He snarled and said, "Now, let's have some fun." Dwiddle placed himself between the coyote and his son. He could not turn his back for even a second while it moved back and forth, taunting Dwiddle and Eldamo.

The coyote lunged several times in feinting attacks to just scare them both. Each time the coyote leaned back and laughed and gave out additional howls. "Are you scared yet? You should be, heh, heh. Your father is a fool and has gotten you in a lot of trouble here. That's what you get for listening to him. He's going to get you killed."

Eldamo screamed back, "That's not true! That's a lie! My father's a good and honorable man." The coyote recoiled at the mention of good and honorable. "Enough of this talk, it's time to shut you both up." And with that, he spun and raced at them, planting his hind legs firmly onto the earth to spring him toward them. He pounced and had just left his feet when a rock flew and hit the temple of the coyote right behind its eye. The coyote went limp in mid-air and fell like a wet rag with a thud to the forest floor. It lay there in a heap, motionless and silent.

Dwiddle had turned and covered his son to protect him from the attack when suddenly he heard a thud and there was complete silence. He turned his head to see the coyote in a heap on the forest floor. His first thought and words were, "What...what happened?" He looked up and there stood Isaiah on the slope with a slingshot in his hand, pointed toward the coyote. Dwiddle nodded at Isaiah, who nodded back.

There was no time to take in everything that had just happened. Dwiddle turned his attention to his son and began to work frantically to free his leg from under the log. He removed several logs and carefully turned his son's leg until it was free from the pile. They hugged and then quickly began to climb back up the slope. As they got to the top, the point-fox said, "We must hurry, we have no time left before those coyotes and wolves will be here." And with that, they all ran but now took no time to carefully pick their way through the forest and hide in the shadows. They all knew that they must create distance for themselves from this place and the wolf and coyote packs.

The band of five now ran for their lives, and they could hear howling in the distance. At one point, there was a pause, and then suddenly, many howls all at the same time came from the same direction. They seemed to be angry howls. Howls that worked themselves up into a frenzy.

Dwiddle turned to Isaiah and said, "They found the coyote."

CHAPTER 13

THE CAVE

They continued to run as hard as they could. They dodged trees, climbed over rocks, and jumped over streams. They all knew they must create distance. The entire time, they heard howls behind them that continued to come closer and closer. They came to a steep incline alongside a rock face, and the point fox stopped and called out to Dwiddle and the others. "We can climb that incline, but I fear it will take everything we have left to just climb it. "We have one other option," exclaimed the point-fox. The foxes looked at each other and then at Isaiah.

Dwiddle spoke up, "I'm not sure he can make it."

"But it may be our only chance," replied the point-fox.

Isaiah sensed that he was part of their conversation and blurted out, "can't make what? Are you talking about me? What are you talking about?"

Dwiddle turned and said, 'Yes, there is an option that we foxes have taken through these hills and mountains over the years. It is not easy, even for foxes, but for a human, I'm just not sure it's even possible."

Isaiah jumped in, "If there's even a remote possibility, we must try."

"He is young and much smaller than a grown man. He just might be able to do it," pondered the point-fox.

Suddenly, they heard a mix of coyote and wolf howls below them just down the hill. They turned and all looked at each other, and Isaiah spoke, "Let's do it." And they all nodded in agreement.

With that, the point-fox ran behind a large rock and began to climb up the steep hill. They all followed him, and they soon found two large boulders with a separation between them that formed what looked like a cave opening. The point-fox went through the opening and then poked his head out and said, "This is it, come with me." The entire group followed him into the cave and its shadows. It took a minute for Isaiah's eyes to adjust, but soon he found himself in a large cavern with high ceilings. It was clear that this had been used for years as a refuge from enemies and weather, as there were signs of campfires, supplies, and even old blankets all around the cave. The point-fox said, "We must keep moving; the wolves and coyotes know of this place and will be sure to check it out."

Isaiah wondered to himself, *If they already knew about it, have we just walked ourselves into a trap?*

The group proceeded deeper into the cave, and it became harder to see even for the foxes, so Dwiddle took a piece of cloth out of a pouch he had on his belt and fashioned a torch with some wood he had found at the entrance of the cave. He lit the torch, and the cave lit up so that they could see the trail through the cave.

Isaiah immediately noticed that the cave had become narrower and that it turned and twisted as it went deeper into the mountain. The cave floor sloped downward and had become slippery as moisture ran off the walls. It was at that moment that the hair on all their backs stood straight up as they heard howls echoing through the cave. They were here. The pace quickened as they all realized time was very short. The wolves had picked up their scent and were tracking them, especially man scent, Isaiah's scent. The howling increased and was amplified by the cave.

Isaiah called ahead to Dwiddle, "How much further?" He had no idea what was ahead of them or exactly where it led. He only knew they were going deeper into the mountain, and the cave was getting smaller with each step they took.

Dwiddle responded, "Just a bit farther, we must hurry." But by now, Isaiah was so hunched over that he was almost crawling. Of course, though, the foxes were still quite mobile as they were much lower to the ground and could move quickly. The growling and howling from the wolves and coyotes continued to intensify and seemed to be only around the last bend in the cave. Unexpectedly, the floor stopped.

Isaiah, who was now on his hands and knees crawling, was stunned. There was no more floor, only rushing water in front of him, which flowed over his hands and knees into darkness and a solid granite wall some fifteen to twenty feet away. He spun around and looked frantically for Dwiddle and the other foxes. His eyes adjusted, and he saw them all standing in a line on a small ledge no more than eight inches in width that ran alongside the rushing water. The ledge led to a small hole just big enough for a fox to squeeze through. Isaiah slid into the flowing ice-cold water, which came up over his knees, but allowed him to stand up and face the row of foxes. The point-fox turned toward the hole and squeezed his body through the opening. Another followed, and Eldamo started to protest and say he wanted to stay behind with Isaiah. Dwiddle instantly stopped him and demanded that he follow the others. It was now Dwiddle and Isaiah alone, with rushing cold mountain water now up to Isaiah's waist. The howling was nearly on top of them. They would be here any moment.

Dwiddle looked at Isaiah through scared eyes and said over the roar of rushing water, "You must trust me." He went on, "Look at this water, it's flowing very swiftly, it will come out the other side. You must hold your breath and swim under the rocks."

Isaiah looked at him incredulously, "Have you ever done it?" he yelled over the roar of the water.

"Well, no, never had to. I always fit through the hole in the wall," replied Dwiddle.

Isaiah yelled over the roar, "How do you know it's open enough for me to get through below the water?"

"I don't know, but would you rather face them?" he gestured over his shoulder to shadows of wolves and coyotes who were about to come down the tunnel behind them.

The wolf and coyote howls were now deafening as they were so close in the cave. Isaiah yelled, "Go, I'll meet you on the other side!"

Dwiddle went to the small opening in the wall and, just before diving through the hole, turned and said, "God be with you…my brother," and then threw the smoldering torch on the ledge and dived headfirst into the small opening and squeezed his body through.

Isaiah stood alone in the cave with ice-cold mountain water now up to his chest. He worked his way over to the granite wall, which was where all the water seemed to disappear under. He could hear the roar of water and thought for a second, *what if it's not large enough for me to get to the other side, or what if I hit my head, or if it just doesn't open up. I'll drown.* Fear gripped him, and combined with the cold water, he stood frozen in the water for a moment. Then suddenly he heard the Voice, "Do not fear, I am with you always. Trust me, Isaiah, I've got you." Suddenly, a peace came over him.

The wolves and coyotes were now at the water's edge and in a frenzy. They growled and snarled at Isaiah. One yelled, "There he is!" They wanted to kill him. The wolves and coyotes, though, were hesitant to get in the cold water, and none could fit through the small opening in the wall. They were all at a dead end. The leader of the pack came through the now crowded cave and screamed at the wolves and coyotes, "What are you waiting for? Get in there and kill him." He threw a couple of wolves close to him into the icy cold water, and they immediately yelped from the cold and began to panic as the current was very fast. They dog paddled to just survive and couldn't grab Isaiah. The leader cursed them and threw a coyote into the stream that had wandered too close. Isaiah was now in the water with two wolves and a coyote.

Isaiah turned toward the wall and took three deep breaths, one…two…three, and dunked under the water into total darkness. He kept his hands in front of him to keep in contact with the wall. He could feel the water pressure that forced him toward the wall, and suddenly his feet went out from under him, and he was swept up in the current and dragged under the wall. It was pitch black, and the current was very rapid; it tossed him head over heels, and he suddenly lost all sense of up and down. He thought in his mind of the times back on the farm where he and the other kids had held contests to see who could hold their breath the longest under water. He had been the undisputed champion.

He could do little to resist the current, but he decided to just relax as best he could and let it carry him in the total darkness. He prayed, "Help me find the other side." His lungs began to burn as his oxygen supply began to run out. From experience, he had learned not to panic but let a little out of his lungs, so he exhaled, and it brought some brief relief, but he was now almost completely out of oxygen. He fought the urge to flail away and try to swim to a surface that didn't exist. The current caught him one more time and tumbled him forward, and suddenly he saw light above him through the water. He now knew which direction to go and rapidly began to swim toward the light and surface.

His head burst out of the water, and he took a huge breath of fresh mountain air. The air rushed into his lungs and cleared his head as he looked skyward at a beautiful cloudless blue sky. The burning sensation in his lungs now quickly departed, and he enjoyed the refreshing cool waters along with the sunshine. He looked skywards and said, "Thank you, you are with me always."

As he gained his strength, he rolled over on his back to get his bearings and realized he was in a swift river. He looked up and saw the other four members of their band. They were excited to see him and ran along the shore calling out to him. He couldn't quite make out what they were saying, but he was so thankful to be alive and see that all his new friends were also alright. He waved to them on the shore, and they continued to point and yell. He still couldn't quite make out what they were saying, but he did see them point at something. He rolled over and noticed that the river looked a bit odd; it just seemed to disappear.

It was then that it hit him; they were yelling, "Falls!"

Isaiah began to swim frantically to get to shore, but it was too late, and the water carried him over the falls, and he fell a hundred feet to a pool below the falls. By God's grace, he had no broken bones or contusions. He was just a little sore. He dragged himself to shore and collapsed. His four companions swiftly worked their way down the cliffs and soon stood next to sopping wet Isaiah, who was now seated on a log. They looked at each other and finally Isaiah smiled and said, "What an adventure," and they all laughed and hugged one another.

CHAPTER 14

OHTARA

The small band worked their way home with the dangers of the wolves and coyotes well behind them. They arrived back at the den long overdue, and Sarta, Selda, and Ion raced out of the door and threw their arms around Dwiddle and Eldamo. They were truly worried and so thankful to see them.

Sarta looked at Isaiah and said, "Isaiah, it is so good to see you. I am so thankful that you all came home safely. We were worried that something had happened."

Isaiah smiled and said, "Thank you, it is good to be back," and he then turned and headed into the den, but stopped and asked, "If you don't mind, I 'd like to lie down and rest a bit…if that's ok."

"Why of course, I am sure you are exhausted," responded Sarta.

Isaiah simply nodded and turned and went through the hut door and went straight to his bunk. Isaiah lay down but knew something just wasn't right. He was cold, but he was also hot. He tried to close his eyes and sleep and not turn over on his increasingly sore shoulder. He finally drifted off to sleep and slept several hours.

Isaiah heard some noises in the hut and slowly blinked his eyes and opened them a bit to see the room lit by the warm glow of the fireplace. He felt worse than he did before he fell asleep, and his eyes slowly focused to see Eldamo, who stood over him, calling his name, "Isaiah, Isaiah...Isaiah, wake up." He heard Eldamo turn to his mother and urgently say, "Something's wrong, mother, something is not right with Isaiah, come quickly." Isaiah heard Eldamo but was unable to even respond; every muscle and joint in his body was in extreme pain and discomfort.

Sarta ran over to Isaiah's bunk and took one look and gasped, "He's sweating profusely," and held her hand to his forehead, "he's on fire, quick, Eldamo, get me a rag and some cold water." Eldamo ran to the well to get water, and Dwiddle, who had been sitting by the fireplace reading, sprang to his feet and joined Sarta beside Isaiah's bunk. "This is not good, no, not good at all," she said to herself and then turned to Dwiddle and asked, "Are any of the rest of you sick?" to which Dwiddle responded, "No, neither I nor Eldamo are sick, and I just saw our other companions and they are just fine."

"Here, help me get another pillow under him," and Dwiddle reached around to help support him while Sarta placed another pillow behind Isaiah. Suddenly, Isaiah let out an agonizing moan of severe pain. Sarta and Dwiddle stared at each other in shock but didn't say a word. Together, they rolled Isaiah on his side, and she began to pull his shirt up over his head. She got it up above his head and asked Dwiddle to bring over a lamp from the table. She lifted the lamp up to see Isaiah's back, and she let out a gasp, "Oh, my, oh my, this is not good, no, not good at all, I've never, I've never seen anything quite like...," and she stopped to not scare Isaiah or the kids. She turned and looked at Dwiddle with genuine fear and then motioned with her eyes toward Isaiah's back. Dwiddle took the lamp and held it closer and then leaned over to view Isaiah's back. His eyes got very large, and he stood straight up. Isaiah's back was swollen around the dagger hawk wound with a deep red color radiating the entire length of the scar. There was so much swelling that his skin looked ready to split. Dwiddle motioned for Sarta to come closer as they stepped away from Isaiah's bunk.

Sarta spoke first and said, "Infection has set in, a very bad infection. It never completely healed after the dagger hawk attack. The toxin left his system, but now infection has set in that is even more dangerous than the toxin." She stopped as if to collect her thoughts and then looked straight into her husband's eyes and said, "If we don't do something, and I mean quickly…He will die." Dwiddle's eyes got large at the words of his wife. He knew her so well; she never exaggerated. She had treated many wounds and sicknesses for years and knew what "bad" looked like and meant. Dwiddle looked at her and said, "We must get help. We must get Ohtara."

Sarta began to apply cold rags to Isaiah's face and forehead in an effort to quench the fire that burned inside Isaiah's body. She knew she was in a race for his life.

As she applied cold compresses to Isaiah's head, she called for her daughter, Ion, to go to neighbors and ask if they had any ginger, echinacea, or mukad honey, all good for fighting infections. Ion ran out the door and down the trail to another den. Meanwhile, Dwiddle came into the room with a jacket already on and said, "Pray that I find Ohtara at her home or learn quickly where to find her." With that, he embraced Sarta and was out the door into the darkness of night.

As he stepped through the door, the cool night air hit him in the face, and he pulled his jacket collar up around his neck and face. Traveling at night was not uncommon for Dwiddle, but it was always dangerous. There were many predators who lurked in the woods at night. They looked for easy, unsuspecting prey. He looked around and thought to himself, *I need to be careful, but I must go fast, very fast.* He hurried down a narrow trail that led from his den to a dried riverbed. Usually, he avoided main trails because there was too much traffic on them, especially wolf traffic, but tonight he might need to take the risk.

Meanwhile, Sarta continued to apply cold compresses, and Isaiah drifted in and out of consciousness. Ion burst through the door with several clay jars and said, "I got some!" She laid the jars on the table, and they were each labeled with their contents. Sarta quickly opened each jar, took a portion out, and put it in a bowl. She ground them together and poured them into a tea strainer and then poured hot water through the strainer into the cup. The tea was steaming hot, and she needed to let it cool a bit. She had to be very careful with Isaiah's temperature. He already had a high fever, and she didn't want the hot tea to raise it any higher.

After a while, the tea had cooled sufficiently, and Sarta propped Isaiah up and said, "Isaiah, I have some tea I want you to drink. Come on, stay awake." Isaiah drifted in and out, and she struggled to get his attention. Finally, Isaiah came awake enough that he responded, "Oh yeah, of course."

Sarta held the cup to his lips and encouraged him to drink it all. He slowly sipped it and shook his head at the bitter taste, but he finally adjusted to the taste and continued to sip it until it was all gone. Isaiah looked at Sarta and whispered, "Thank you...Thank you so much." Sarta simply smiled and nodded and helped him lie back down on the bunk. Sarta knew the herbal tea would not cure the infection; it would only slow it. She knew that everything now depended on Dwiddle. He must find Ohtara. She continued to apply cold compresses and prayed.

* * *

Dwiddle headed north toward the castle and town. He knew his best chance of finding Ohtara would be at her home on the edge of the town. The dried creek bed gave him some cover from predators, which included late-night wolf patrols. Over the last year, wolf packs had grown in number and aggressiveness. They terrorized shepherd's flocks and killed sheep at will and had cut off whole regions from needed supplies. They had forced entire villages and communities to bow to their rule.

The wolves, though, had still not taken the city or castle of Endemar, but there were rumors of spies lurking throughout the city. The rumors were that the spies had been looking for weaknesses in the city defenses. As a result, there was much fear and turmoil in the city, and that made it a dangerous place.

The dried-up creek bed came to a bridge built over it, and Dwiddle paused to consider his options. He could stay in the creek bed and work his way toward the city or take what now had become a road and move much faster. He stopped, looked both ways, and listened carefully for any sign of wolves or other threats. He knew the road would allow him to move much faster, but it also presented a greater risk. He took a deep breath and prayed, "Please protect me," and climbed up out of the creek bed and onto the road. He must take the risk; time was running out for Isaiah.

Dwiddle scampered down the road and tried his best to stay in the shadows. The night was clear with a star-covered sky and a full moon. What was normally beautiful now made him very nervous and on edge. He listened carefully and swiveled his head constantly so as not to be surprised since the full moon was like a spotlight pointed directly on him. He pressed forward through the night and moved as quickly as possible.

A light appeared down the road, and he came to a complete stop and hid in the brush just off the road. He crept closer to get a better look and realized it was an old tavern that he had visited in the past. He knew the owner and thought, *perhaps he might have an idea where I could find Ohtara.* He was closer to the edge of the city and had begun to see cottages and an occasional business. As he watched, the tavern door opened and three patrons came out: a fox, a possum, and a groundhog. All three headed in the opposite direction and were clearly headed home. Dwiddle thought, *now is my chance to slip inside. I am sure there is no one left at this hour but the owner.*

Dwiddle crept close to the building and tried to peer through a window to assure himself that only the owner was present. He could only see the owner dimly lit by the fire in the fireplace. He was behind the counter with a rag cleaning the top as if about to shut down for the evening. *Good,* thought Dwiddle, *everyone has left, and he is about to close up.* With that, Dwiddle reached for the handle on the door and turned it. He quickly opened the door and slipped inside, keeping his back close to a wall and in the shadows.

The owner didn't even look up but pronounced, "Sorry, we're closed for the night." Every nerve in Dwiddle's body was on high alert as he sensed danger.

"Ah, ah," he stammered, "Morely, it's Dwiddle." Morely was a middle-aged Otter who had run this establishment for many years.

Morley looked up and squinted to try to see in the dimly lit room. "Dwiddle, what are you doing here so late?" He said nervously as he looked to his right.

Dwiddle, now fully committed and relieved that Morley recognized him, blurted out, "I am on a mission to find Ohtara. I have a Journeyman at my house who is very ill, and we must find Ohtara. Do you have any idea where she may be?"

Morley now seemed very uncomfortable and stammered, "No, no, no - I have no idea, you need to leave though; right now, we are closed!" Dwiddle was taken aback at Morley's inhospitable behavior when suddenly from the other side of the room came a voice out of the shadows, "Morley, you scum bag. You just let any kind of vermin wander into your place in the middle of the night." A figure stepped out of the shadows toward Dwiddle and became dimly lit by the fire. It was a large gray wolf.

"So, you have a Journeyman at your house and he's sick…now that is very interesting," snarled the wolf as he slowly walked toward Dwiddle. "And you want to find Ohtara," growled the wolf with absolute contempt. "He must be bad, really bad if he needs Ohtara," continued the wolf, which was now within just a few feet of Dwiddle with its teeth bared. Dwiddle could feel the wolf's heavy breathing in his face and expected him to pounce at any moment.

"Hey, I don't want any trouble in my place," yelled Morely.

"Shut up, Morely," responded the wolf as he weighed his next move. The tension in the room was extreme, and Dwiddle was trembling and sweating heavily. "Let's have some fun," chuckled the wolf.

Dwiddle had back peddled as the wolf drew closer and now was in a corner with the front door across the room from them. There was no chance of bolting for the door and into the night. Suddenly, the door flew open, and a silhouetted figure stood in the doorway wearing a long-hooded coat. Both Dwiddle and the wolf stepped back at the sudden entrance. A voice came from the silhouetted figure, "Hello, Dwiddle, it's been a while." It was Ohtara.

The wolf growled and proceeded to move closer toward Dwiddle when suddenly a knife, a dagger to be exact, flew through the air and embedded in the wall right below the wolf's chin. The wolf froze, and a small trickle of blood appeared and dropped from his chin where the knife nicked him.

"The next one won't be so generous," said Ohtara.

The wolf backed away and growled in disdain as it ran out the door just as Ohtara stepped further into the tavern. Dwiddle let out a deep breath and thought he was going to pass out. "Thank you, Ohtara, it is so, so good to see you," said Dwiddle.

Ohtara responded with a chuckle, "And you, too, my friend. What brings you to town in the middle of the night?"

Diddle immediately began to explain Isaiah's dire condition, and before he could finish, Ohtara grabbed his arm, "Dwiddle, we must go quickly!" As she ran out the door, she shouted over her shoulder, "Morley, sorry about the wall."

Ohtara firmly held Dwiddle's arm and ran into the night air, stopped, and whistled. A magnificent white stallion raced out of the dark and came to an abrupt stop right in front of her and Dwiddle. She reached down, swept Dwiddle up, placed him on the horse, and, in one motion, mounted the stallion herself. She yelled, "Aranco, ride fast!"

Ohtara rode swiftly down the road in the direction of Dwiddle's den. Dwiddle held on as tight as he possibly could. He had never been on a horse before, let alone travelled this fast. Ohtara urged her horse, Aranco, to press on. She asked Dwiddle to show her where to get off the road to get to his den. Dwiddle simply nodded, but when they came to the old bridge over the dry creek bed, Dwiddle yelled over the galloping sounds of hoofs, "Here it is, this is where you leave the road and follow the dried creek-bed."

Ohtara brought Aranco to a stop, reviewed the situation, and then slowly edged the horse down into the creek-bed. They would have to go slower, but they still were much faster than on foot.

* * *

Sarta continued to hold vigil over Isaiah, who slipped in and out of consciousness. She applied cold compresses and prayed. Selde and Ion had long ago fallen asleep, but Eldamo remained awake and got new cold compresses and anything else his mother needed.

Sarta was exhausted and fighting sleep herself when the door to the den burst open and Dwiddle ran in with Ohtara right behind him. Sarta looked up, and tears filled her bloodshot eyes. She was exhausted, but so grateful that Ohtara had arrived. All she could say was, "Thank God."

Ohtara gave a brief smile to Sarta and then asked, "How is he?"

Sarta rolled Isaiah over to see his inflamed back and explained that she had given Isaiah ginger, echinacea, and mukad honey tea, and he had stabilized some. Ohtara nodded in approval and responded, "Good work, Sarta, you saved his life." She then calmly turned to Dwiddle and in a forceful voice said, "Dwiddle, go to Aranco and get the bag attached to his saddle and bring it in here. Dwiddle didn't hesitate and ran outside to Aranco and found a brown weathered bag attached to the horse's saddle and brought it to Ohtara.

Ohtara opened the bag and removed a clay jar and asked Sarta to roll Isaiah over onto his side so they could get to his back and the inflamed area. Sarta complied and turned Isaiah onto his side and pulled his shirt up. Ohtara opened the clay jar, stuck her fingers in the jar, brought out a big lump of salve, and began to apply it directly to the wound and infected area. Isaiah jerked at Ohtara's touch, and she calmly and almost at a whisper said, "There, there, it will hurt a bit, but give it time, and you'll be thankful." After spreading the salve over the entire bright red, swollen area of Isaiah's back, she stopped and placed both her hands directly on the wound. Isaiah flinched once again but did not protest. With her hands on the wound, she lifted her head toward heaven and began to pray, "Father, this is Ohtara, your watchman, called to protect and watch over journeymen. You are our creator; you made every bone, every muscle, and every nerve in our body. I come to you this night to ask that you heal this young Journeyman and remove this infection from his body. Restore his body and strength so that he may continue his journey. Thank you, Amen."

As Ohtara prayed, the area under her hands began to glow, not the red glow from the infection but a bright white light that lit up his back and filled the room. Sarta, Dwiddle, and Eldamo looked on in wonder as an incredible peace settled over them and their home. No one said a word; they couldn't.

Slowly, Ohtara removed her hands, and the glow diminished until it went away. The swelling on Isaiah's back began to diminish, and the color of the skin also began to return to normal. She looked up and whispered, "Thank you."

After a time of complete quiet and stillness in the room, Ohtara turned to Sarta and said, "Let's let him rest now, and in the morning, I will take him to my home to fully recover. By the way," she asked, "do you have anything to eat?"

CHAPTER 15

THE RIDE

Late the next morning, Isaiah managed to pull himself up in his bunk and look around the hut. He had very little strength, but he actually felt much better. The fever had broken. The events of the night before were nothing but a blur in his mind. The fever had caused him to hallucinate and drift in and out of consciousness. He was unsure of what had actually happened and was real, and what was nothing but a dream.

Sarta came into his room and said, "Good morning, Isaiah. It is so good to see you are better."

"Yes, I do feel better, but uh, what exactly happened last night? It's kind of all a blur to me." Sarta smiled and sat on the corner of his bunk to fill him in on the events of the previous night. As she was filling him in on the events, Ohtara walked into the room and jumped on the end of the bed and asked, "How are you this morning, Isaiah?"

Isaiah was stunned because he thought this girl was nothing more than a character in his dream. He had remembered a beautiful young teenage girl being present and praying over him, but he thought it was all simply a dream. "Why, why, much better, thank you," he stammered.

Ohtara stuck out her hand to shake Isaiah's hand and said, "Let me introduce myself, my name is Ohtara, watchman of the orchard and…an occasional Journeyman."

Isaiah shook her hand and responded, "My name is Isaiah, but it appears you already know that." Ohtara simply smiled and nodded, and Isaiah continued, "Sarta was just telling me that you were responsible for my getting better."

"No, not really," responded Ohtara, "I may have helped a little, but the real credit goes to Sarta and Dwiddle and answered prayer." Isaiah smiled and, for the first time, took notice of her. She was a very beautiful girl who he guessed was in her late teens. She had hazel green eyes and light auburn hair braided on the sides but pulled back and allowed to flow down her back. She wore a long brown hooded coat that reminded him of Iswa and his coat. She also wore leather boots that came up to her knees with pant legs that gathered at the top. She had on a loose-fitting shirt that was neatly tucked into the pants with a brown belt around her waist. It was the brown belt that particularly caught his attention. Tucked in one side were several daggers, and on the other side, she had a short sword in a sheath. As Isaiah ate some breakfast, she sat on the end of the bed, talking and fidgeting with her necklace.

As the morning progressed, Isaiah became a bit stronger, so shortly after noon, Ohtara decided it was time to leave with Isaiah for her home on the outskirts of the city. She asked Sarta and Dwiddle to help get Isaiah out to her horse, Aranco. They obliged and lifted him onto the saddle. Ohtara turned to Sarta and Dwiddle and smiled and pulled them both to her in a hug. "God bless you for what you did," she whispered. Dwiddle responded, "And God bless you for coming. Go with God's grace." And with that, Ohtara put her foot in Aranco's stirrup and hoisted herself up in the saddle behind Isaiah.

Ohtara was comfortable making the journey back to the city while there was still daylight, but after dark was another issue, especially while she had a still weak Isaiah with her. They rode for over an hour through dry and wet creek-beds when she decided to stop and give Aranco and Isaiah a rest. Aranco drank from a nearby stream as Isaiah and Ohtara sat under a tree and talked.

"So, Isaiah, where do you want to go?"

"I am on my way to the Land of Integrity," stated Isaiah, "but I seem to have gotten a bit distracted and off course."

"Really, why do you say that?" responded Ohtara.

"Well," replied Isaiah, "I went on a mission to deliver supplies and nearly got killed by wolves, fell over a hundred-foot waterfall, and nearly died from an infection caused by a dagger hawk. None of that seemed to have anything to do with the Land of Integrity."

Ohtara laughed and said, "Well, you certainly have had your adventures. But as you look back on them, what have you learned?"

Immediately, Isaiah stopped and looked at her inquisitively. *He had heard these words before from Iswa. What have you learned?* He stammered a bit to respond since the events of the last few days had not been conducive to quiet introspective analysis.

Before he could answer, Ohtara continued as if it were a rhetorical question. "Dwiddle used to work for me, but when the wolves returned and the attacks started, he chose to go back to the woods." She continued to stare out at the stream, "he deeply cares about people and feels called to help in any way he can. However, in the city, he heard a lot of politicians give speeches. They would say this and that about the wolves, but few would do anything to stop their attacks. Dwiddle simply could not be all talk, no action. It just didn't fit his character. It was not the way of integrity." She continued, "Dwiddle is respected throughout the whole forest for his honesty and being a fox of his word. If he says he will do something…he will do it."

Isaiah sat quietly and listened and thought about Dwiddle and Sarta and the sacrifices they had made to help others.

Ohtara quickly sat up and turned her head to listen. Aranco let out a loud whinny. She was now on high alert and whistled for Aranco to come. With a sense of urgency in her voice, she said, "We've been here too long, we must go...now." And with that, she boosted Isaiah back onto Aranco and swung her leg over the saddle behind him.

They finally reached a road, and she turned Aranco onto the road that led to the city. They could move much faster now if needed, and she sensed that might be the case. Suddenly, from above, she heard a screech of a dagger hawk. Isaiah heard it too and began to tremble. His first experience with a dagger hawk had not gone well, and he certainly did not want a repeat of it. Ohtara called out to Aranco, "Ride fast, Aranco, ride fast!"

Isaiah held on as tightly as he could as Aranco galloped at top speed. Ohtara leaned into Isaiah and calmly said, "Hang on, Isaiah, this may get a bit rough." Just as those words came out of her mouth, they both caught a glimpse of movement from the trees on both right and left sides. Moving fast out of the woods was a pack of wolves. The dagger hawk had been their scout, and now they were trying to execute an ambush. Ohtara reached around Isaiah and pulled two swords out of sheaths that were attached on each side of the saddle. In a fluid motion, both swords were out of their sheaths and in Ohtara's hands. As Aranco galloped hard, Ohtara twirled each sword in her hands as she positioned them to defend against the wolves that now chased from behind, as well as those ahead of them. She realized that as long as Aranco could keep up this pace, the wolves could not catch them from behind. However, the wolves just coming out of the woods were ahead of them and had an angle of attack that could give them trouble.

Ohtara saw that the wolves that had just emerged out of the woods were going to intercept them in another thirty yards. She quickly pulled Isaiah to one side of Aranco and yelled, "Keep your head down," and just as they reached the point of interception, a wolf leaped from a rock directly at Ohtara and Isaiah. Ohtara leaned back and spun her sword to deliver a clean blow right below the rib cage of the wolf. There was a yelp, and the wolf fell dead in the middle of the road. She then turned her attention to a wolf that came at them from the other side, and she spun her sword in that hand, leaned over Aranco, and came down onto the top of the wolf's head just as it got to the side of her horse. It also went down motionless in the center of the road. This seemed to discourage the rest of the wolf pack, and they broke off their chase, but Aranco continued to gallop at top speed to gain distance.

Finally, after several miles, Aranco slowed his pace to a trot, and Isaiah began to raise up and look around when, without warning, he heard the high-pitched screech of a dagger hawk. Ohtara screamed, "Enough of this!" and turned in the saddle just in time to sling one of the swords into the attacking dagger hawk's chest. The sudden blow stopped the hawk in midair, and it dropped straight to the ground like a rock.

Isaiah was out of breath, witnessing what had just happened. He had never seen anything like what Ohtara had just done. It was so extraordinary that it was difficult to process in his mind just what had occurred. The adrenaline rush he had from the danger began to drain from his bloodstream and, combined with the fact that he had not yet completely recovered from the infection, caused him to feel very weak and woozy.

Ohtara grabbed onto him as she felt his grip on Aranco loosening. "Hang on, Isaiah, it won't be much farther now, we're almost home," whispered Ohtara.

Isaiah was still awake when they arrived at Ohtara's home. On the way, they had passed several sentry points manned by city guards. When they arrived at Ohtara's home, there were very large gates with additional sentries and a long lane lined with trees that led to the house. They turned into the lane on Aranco, and the horse walked steadily but clearly tired up the lane to the house. When Isaiah saw the house, he was stunned. To call it a house was inadequate. It was a massive palace made of brick and stone with at least three floors. There was a large circular drive that led to front steps that rose to massive, ornate wooden doors. The green grass in front of the house was immaculately kept, and there was a beautiful fountain with a sculpture of a stallion in the middle. Spires rose above the house at multiple points, and each flew the flag of the kingdom.

As Aranco came to a stop in front of the house, several individuals ran out to greet Ohtara and help Isaiah dismount from Aranco. Ohtara embraced each one and then went to Aranco and hugged his neck and said, "Thank you, my old friend, get some much-deserved rest," and Aranco went off to the barn. She turned to the house servants and said, "Please take my friend, Isaiah, up to one of our guest rooms. He is very weak and needs rest." With that, they carried Isaiah up the steps and took him to a beautiful guest room where he lay on the softest bed he had ever slept on. Within seconds, he was sound asleep.

CHAPTER 16
THE MARKET

Isaiah woke up, and his first thought was that it had all been a dream, but then he looked around the room and realized he was in this exquisite room with high vaulted ceilings. It was not a dream.

The door to the room opened, and Ohtara walked in and said, "Good morning, sleepy head. I hope you slept well and are feeling better." Isaiah, still disoriented, stammered, "Well, yes, I do feel much better, just a bit stiff from the ah…ride last night." Ohtara laughed and said, "Yes, that was a bit intense, but we're here now."

Isaiah looked around the room and propped himself up on the pillows behind his head. He was in a poster bed with a canopy over the top. The windows were tall and covered with beautiful layers of curtains. The furniture was finely crafted and made from marble and cherry wood. This all sat on top of inlaid wooden floors. There was a couch and a fireplace in the room with magnificent paintings on the walls of people who looked very important. Quite simply, it was breathtakingly beautiful, and Isaiah was confused. *Where was he?*

Isaiah gathered his thoughts and words and finally asked, "Where exactly are we at?"

Ohtara responded matter-of-factly, "At my home where I live and work of course. Oh, there will be plenty of time to show you around, but we first must get your strength back," and with that she bound out of the room and an otter, that he found out was named Otto, stayed behind in the room. Isaiah couldn't help but smile at his name, Otto the Otter.

Otto was middle-aged with gray whiskers and wore wire-rim glasses that made him look both distinguished and wise.

"Good morning, Isaiah. I am very happy to see that you are recovering. I have worked with Ohtara for many years and am here to help you fully heal and recover your strength. I will also help you become acclimated to the city of Endemar."

"Endemar, are we in Endemar!" Isaiah bound out of bed and ran to the window and threw the curtains back. "Is that Endemar?"

Otto chuckled and responded, "No, those are the lawns and barns for the manor house. We are actually outside the city, but in time we will travel into the city."

Isaiah returned to the bed, and Otto brought him some breakfast, which tasted wonderful and made him realize just how hungry he was.

The first day, Isaiah stayed mostly in bed and rested, and slowly regained his strength, but he began to feel stronger after a good night's rest. On the second day, he rose early and ventured out of his room and into the wide halls of the home. He walked to a grand staircase that led to the first floor and descended the stairs. The staircase opened into a grand entrance that led to a large dining hall with a stone fireplace at one end and high ceilings with bright colored tapestries hung along the walls. The living area contained several large couches and oversized chairs arranged in sitting areas to promote conversation. It also included a large fireplace with a massive painting of whom he assumed was the owner, over the mantle. The large windows were framed by ceiling-to-floor curtains. He stood in the opening to the large dining room, and a young girl with her brown hair tied back in a ponytail, bound by him with a clipboard in one arm. As she went by Isaiah, she said, "Good morning, Isaiah. I hope you are feeling better." He had never seen her before, but she obviously knew who he was. A servant then greeted him and offered him a chair at the large table for breakfast. He sat at the table, overwhelmed at the sight of it all.

Ohtara came into the dining hall where Isaiah was now seated for breakfast and said, "Good morning, Isaiah. I think it's time we get you out and about in the Kingdom."

Otto overheard this and spoke up, "Tara and I are on our way to the plaza to sell some fruit. He can accompany us if he wishes."

When Isaiah heard the word plaza, he immediately remembered the words of Luc, that he had hidden the box in a well in a plaza. Isaiah jumped at the offer and said, "I'd love to go. I need to get out."

They agreed to meet and at precisely nine o'clock Otto walked into the grand entrance and said, "This way, Isaiah," and showed him to a wagon parked in front of the house. The young girl with the ponytail was already up on the wagon, and he soon found out her name was Tara. Otto and Isaiah climbed aboard, and off they went toward the city market.

Isaiah found out that Tara was just a couple of years older than him and worked at the house. He determined that she was a sort of personal assistant who helped in any way she could with daily chores and day-to-day management of the house.

They entered the city gates, and the sights and sounds were overwhelming. Cobblestone streets wound throughout the city, and small shops lined the streets with residences above. Flower boxes hung from windows with red, yellow, and blue bouquets of flowers cascading down from the boxes. The roofs of the buildings were covered with red clay tiles. Occasionally, the street would open to a plaza area where vendors would sell vegetables, fruits, and other goods from wagons and carts. Isaiah had never seen anything like this as hundreds of citizens moved in and out of the plaza areas. He began to understand how Luc could not remember which plaza he had hidden the box.

The inhabitants of Endemar were made up of humans, foxes, raccoons, squirrels, and others from the animal kingdom. All were moving about, talking, buying, selling, and living life with their families and friends. In this world, it was completely normal, and Isaiah had come to accept that fact.

"This is a good spot, said Otto, "Let's pull the wagon in here and set up." Otto maneuvered the wagon into an empty spot and disconnected the horses from the wagon. He reached into the back of the wagon and pulled out a table and a balance scale. The scale consisted of two balance plates suspended by chains. Standard weights are placed on one side for a desired weight, and then goods are placed on the other scale until the balance is perfectly level, which indicates the goods weigh the same as the weights.

Shoppers immediately began to gather around Otto's wagon and buy fruits. They would typically ask for five or ten pounds of some type of fruit, and Otto would place weights on the scale for the desired weight, and then the shopper would select their fruits from the wagon and add to the empty scale plate until the entire scale was perfectly balanced, which indicated they had exactly the desired weight. This went on and on for several hours, and the contents of the wagon steadily diminished.

Otto did the weighing and collection of payments while Tara continually rearranged the fruit on the wagon and helped customers gather fruit. Isaiah helped get set up but then asked Otto if he could look around a bit. Otto readily encouraged him to explore the area and told him they would be there for several more hours.

Isaiah saw an opportunity to explore the area for wells that could be the possible hiding place for Luc's box. He took off across the plaza and took in his new surroundings. He was amazed at the sights and sounds all around him. It was all so different than anything he had ever seen. One vendor sold fish from a wagon that contained hundreds of fish. Another sold bright colored rugs and fabrics from far away, while another sold copper kettles and pans. The plaza was filled with people, animals, colors, and sounds so different than home. He crossed the large plaza and had not seen any obvious wells but came to a street that led away from the plaza and decided to ask someone. They told him this plaza did not have a well, but a couple of blocks away was another plaza with a well. He immediately followed their directions and headed down the narrow street.

He had walked a distance down the street and came to a place where the street split into two different directions. He paused to contemplate which direction to take when a gloved hand went over his mouth and pulled him quickly into a dark alley and pinned him against the wall. An individual in a hooded coat had grabbed him. Suddenly, he heard a voice he recognized, "Isaiah, it's me, Luc."

Isaiah spun around and grabbed Luc, "It's so good to see you, my friend. It is good to know that you're ok."

"Well, for now, I'm safe, but everyone seems to be after me. This place is very dangerous."

"How can I help?" asked Isaiah. "Are you looking for the well where you hid the box?"

Luc acknowledged that he had been trying but had not yet found it.

"I am getting familiar with the city and can move about more freely than you. Can you remember anything else about the location of the well? Any clue would be helpful," said Isaiah.

Luc leaned back and shook his head, "I don't know, the one thing that keeps going through my mind is that I remember a gate, a large iron gate nearby. I had to climb over it because it was locked."

"Alright, that's something. I will use that as I look around. How will I get a hold of you?"

"You won't, I'll get ahold of you, and one more thing. Rumor has it that Ohtara helped get you out of the woods. Is that true?"

"Yes, she helped save my life."

"Don't trust her. Tell her nothing about you, me, or the box. She is very dangerous. I mean it, very dangerous," said Luc while he looked intently at Isaiah.

"But she can help you," protested Isaiah.

"No, Isaiah, she is very dangerous, now promise me. Promise me you'll say nothing to her or that friend of hers, Otto." Isaiah shook his head in disagreement but finally relented and nodded affirmatively that he would keep this between the two of them for now. Luc let go of Isaiah and slipped down the dark alley and was gone, off to do what he does best...hiding.

Isaiah continued down the street and thought about their conversation. It bothered him greatly that Luc had described Ohtara as extremely dangerous. Ohtara had been nothing but kind and caring to him.

He used the rest of the morning to explore several small plazas in the area, but none had a well that could provide a hiding place, nor did any have iron gates nearby. As noon approached, he returned to the plaza where Otto and Tara were still selling fruit.

Tara looked up from rearranging fruit and asked, "Did you enjoy yourself?"

"Ah, yes, of course, I enjoyed looking around. It was very interesting," responded Isaiah while still thinking about his conversation with Luc.

"I am off to lunch. Can you help Otto out and rearrange the fruit for customers?" Isaiah happily said yes and took over her duties of pulling fruit forward so customers could reach it. He noticed the wagon only had a third of the fruit left to be sold.

Isaiah overheard Otto say, "Oh no, Mrs. Nettles overpaid me by several dollars. They must have stuck together." He quickly turned to Isaiah and said, "Can you hold things down here? I must find her." Isaiah had watched Otto earlier in the morning but had not been involved in the weighing or payment process, and he responded somewhat hesitantly, "Sure, ah, no problem." Otto reassured him that he would do fine, and he promptly disappeared into the crowd.

Isaiah began to weigh fruits and collect money, and he established a rhythm that made him more comfortable. Many customers immediately asked about Otto's whereabouts, and it became clear that Otto was not only well known but highly respected by the community. As the quantity of fruits diminished further in the wagon, he began to wonder where Otto had gone. A nineteen-year-old teenager, who he later found out was named Pilu, walked around the corner of the wagon, picked up an apple, and took a big bite out of it. He came up and started to talk to Isaiah. Pilu was confident, brash, and aggressive, and finally asked about Otto.

"Where's old Otto? I don't see him today."

"Otto had to run an urgent errand. He will be back shortly." Isaiah replied,

"Oh, that's too bad, but I suppose you and I can just do business," grumbled Pilu. "You see, every week I come about this time and buy the remaining fruits from Otto for half price. It lets him finish up the day early by emptying the wagon. I suppose we can just do the transaction, just the same. Shall we settle up?"

Isaiah was immediately uncertain about what Pilu told him. He didn't know anything about this "deal" that Pilu claimed existed between him and Otto. However, he also did not want to upset Pilu or anger Otto. He wished Tara were back from lunch, but she was nowhere in sight.

Isaiah hesitantly responded, "Well, I am not so sure. I don't know anything about a deal; I was just asked to watch the wagon and sell fruits until he returned."

Pilu became more insistent and urgent, "Oh, come on, you don't want to upset old Otto. If you don't sell, then he and you will be here several more hours to get rid of the remaining fruits. That will not only be a big problem for Otto but an even bigger problem for you. Otto will not be happy."

Isaiah was still uneasy and responded, "I... I am not sure, I guess it could be a problem."

"Of course, it would be just as I said. He'd be very unhappy. Old Otto and I do this all the time," urged Pilu.

Isaiah was just about to agree to the deal when he heard the Voice ask, "Is this an accurate description of Otto? Would he really be mad at you if you didn't do this deal?"

Isaiah stopped short of agreeing to the deal and said, "I am sorry, but I simply cannot do it. You will have to wait until Otto returns."

Pilu became very agitated, "That's absurd, I am leaving, and there will be no deal today, so you can face Otto's wrath! I give you one final chance."

The last words, "Otto's wrath," jumped out at Isaiah. Since he had met Otto, there had never been any evidence that suggested that he would pour out his wrath on anyone. He came across as gentle, kind, caring, self-controlled, and even loving.

Isaiah immediately responded, "That's the way it will have to be. Thank you for the offer."

Pilu turned and let out a loud, "Humph," that showed his disgust, and stormed off into the crowd after tossing the half-eaten apple back into the wagon.

Isaiah stood beside the wagon with the fruit as customers continued to look over the fruit. He knew he had made the right decision. Just then, Tara returned and asked if everything was ok.

Twenty minutes later, Otto showed back up at the wagon, and Isaiah was very glad to see him. He filled him in on the conversation with Pilu, and Otto simply listened quietly while he shook his head from side to side. After Isaiah had told him the whole story, he looked Isaiah in the eyes and said, "Well done."

Otto went on to explain that Pilu ran a local street gang and constantly ran schemes and used theft, extortion, and intimidation to make money. He saw Isaiah and tried to take advantage of him. Otto then said, "Let's close up shop for the day. We've sold enough."

Isaiah was fine with that but said, "We still have some fruits that we could sell; don't we want to stay and sell them?"

Otto responded, "I think I know a better use for the remaining fruits." He winked at Tara, who smiled, and with that, they closed the shop for the day and hitched the horse up to the wagon.

As they left the market, Isaiah asked if he had found Mrs. Nettles, to which Otto replied laughingly, "Oh yes, finally, turned out that she went to her sister's house a couple miles outside of the city and by the time I got there she had gone back to her house on the edge of the city. We all got a good laugh about it, and I thanked her for helping me get my exercise for the day."

Isaiah was amazed at his attitude and cheerfulness about what some might have thought was a waste of time and effort. He simply did not view it that way. He was also impressed that Otto would go to these lengths to return a couple of dollars. He had begun to understand the basis for the community's respect and love for Otto.

As they pulled out of the plaza, Isaiah asked Otto, "Are there many wells in these plazas?"

"Humm," replied Otto, "Not this one, but many plazas do have wells."

Otto turned the wagon down a small dirt road on the outskirts of the city. He pulled the wagon up to a two-story stone house surrounded by grass and trees. As soon as he stopped the wagon, he and Tara jumped down, and almost simultaneously, a group of kids ran out of the building. Otto laughed and hugged the kids, and a woman came behind them who smiled and greeted Otto. Tara also hugged the kids and pulled out the candy she had bought in the market and began to pass it out. This was clearly not the first time this has happened.

"Hello Otto, it is so good to see you," said the woman.

Otto replied, "And you, too, Elendil!"

Otto introduced Isaiah and then turned his attention once again to the kids. There were twenty in all, and they were very excited to see him. He told them to come with him to the wagon, and he proceeded to unload the remaining fruits. The older children carried them into the house while the others tagged along and giggled with Tara, who held the kids' hands. As Isaiah watched this scene, he couldn't help but think of Purposeville and Riddle. He looked on and smiled.

"Otto, thank you so much. What can I ever do to repay you?" asked Elendil.

Otto simply smiled and said, "Your friendship is always enough." And they laughed together.

It turned out that the house was an orphanage, and every week Otto dropped off the last portion of his wagon instead of selling the fruits in the market. It was always a tremendous blessing to Elendil and the children.

Isaiah could not help but think, *What would have happened if he had sold the remaining fruit to Pilu?* It made him shudder.

Otto, Tara, and Isaiah returned to the large house at sunset and had some dinner, where Otto filled them in on more history about Endemar. He explained that the kingdom was currently run by a Regent whose name was Theron. He was a human who had the responsibility to administer the kingdom in the absence of a monarch. The previous king had died a number of years before, and his only child was a minor and could not rule, so a regent was assigned to rule until the king's heir was of age. He went on to explain that the king's child had been hidden away to protect them from enemies.

He also talked about the current troubles in the kingdom. The wolves had killed, destroyed, and created mass fear. Every week, the wolves grew stronger as more and more wolves came to Endemar Forest. They had now begun to attack and kill sheep even though they were protected by shepherds and sheep dogs. They even threatened to overrun the entire kingdom, which included the city of Endemar. The city had grown very restless. Isaiah sat and listened intently. He had seen up close the evil of the wolves.

Isaiah asked, "Is there anything that can be done to stop the wolves?"

Otto smiled and said softly, "Yes, there is always a way."

As they prepared to retire for the evening, Otto turned to Isaiah and thanked him for his help and once again acknowledged him for not having been taken in by Pilu's scheme. Isaiah started to turn to head to his room, and Otto stopped him, "One more thing, can you help me again tomorrow?"

Isaiah responded, "Why of course, Otto, I would love to: more fruit to sell?"

Otto looked at him with a sly smile, "No…tomorrow we kick the hornet's nest," and with that, he turned and headed to his room.

CHAPTER 17

THE HORNET'S NEST

Isaiah was already wide awake when the first sunshine came through his window. Otto's words had stuck with him, and he carefully mulled them over. He quickly descended the grand staircase and found Otto had already eaten his breakfast.

"Good morning, Isaiah," said Otto cheerfully. "Are you ready for a new adventure today?"

Isaiah laughed and asked, "Of course, where are we off to today?"

Otto simply responded, "You will see, you will see." And with that, Isaiah finished breakfast and headed out the front doors. Once outdoors, Isaiah immediately noticed a carriage with a driver. Otto greeted the driver and said to Isaiah, "We don't need the fruit wagon today, just a ride back to the market, so, shall we?" And with that, he pointed his open palm toward the carriage to allow Isaiah to climb in first.

The carriage proceeded back into the interior of the city toward the same mall they had been in the day before, but this time Otto had the driver stop the carriage several blocks from the mall. "This will do; we'll get out here. Stay close to me, Isaiah."

Otto hurriedly got out of the carriage, grabbed Isaiah's arm, and guided him under a covered portico and down a back alley. Otto looked both ways carefully as if he expected someone or something. They crossed several streets, stayed in the alley, and took great care to keep close against walls and in the shadows. Finally, they came to an alley that came out on the mall, and Otto abruptly guided Isaiah behind several large crates that provided cover so they wouldn't be seen.

Isaiah was a bit surprised by all this sneaking around and finally asked Otto, "What are we doing? This is right back where we were yesterday, but we have no fruit to sell?"

"We're not here to sell today, we're here to watch," replied Otto in a whisper, and with that, they settled in behind the crates to watch the market.

Isaiah was still a bit confused and asked, "Watch what exactly?"

Otto replied, "Look out toward the market and watch with me and see if anything looks strange to you, something just doesn't feel right." So, with that, the two of them sat there in silence and just watched vendors sell their fruits and vegetables as customers came and went.

Time went by, and finally Otto let out an audible sound, "Hmm, did you notice that?" Isaiah wasn't quite sure what exactly he referred to. Otto went on, "Watch the vendor in that fruit stand sell his fruit." Isaiah turned his attention to the specific vendor and simply watched. The vendor placed his weights on one side of the scale, and the customer placed their fruit on the other to get a weight. The vendor then charged them for the weight of the fruit they had put on the scale. This was the same process Otto used, and Isaiah didn't see anything unusual.

"It looks pretty normal to me."

"Yes, basically what we do, but look at the amount of fruit the customer has in his basket after it was weighed. That customer bought five pounds of fruit, but that is the smallest five pounds I have ever seen, and I've sold fruit in this market for nearly twenty years."

Isaiah redirected his attention to the basket and saw what Otto referred to. He himself had only sold fruit for the first time yesterday, but the amount in the basket was notably less than similar quantities they had sold just yesterday. He whispered to Otto, "How can that be?"

Otto quietly responded, "And that is the right question."

They continued to watch this vendor for some time to understand the apparent weight discrepancy. At first, Otto thought the counterweights used by the vendor might be wrong or mislabeled, but a constable routinely checks the vendor's scales. They saw this specific vendor pass that test each time.

After they watched the vendor for well over an hour make dozens of transactions that all looked the same, with the amount of fruit always appearing less than what is typical, Otto suddenly said, "Of course, that's it, ...a very old scam but still effective." He turned to Isaiah and said, "At the next transaction, watch the vendor at the table very carefully and tell me what you see."

Isaiah watched very carefully and saw the vendor add weights to his side of the scale, and then the customer placed the fruit on the scale until the scale was level. Nothing looked out of the ordinary, and he was a bit perplexed. Otto sensed this and spoke. "Look carefully at his right-hand next time and tell me what you see."

The next customer stepped up, and Isaiah watched intently. He noticed a very subtle move by the vendor with his right hand. The vendor talked away to the customer and placed his right hand under the table very quickly as the customer put their fruits on the scale. When the customer went to remove their fruits, he once again slid his hand under the table. The entire action happened so quickly and smoothly that unless you looked for it, most people would never notice.

Otto explained what Isaiah had just witnessed. "The vendor has a magnate under the table that creates a slight pull downward on the customer's side of the scale. As the customer places their fruit on the scale to be weighed, the vendor reaches under the table and slides a cover off the magnet, which allows a slight downward pull on the scale. The scale incorrectly weighs what is on the scale by indicating there is more on the scale than is actually there. As a result, the customer over-pays for what they really get. They have been cheated." Isaiah shook his head in disbelief, and Otto continued, "The vendor has to become quite skilled at sliding the cover on and off at exactly the right moment the customer places their fruit on or removes it from the scale."

Isaiah immediately started to get up from behind the crates and run across to confront the crooked vendor when Otto grabbed his arm and pulled him back. "Hold on, we now understand what he is doing to cheat people, but we need the right people to actually see him doing it," said Otto.

Isaiah looked at Otto a bit puzzled by what he meant, but Otto went on, "We need to get the constables to catch him in the act. We must have a plan."

Otto knew nearly everyone in the marketplace, including the constables who kept order and routinely checked the scales of vendors. He watched this vendor a bit longer and realized he had a lookout who watched for constables. He would signal the vendor, who would simply not use the technique while the constable was in the area. They must be very sly to catch this vendor cheating.

After years of selling in the marketplace, Otto knew each of the constables very well and looked around to see who was on duty today. He found two constables he knew and pulled them aside to explain what he had seen. They expressed concern but agreed that they needed to catch the vendor in the act of cheating, so they created a plan.

One of the constables would put on a disguise to get close to the vendor's table while Otto would watch and signal when the cover had been removed from the magnet. They had one problem; they needed a distraction to get the vendor to leave the table without re-covering the magnet. Otto said, "I am just not sure how we can distract him long enough." Isaiah quickly responded, "I know how, leave it to me. Just signal me when fruit is on the scale." Otto looked at Isaiah and then the constable and nodded, "Let's trust him."

Later in the afternoon, everything was in place. The constable had successfully disguised himself and was hidden among customers at the fruit stand, totally undetected. Otto hid behind the crates undetected and had a clear view of the table and the hands of the vendor. They now simply needed to wait for Isaiah's distraction. Soon, Otto saw Isaiah walk across the plaza, bouncing a ball off his foot just like any other kid on a sunny afternoon. Nobody paid him much attention as he went behind the fruit wagon. Isaiah suddenly peered around the wagon just enough to see Otto but not be seen by the vendor.

It was now or never; Otto signaled the constable that they were ready, and the disguised constable went to the table and said to the vendor that he wanted to purchase five pounds of fruit. Just as planned, the vendor put a five-pound weight on his side of the scale and instructed the disguised constable to put his fruits on his side of the scale. As he placed the fruits on the scale, the vendor reached under the table and slid the cover off the magnet. Otto gave the signal, and Isaiah immediately grabbed and released the brake on the wagon and gave it a shove. He then yelled, "Hey, the wagon's moving!" The wagon with fruit had suddenly started to roll forward, and people began to scream, "Stop the wagon!" The vendor instinctively leaped to his feet and nearly toppled the table. He sprinted to the front of the wagon to reengage the brake. He stopped the wagon and glared around to look for anyone who had released the brake. Isaiah had slid into the crowd undetected.

The vendor resecured the wagon and returned to his table, where the customer still waited. He sat down and looked at the scale, and immediately fear gripped him along with confusion. He realized that in the excitement, he had not put the cover back over the magnet before he left the table. Sitting on the scale was not fruit but a five-pound weight, a constable's standard weight to be exact. The disguised constable stared down at him with both hands on the table and leaned forward and said firmly, "Place both of your hands on the tabletop and don't move them." Between them was the scale, and it indicated the constable's five-pound weight was heavier than the counterbalance weight provided by the vendor. The constable reached up and pulled his disguise back to reveal his identity.

"Now this is interesting," said the constable. "Either my standard weight has somehow gotten heavier than five pounds, or we have a problem with this scale and your counterweights." Beads of sweat appeared on the vendor's forehead, and he stammered, "Why...I don't know what you are talking about." By this time, a crowd had begun to gather around the table, and people began to realize the vendor's scale was incorrectly weighing fruit. A voice from the crowd yelled, "Cheater!" Another called, "Crook!" and with that, other people began to yell and press closer to the vendor's table. The constable walked around the table and looked under to see the magnate and cover. The constable blew his whistle for assistance from other constables, who rapidly came to assist, and the vendor was taken into custody and taken away with the evidence. As the constable left, he turned to the crowd and said, "Well, it looks like you've all been cheated. Take and divide up the remaining fruit among yourselves," and the crowd descended on the wagon and emptied it in short order.

Isaiah had worked his way around back alleys and returned to the side of Otto. They looked at each other and smiled. Otto said, "Well done, Journeyman, well done."

It was time to head home, and Isaiah was very happy that they had exposed and stopped the crook's scheme. They stood up from their hiding place and began to walk away when both Otto and Isaiah caught a view of someone on a rooftop staring down at them. They both looked and saw Pilu and several other rough-looking characters who stood and glared down at them with scowls on their faces. Pilu was busily writing in a black notebook he always carried with him, which justified his underworld nickname, "The Bookkeeper."

Otto spoke, "I think we just broke up one of Pilu's schemes."

"Yes, I think you're right, and they don't look very happy," responded Isaiah

"It is time to go, we've kicked the hornet's nest," and with that, they slipped out of the mall and headed back through alleys to their waiting carriage and home.

* * *

Before dinner, Isaiah walked through the massive two-story library and exited onto a long, broad corridor that had large French doors that opened onto a covered veranda. The corridor was lined with beautiful tapestries and very plush furniture. He exited to the veranda and found that it overlooked a massive, beautiful orchard filled with various kinds of fruit trees. It was an exquisite scene with the trees blooming and all carefully manicured. He walked down a stone stairway into the orchid and found a wide brick pathway that proceeded from the house through the heart of the orchid. He decided to keep walking and explore this beautiful, peaceful setting.

He traveled some distance and was now surrounded by fruit trees and heard a voice, "Beautiful, isn't it?" He turned to see Ohtara behind him, and he replied, "Yes, it is and very peaceful."

Ohtara smiled and said, "Then let me show you something."

They walked a bit further, and suddenly, there was a massive stone and glass structure in front of them. They walked inside, and he found himself standing in a cathedral with an extremely high ceiling and stained-glass windows that separated the last light of the day into multiple brilliant colors that were spread across the floors, walls, and altar at the front.

"Wow, this is beautiful," said Isaiah in a whisper.

"Yes, it is," replied Ohtara. "This was built many years ago on the property as a place for worship, meditation, and quiet solitude. You don't have to be in a place like this to hear from the Voice, but it sure is nice to have a place like this to come to."

There was a deep peace present, and Isaiah didn't want to leave, but Ohtara said, "Follow me," and proceeded directly through the cathedral to the back, where she opened a set of large wooden doors. She stepped out of the doors and pointed out at another orchard with a high wall built around it and a brick pathway that wound directly through the middle toward the back. "We call this the Orchard within the Orchard. It is a special place for prayer and meditation. The gardener responsible for maintaining it is Otto.

"Of course," said Isaiah with a smile.

She turned to Isaiah and asked directly, "Isaiah, what is your mission in Endemar?

Isaiah looked at Ohtara but did not know how to answer. The direction he had gotten had been clear, but he was afraid it would sound crazy to Ohtara. He also remembered Luc's words regarding Ohtara but had dismissed them as irrational and unfounded. He gathered his thoughts and responded.

"Ah...the Voice told me to save the kingdom." There was silence for several seconds as he tried to assess how Ohtara reacted to his declaration. He decided not to mention saving Luc because he had already saved him on the island.

Ohtara simply stared at Isaiah as if measuring him and the words he had just spoken. "Ok...that is a very serious, yes, very serious mission. We must make sure you are well-equipped. Did Iswa tell you about anything you needed to obtain to achieve your mission?"

"Well... yes, he did," replied Isaiah. "He said I needed to obtain the Sword of Integrity, and it would come to me if I was worthy."

Ohtara nodded in affirmation of Iswa's assessment and then turned and pointed toward the path that ran through the orchard. "Isaiah, that path will lead you to the back gate of our property. Beyond that gate, you will meet your final challenge to achieve the Sword of Integrity. Take note that you do not obtain the Sword, but rather it chooses you, so even though you may make it to the Sword, it still will ultimately accept or reject based on the integrity shown. When you are ready to make that journey, it begins right here."

Isaiah simply nodded and stepped down the steps in silence into the orchard to gather his thoughts. Finally, with tears in his eyes, he turned to speak to Ohtara, but she was gone.

Isaiah spent some time in the orchard and listened to the Voice and enjoyed the peace and solitude while he considered his next move. *Was he ready? Would he be found worthy?* He headed back to the house for evening dinner with Ohtara, Otto, and a new individual, a human named Erestor.

CHAPTER 18

REGENT THERON

It turned out that Erestor was a senator in the kingdom and served on the inner council in ruling the Kingdom with the Regent Theron. He was a middle-aged man with black hair sprinkled with flecks of gray. His beard was manicured carefully and much grayer than the hair on his head, which made him look distinguished. Erestor was a jovial man who enjoyed laughter and storytelling but also exuded wisdom and seriousness when needed. He wore a green velvet coat with polished high black boots that made him look distinguished and important.

The four of them sat for several hours at the formal dining table in front of a blazing fire in the fireplace. The table easily could have sat twenty-five, but tonight there were only the four of them. Stories were told, and there was much laughter, but also a few minutes of quiet reflection as they remembered friends no longer with them. Isaiah felt privileged to just sit and listen and soak in the stories. He learned that Erestor had not always been a politician but had led a very adventurous life, which included exploring various strange lands and overcoming numerous adversaries and challenges.

Isaiah could have listened to his stories all night long, but Erestor turned to Isaiah and, in a jovial voice, asked, "So, young Journeyman, what adventure are you on?"

Isaiah didn't really want to talk about himself but replied politely, "I am on a journey to the Land of Integrity."

"Oh, that's a very serious journey you are on," replied Erestor as his voice and mood turned more serious, and he continued. "I think it would be good for you to accompany me to the Senate tomorrow. What do you think, Otto and Ohtara?"

They both looked at each other, smiled, and nodded affirmatively, and Ohtara quickly added, "I think that would be enlightening for him."

"Good, then Otto will accompany him to the castle at nine tomorrow morning," declared Erestor, and with that, plans were set that Isaiah would be off to the castle in the morning.

Erestor turned to Ohtara and Otto, and his tone got more serious. "I do need to make you aware that there is great fear in the kingdom, and with that fear has come many rumors. The rumors not only include stories of spies looking for weaknesses in our defenses but also claims that spies are deliberately stirring up fear and discord. In fact, today there was even a rumor that wolves had been seen in the city."

Both Ohtara and Otto listened intently to Erestor's accounts of events. Otto finally spoke. "I am not surprised by these rumors, whether they are true or false, they reflect the current state of the kingdom, as the time draws near."

Isaiah listened quietly and did not want to interrupt. The conversation had turned very serious, yes, very serious, but what did Otto mean when he referred to, as the time draws near?

Erestor, who always seemed to be on the move, abruptly stood up and said his goodbyes and quickly headed toward the door and his awaiting carriage. Both Ohtara and Otto followed him to the door and his carriage, and as he pulled away, Ohtara turned to Isaiah and said, "You must get your rest tonight. Tomorrow will be a busy day."

Isaiah went to his room and lay on his bed and stared at the ceiling but couldn't shake the nagging questions. *Am I ready to go up the mountain? Am I worthy? What does, as the time draws near mean?* He finally slipped off to sleep, resolved to probe this last question with Otto in the morning.

Isaiah awoke early the next morning and was already at breakfast when Otto walked into the breakfast room wearing a white lab coat and carrying a flask. Isaiah was taken aback by the lab coat and looked at Tara, who had just filled her plate with fruit. She smiled and said, "Oh, you probably didn't know that Doc Otto used to teach Chemistry and Biology at the university." Isaiah looked at Otto in surprise, and Tara continued, "Oh yes, he taught for many years until Regent Theron shut the university down. He said it was too expensive and unneeded."

"Are you ready for your visit to the castle today?" asked Otto. He quickly interrupted the discussion so as not to open old wounds. Tara had been one of his prize students.

"Absolutely, Senator Erestor is a very interesting man."

"Yes, he is, very interesting indeed," laughed Otto.

"Good," replied Otto, "then as soon as you are done with your breakfast, I have a carriage waiting and ready." And with that, Isaiah quickly finished his breakfast, and they were in the carriage headed for the castle.

They had traveled a short distance in quiet when Isaiah decided to broach the question with Otto. "Otto, last night when we were all in the dining room, you said, 'as the time draws near.' What time did you mean by 'the time draws near?'"

Otto smiled in a reflective manner and said quietly, "We are approaching Ascension time."

"Ascension time, what is that exactly?" asked Isaiah.

"Ascension time is when a sovereign takes their place as the rightful King or Queen of the kingdom. We are approaching this time in Endemar."

"But I thought Endemar had a Regent already," asked Isaiah.

"Yes, we have a Regent, but a Regent is not a King or Queen," replied Otto. "They are appointed to administer the kingdom until an heir is found, or an heir reaches the appropriate age. They simply handle day-to-day administration but must turn it over at the time of Accension."

Isaiah thought about what Otto had just told him and asked, "What defines the day of Ascension in the kingdom?"

"It is the day the King's heir turns eighteen years old," responded Otto.

'So, the heir will soon turn eighteen years old. Am I correct that the Regent then must step down?" asked Isaiah.

"Yes, you are correct, or at least that's what is supposed to happen," replied Otto.

He continued, "There have been times in history when enemies have seen the Ascension as a time of vulnerability for the kingdom and have tried to take over or greatly damage the monarchy. The tension and tactics we have seen in the kingdom the last several months are very typical of the enemy's tactics, but we also have seen a new, never-before-seen level of treachery."

Their attention was drawn to the castle as they approached it. Stone walls at least thirty feet tall encircled the entire castle, with guard towers positioned at strategic points along the walls. They entered through two huge, massive wooden gates and pulled into a large courtyard with beautiful, manicured grass surrounded by a crushed gravel pathway for the horses and carriages. Opposite the gates were stairs that led to a massive set of heavy wooden doors. The carriage stopped in front of the doors, and guards saluted them while servants helped them down from the carriage. Isaiah tried to take in all the sights and sounds around him. His head swiveled constantly, and he found the whole experience overwhelming. He looked around at the scene of guards, horses, and castle walls and knew this was completely new to him compared to his hometown of Providence. One thing was very clear to him: he was about to experience something completely new.

They entered the main building of the castle and crossed a massive foyer filled with wood beams, flags, and artwork. Ornate, colorful tiles formed the kingdom of Endemar's crest in the foyer floor. They were met by Erestor, who swiftly walked across the massive foyer, shook their hands, and urged them to follow him, "We must hurry, come with me to the Grand Hall. The Regent is about to give a speech."

They hurriedly followed Erestor into the magnificent Grand Hall that fully lived up to its name. The ceilings were easily sixty to eighty feet tall with exposed wooden beams. Flags that represented each region hung from the beams. At the front of the Grand Hall was a speaker's podium, and a very large oval table filled most of the floor space. The senators sat at this table throughout the legislative sessions to discuss and debate policies and laws. Isaiah noted a very distinct feature behind the speaker's podium. Approximately twenty feet behind the podium was a set of seven steps that led to a massive, ornate gold throne. Above the throne hung a massive red tapestry. The red tapestry had a coat of arms stitched into the fabric along with the words, "The Kingdom of Endemar - Land of Integrity." Brass pipes for a massive pipe organ rose majestically on each side of the bright red tapestry.

Isaiah watched as senators, military people, and visitors entered the Grand Hall. The senators, who included Erestor, assumed their assigned seats around the large table while visitors ascended stairs to sit in a balcony which wrapped around the Grand Hall. Once seated, trumpeters played a fanfare to announce the arrival of the Regent, and everyone stood. Regent Theron stepped up to the podium and motioned for everyone to be seated.

Theron began to speak, "My fellow citizens of Endemar, I come to you today with a heavy heart. We received word this morning that last night, there was a massive attack on shepherds and their flocks to the east. Many sheep were killed, and some shepherds were severely injured. I have sent troops to the region to find the guilty parties and bring them to justice." Some of the senators yelled, "Here, Here," as a sign of support for the actions of the Regent. Others simply sat quietly, shaking their heads. The Regent continued, "This unlawful act will be met with force. We will not tolerate this, and I will bring the full force of Endemar down on those responsible." He went on for ten minutes with the same theme that he had control and would resolve the current problems, but suddenly his tone changed.

"As you well know, my fellow senators, we are rapidly approaching the Ascension when the heir to the throne will be announced, but I would offer up the following for consideration: Is it the right time for such a dramatic change?" Otto leaned forward in his seat to listen intently to every word that came from Theron's mouth. Isaiah could see Erestor, who sat at the large round table, do the same. As Theron said these words, he had walked casually back toward the elevated throne and gestured with his open hand toward the throne as he said the words, "Is it the right time?"

Everyone in the room knew what he was suggesting, delaying the Ascension ceremony, but he didn't stop here he walked up the steps to stand beside the huge throne and then said, "consistency in leadership is vital at a time of crisis. We must have stability, we must have security," and then he proceeded to sit on the throne. There was a notable gasp among senators, and a murmur ran through the audience in shock. Theron then sprang to his feet and said, "But of course, we should not let our enemies thwart our very heritage," and he smiled, and there was laughter among his supporters, but Isaiah looked at Erestor, who was now even more focused and stared directly at Theron.

The speech ended with applause, and Theron then mingled with the senators, shook hands, and exchanged greetings while visitors filed out of the Grand Hall. As Isaiah and Otto were descending the stairs from the balcony, Erestor called out to them to come over to where he was standing. As they arrived by his side, Theron saw them and walked over to Erestor with his hand extended. "Hello, Senator Erestor, and who do we have here?" he asked as he looked directly at Isaiah.

"This is young Isaiah, a Journeyman, who is visiting with us."

"Hmm," responded Theron, "You wouldn't by any chance be the young lad who broke up that criminal scheme in the marketplace yesterday?"

"Well, yes and no," replied Isaiah. "Otto and the constable did most of the work. I just created a distraction."

"Well, of course, Otto and the constable were a part of it too," he responded as he nodded toward Otto. Otto simply gave a small smile in reply. "Excellent work, yes, excellent. We will have to find some way to reward you," Theron continued and turned to respond to an aide who whispered into his ear. "Well, must be off, kingdom business. "Good day, gentlemen, and very nice meeting you, Isaiah," and with that, Theron proceeded to exit the Grand Hall through a private set of doors with two guards posted.

Isaiah turned to Otto and Erestor and said, "He seems like a very nice man." Neither Erestor nor Otto responded to the comment but looked at each other with concerned looks.

* * *

Theron burst through his office door and turned to his aide, Felix, who had followed him into his inner office. "So, that is the brat that cost me thousands yesterday!"

Felix responded nervously to the outburst, "Well, yes, he was, along with Otto."

"That meddling old otter just won't leave things alone. He always must have things all prim and proper, above board. He just can't accept an entrepreneur making a little extra money by taking advantage of the market and demand," ranted Theron. "And for Pilu, how incompetent can that greedy vermin be. He ruined a perfectly good scheme. He lost us thousands. Let him know he owes us, and I mean bigtime!" The aide, Felix, simply listened and nodded affirmatively. He knew that when Theron got in this type of mood, it was best to simply agree and not try to talk.

* * *

Isaiah, Otto, and Erestor walked outside the castle in silence until they were away from any prying ears. Erestor spoke first, "The game has changed. Theron gave the boldest statement yet regarding his intentions."

"Yes, it's very clear what he wants to have happen. It's just unclear if he has the backing of enough senators yet," responded Otto.

"There are those in the senate who support Theron no matter what, and there are those who are very scared by the recent turmoil and threats from the wolves. They may just agree with him, to delay the Ascension and maintain him as Regent until the turmoil ends," said Erestor.

"Theron has always been the complete politician, but what can we do to stop him from delaying Ascension Day?" asked Otto.

Erestor nodded and rubbed his chin as he contemplated their next move on the political chessboard. "We must get ahead of him and figure out what he is up to and his ultimate plan. We need to follow Felix. Theron won't deal directly with any potential co-conspirators, but he often uses Felix as his go-between. Yes, let's follow Felix."

Otto looked at Erestor and said, "We must make Ohtara aware."

Erestor agreed and said, "Yes, quickly, time is short."

CHAPTER 19

THE CHASE

They all agreed that Otto and Isaiah should head back to the house to brief Ohtara on the events of the morning and the proposed delay of the Ascension. Erestor would assign trusted colleagues to keep an eye on Felix and keep him informed as he went about his business as senator.

Otto and Isaiah headed down to the center of town, where they could hire a carriage to take them back to the house. They walked past the massive gates and were swallowed up by the cobblestone city streets and alleyways filled with people. People were busy buying and selling, and Isaiah noticed that there was a notable tension in the air. The attacks by wolves the night before had created panic buying as people were stocking up for a worst-case scenario. With the panic buying, prices had soared, and sellers were making a very good, if not extreme, profit.

Otto turned to Isaiah and said, "This is not good, not good at all. The panic buying has driven up prices and will also shorten inventories, which will drive prices even higher. Then more panic sets in, and people will start to turn on one another out of fear."

Isaiah watched the frenzy building in front of them. People were overbuying, and others then couldn't get anything and became angry. Then people began to push and shove, and angry words were exchanged. This quickly evolved into fighting, and the constables had to break up a fight between two raccoons trying to buy food for their families.

Otto grabbed Isaiah's arm and said, "This way, quickly," and they turned down an alley to get away from the commotion. They had gone halfway down the alley and turned onto another desolate alley when Isaiah spoke, "This is crazy. People are fighting their neighbors."

"Yes," replied Otto, "this is what happens when fear grabs hold of a community: people turn on each other. We must pray for peace to settle over the city."

Without warning, they heard a voice, "Look who we have here." They both recognized the voice, and both turned to look behind them at Pilu, who stood in the opening of the alley that they had just turned down. There was no return in that direction. Pilu was surrounded by ten of his associates. Some snarled and growled while others held clubs that they patted in anticipation of what was about to happen. "You two cost me a lot of money yesterday. You should have minded your own business, but no…You decided to interfere, and that is going to cost you…dearly."

Otto looked at him and stood as tall as he could and spoke calmly but directly, "You shall not harm us. We are on a senatorial mission."

Pilu laughed, "A senatorial mission, for your old friend, Erestor? Hah, who cares! Erestor will soon be history. Get them boys." And with that, Pilu's associates charged after Otto and Isaiah.

Otto and Isaiah turned and ran down the alley to keep away from the mob that chased them, but they were gaining steadily. They rounded a corner, and Isaiah saw some empty barrels in the alley and grabbed them as he ran by and threw them into the path of the pursuing mob. This only slowed them, and they kept coming. The next alley turned left, and they had no choice but to take it.

As they turned into the alley, they saw a staircase, and Otto grabbed Isaiah's arm and pulled him up the staircase. It led to an outdoor covered walkway that ran across several buildings, and half of the pursuing mob followed them up the stairs while the others stayed below in the alley. They reached the end of the walkway, and there was nowhere to go; it simply ended, and they looked out over a railing. The pursuing mob was nearly upon them, and Isaiah said to Otto, "Trust me," and grabbed Otto around the waist and leaped off the walkway into mid-air.

For a moment, Isaiah remembered swinging out on a rope over the lake with his brothers back at the farm. He relished those days of freedom and boys just being boys on a summer day. That, though, seemed like eons ago now. Isaiah had reached up with his right hand and grabbed a rope connected to a hoist just off the walkway, and while he held onto Otto, they both swung across to a lower roof, where he let go, and they tumbled across it.

This stopped the pursuers on the walkway, but there were still pursuers below continuing to chase them. They regained their footing and raced across the rooftop. They found a stairway off this rooftop and raced down it into yet another alley that turned right, but suddenly it led to a dead end. They turned to retreat, just in time to see the pursuers at the entrance to the dark alley. All of them were huffing and puffing and out of breath, but now angrier than ever. Pilu suddenly appeared behind them, out of breath, with his hands on his knees. "Are you done playing games? There is no way out."

Otto responded, "There is always a way," to which Isaiah had to admit to himself that he wasn't so sure about that argument. He reached into his pouch and pulled out his slingshot with a handful of rocks. He decided that if there was to be a fight, stones would fly. He loaded the slingshot and aimed it at the pursuers, who had now all rejoined. He thought to himself, "At least I can take out a few before they get to us."

A voice came from the shadows that he recognized, and it instantly sent a shudder down his spine. "Hello, Isa..iah," came the voice, drawn out and deliberate. He turned in time to see squinting, threatening yellow eyes coming from the dark shadows. It was Temp.

Instinctively, Isaiah put himself between Temp and Otto. "What...what are you doing here, Temp?"

Temp laughed and said, "I am everywhere. I go where I please and when I please. Maybe the better question is, what are you doing here, Isaiah?"

Isaiah stammered, "On...on a mission for a senator."

"Well, it appears that there may be some sort of disagreement with these...ah.... gentlemen," laughed Temp as he took a step from the shadows toward Otto and Isaiah.

"This is none of your business, Temp. Stay out of this, you hear?" yelled Isaiah emphatically.

"Everything is my business if I want it to be, and I... want...this... to be," said Temp with a deep growl.

Isaiah turned toward Temp and pointed his slingshot in his direction, to which Temp became highly irritated. Temp roared, "You challenged me one other time, Isaiah, and I told you, not that day, but someday. Perhaps this is that day and the place that we let your challenge happen, shall we?"

"Hello boys," came a voice from above.

Isaiah turned to see Ohtara standing above them on the flat rooftop, wearing her long coat with leather boots and two swords attached to the belt that went around her shoulder and waist. The coat was open and fluttering like a flag, and her hair, though pulled back, was also flowing in the breeze. She had a bit of a smirk on her face but also had fire in her eyes as she looked intensely back and forth between Pilu's gang and Temp. Pilu and his mob took a notable step backward as the odds had just changed dramatically. Temp also began to growl and snarl, but stepped back into the shadows, noticeably reluctant to tangle with Ohtara.

Ohtara came down the steps from the rooftop and asked Isaiah and Otto, "Are you alright?" to which they immediately replied that they were unharmed. While she kept her eyes on both Pilu's group and Temp, she told Otto and Isaiah to go up the stairs to the roof. She then turned to Pilu and yelled emphatically, "Get out of here," and they immediately turned and ran back down the alley with Pilu trailing behind. Ohtara's reputation and skills were well known throughout the kingdom. They were the subject of legends and tales. Pilu and his associates did not want to learn first-hand if they were true.

Ohtara then turned to Temp, who was now back deep in the shadows, growling and snarling at her. She stepped toward him and sternly said, "This is not the day for Isaiah to challenge you, but there is a day coming, in the not-too-distant future, when he will be ready, very ready. Now…get!" and with that Temp turned and ran down a narrow opening between buildings and disappeared under an iron gate. Ohtara stood alone in a quiet, desolate alley.

Ohtara called out to Otto and Isaiah, who were on top of the roof. "Come on down, it's all clear, and they descended back down the stairs to the now quiet alley. Otto and Isaiah both greeted her with hugs and thanked her for her help. Ohtara looked at Isaiah and said, "Isaiah, you were very brave to stand up to Pilu and his gang as well as Temp, but let's get out of here." Otto agreed that they needed to go but stopped her and said, "Yes, we must go, but we also have an urgent message for you from Erestor."

Otto briefed Ohtara on the events of the day at the castle that included Theron's proposal that the Ascension should be delayed, which included his not-so-subtle theatrics of sitting on the throne. Ohtara listened quietly in deep reflection. Isaiah noticed that her deep reflection indicated a much deeper understanding of what was happening. There was a secret here that he was yet to understand.

Otto also told her that Erestor had people follow Felix. Ohtara agreed that following Felix was a good idea since he was always in the middle of Theron's business, whether it was about politics or making money. Felix's whereabouts and contacts would help us understand what Theron is up to. For now, though, they would return to the house and wait to hear from Erestor.

CHAPTER 20

REFUGEES

It was after sunset when they arrived back at the house. Thankfully, there had been no more incidents, and the trip home was uneventful. Ohtara, Otto, and Isaiah all sat in the library in front of the large fireplace while outside it started to rain. The darkness of the night had fully set in, and it was now pitch-black outside. It was a night to stay in and stay warm as the rain began to pelt harder against the roof and windows with an occasional clap of thunder and lightning.

The glow of the fireplace was the only light in the grand library and reflected off each of their faces. Isaiah looked deep into the fire and asked almost to nobody, "I wonder who told the Regent about the events in the marketplace?"

Otto looked at him and replied, "What do you mean?"

"Well," continued Isaiah, "do you remember the words of the constable? He said that he and the other constables wanted to keep this very quiet so they could see if there was a bigger conspiracy going on."

"Humm, interesting point, he did ask us not to discuss it with others," reflected Otto while rubbing his chin.

"Oh well, I guess he is the Regent and probably was told about it," replied Isaiah.

"Yes, possibly, but not something you would expect being brought to a man as important as the Regent. There are far more important matters he needs to worry about. Very interesting, yes very interesting indeed," responded Otto.

Their train of thought was interrupted by a rapid pounding sound at the front doors, and all three looked at each other and jumped to their feet. This was not a normal knock but a pounding of desperation. A call for help.

Otto opened the large doors of the mansion, and a figure practically fell at his feet. He was soaked from head to toe even though he had on a rain poncho. Ohtara reached down to help the stranger to his feet. She helped him gather himself and stand, and he then pulled back his hood, and all three were shocked.

"Dwiddle, my friend, come in," cried Ohtara.

Dwiddle was soaked and managed a very tired smile and said, "Thank you, but can we all come in," and he turned to look down the steps and there in the pounding rain was a small huddle of Sarta, Eldamo, Ion and Selde all soaked but trying to stay dry under a poncho being held over their heads."

"Oh my, of course," cried Otto, and he ran down the steps with Isaiah right behind him to help Sarta and the kids into the house.

They got the entire family into the house and by the warm fire to dry out. Otto ordered food from the kitchen to be brought to the library, and servants brought hot food immediately, along with blankets and towels. The entire family ate the food as if they had not eaten in days.

"My friends, what has brought you here in the middle of a rainy night?" asked Ohtara.

"The wolves, coyotes, and mercenary thugs," replied Dwiddle. "The numbers have increased week-by-week, and two days ago, a patrol found our den. We barely made it out alive. They raided it and stole all our food and supplies before they set it on fire. We have been on the run for two days and finally decided to come here to ask if we could stay overnight and simply rest."

"Of course," replied Ohtara. "You are welcome to stay as long as you like; you are family. Please, accept our hospitality."

Dwiddle looked at Sarta, and a sense of relief flooded their faces as the reality of shelter, food, and safety hit them. They both managed weak, tired smiles, and together said, "Thank you."

The house staff got the entire family into their bedrooms and put the children to bed. Dwiddle and Sarta had both finally dried out and warmed up by the fire. They had their paws wrapped around hot tea and had begun to finally relax when Dwiddle spoke up, "As I said earlier, the number of wolves and coyotes has increased rapidly, but this is not a random event; there is an organized effort to import more and more into Endemar forest. I don't know who is behind it, but the numbers and their organization suggest an army is being assembled. A full-scale invasion is imminent."

"Have you seen Kingdom troops in the woods to drive them off?" asked Ohtara.

"No, that's the strange thing. There are very few troops in the area, and those that are there act like they want to avoid the wolves at all costs. In the meantime, the numbers just grow larger, and the attacks and raids have just continued and become more aggressive," explained Dwiddle.

Ohtara looked deep into the fire and reflected on this news and its meaning.

Dwiddle continued, "I also received an interesting piece of intelligence from one of my associates a few days ago. He was at the old Tavern late one night last week and heard talk of a very important ship on its way to Endemar in three days from tomorrow.

He didn't get any information on, 'why' it was so important, but they said it was the final piece before the Ascension ceremony."

Both Otto and Ohtara leaned forward and listened intently to every word from Dwiddle. The news of the ship brought Ohtara straight up in her chair with eyes wide open. This was news nobody expected. "We must quickly find out what that is all about," said a concerned Ohtara.

"And inform Erestor of this news immediately," added Otto.

Isaiah sat in a chair and listened intently to Dwiddle's account of how the wolves, coyotes, and thugs looted and burned homes and terrorized people. He cringed when Dwiddle described the killings of those who resisted. He thought about the families that they had delivered food to and wondered about their fate. Inside, he felt a stirring in his spirit. It started out as anger, pure outrage, but evolved into a burning commitment as the Voice began to speak very clearly to him. "Isaiah, this must stop. I have called you to save the kingdom. It is time to climb the mountain, climb now."

While the others continued to talk, Isaiah stood up, grabbed his jacket, and headed out the glass doors to the veranda. Ohtara noticed him get up and head out, and Otto started to follow, but she grabbed his arm and said softly, "Let him go, it is time."

Isaiah stepped onto the veranda, and the rain was still coming down hard, and lightning bolts repeatedly split the sky. He gathered his jacket around him and made sure his pouch was secure over his head and shoulder. He patted the pouch to assure himself that his sling shot was securely inside and then stepped off the veranda and began to walk the brick path to the cathedral and the path toward the back property gate.

He reached the back gate, opened it, and stepped onto a trail that led directly into the woods and up into the mountains. It was not lost on him that as he took his first step out of the gate, a huge bolt of lightning cracked across the sky, followed by a loud roll of thunder. He climbed up the trail, and with each step, it seemed to get steeper. He found himself completely enveloped by woods to the point that he could no longer see the light from the big house. He continued to climb and was now on the side of the mountain away from the house. The house would no longer provide a reference point. He was alone with his thoughts and fears.

The climb continued to get steeper, and in the darkness and rain, it had become even harder to climb. The lightning bolts now came faster, and he appreciated that they provided some light to navigate the increasingly difficult trail. The downpour of rain had turned a once gentle mountain stream into a torrent of rushing water that could easily carry someone away if not carefully crossed. Despite the severity of the storm, he continued to hear the Voice say, "Climb now, climb now."

Rain continued to fall, and Isaiah came to one of the mountain streams, which was now a mountain river with rushing, turbulent water. He stopped and took a deep breath as memories of his past and dealing with a raging river flooded his memory. The water formed a torrent that ran very fast and carried tree limbs, silt, and even whole dead trees. Wading across was out of the question. It simply was too dangerous. He pushed the memories aside and searched for a crossing point but then froze when he heard a long wail of a wolf. It all felt so surreal, wolves, he thought, not wolves again. The irony of how he started his journey to Endemar immediately hit him. Chased by wolves to cross a river. This time, though, he felt both peace and confidence. He heard the Voice say, "Climb now, I've got you." He looked around, and a bolt of lightning flashed, and he saw a tree upstream that lay across the raging river of water. He climbed through fallen trees and boulders until he got to the tree that crossed the river. He took a deep breath, looked to the sky, and said, "I will climb now, you've got me," and stepped onto the fallen tree stretched over the wild river. As he did, he heard another howl, now much closer, but he refused to let it distract him. He took a step and then another. With each step, he grew even more confident and walked calmly across the fallen tree to the other side of the river and the trail. He stepped on the ground and noticed that the rain had begun to subside.

On the other side of the river, the ground quickly became even steeper, and he soon began to climb a sheer rock face. Isaiah was thankful the rain had nearly stopped. He grabbed for rocks to hold on to while searching with his feet for footholds. He slipped several times and nearly fell as it took all his strength. He was breathing heavy as he pulled his body up one rock at a time but finally reached the top of a plateau and crawled over the edge and rolled over on his back to catch his breath. Suddenly, he heard a noise that jolted him to his feet. It was the sound of a hawk nearby, very nearby, and from the sound of it, a very large hawk. His head swiveled side to side to find the hawk when, out of the corner of his eye, he saw an eruption of water into the night sky. He spun around to see the largest bird of any kind he had ever seen in his life. He felt an instant pit in his stomach. The bird was a dagger hawk, and it was as big as a house. The hawk had stood up from its nest and shaken water off its wings. It had been sitting in its nest during the storm and was now shedding the water in preparation to fly.

Terror welled up inside Isaiah, and his eyes darted back and forth as he assessed his options. He was totally exposed on the flat plateau but dived to his belly in an effort not to be seen. His eyes were drawn to a cave entrance immediately underneath the dagger hawk's nest. The nest looked like it was positioned so the dagger hawk could guard it to prevent entry. A green glow, that Isaiah recognized immediately, came from the cave. He instantly knew...this was the right place.

Isaiah quickly spanned the plateau to assess his options. On one hand, he could try to climb back down the rock face, but he would be totally exposed and have no free hand to even try to defend himself. His only other option was to sprint directly toward the cave entrance and get inside before the hawk saw him and attacked. He chose the latter and took a deep breath and tried to time his sprint when the hawk looked away. It might give him precious extra seconds to get to the cave.

The dagger hawk threw its head back and screeched once more into the night air and shook its enormous wings one more time to expel water. Isaiah saw his chance and sprang to his feet and made a beeline directly toward the cave opening. He sprinted as hard as he could, but the dagger hawk suddenly jerked his head around and saw Isaiah running directly toward him and the cave. He let out a deafening screech and leaped out of his nest and down onto the plateau in front of Isaiah, which completely blocked his path to the cave. Isaiah skidded on one knee to a stop approximately twenty feet from the giant hawk. The hawk lunged at Isaiah with its enormous beak in an effort to grab and crush him. The point at the end of the hawk's beak was like a spear being thrust over and over again at Isaiah, who had to spin and dive to avoid being impaled as the hawk got closer and closer to him. The dagger hawk began to flap its wings, which created such force that it nearly blew Isaiah over. The hawk fluttered into the air and raised its enormous, venom-filled talons toward Isaiah. He was going for the kill, and Isaiah had no doubt that the venom in those talons would not just disable but would kill their prey.

Isaiah looked to his left and an opening, a trench, a fissure in the plateau rock caught his eye. He sprinted toward it and slid into the opening just as a giant talon crashed down on top of him. The opening was just wide enough for him to slide through and drop into a trench that was no more than six feet deep. Isaiah was breathing hard, and he looked up and saw the underside of an enormous talon with venom dripping from the tips. He immediately began to check himself for scrapes or cuts from the talon. The only thing he found was that his jacket had been torn by the talon, but it had not touched his skin. *That was too close for comfort,* he thought to himself as he pinned himself against the trench wall.

The dagger hawk was now enraged and frenetically pecked with its beak down into the fissure. The pecking continued over and over again, and Isaiah backpedaled and scrambled to get away. The fissure twisted and turned across the plateau, and as Isaiah fled, the hawk continued to pursue and thrust with its beak. Isaiah stumbled and fell on the floor and found himself in a wider and shallower section of the fissure, which left him completely exposed. He jumped to his feet and once again pinned himself against the nearest wall to find some protection, but there was no hawk, only the sound of rain which had begun to fall again. The atmosphere became very strange as the air instantly became very cold, and he could see his breath. Isaiah was wet from the rain and began to shiver as the temperature dropped. A lightning bolt raced across the sky, and thunder clapped. The dagger hawk was no longer seen or heard anywhere. Isaiah felt a strange presence, a dark presence, and it was then that he noticed a black onyx rock that looked like an altar right in the middle of the space between the fissure walls. He cautiously crept toward it, and then he heard a voice, not the Voice, but a sinister, cold voice. A voice that dripped with contempt and was filled with accusation.

"Isa... iah, what are you doing here? You don't belong here," hissed a low, gravelly voice.

Isaiah spun and demanded, "Who is it? Who are you?" A black shrouded form appeared suspended in the air and was moving toward him. He stepped back and shouted, "Stop, don't come any closer!"

"Isa... iah, I am truth, I am reason. You don't belong here; you are only a boy. What is going on here is too big for you. You need to leave right now. In fact, yes, in fact, I can send you back to your family right now, and this will all be nothing but a distant memory, a dream that will soon fade."

The figure raised his arm and pointed toward the black onyx altar, and Isaiah moved closer and saw his brothers with his mom and dad at the dinner table, enjoying dinner and laughing. He gazed for a moment and began to long for a return to a simpler life. He watched further and saw his friends swimming in the lake and shooting their slingshots.

"Don't you miss your family and friends, Isaiah? All you have to do is say yes, and this nightmare, this pain, will all be over, and you will be back home and safe. Just say the word, Isaiah."

Isaiah gazed a bit longer and continued to watch his family and friends, and a tear appeared in the corner of his eye as homesickness began to overtake him. As a tear began to trickle down his cheek, he heard the Voice say to him, "Save the kingdom, save Luc." Isaiah closed his eyes, took a deep breath, and came back to reality.

"No, I have a mission to complete."

"Well, your mission is a farce, it is destined to failure, don't be a fool," shouted the dark voice. "That old man, Iswa, has brainwashed you. He has confused your thinking and sent you on a disastrous mission. Why don't you join us? We are going to win; it is just a matter of time and playing it all out. Isn't it better to be on the winning side? Join us and you can reign with us," said the dark form as he motioned again toward the black onyx altar. This time, Isaiah saw images of the kingdom being overrun by the wolves and thugs who rampaged both homes and businesses. "We will establish a new world order, a good order, where there is no strife, no chaos. Join us, Journeyman, join the cause and rule with us in a new world order."

Isaiah stepped back when he saw the images and looked directly at the dark form. "Oh, I know who you are, you are the Prince of Darkness, the dark force behind Temp and the thugs who have been stealing and killing. You are a liar, a deceiver. You destroy, you cheat, and nothing truthful comes from your lips." As Isaiah went on, he got bolder and took a step toward the dark form, which recoiled with each word he spoke. "You know I speak the truth, that you have no power over the light and the Voice. You are right about one thing; I am a Journeyman. I have made a promise, and my integrity is not for sale!"

The dark form became enraged and shouted, "So be it then, you must die...I leave you to my dagger hawk," and he raised his arms above his head in a swirling motion, and his whole form swirled away. As he swirled away, Isaiah heard the deafening screech of the dagger hawk as it descended to finish him off. He looked for cover but was now completely exposed. He remembered something he saw in the images shown to him; his friends shooting their slingshots and remembered that he still had his slingshot in his pouch. It would do little good with the heavy, almost steel-hard feathers on the dagger hawk, but the hawk had to peck down into the fissure at Isaiah. He suddenly had an idea and grabbed his pouch and quickly retrieved his slingshot with several rocks.

The hawk arrived above him, screaming with talons poised to reach down and grab Isaiah and tear him to pieces. If he could get his talons wrapped around Isaiah, he would not wait for the venom to take its effect. The hawk lunged at Isaiah with its talons, but he was able to dive back into a narrower section of the fissure. The hawk landed and stabbed with its beak into the fissure and just missed its intended target. Isaiah spun away, pulled back his slingshot, and let a rock fly.

The rock flew straight and, with all the force possible generated by the sling, penetrated the eye of the hawk, who fell backward and landed on its back, where it screamed in pain. The dagger hawk stumbled to its feet and flew off but continued to scream in pain. Isaiah saw his chance and climbed out of the fissure and ran as hard as he could toward the cave entrance and the green glow. When he reached the entrance of the cave, he tumbled down a passageway to get as far away as possible from the entrance.

Isaiah sat on the floor of the cave, breathing hard, and looked around. He was confident from the size of the cave passageway that the dagger hawk could not follow. He looked around and saw a pure white, thick liquid flowing from a rock into a pool, and he was reminded of the white salve that Ohtara had used on him. He wondered if this was where she got it. He stood to his feet and followed the cave tunnel deeper into the mountain. The tunnel was well lit by a soft green light that seemed to emanate from everywhere.

As he moved through the cave, he came to a large pool of water with a distinctly bright green glow. What really caught his attention, though, was what was above the large pool, a bright, shiny sword with a gold inlaid handle. It floated in the air some twenty feet above the water surface. The entire chamber glowed with various hues of light that danced off surfaces and created a beautiful though somewhat disorienting scene. He had obviously arrived at his destination.

Isaiah stood at the edge of the pool and realized he had made the journey but was now lost regarding what he should do next. Both Iswa and Ohtara had told him that the Sword of Integrity chooses who is worthy. *So, what was he to do now?*

He stepped back, took a deep breath, and then slowly exhaled as he looked at his surroundings. The scene was breathtaking. He had nothing to compare it to. The lights reflected off crystals in the cave walls and scattered light throughout the entire chamber. The bright green glow from the pool mesmerized him, and he couldn't take his eyes off the Sword of Integrity suspended in the air above the pool. Despite the disorientation, there was a peace that permeated the entire cave. A peace that wrapped its arms around you and pulled you close. A peace that let you know you were in the right place at the right time. A peace that humbled. Isaiah dropped to his knees in reverence on the sand-covered floor of the cavern. As he knelt, he heard the Voice speak to him, "Trust and follow the instructions." He looked up toward the ceiling and said, "What instructions? What am I to do? He dropped his head and shook it in confusion but then noticed writing appearing in the sand in front of him. It read,

Those who walk straight and fully immerse themselves
in the waters, making themselves available to the sword,
shall be determined to be worthy or not.

But a caution to the unworthy.
Those who are unworthy face the penalty of the sword.

He sat back and read the words aloud several times to process the meaning. *"Those who walk straight* means they will not deviate. *Fully immerse themselves* implies being completely under. *Making themselves available."* He couldn't quite understand what he was called to do, but he determined he should walk straight into the water until under it and then somehow make himself available. But he stopped and read it again and took note of the caution, a caution to the unworthy. A caution that was ominous and talked about a penalty of the sword. He contemplated what this could mean, but he certainly didn't want to find out.

Isaiah stood, took a deep breath, and walked to the edge of the glowing green water. He looked up at the sword suspended above the pool of water with green and white lights reflecting off its shiny surface. He took another deep breath and looked down into the glowing green pool of water and caught a glimpse of something under the water on the bottom. He looked closer and quickly took a step back from the water as he realized what it was...bones, human bones. The scene was unsettling, and fear gripped him. His eyes darted quickly around the cave as he was hit with a sudden feeling of panic that raced through his mind. He said to himself, *Get out of here. What are you doing here? You don't belong here. You're going to die. Run.* The caution to the unworthy became clearer.

The Voice began to speak calmly and softly, "Isaiah, haven't I brought you here, haven't I rescued you from the wolves, conquered the coyotes, and healed you when near death. Trust me, Isaiah, trust me now."

A peace came over Isaiah, and he took a deep breath and walked to the edge of the glowing green water. He looked up again at the sword suspended above and then looked ahead at the large pool. He had no idea how deep it was, but it was large and in the center of the cave chamber. He took several deep breaths to clear his lungs and walked straight into the water toward the center of the pool, which appeared to be directly below the sword. The water was warm and felt really good to his muscles and joints after his climb through the night and battle with the dagger hawk. The pool got deeper with every step, and he soon stood with water up to his chin. He paused and took three deep breaths. He knew that from this point forward, he must hold his breath. Isaiah looked up at the sword and then stepped forward, which immersed his head under water.

The sensation was initially disorienting. He stood underwater in the glowing green pool of water, but he knew he had to proceed forward, so he continued forward and walked deeper and deeper.

He looked up and found himself directly under the sword, and he thought, *Now, what?* He reviewed in his mind what the writing had said,

> *Those who walk straight and fully immerse themselves in the*
> *waters, making themselves available to the sword, shall be*
> *determined to be worthy or not.*

He had walked straight forward and fully immersed himself but now wondered how he could make himself available. His air had begun to run out, and his lungs now began to burn. His mind raced, *Make himself available, make himself available, make...* "Give him your hand," whispered the Voice. Isaiah looked up and lifted his hand toward the sword with an open palm. His hand penetrated the surface of the water, and the sword began to vibrate, and it rotated in space and descended slowly toward the water until the handle nestled firmly in Isaiah's hand. He grabbed hold of the handle with his last bit of air in his lungs, and suddenly the glowing green water all around him turned into a green mist, and fresh air rushed into his lungs. A surge of strength and clarity rushed through Isaiah's body, and he now stood in an empty pool with no water or bones and only a green mist hanging across him up to his waist. He looked heavenward and said, "Thank you."

The green mist swirled around him, and he heard the Voice proclaim loudly, "You have been found worthy, now you have what you need...Go...Complete your mission, Journeyman."

The mist lifted and moved back up the tunnel toward the entrance, and Isaiah followed it out of the cave. He held the sword in his hand as he climbed out of the cave, and when he reached the entrance, he found absolute stillness with no sign of the dagger hawk or the dark force. He was not surprised and climbed down from the mountain and returned to the back gate of the property.

The first sun rays had just come over the mountain and hit the trees when Isaiah walked through the back gate. He looked up, and Ohtara stood there with an understanding smile and nodded. He smiled back and returned the head nod in a silent communication that said they understood each other in a new way. The sword was still in his hand, and Ohtara finally spoke, "Well done, Journeyman."

CHAPTER 21

THE THREAT

Later that morning, Ohtara, Otto, and Isaiah went back into the city to meet Erestor and inform him of the intelligence report from Dwiddle. They reached Erestor's office in the castle and were immediately ushered inside by his assistant.

Erestor carefully looked both ways out of his door before he closed it completely and uncharacteristically locked it. As he closed it, he whispered, "There are spies everywhere, and near panic and chaos throughout the castle. We must be careful." He proceeded to fill them in on what they had found out about Felix. "Felix spent most of the night going from senator to senator and lobbied them to agree to delay the Ascension ceremony. He used Theron's argument that it was way too dangerous a time to change leadership. Especially to someone that none of us know."

Isaiah took note of the statement, *especially to someone whom none of us knows*. He wanted to learn more about this later and made a mental note to ask Otto.

Erestor continued to explain that some senators had agreed with Felix's argument and pledged their vote of support. Others were more skeptical, and then some, like Erestor, practically threw him out of their office. Felix had long been seen as a political animal who lived and breathed politics. He bought and sold favors. More than once, he had lied to get votes and left people devastated at his betrayal. He essentially does Theron's bidding while keeping the political dirt away from Theron. He was not well-liked and barely tolerated by many.

Ohtara and Otto were both well aware of Felix's background and mode of deception and nodded affirmatively as Erestor went through Felix's background. Erestor stopped and said, "Interestingly though, in the middle of the night Felix left the senator's office and traveled down several dark streets and alleys until he came to a very small tavern. He stopped, looked around, and then went inside. We do not know what he did or who he saw in there, but after twenty minutes, he left and returned to the castle."

"Very interesting," said Ohtara. "If he returns tonight, we need to find out who he meets with and why. We need to get someone in that tavern tonight, someone who won't be spotted."

Ohtara turned to Erestor and said with a very serious tone, "I need to tell you one more thing," and she proceeded to tell him about the very important ship on its way to Endemar shores. Erestor listened intently, and his eyes got bigger when Ohtara mentioned, "The very important ship... in three days."

They decided to divide up and have Ohtara and Erestor keep track of Felix and his whereabouts, while Otto and Isaiah would pursue the mysterious ship story. Otto and Isaiah left Erestor's office and headed toward the coastal town of Gebil, about five miles outside of Endemar. Otto knew a number of fishermen who worked out of here and thought one of them might have some more information on any expected mystery ships. Isaiah already knew one resident of Gebil...Luc.

Ohtara went with one of Erestor's people to have him show her the location of the tavern that   Felix had visited in the middle of the night. They went to great effort to be very discreet so any lookouts might not identify them.

* * *

Inside the castle, Theron was briefed by Felix on his night's work. "I think we have twenty senators ready to vote for delaying the Ascension," declared Felix.

"That's not enough," screamed Theron, "we need at least twenty-six of the fifty senators to vote for a delay. You're not trying hard enough! Now, get out there and get those final six votes and do whatever it takes, you hear me, what...ever...it...takes!"

Felix cowered at the berating from Theron. He had been the receiver of many in the past, but the intensity had gotten higher as the Ascension Day approached. He knew that the bottom line was that Theron had no intention to give up power easily. He had seen Theron's lust for power, money, and prestige consume him over the seventeen years he had been Regent. He had become the consummate politician; he would tell people what they wanted to hear but then do what was most beneficial to himself.

Felix stammered, "Yes, yes, Regent Theron. I will try harder. Perhaps we could offer a few well-placed bribes to get the votes."

"Of course, you imbecile, we should use bribes, if that is what it takes, then do it," barked Theron.

"Yes, sir, said Felix, "and uh...on a positive note, Pilu reported that sales were at an all-time high yesterday in the markets. The wolf attack on the flocks sent the city into a frenzy, and people started to panic, which drove prices through the roof. We made a huge profit."

"Well, good, finally some positive news. A little chaos is always good for the pocketbook," replied Theron. "By the way, are the wolves still turning over the food and supplies they steal from people across the countryside?"

"Yes, Regent, just as we agreed, they get a percentage, and we keep the rest to sell back to the citizens of Endemar."

Theron laughed, "I love it, we steal their food and supplies and then sell it back to them. They are all fools."

Theron quickly turned to Felix and grabbed him by the shoulders, looked directly into his eyes, and said, "I know I am demanding a lot, but we must stop the Ascension to avoid the 'Dark Storm Plan.' I need your help to stop that, I'm depending on you, Felix… you Felix." Theron was shaking, and the look in his eyes was wild, fanatical, even maniacal.

Felix was frightened and could only nod affirmatively. He turned and nearly ran out of Theron's office.

* * *

Ohtara had just crossed the marketplace plaza with Erestor's agent when she saw Dwiddle and Sarta in the market buying some supplies and goods for the children. Ohtara hurried over, and they embraced, and she pulled them aside to fill them in on the news from Erestor about Felix's activities. Ohtara explained that they were on their way to a small Tavern that Felix had visited the night before but had to figure out a way to get someone in there who wouldn't be noticed or recognized. Someone who could be very discreet.

"I can do it," said Sarta abruptly.

Both Ohtara and Dwiddle looked at her a bit astonished, and Dwiddle spoke first, "No, no, that would be too dangerous, that's out of the question."

Sarta protested back, "Who's better? Very few people know me in this city, and nobody will pay attention if I slip inside, right, Ohtara?"

Ohtara contemplated her proposal. It did make some sense. Nobody would suspect her as a spy, and they would be outside the whole time. Dwiddle continued to protest, but Sarta pressed on in a calm manner, "It simply makes too much sense. I should be the one."

Finally, Dwiddle looked at Ohtara in an effort to seek help but quickly realized she had come to the same conclusion. Sarta was the right answer. They agreed on a discreet safe place to meet after dark.

Ohtara and Erestor's agent continued to the Tavern, which was down a very narrow alley three blocks from outside the castle walls. It was getting late in the afternoon, and they now simply needed to get Sarta in there before Felix showed up, if he showed up at all.

* * *

Otto and Isaiah jumped on a wagon and headed to the coastal town of Gebil. It was a small fishing village of only four to five hundred inhabitants. There were humans, otters, beavers, and even a few bears who lived and worked out of here. On the way, Isaiah turned to Otto and asked, "Otto, can you explain the Ascension Day to me?"

Otto smiled and said, "Oh yes, of course, I do apologize that in all of the stress, no one has taken time to explain what this day is exactly all about."

Otto continued, "Ascension Day is the day that the King's heir ascends the throne and takes over as the ruling monarch of Endemar. King Aran died eighteen years ago from an illness, but before he died, he instituted the Ascension Day requirements. His heir would not assume the throne until they reached the age of eighteen. Ascension Day would be the day of his heir's birthday."

Isaiah listened intently and finally asked, "So, who is it? And when is it?

Otto looked straight ahead and paused as if he needed to collect his thoughts, and then spoke, "We know when Accension Day is to occur. It is in several days, but the identity of the king's heir has been a very closely guarded secret. The queen died in childbirth, and the king was gravely ill, and he knew his child would be hunted by his enemies. So, he arranged for the child to be taken and hidden. They did not even reveal if it was a boy or a girl to protect the child. Their identity will be revealed at Accession Day."

Isaiah leaned back and listened carefully to Otto's explanation. "So, this is why Theron said, especially to someone that none of us know."

"Exactly, he is playing on people's and particularly senators' fear of the unknown."

The wagon pulled into the town center, which was right across from the wharves where a variety of fishing boats were tied up. They jumped off the moving wagon, and Otto immediately began to look around for anyone he knew. The town was a working town, a bit worn out from heavy weather that pounded rain and waves against the shore and docks. The houses and store fronts also looked weathered with paint peeling and a few shutters missing here and there.

Isaiah looked around and took in all the sights. Fishermen were mending nets while other boats were being emptied of fish and crab. Seagulls dived into the water to catch fish while others stood on the docks and squawked at fishermen to throw them scraps. There was row after row of docks and boats. Isaiah gazed at the sights and took it all in when his eyes caught a glimpse of a figure moving around on a boat several docks down. He moved around to see better and shouted, "Kwidley?"

The last time Isaiah had seen Kwidley was as he pulled away from the shore after he had dropped Luc and him off with the supplies. Their relationship had been short and not very warm, but Kwidley had at least warned him to get off the shore. A piece of advice Isaiah now wished he had adhered to.

Isaiah ran over to the dock, and Kwidley greeted him, "It is good to see you, Isaiah, and I see you are doing well."

Isaiah smiled and replied, "It has been adventuresome to say the least. What brings you to Gebil?"

"Fish, like everyone else. The demand is very high right now, and people are paying top dollar. But maybe the more important question is, what brings you to Gebil?"

By this time, Otto had walked over to the dock that Kwidley and Isaiah stood on, but before Isaiah responded, he turned and introduced Otto to Kwidley, "This is my friend Otto."

Kwidley smiled and replied, "Oh yes, I have heard of Otto and his exploits from my cousin Dwiddle. It's nice to finally meet you." Isaiah was surprised that Kwidley knew of Otto, but was also amused since this was the warmest he had ever seen Kwidley act.

Isaiah continued, "We have received some information regarding a large mysterious ship that is to come here in a few days. We want to validate the story and learn more about it. Have you by any chance heard about this?"

Kwidley's face suddenly turned sullen, and he simply said, "Let's talk, but not here," and he proceeded right past them to the shore. He led them across the city green and down a small street to a single wooden door that he opened and stepped inside with them close behind. It took a moment for both Isaiah's and Otto's eyes to adjust from bright sunlight to the nearly pitch-dark room. As their eyes adjusted, they saw a small lantern burning on a small square table and a fireplace with only glowing embers. Kwidley offered them hot tea and told them to have a seat while he stoked the fire.

He sat down and started, "I am sorry for all the cloak and dagger, but there are spies everywhere these days, and way too many prying ears and eyes on the docks. No secret stays a secret long on the docks. Now, you asked about a mysterious ship, yes?"

Isaiah and Otto both nodded affirmatively and together explained that Dwiddle had brought them the intelligence report from one of his associates, or rather spies. "Do you know anything about such a ship?" asked Isaiah.

Kwidley leaned back in his chair, took a deep sigh, and said, "Not only do I know about it, but I've seen it." Both Isaiah and Otto got wide-eyed and looked at each other, stunned, and encouraged Kwidley to continue.

Kwidley took a deep breath and continued, "Two weeks ago, I was fishing off the banks on the northernmost end of the kingdom, and I rounded a very remote peninsula and found a protected cove on the back side, so I sailed up it, dropped my nets because fish often gather in such spots. As I drifted back into the cove, I heard some noise and pulled over into the marsh grasses to have some cover. Then I saw it," and Kwidley paused to collect his thoughts. "It was not a merchant ship; it was a huge ship meant for one thing and one thing alone…war." He let the words sink-in and then continued, "it was three-hundred feet long and at least seven-hundred tons loaded with canons and rigged to carry troops, lots of troops, and it was being readied to sail."

He paused, and Isaiah and Otto let his words sink into their consciousness. A fully battle-ready frigate was up the coast and being readied to sail. Otto turned to Kwidley and asked, "Do you know anything more about where it is headed, or when it is to leave port, or who owns the ship?"

Kwidley looked directly at Otto and said, "I heard rumors today that fishermen have reported a huge frigate was seen sailing south toward us. It's underway and other than a government, only one man on the coast could build, own, and operate such a ship … Monsieur Dubois."

Monsieur Dubois was a shadowy figure who controlled much of the commercial shipping on the coast. Quite simply, nothing of any significant amount got shipped without his involvement and approval. There had been rumors for years that he had been involved in piracy on the open seas, but he was never arrested.

"Find Dubois and you will find many answers to your questions," stated Kwidley.

Otto and Isaiah left the small room and returned to the bright sunlight. Otto turned to Isaiah and emphatically said, "We must get back to the castle with this information as quickly as possible."

Isaiah agreed but suggested they split up and that he would look for leads to finding Monsieur Dubois while Otto gets word to Erestor and Ohtara about the frigate. They agreed that he would meet back with Otto at Erestor's house at noon tomorrow.

CHAPTER 22

CONFESSION

Total darkness had fallen, and Erestor joined Ohtara and his man in hiding across the street from the tavern. Ohtara had met with Sarta and a very nervous Dwiddle to give her instructions. Ohtara asked her to simply signal them once Felix sat down with someone. They would take it from there. Her signal would be to raise a blind on a window in the tavern.

At ten-thirty sharp, Sarta walked down the street and entered the small tavern. The owner was a large, surly-looking groundhog who was cleaning the bar top and served food when the kitchen prepared it. He looked tired and somewhat disinterested in the people eating at tables. She looked around and saw a fire burning in the stone fireplace and several small tables dotted around the wooden floors. The ceiling was low with large wooden beams that crossed from one side of the room to the other. It had a definite rustic look by necessity rather than design.

Sarta saw an open table right by the window and she thought to herself, *Perfect...that'll work,* and quickly slid into a seat. She took her time and looked over the menu provided by the owner and finally selected some food so as not to become conspicuous.

There were only a few guests in the tavern at this time of night, and she hoped none would leave, so she could simply blend in and not be too obvious.

At exactly eleven sharp, the front door of the tavern opened and in walked a man with a large overcoat and a hood over his head. The man glanced around nervously and then lowered his hood. It was Felix. Sarta tried not to stare, but she wanted to get a good look and see where he was sitting, but then, to her complete surprise, he walked through the tavern, pulled back a curtain, and went down a small hallway. *Oh no,* she said to herself, *what do I do now? I've lost him.* She hurriedly looked around the room and saw the owner follow Felix through the curtain to a small table tucked in the very back, just out of her sight. The owner returned behind the bar and continued cleaning, but she noticed he gave an order to the kitchen. *Felix must have ordered food but is that it?* she thought. *Does he simply come here for a late dinner, and all of this is for nothing?* The owner stepped away from the bar top to a table to finalize a guest's check. Suddenly, the kitchen put two plates up on the window counter, and she saw a chance. She jumped to her feet, grabbed an apron that hung by the bar, threw it around her waist, and grabbed the two plates out of the window. She dipped behind the curtain and headed to the table where Felix was seated. She rounded the corner, and Felix was seated with his back to her, and another individual was seated across from him. She quickly placed the plates in front of each of them and avoided eye contact. She was about to slip out when Felix looked up and asked, "Are you new here?"

Sarta froze but composed herself and smiled, "Why, a matter of fact, I am, my first night."

"Humph, about time that old groundhog gets some decent help around here," grumbled Felix.

Sarta laughed and quickly moved back up the short hallway and took off the apron as she walked. As the owner returned from the guest table to his place behind the bar, she slid back into her seat by the window. She reached up and raised the blind on the window.

Ohtara and Erestor saw the blind go up and moved out quickly and darted across the alley and through the front door. As they came in, Sarta exited and whispered, "In the back, past the curtains," and she exited into the arms of Dwiddle, who waited outside. Ohtara and Erestor walked straight through the curtains to the back and the round table, where Felix was sitting with his back to them. They immediately recognized Pilu across the table from Felix, whose eyes got big when he saw them come through the curtain. Felix, however, was oblivious with his back turned to the hallway.

Erestor placed both his hands on Felix's shoulders with a firm grip and said, "Well, look what we have here. The Regent's Chief of Staff is having dinner with a known criminal who has been gouging the public in the markets."

Ohtara sat down on a chair between them and said, "This certainly doesn't look good, no, not at all. Perhaps we should let the other senators know about this. It might just open some eyes to who they have been dealing with."

Felix's face was red, but he tried to fall back on his ability to lie and maneuver out of awkward situations. "So, what?" he said, "I ran into an old friend tonight from our school days, and we were simply catching up on family."

Pilu, who was not a good liar, quickly added, "Yeah, we're just catching up on family." To which Ohtara responded sharply, "I know you, Pilu. You have no family, only associates that you use and destroy at will," and with that, she stood up, grabbed his throat, and pinned him back against the wall while she reached inside his coat pocket and pulled out a small black book.

"Aw, yes, this appears to be what we need," said Ohtara, and she showed it to Erestor, who still had a firm grip on Felix.

"Perfect," said Erestor, and he released his grip on Felix and threw his leg over the fourth chair and sat opposite Ohtara. She threw Pilu back into his seat and sat down herself.

Ohtara handed the black book to Erestor, who began to thumb through the pages. "It appears that this little book provides the methods and names of vendors you have used to cheat people, as well as the amount of money you share with Regent Theron as your partner," stated Erestor.

Ohtara, who had taken the book back and was paging through it, chimed in, "Oh yes, but don't forget this line item, which also gives the amount skimmed off to pay directly to Felix."

Erestor continued, "So, how do you two think it's going to go down when we share this with the rest of the senate? Not to mention the public, when they learn what you have been doing. Or, for that matter, Felix, how do you think your boss, Theron, is going to take it when he finds out you've been stealing from him?"

"I wouldn't want to be you. There will be nowhere to hide, and I mean nowhere!" said Erestor sternly.

Erestor looked at them both and then said with a low, very intentional voice, "You are going to both come clean and tell me everything you know. Right now...do you understand?"

Just as he finished, a dagger was planted point down into the center of the table by Ohtara, with a loud thud. She looked at each of them and said, "You can cooperate or make it very rough on yourselves."

Felix was very nervous, and beads of sweat appeared on his forehead. He sensed it was checkmate. He feared Theron tremendously but was terrified of what Erestor and Ohtara could do to him. They could simply make him disappear, buried in the depths of the prison system for his crimes. He had no other option but to cooperate and try to make a deal for his cooperation. He was a politician at his core and now sensed that he needed to negotiate a better outcome for himself. He stuttered, "I don't know anything about this, I'm innocent of any wrongdoing."

Pilu exploded, "You're not going to pin this all on me. It was you and Theron's idea anyway. I just did what they told me, and I didn't have anything to do with the wolves... no, that's not me at all, not at all."

"Shut up, you fool!" shouted Felix.

Ohtara and Erestor looked at each other, and Ohtara turned to Pilu and pulled him close by the collar and said, "Tell me more about the wolves." He started to deny that he had any real knowledge about the wolves, and Ohtara grabbed Pilu's right hand and slammed it on the table, and with one motion, grabbed the dagger and planted it between his thumb and index finger with a loud thud. A small trickle of blood ran down his index finger. "The next one won't be so generous...now talk!"

Pilu's eyes were fixed on Ohtara, and he listened to her intently with real fear. Sweat ran down his face, and he knew she was not to be tested. There was silence in the room, and Pilu began to shake, but finally spilled out everything he knew about how the wolves had been brought to Endemar by Theron to create havoc and chaos. He explained that the wolves and coyotes were supposed to terrorize the countryside and create mass fear so that prices would soar, and a huge profit could be made. The wolves and coyotes would be allowed to keep a portion of the food and goods they stole, but the rest would come back to Pilu and be sold by the vendors. The citizens of Endemar were unknowingly buying back their own goods.

Felix sat with his head down, completely distraught, as any chance for negotiation rapidly slipped away. He finally spoke, "There is one other thing, but I need something in return for it."

Erestor said, "Go on."

Felix looked around and continued, "I...I need immunity from prosecution." He thought he would swing for the fences, but Erestor wasn't buying it.

"The most you will get from me is a promise to not let Ohtara take you out back and my good word that you cooperated, that's all, period," responded Erestor sternly.

Felix dropped his head and spoke slowly, "There is something else. I don't know any details because Theron insists on keeping his business separate, with only him knowing everything. But there is something else going on. Theron always has plans and then backup plans. He has never shared any details regarding what it is."

Ohtara spoke up and said, "Tell us everything you do know."

Felix continued, "That's the issue, I don't know any details. Theron has only mentioned it once to me. He calls it the Dark Storm Plan."

At that point, four constables walked into the tavern and came directly to the table. Erestor told them to take these two and keep them under wraps for a few days until we get to the bottom of all this.

CHAPTER 23

MONSIEUR DUBOIS

Otto returned to the city and headed directly to Erestor's house to warn him and Ohtara about the frigate. Erestor and Ohtara had just arrived back from their interrogation of Felix and Pilu, and the three of them went into Erestor's library to discuss their next move.

"Welcome back," said Erestor as Otto stepped into his library. "Where's Isaiah?" Otto quickly filled them in about everything they had learned about the large frigate headed for the shores of Endemar and then said, "Isaiah stayed behind to find out how to contact Monsieur Dubois since we were told he could provide some answers."

When she heard this, Ohtara leaned forward, and the expression on her face changed to concern. She knew who Monsieur Dubois was and had dealt with him in the past. He was ruthless and would not stop at anything to make money or obtain more power. He was bad news, very bad news. Ohtara stood up and leaned forward on her hands toward Otto and very deliberately asked, "What exactly was Isaiah going to do? I hope he wasn't going to try to make contact with him."

Otto paused and looked at Ohtara and said, "I don't think so. We only talked about finding leads for how to contact Monsieur Dubois, not actually trying to make contact."

Ohtara turned to Erestor and asked, "Can you handle things here if I go to Gebil?"

"Of course ... go!" said Erestor

Ohtara ran out of the library and out the back to a paddock behind Erestor's house. Ohtara had brought Aranco there earlier in the day, and she now needed his speed. She jumped on Aranco and said, "Run fast, old friend, I fear we may already be too late."

* * *

Isaiah had gone back to the docks and looked for Kwidley but could not find him anywhere, so he went into a tavern and decided to ask the owner for some help. "Excuse me, sir, but do you by any chance know a man named...Monsieur Dubois?" The owner scowled back at him, obviously not happy. At the same time, several rogue-looking patrons who sat at tables turned and glared directly at Isaiah. The whole tavern went silent. The question had obviously struck a nerve. Finally, the owner scowled and said gruffly, "Who's asking?" Isaiah was taken aback at the nature of the question and was just about to answer him when the door to the tavern opened and Kwidley stepped inside.

"Nobody is asking," snapped Kwidley, "nobody at all. "He turned to Isaiah and said, "There you are, I've been looking all over for you. It's time to cast off. We must go now." And with that, he literally put his arm around Isaiah's shoulders and pushed him out of the tavern and into the street. Once in the street, he dragged him around a corner of the building and pinned him to the wall with a forearm.

"What are you doing? Do you want to get killed?" he screamed into Isaiah's face.

Kwidley took a deep breath and calmed a bit, and then continued, "Listen, there are two kinds of people in this town, those that hate Monsieur Dubois and those that work for Monsieur Dubois. Both will kill a man for simply asking questions about him...people just don't speak that name if they want to continue living."

Isaiah stared wide-eyed at Kwidley and simply nodded and said, "Uh huh, I get it."

Kwidley stared at him to make sure he understood the message and then finally said, "Ok, come with me," and they both ran down an alley that led them to the edge of the town with a dense forest about fifty yards away. "Take this path until you come to a small cabin. Knock on the door and say Kwidley sent you. You can get answers to your questions there. I'll wait for you right here."

Isaiah looked at him a bit confused but decided to trust Kwidley and follow his instructions. He ran across the open field through tall grass until he reached the edge of the woods, where he found a small path. He looked back, and Kwidley motioned for him to keep going while at the same time he looked nervously around. Kwidley was obviously spooked by Monsieur Dubois and his people.

It was late in the afternoon as he entered the woods, and it became darker under the forest covering as it blocked all direct sunlight. He decided he must hurry, or he could be lost in a very dark forest. He had gone about a half mile when the trail seemed to split, and he stopped to get his bearings. Suddenly, a hand grabbed his shirt and pulled him down into a dry creek bed. His first reaction was to fight, but then he heard a voice, "Isaiah, it's me, Luc."

Isaiah spun and embraced Luc, who said, "Follow me, I can get you to the cabin undetected."

They moved in silence for another mile when they stopped and looked straight ahead at a small cabin that sat beside a small pond surrounded by trees. It was a beautiful scene with trees surrounding the very still pond, and it made it all seem so serene.

Luc leaned over and whispered, "That is the cabin, but I can't go any further."

Isaiah nodded and proceeded to the cabin. He stepped cautiously on the porch to make as little noise as possible and then knocked lightly on the cabin door. There was no response initially, but finally, he heard a voice that said, "Who is it?" He paused for a second but then remembered Kwidley's instructions, "Kwidley sent me," he said in a soft voice. There was silence that seemed like minutes. "Come in," said a voice from behind the door.

Isaiah opened the door and slowly stepped into a mostly dark cabin with only a small fire burning in the fireplace. An individual sat in the corner completely emersed in shadows. Isaiah could only see the silhouette of someone. It was obvious they had no intention of Isaiah seeing their face. Isaiah started to speak, "My name is..." but he was immediately cut off by the shadowy man, "No names...just questions and answers," the shadowy voice commanded. Isaiah realized he had to be very efficient with his words because he had no idea when this individual might shut off their meeting.

Isaiah formulated his thoughts and said, "I need to find Monsieur Dubois."

The voice chuckled and said, "Nobody finds Monsieur Dubois...or lives to talk about it."

"Why are you looking for him?" continued the voice.

Isaiah swallowed hard and wondered if he should disclose what he had heard from Kwidley. He whispered a short prayer. He took a deep breath and felt prompted to continue, "We have received information that a large frigate, rigged for war, is up the coast and heading here. We were told nothing happens on this coast without

Monsieur Dubois's approval or knowledge. We believe if we find him, we find answers."

There was a long silence, and Isaiah could only hear the crackling of the fire and his own breathing.

"Come closer," and Isaiah took several steps closer toward the silhouetted figure in the dark.

"You have found answers," spoke the voice from the shadows.

A chill went down Isaiah's back as the realization of those words sank into him.

"Before you say another word, Do you understand that being here is highly unusual, even dangerous. Many men have lost their lives while trying to be where you are standing right now, but you are standing here before me, alive and well... for now. That should give you reason to ask, why you, why now, why here?"

Isaiah stood before him, silent and listened to each word, but before he could say anything, the silhouetted figure continued, "I pay my debts, and I am indebted to you for saving my son's life."

Isaiah was stunned and confused. He began to stammer in response, "Saved...saved your...your son, what?"

Just then, he heard another voice, "Hello, father, I brought him to you, just as requested," and Luc appeared beside him out of the shadows of the cabin.

Isaiah was shocked at the revelation that Luc was Jean Luc Dubois, the son of the notorious underworld figure, Monsieur Dubois. He now wondered what would happen next; was this all a ploy by Luc and his father to trap him?

"Now, what is it you wish to know and, more importantly, why do you wish to know it?" continued Monsieur Dubois.

Isaiah's mind was racing, and his heart was beating fast as he carefully considered how to respond. Finally, he said, "We want to know whose ship it is and what their intent is."

"Who is 'we'?" thundered Dubois.

Isaiah gulped and took a deep breath, "Well... my friends and I: Senator Erestor, Otto, the keeper of the garden, and Ohtara, the watchman."

"Augh...not Ohtara, she has been nothing but trouble to me and cost me a lot of money. We have had more than our share of run-ins over the years. Why would I help her? She has been nothing but trouble for me, a real pain for my business," he snarled.

Dubois continued, "As for Erestor and Otto, they also are major pains. They always want everything done prim and proper, by the book, all legal ...augh, makes me sick. Why would I help them?"

Isaiah felt a surge of panic well up inside him. He thought, *What do I say now? He despises Ohtara, Erestor, and Otto. He considers them his enemies, and I can now only assume he views me as his enemy.* Isaiah took a deep breath and opened his heart to hear the Voice speak to him.

A peace settled over Isaiah, and he began to speak, "Monsieur, this is about much more than past differences and even business. Many citizens have been hurt already, and if war happens, many, many more will be killed and injured. Many children will become orphans. If you can do anything to stop this, would you please help?"

There was a long silence in the room, with only the sound of the crackling fire. Isaiah looked at the silhouetted figure in the corner and noticed that he raised his hand to his eyes and wiped them. Finally, the silence was broken by Dubois, "I will help...for the children." Isaiah had no way of knowing that Monsieur Dubois had been an orphan.

Dubois continued, "The ship has been under construction for over two years in a cove to the far north. The funds had been secretly syphoned from the Endemar treasury by none other than Regent Theron himself. He has no intention of surrendering his power on Ascension Day, but rather, if need be, he is prepared to lead an attack on the kingdom and the new monarch. His first plan has always been to delay Ascension Day by creating instability in the kingdom with the wolf attacks on villages. He wanted to make people afraid of change at this unstable time; thus, the senate would allow him to stay in power for one to two more years. However, Theron always has a backup plan that he will execute if necessary. That backup plan, if necessary, is to lead a coup to overthrow the monarchy and name himself king."

Isaiah listened dumbfounded at what Monsieur Dubois told him. The Regent had passionately made public speeches against the wolf attacks and made promises to do everything he could to stop them. It now appeared to all be a lie. A carefully orchestrated ploy to gain more power and riches. The Regent was the one behind the wolf attacks all along!

Dubois continued, "I will neutralize the ship, but you must find a way to keep the troops on the ship. My sources say they will only leave the ship and attack when Theron gives a signal. I do not know what that signal is, but you must delay that from happening as long as possible, to assure my people are in place."

There was silence once again, and then Dubois spoke, "By the way, the ship's name is Dark Storm."

Isaiah listened intently and then responded, "We will do our best, but it would really help if you would come forward and speak to the senators; it would carry great weight if you helped confront Theron."

"Hah, hah, that's not going to happen," declared Dubois. "I will never expose myself to that useless group of politicians. Half of them I've paid off with bribes, and half want to kill me."

There was silence, and then Isaiah spoke, "Sometimes doing the right thing is difficult, and has a high cost."

Dubois suddenly declared, "Our business is done here." Isaiah took the cue to leave the cottage, thanked him for his cooperation, and turned to leave. As he turned, his long coat swung open and exposed the handle of the Sword of Integrity.

Dubois suddenly said, "Stop, wait, where did you get that?" as he pointed with a shadowy, shaking finger toward the sword. "Is that... is that what I think it is?"

Isaiah turned back toward Dubois and opened the coat, revealing the Sword of Integrity. "Yes, it is the Sword of Integrity."

"How... how did you get that?" stammered Dubois with a shaky voice.

"I climbed the mountain, and it chose me as worthy...for doing the right thing." Isaiah opened the door and turned for one last look at Dubois' shadowy silhouetted figure, and nodded, and for just a moment, he thought he saw a smile appear.

It was now completely dark outside, and Luc led Isaiah back to town. They finally saw some lights from the town and came to the edge of the woods. Isaiah spun around and pressed Luc against a tree and said, "Now, it's your turn. I need answers. Were you playing me all along? Is there a box? If so, I need to understand what this is all about. Why is everyone after you? Who did you steal this from? I must get back now with this information, but the next time we meet, be prepared to answer these questions." With that said, Isaiah turned and walked across the fifty yards of tall grasses to the alley.

He had no sooner reached the alley when he heard Kwidley's voice, "Isaiah over here," and he saw Kwidley hiding behind some crates in the alley. Kwidley continued, "Follow me and stay close." They moved quickly down the alley, and in a few minutes, he found himself back inside the small room Kwidley had taken them to earlier. Isaiah sat down and explained everything that happened in the cottage. Kwidley sat in the chair and shook his head at every detail.

"We must get this information to Erestor and Ohtara as quickly as possible." Kwidley agreed but cautioned that it was very dangerous to travel late at night in the town. They started to discuss possible ways to slip out of the city when they heard galloping hooves against the cobblestone streets, followed by the whinnying of a horse as it came to a stop. Kwidley went to the door and cracked it open, and saw a magnificent white stallion reared up on its hind legs with a distinct rider in complete control. Isaiah, who had been looking over Kwidley's shoulder, burst by him and went outside and yelled, "Ohtara!"

Ohtara brought Aranco right down the street to Kwidley's door and dismounted and grabbed Isaiah in a tight hug. "Are you alright?" she said with an urgency in her voice.

"I am fine, but I have some critical information to share with you and Erestor. We must get back to the city as fast as we can. It cannot wait. Time is of the essence. We must go now," said Isaiah with emphasis in his voice.

There was a tone that Ohtara had not quite seen before in Isaiah, a strength, a firmness, a deep commitment, and a confidence. She looked at him and smiled, 'Let's go," and hoisted him onto the back of Aranco. The commotion of Aranco and Ohtara galloping through the streets had created some interest among local ne'er-do-well characters who had decided to come out of the taverns and investigate what was going on. Ohtara had her back to them, and they started to shout and threaten her and Isaiah.

Ohtara spun around, and instantly two swords came out of their sheaths and spun in her hands and landed just under the chins of the nearest two approaching tavern characters. She looked them firmly in the eyes and said, "Not tonight, boys, just don't have the time or patience to deal with you... Now get! Their eyes got huge as they realized who she was, and they began back peddling, and before long, the street was completely empty. She climbed on Aranco, and she and Isaiah galloped off into the night toward Endemar.

CHAPTER 24

SIGNAL FIRE

Ohtara and Isaiah returned to Erestor's house well after midnight, but both Erestor and Otto were still up and discussing plans. Ohtara and Isaiah had ridden so hard on Aranco that they did not get a chance to debrief each other on what they each knew, but now in Erestor's library, they all began to lay out the facts. Ohtara and Erestor shared the information they had gotten from Pilu and Felix. Information that indicated that Regent Theron created the current crisis with the wolves, which included stealing both food and goods while also price gouging and cheating people in the marketplace. They all shook their heads as the details were shared about the numerous schemes to make money and create fear and chaos.

Once they had shared the details, Erestor said, "Theron is a master politician. He always has plans and backup plans in case the first plan doesn't work. He does not want to give up power. He is drunk with it and will do just about anything to keep it."

Isaiah spoke up and said, "I think I can fill in some gaps, I talked to Monsieur Dubois and..."

"What do you mean you talked to him?" came a stunned Ohtara response. He proceeded to tell them about his time spent with Monsieur Dubois. All three sat there with their mouths wide open in shock. They all knew just how dangerous Dubois was, and the thought that Isaiah had actually met with him in person was incredulous to them.

When Isaiah finished, Ohtara spoke up, "I just don't know if we can trust Dubois. He has a long history of deceit and deception. It all could just be a trap to benefit himself. Everything with him is about business…his business."

Erestor agreed with Ohtara's concerns and expressed similar skepticism. "Is anything he's telling us true?"

Isaiah listened carefully and then quietly but firmly said, "I trust him."

They all stopped talking and looked right at him. Ohtara again saw what she had seen earlier that evening in Gebil. He had a new strength, firmness, deep commitment, and confidence.

Isaiah continued and asked, "What did Felix tell you about Theron's backup plan?"

Erestor responded, "He mentioned something about a plan called Dark Storm, but he had no details at all. That could have been made up by Felix to try to buy time or make us believe he was actually cooperating. We have no idea what that is about, nor do we have the time to sit around speculating. It is a nonstarter to chase that weak link."

Isaiah smiled and said, "I don't think it's as weak a link as you might think. Monsieur Dubois told me the name of the frigate is… Dark Storm."

They all stared at Isaiah in silence as his words sank in. Felix, who had no connection to Monsieur Dubois, had told Erestor and Ohtara about a backup plan called "Dark Storm," but swore he didn't know any details, and for all practical purposes, he probably was telling the truth. Theron was well known for keeping subordinates uninformed of all his plans. It was due to his deep paranoia.

On the other hand, Monsieur Dubois, a powerful underworld character who controlled the coast and shipping, told them all about the frigate, its funding, construction, and purpose. Exactly what you would expect from him and his control of the coastal activities. However, the name of the ship, Dark Storm, aligned with the name Felix had shared for the backup plan. Dark Storm was both a plan and the name of the ship that Theron planned to use to seize control of Endemar. Monsieur Dubois's claim that Theron had planned a coup attempt using an armed-to-the-teeth frigate loaded with mercenary troops now seemed very feasible.

Isaiah said, "We have one day to figure out how to stop Theron from signaling the ship to attack. Monsieur Dubois has promised to stop the ship if we buy him the time needed. We must trust him and figure out how to stop that signal from happening!"

Erestor, Ohtara, and Otto all looked intently at Isaiah. The only sound was from the crackling fire in the fireplace. No one spoke until finally Ohtara said, "Ok, let's do it Isaiah's way. We will trust Dubois."

***

The next morning, the castle was abuzz with senators and staff. Senators were huddled and intensely talking about Ascension Day while staff were running back and forth, keeping senators updated on the most recent news, as well as plain gossip, as uncertainty and confusion hung over the senate. Ascension Day was scheduled for the next day, and the issue of a delay was still on the table. Erestor had successfully gotten the vote moved back to the morning of Ascension Day. The Senate would take a vote on a proposed delay, and if defeated, the Ascension process would proceed as planned at twelve noon. Erestor knew that if he delayed the vote, it would also delay any action by Theron to enact his backup plan called Dark Storm.

Crowds had grown in the city for several days in anticipation of Ascension Day, and vendors were selling everything from food to souvenirs. Rumors ran rampant through the crowds, and some people even placed bets on who the next monarch would be. The crowds were nearly shoulder to shoulder in the streets, and Ohtara wondered how many were being taken by either corrupt vendors or pickpockets.

Theron worked the floor of the senate, talking to senator after senator, and seemed particularly nervous. He continually looked around and made a few comments regarding the absence of Felix, whom he couldn't find anywhere. He said to no one in particular, "Where is that little vermin. Just when I need him, he is nowhere to be found." He worked the room in his usual skilled manner. He laughed at the right time, joked with senators, patted backs, and handed out meaningless, insincere compliments, all to influence votes. This continued throughout the entire morning with a few brief exits to go back to his office.

Erestor pulled several senators aside to have very private conversations. He wasn't quite ready to lay all the evidence on the table. He was afraid it would lead to a very long delaying tactic by Theron, so he worked to convince senators that they simply needed to move on with the Ascension Day process the next day.

Ohtara walked the entire castle's defenses and checked to see if they had the right armaments and troops in place if they needed to defend against an attack. The entire time, she kept her eyes open for some possible way Theron could signal the ship to attack.

Otto and Isaiah went to the rooftops of the castle to see if there was anything new or different that could be used to signal a ship in the bay. It was very clear from this vantage point that they could see the harbor, which meant the ship would also be able to see the spires of the castle. This seemed like the most logical place to signal a ship in the harbor. They both carefully walked the area but saw nothing that seemed to be out of the norm.

Theron continued to work the Senate floor all afternoon, telling senators how he was stopping the wolf attacks and that Endemar needed his consistent leadership right now. The time for a new monarch would come in due time, and he would be fully supportive of whoever that would be. His love and passion for Endemar were what motivated him.

The day came and went with no discovery of how Theron would signal the ship from the castle to begin an attack. Erestor, Otto, Ohtara, and Isaiah all met back in Erestor's office and shared their lack of findings.

Isaiah spoke first, "There is just nothing obvious regarding Theron's plan to signal the ship. What are we missing?"

"Maybe he isn't signaling the ship but going to the ship," said Otto. "Or perhaps, he is having someone else go to the ship with his orders."

Ohtara spoke up, "With Theron's desire to control everything, I don't see him turning this task over to anyone else. He's simply too paranoid."

Erestor said, "Ok, let's walk through the Accension Day process, and perhaps that could lead us to some answers." Tara, who had come into town to help, proceeded to read aloud through the documents that described the entire day's process and subsequent coronation and celebration."

Otto suddenly stopped her and asked, "What did you say happens at nine o'clock?"

Tara stopped and went back and reread aloud the last section, "at nine o'clock, the signal fires are lit on top of the castle to announce to neighboring kingdoms that a new monarch of Endemar is in residence."

Otto rubbed his chin in deep contemplation and then continued, "Hmm…perhaps that is how he plans on doing it. What if he plans on using Endemar's own signal fires to signal the ship?"

"But wouldn't that be too risky? What if he wants to call off the attack? They are going to light the towers, anyway," said Erestor.

"Yes, you are correct, but what if there was something unique that he could do to the fire to send a signal?" responded Otto.

"Like what?" said Erestor.

Otto went on, "Well, I noticed something today when we walked around the roof. Workers had prepared the signal fires for the Ascension Day celebration, and in each of the four towers, there were a number of clay jars stored in small closets. I looked in the jars and they contained a yellow brown powder. I recognized it as copper chloride, which I have used in the orchard as a fungicide."

"Yes, go on," said Erestor, who did not quite understand what point Otto was trying to make.

"Re-read the section that describes the signal fires that are to be lit at nine o'clock," asked Otto.

Tara returned to the document that had been provided by the staff: "The signal fires shall be blue fires."

"Yes, blue," said Otto. "Tradition dictates that blue fire signals a monarch is in residence. Blue is the color of royalty."

Erestor still wasn't quite sure and was confused. He still didn't understand what point Otto was trying to make and was now impatient, "So what, what has the color blue got to do with signaling the ship?" he said.

"Well," responded Otto, "in the tower closest to the bay, number four, I noticed something else besides the yellow brown powder; there were also several jars with a distinct white powder. It appeared to be strontium, and this was the only tower with this substance."

Tara, who had worked with Otto for years in his lab, suddenly saw what Otto was getting at and let out a loud, "Oh, yes, I see, of course."

Erestor, now exhausted by the chemistry lesson, said, "But what does it all mean?"

"Strontium burns very differently from copper chloride. Strontium burns a very bright crimson red and is often used in fireworks," replied Otto. He continued, "It is very interesting that the only tower to have strontium, which burns crimson red, is the one closest to the harbor. Is it possible that he will not signal the ship directly, but rather the color of the fire in the signal tower will be the signal to the ship? If so, Theron will direct the fourth tower crew as to which jar to use, copper chloride or strontium?"

Everyone looked straight at Otto in astonishment at his perception and insight. Finally, Erestor said slowly, "That...could...work."

They all agreed that Otto's theory was one possible way to send a signal to the ship, and the evidence certainly supported the idea of a different color flame being used from the fourth tower. They also decided to look for other alternatives and, most of all, keep constant surveillance on Theron.

Erestor turned to Otto and Isaiah and asked, "Do you think you could get the strontium out of that tower?"

Otto and Isaiah looked at each other and adamantly replied, "Absolutely." It was late in the afternoon, and Otto and Isaiah needed to act without delay to sneak up to the roof undetected and remove the strontium.

CHAPTER 25

THE SWITCH

Isaiah and Otto filled backpacks with supplies they needed and headed toward the castle. They took a carriage from Erestor's house and stopped a couple of blocks from the castle in a plaza. This way, they could be more discreet in their approach to the castle. As they got off the carriage, Isaiah saw something in an alley off to his right. He grabbed Otto's arm and stopped him. "Otto, wait here a minute, I want to check something out."

Isaiah went into the alley and looked around and whispered, "Luc, are you here?"

From a dark recess of the alley, Luc stepped forward and said, "Isaiah, I think I found the well. I found a well two blocks from here, which may be the one that I hid the box inside, but I need some help to check it out. Can you help me?"

"Of course, I can help you, but I have an urgent matter I need to address. I need to get to the ramparts of the castle as quickly as possible and do it without anyone seeing me."

"That may be a problem," stated Luc.

"What do you mean...a problem?"

"Regent Theron ordered the entire castle to lock down until the Ascension Day ceremony tomorrow. Nobody comes in or out. It is a fortress tonight."

Isaiah grabbed Luc by the arm and said, "Don't move, I'll be right back. I may need your help first." He ran out to Otto and brought him back to the dark alley and called for Luc to come out of the shadows. "Otto, this is a friend of mine, and he just told me some disturbing news." Luc repeated his information to Otto, who began to shake his head and say over and over, "This is not good, no, not good at all."

Isaiah turned to Luc and said, "Wait a minute, Luc, you are an expert...at...a... You know, at getting in places." He felt awkward saying Luc was an expert thief. A cat burglar, to be exact, who was very skilled at breaking into places and stealing things. "Luc, you can help us get into the castle, right?"

Luc's eyes went back and forth to Isaiah and Otto as if looking for something, and then he asked, "Why exactly do you need to break into the castle?"

Isaiah turned to Otto and hesitated, not quite sure how much to divulge, but finally spilled out, "We believe there is a plot to overthrow the new monarch, and a signal will be sent from one of the ramparts tomorrow night. We intend to stop the signal from being sent. Will you help?"

"Ok, let me get this right. You two want to break into the castle, a fortress guarded by many troops, and do something to stop something that may or may not happen and then sneak back out. All without being detected by anyone...correct."

Isaiah smiled, "Well...yes, that sums it up pretty well."

"Then nope, it's not my problem. Sorry, can't help you. I've got more important matters to attend to. Like staying alive. Besides, it would take perfect timing and ability to move quickly to have a chance."

"But there is a chance, you say?" blurted out Isaiah.

"There is a way, but once inside, you have to move quickly and quietly to avoid guards and detection, and you must know where you're going."

Otto listened carefully and then spoke, "It seems that you have a lot of knowledge about what it takes to be successful."

Luc looked back at him and peered intensely into his eyes but did not respond to his comment.

"Besides, as I said, not for me. I have other things to do and really don't care much about the kingdom of Endemar and what happens here. I don't want to be involved."

Isaiah gave out a loud sigh of frustration and then looked at Luc and said plainly, "Your father thought it was important enough to help us understand the Dark Storm plan."

Otto's eyes got very large when he heard Isaiah. He suddenly came to the realization of exactly who Luc was.

Luc was very silent as those words sank in, and Isaiah continued, "Doing the right thing can sometimes be very hard, even inconvenient. It can be risky and even have a cost, a very high cost, but it's still the right thing to do."

Isaiah looked at Luc and smiled while continuing, "And besides, when this is all done, I'll help you find that stupid box so you can do whatever you are going to do with it."

Luc looked at both and took a deep breath and finally said, "Ok, I'll help you. Follow me."

Luc led Isaiah and Otto down a series of alleys. Otto was perplexed because they were nowhere near the large castle gates but rather stayed in the dark shadows of alleys. They worked their way around the walls of the castle toward the far east side. This area outside the east walls was known to be an area filled with rough characters and small seedy taverns. It was not a place people typically went to alone. Neither Isaiah nor Otto realized that this was the exact area that Ohtara and Erestor had nabbed Felix and Pilu.

Luc came to a door in the alley and gave a gentle tap, three times, and then paused and followed with two more quick taps. The door opened, and he shoved both Otto and Isaiah into a small, dimly lit room and closed the door quickly behind him. An old woman had opened the door, and Luc immediately put some coins in her hand, and she disappeared up a set of stairs with no words exchanged. Isaiah realized they were now inside a dark underworld of alliances, favors, betrayals, and bribes. Caution was important for survival.

Luc turned and, in a whisper, said, "We can enter the castle from here, but are you sure you want to do this. It's very dangerous." Isaiah looked around, confused, and thought to himself, *How do we enter the castle from here?* Together, he and Otto nodded that they wanted to proceed.

When he saw their confusion, Luc whispered again, "Years ago, secret passages were put into the castle to allow certain people to go in and out undetected or even escape if necessary."

Luc walked over to a large stone box built into the wall beside the fireplace. He reached in and began to remove pieces of wood that had been stored. He set them on the floor to the side. When empty, he reached into the box and removed several stones that made up the floor. As he removed them, you could see an opening appear that descended underground. It was pitch black, so there was no way to know how deep it went or where it led exactly.

Luc grabbed an oil lamp near the fireplace and lit the wick. It immediately lit up the room brighter so Isaiah could now see the surroundings a bit better. It was a simple room with nothing but a table and chairs across from a fireplace. There were no pictures or any personal items present. The room seemed intentionally left very plain. A staircase led up to a solid wooden door that the old woman had gone through.

Luc climbed into the hole while he held the lamp and said, "Follow me." He disappeared down a ladder into a storm sewer where water ran down the middle and narrow walkways ran along each side of the sewer. Otto and Isaiah were soon by his side with the light from the oil lamp that created shadows on the rounded brick ceiling of the sewer. Luc held his finger to his lips to signal silence and proceeded to walk down the walkway. As they walked, Isaiah's eyes caught some motion on the floor. It was rats, many big rats. The rats scurried around and foraged on the walkways and made a continuous squeal as they competed for food scraps. Isaiah had to nudge them away with his foot to have a place to step. Each time he nudged the rats, they squealed and climbed over top of each other and his foot. Isaiah looked up and noticed Luc reach down and pick up a fat rat by its tail and put it in his pouch. He turned to Isaiah, smiled, and said, "Never know when one of these may prove useful."

As best Isaiah could tell, they had passed under the street that separated the house from the castle wall. They walked further on the walkway, nudging rats as they went, until the lamplight lit up a solid stone wall. However, there was only this wall with a small, curved iron grid in the middle of the wall that allowed water to continue to flow. He turned to Luc and whispered, "What do we do now?" Luc pointed to the corner where the wall and the ceiling met. There was a length of rope hanging down. The rope disappeared into a slot about three feet in length. If Luc had not pointed it out, he would have never noticed the rope. It was cleverly camouflaged into the corner where the two walls met. Luc pulled on the rope, and an opening in the ceiling appeared, and a ladder began to descend.

They all climbed up the ladder and found themselves in a dark chamber where Luc extinguished his lamp and slid open a panel in the wall that allowed light to come into the chamber. Luc turned toward Otto and Isaiah and whispered, "Good, no guards, now stay very close to me."

A hidden door in the wall was opened, and they all stepped into a storage room in the bottom cellar of the castle. There were barrels stacked everywhere, and it took Isaiah a minute to gain his bearings. Luc turned and said, "We need to get to the ramparts quickly. I know another direct way up that few know about." He took off and moved rapidly out of the storage area and up a flight of stairs to a hallway that led to a library. He slipped into the library after he checked to make sure no one was inside and pulled several books out of a large bookcase. Isaiah thought it was a strange time to look at books, but there was a popping and creaking sound, and the bookcase moved. At the same time, he heard voices in the hallway. Luc spun and whispered, "Quick, get in here," and shoved both Isaiah and Otto behind the open bookcase. He pulled it closed behind him as they heard the library door open.

"This is a hidden stairway that goes all the way to the ramparts, but it also goes right by Theron's office, which connects to it. We must be very quiet."

They all quietly moved up the steps but stopped several times to check for any sign of Theron or his guards. They got to an upper level, and Luc threw his hand up in the air, signaling to stop, and they all pinned themselves against the stair wall. The hidden opening to Theron's office was wide open, and light from it flooded the stairway. To make matters worse, they could hear Theron's bellowing voice. "We haven't found that little thief yet, but when we do, we'll kill him. That will solve an immediate problem. I can't have him out there talking. We must clean up this loose end."

A low gravelly voice responded, "Of course, you're right, Regent Theron. Kill him, leave no loose ends. Have you found the box yet?"

The hair on the back of Isaiah's neck stood up. He recognized that voice and worked his way along the stone wall until he was next to Luc. Straining to see into the room, he saw a tall, thin man with black hair down to his shoulders. He recognized immediately that it was Temp. Temp now as a man.

Temp was a master of deception, who knew when to flatter, when to lie, and when to push. He was doing all three, playing to Theron's ego while simultaneously lying and pushing him to action to create more chaos and bring down the kingdom of Endemar. Luc turned to Isaiah and whispered, "We must get out of this stairway right now. It's obvious that this is the way that man came in here, and he's going to leave the same way, and that could be any minute." Isaiah's heart was racing, and he wanted to explain who the man was, but he didn't have time. He totally agreed with Luc's assessment. They must get out of here right now.

Luc reached into his pouch and whispered, "Be ready to move. I am going to see how Theron likes rats." With that, he took the rat out of his pouch, reached for the door opening, and placed it on the floor of Theron's office. The rat sat there a second and blinked its eyes while it got its bearings now that it was in a well-lit room. It then began moving around and giving a soft squeak. Suddenly, there was a thunderous shout, "Blasted rats," yelled Theron, and he kicked the rat out of the opening and back into the stairway and slammed the bookshelf closed to seal the office. Luc turned to Isaiah and Otto and smiled, "I guess he doesn't like rats, let's go."

They all raced up the stairs and found themselves in a closet on the ramparts. The night air that blew into the closet was refreshing, and Luc looked across the ramparts at the signal tower and said, "That's the one you want, but we have a new problem. There are two guards posted at the only door."

Isaiah looked over the situation and asked, "Can we create a diversion to draw those two guards away from the doors?"

"How about an explosion or fire?" asked Otto.

"That would draw too much attention," stated Luc. "I'll create a diversion; you two, just be ready to move. If I'm not back here, tie this rope around a pillar on the tower and climb down the rope and get away as fast as you can." Luc reached into his pouch and pulled out a rolled-up rope of considerable length and handed it to Isaiah. "What about you?" asked Isaiah.

"Don't worry about me, and besides, someone once told me, doing the right thing sometimes has a high cost." With that, Luc slid out the door and was gone into the darkness.

Isaiah looked at Otto, who intently stared at the door to the tower. A few minutes went by, and they heard a loud noise of clanging like a bucket being kicked across the cobblestone rampart walkway. "Heh, who goes there?" yelled a guard. "Stop or...I said stop," he continued and turned to the other guard and said, "Let's get him, he's getting away." The second guard was somewhat hesitant to leave his post but finally joined in the chase. Isaiah could see Luc running on the ramparts, but he stayed far enough ahead that they could not catch him but still see him. He started to taunt the guards to keep them pursuing him. Isaiah just shook his head in amazement at Luc's brazen boldness.

When the guards left, Otto and Isaiah bolted out of the closet and raced toward the signal tower door.

The signal towers were stone structures located on each corner of the castle that rose high above the ramparts. The fires were lit in large fire pots that sat on stands at the top of the tower. When they got to the signal tower, they opened the door and stepped inside the tower. They were in total darkness except for some light from a full moon that came down the stairway from the above platform.

Otto said, "We must get up to the small closet at the top." Isaiah nodded, and they moved quietly up the winding stairs, being careful not to stumble or make noise. They reached the platform and saw the fire pot in the center of the platform, and over on one side, a small storage closet. The full moon now helped them see quite clearly, but it also made them exposed since they could be seen more readily. They crawled on the floor across the platform to the closet and opened it carefully. Isaiah was thankful that Otto was along because in the dark, he could never have told the difference between the chemicals.

They suddenly heard a voice below, "I need to do my rounds, I'll start with signal tower one," said the sergeant at arms. Isaiah looked at Otto and said, "We must hurry, we are number four!"

Otto reached into the closet and pulled out three clay jars and opened the lids. They were strontium, and he immediately began to empty the chemicals into a burlap bag he had brought with him. He then reached into the backpack he had asked Isaiah to carry and pulled out a bag of copper chloride and refilled each empty jar.

Isaiah said, "Good, let's go," and started to crawl back toward the stairs.

Otto grabbed his arm and whispered, "Not just yet," and proceeded to take his backpack off. He reached inside and took out a smaller bag and started to spread a thin layer of white powder on top of the copper chloride he had just put in the jars.

Isaiah looked at him, perplexed, and asked, "What's that for?"

Otto whispered, "Calcium chloride burns blue but is white in color. We don't want them to be alarmed by the yellow brown color of the copper chloride we just put in the jars. Hopefully, they will just see the white powder and not think a thing about it."

"Makes sense," responded Isaiah, "but why didn't we just bring calcium chloride instead of copper chloride in the first place?"

"Calcium chloride weighs less than copper chloride. Didn't want anybody to notice weight difference," replied Otto again in a whisper.

Isaiah was amazed at Otto's knowledge and attention to detail. They both froze when they heard the door to the tower open below them.

Isaiah said, "Otto, quick, get in the closet!" Otto started to protest but realized there was no other option and squeezed into the very small closet. He turned to motion for Isaiah to join him, but Isaiah looked at him and said, "It won't work for both of us," and closed the door on the closet. The sergeant of arms' steps could be heard coming up the stairs one after another. Isaiah looked around for any possible hiding place and quickly determined there were none. He ran to the edge of the platform and looked over the stone rail. The sergeant's steps were now very close to the top, and he slung his leg over the stone wall, searching for any ledge or foothold.

The sergeant reached the platform and looked around. He was fuming mad that the two guards had left their posts. He stopped and took his time to admire the view and then went back to the stairs and descended and exited through the door. Otto opened the closet door and whispered, "Isaiah, Isaiah." There was no sound. He crept out and continued to call, "Isaiah, Isaiah." Finally, he heard Isaiah say, "I'm up here," and Otto looked up into the rafters of the roof to see Isaiah hugging a beam. Isaiah shinnied back down a stone column and decided there was no going back down the stairs onto the ramparts. He pulled out the rope that Luc had given him and securely tied it around a column as instructed by Luc. Just as they were both about to descend on the rope, they heard a commotion and looked out across the ramparts. Luc was standing on the top of the stone rampart railing and was surrounded by many guards who were all trying to grab him. He taunted them and jumped from side to side to keep them from grabbing him, but suddenly, he lost his balance, and as the guards reached to grab him, he fell backward off the railing and disappeared into the darkness.

Isaiah let out a loud, "No, Luc, no," but Otto grabbed his arm and said, "We must go now, Isaiah, come."

CHAPTER 26

THE BOX

They both climbed down the rope and disappeared into a maze of streets and alleys without saying a word. They finally came to the plaza, and Isaiah broke the silence with tears flowing down his face, "No one could survive that fall. It's my fault, I talked him into it." Otto tried to console him, but Isaiah was distraught and sat on a low wall and just stared at the ground. Otto put his hand on Isaiah's shoulder and softly said, "We still have work to do. We must get back to the house and meet up with the others." They were about to leave the plaza when they heard a voice saying, "Leaving before we find that stupid box?"

Both Isaiah and Otto swung around to find a grinning Luc leaning against a lamp post. They both grabbed him and hugged him with tears of joy. "But how? We saw you, we saw you fall from the ramparts," stammered Isaiah.

Luc smiled and said, "Two ropes, I gave you one and I kept the other." They all started to laugh, and Isaiah turned to Otto and said, "I'll meet you back at the house. I need to help my friend."

Luc led Isaiah down a back alleyway to a plaza a few blocks away and pointed to a well in the middle of the plaza. "I remember seeing some of these buildings as I ran that night, so I wonder if that is the well," said Luc.

"How can we know if it's the right one?"

"Halfway down the well, there is a red 'X' painted on the wall. If we find the "X," then we have the right well and must continue to go down until we find a chamber, a sort of cave that comes off the side before you reach the water."

"Ok," replied Isaiah, "let's walk over and just look in the well."

"It's too far down. One of us will need to be lowered into the well and look for it," replied Luc.

Isaiah began to see why this was a two-man job. He was smaller than Luc, and it would be easier for Luc to lower him on a rope instead of Isaiah trying to raise and lower Luc. They came to the well, and since it was late, there were very few people in the plaza. Luc had his hood over his head so as not to be recognized since he was still a wanted man, though some may have now thought he had died in the fall.

Isaiah looked at Luc and asked, "Can you lower me on the bucket rope?"

Luc nodded affirmatively, and Isaiah climbed up on the edge of the well, put a foot in the bucket, held tightly to the rope, and nodded to Luc, who began to lower him into the dark well. It was very dark, but Luc had handed him a small lantern to light after he went down into the well, and it provided enough light to see the walls. He descended farther and farther but saw no sign of a red "X" on the walls. He was about to signal to come up when he heard voices above. "Hey, boy, get me some water for my horse."

Isaiah looked around and realized he had nowhere to go; he couldn't go up, and he couldn't go down. He saw a small rock ledge jutting out on the wall and decided to try to step onto it. It held his weight, and he found a handhold and took all his weight off the bucket. He knew Luc could feel his weight come off and heard him say loudly, "Uh...sure, officer, just give me a minute." The bucket dropped down into the water, scooped up a bucket full, and was lifted quickly by Luc.

The officer's horse drank the water, and the officer moved on with his patrol, but none of them ever realized that Luc was a wanted man. Isaiah's fingers were very tired from hanging on to the rocks, and as a result, his grip was getting very difficult. He was about to lose his grip when Luc dropped the bucket and whispered, "Get on."

Isaiah returned to the surface and reported there was no sign of an "X" or chamber. Luc sat on the ledge and let out a large sigh, "I was sure this was it."

"Ok, do you remember anything else about that night?"

Luc just shook his head no.

"Did you say there was a large iron gate?

Luc nodded, "Yes, there was."

"Was there anything unique about that gate?"

"Now, that you mention it, there was a sculptured stallion attached to the middle of the gate."

Isaiah spun and looked at him, "A sculptured stallion?" Luc just nodded.

"Come with me. I think we may have just found your well." Isaiah grabbed Luc and dragged him across the plaza and down an alley. They came to a turn, and Isaiah paused, but then went left and went down the dark alley at a trot. He looked both left and right while he talked to himself with Luc trailing behind, "Yes, it was around here. Several days ago, I had a run-in with some of Pilu's men, and then Temp showed up and... then Ohtara was there... and then Temp ran under a gate." Luc trailed behind and tried to follow Isaiah's stream of talk until Isaiah stopped dead in his tracks, pointed, and said, "There's your gate."

They stood in front of a large iron gate with a sculptured stallion on its surface. Luc let out a laugh, "That's it, yes, that's it, and...and the well should be just beyond that gate."

They went through the gate and found a small, isolated plaza with a well on one corner hidden in the shadows. The plaza was very quiet and dimly lit by a few gas-burning street lanterns. No one could be seen on the plaza or connecting streets. A stone bridge crossed over a canal that split the plaza in half. Luc looked it all over and said, "Yes, yes...this has got to be it. Are you willing to go down again?"

Isaiah smiled and climbed up on the well ledge and waited for Luc to position the bucket. He descended with the lamp, and halfway down was a large red "X" painted on the wall. He became very excited and whispered up to Luc, "The X, the X," and descended further until his light illuminated a chamber with a gray weathered box sitting squarely in the middle.

Isaiah grabbed the box and put it inside a burlap bag, and Luc pulled him to the surface. They collapsed under the moonlight in this small plaza, and both laughed quietly. They had finally recovered the infamous "box."

Isaiah turned to Luc and said, "ok, you need to answer some questions. What is this all about?"

Luc took a deep breath and said, "I owe you an answer, so here goes. For the last year, I have run with a street gang that had...shall we say...a dubious reputation. They ran illegal schemes, did petty theft and extortion, and, occasionally, some major thefts for underworld groups. The leader's name was Pilu."

Isaiah's head snapped around and looked directly at Luc, "You worked for Pilu?"

"Yes, I worked for Pilu for a while. I was trying to prove something to my father and myself. You already know my father is a big player in certain worlds, and I was frustrated that he hadn't included me in his organization, so I was out to prove to him that I could handle myself."

"So, you became a thief?" responded Isaiah.

"Well...yes, but I was or am a very good thief. You might say my expertise is as a cat burglar. I am good at breaking in and getting out of places undetected. A few months ago, I was approached by Pilu, who said that a potential client had a need for my special kind of skills. Pilu said it paid extremely well, and I saw it as not only an opportunity to make a lot of money but also to enhance my reputation in certain circles. The job was to break into a vault, steal some sort of box, and deliver it to the client. Sounded simple enough, but then I learned that the location of the vault was in the castle."

"So that's how you knew so much about the secret passage and how to navigate around the castle," chimed in Isaiah.

"Yes, exactly. I cased the place for several months, I learned all about secret passages, made late-night explorations, and learned guard schedules and habits. I found out the exact location of the vault and the type of lock. I even learned how to crack that specific type of lock. I developed a plan to get in, steal the box, and get out without anybody knowing that I had ever been there." Isaiah sat there shaking his head in disbelief as Luc unfolded the story.

"I caught a break when I learned that they were doing some painting in the area outside the vault in preparation for Ascension Day. They had erected scaffolding and had tarps hung to block paint splatter. This activity required the guard's location to be moved around a corner into an adjacent hallway. I noticed that the guards had become increasingly complacent and were more and more lax in their duties. They would be easily distracted and sometimes even wander away for long periods of time. They saw no threat to the vault since they knew it was securely locked. One night, there was a festival in town, and I knew they would be shooting off fireworks that night. It was a perfect distraction for the guards. I entered the castle through the passageways and hid in a closet near the vault until the fireworks started, and then I slid under the tarps that provided a screen from the guard's view. Of course, the guards wandered down the hall to watch the fireworks through a grand window. I had paid the fireworks master shooter to position his fireworks at just the right point that they could be seen from that window."

Isaiah interrupted, "And they left their post just as you expected?"

"Well, yes, exactly as I had planned. I had observed these guards for weeks and seen their tendencies and habits. I was confident they would, so to speak, take the bait. They left their post, and I went to work cracking the vault code while under the tarp. Ten minutes later, I was standing in the vault as the fireworks continued to explode outside. The box was locked in a type of safety deposit box. I found the number I had been given and quickly picked the lock and, just like that, I had the box in my hands."

"So now you had the box, how did you get out of the vault and get away?"

"I quickly left the now unlocked vault and made sure I closed it behind me, taking care to make sure it was locked again. Under the tarp with the box, I could see the guards still distracted by the fireworks as the climax of the show began to explode across the sky with multiple bursts and booms. As I left the area, I saw an empty wooden paint crate and put the box inside to conceal it and put it under my arm. It was a good thing I did, because as I rounded the corner to head to the library and the secret passage, a guard stood right there looking up at the fireworks coming through the window down the hallway."

"What did you do then?"

"Well, I offered him a crate to sit on while he watched the end of the fireworks. I had dressed as a painter, and he simply thought I was a painter working late and finishing up some work."

Isaiah laughed, "And that worked?"

"Absolutely, I just acted like I belonged there and watched the rest of the fireworks with him. We had a nice chat and oohed and awed at the fireworks."

"Did he sit on the crate?"

"No, but I did," replied a chuckling Luc. "After the fireworks, I picked up my box and slipped into the library and got out through the secret passage behind the bookcases."

"Amazing, just amazing," said Isaiah, shaking his head. "But what happened after that?"

"Well...everything went south, so to speak. Two days later, I was supposed to turn over the box to Pilu. I was to meet Pilu and give him the box and be paid, but I didn't trust Pilu to pay up. I had been a part of too many of his schemes and scams to know that he couldn't be trusted. So, I insisted, with much protest from Pilu, to only turn the box over directly to the client. I would only accept direct payment. To say the least, Pilu was outraged but had no other recourse and agreed to do it this way if the client agreed.

Several days later, we were to meet in an old warehouse on the east side of the city, not too far from here. I was to bring the box, and a client would bring the gold he owed me. A simple transaction, however, it all went wrong very quickly. I got to the warehouse hours before we were to meet and found a good hiding place in a loft area and just settled in to see who was coming and going.

After a couple of hours, but well before we were to meet, I heard voices from below. I strained to hear and moved closer until I recognized Pilu's voice talking with someone. They were talking about the box and their plans. The stranger wore a hood over their head and turned to Pilu and said, "After I get the box and leave, you will deal with this thief, correct? No loose ends, he must be eliminated, kill him quickly, and get rid of the body so it will never be found." I was stunned that they intended to kill me, and Pilu was not only in agreement but intended to make sure it happened. The stranger turned, and his hood slid back this time, and I was shocked to see that it was Regent Theron who stood there plotting my assassination."

Isaiah's jaw dropped, and he sat there stunned and stared at Luc as these words sank in.

"My father is a sworn enemy of Regent Theron. They hate each other and have had many run-ins over the years. If my father knew I had helped Theron, I would be disowned, so I decided that there was no way I was ever turning this box over to Theron."

"So...so what do you plan on doing now?" asked Isaiah.

"To be honest, I don't know. I would like to just return it quietly to the castle vault and walk away and forget this ever happened, but that's not going to happen. Maybe I'll just destroy it and move on."

"By the way, do you have any idea what's in the box?"

"Not at all, I have tried to open it over and over, but there are seven unique key locks. As much as I have tried, I have not been able to pick the locks or pry it open. Whatever is in that box is accessible only to the right person or persons with the right keys. That's the story about the box, and it's late, and we both need some rest."

Isaiah let out an exhausted sigh and said, "I need to get back to the house. Do you want to come?"

"No, I have a place I can hide out tonight."

The night air was damp, and there was fog that had settled over the city like a blanket. Visibility in the streets was limited, and nearly everyone was now off the streets except for an occasional tavern goer headed home for the night. Luc and Isaiah headed across the plaza toward a bridge when Isaiah heard the Voice say plainly, "Stop." He reached out and grabbed Luc's arm and said firmly, "Wait."

Luc was surprised and a bit confused as fatigue had begun to take over. He turned to Isaiah and saw concern on his face. "Let's get off the street," said Isaiah as he pulled Luc toward an alley. "I am not sure, but something doesn't feel right, and the Voice just told me to stop."

Luc looked at him, now confused, "What voice? I didn't hear anything."

Isaiah didn't have time for a full explanation of the Voice to Luc but simply said hastily, "The Voice of light and truth, I'll explain later." He pulled Luc back into the shadows and said, "There is danger here, real danger."

Luc looked at him, now bewildered. Isaiah looked up at the building they were hiding next to and said, "Let's try to get in this store."

Luc said, "But it's closed."

"That's never stopped you before."

Luc pulled out some tools, and seconds later, they were kneeling beside a counter inside the store. Isaiah turned to Luc and asked, "What would they do if they thought the box was destroyed.

"I don't know, but they may still hunt me to kill me."

"Perhaps, but what if we made them think the box was destroyed? It could change things, right?"

"Uhm... interesting, yes... it could possibly," replied Luc, and he sprang to his feet and started to look around the shop, which contained farmers' goods, tools, feed, etc. He went through several shelves looking at jars and boxes, and finally stopped and said, "Here it is, this could work." He pulled several jars down and sat on the floor next to the box with Isaiah. He pulled out his knife and pried the lid off one of the jars and then moved on to the lid of the old wooden crate.

For the first time, Isaiah saw the real box. It was mesmerizing. It was painted a deep red with gold hinges and adornments. *It certainly looked like it belonged in the castle, but what was it exactly?* It had seven key locks that held the box securely tight. So tightly constructed that you could not detect a seam of any kind to even try prying it open.

Luc pulled the old, weathered paint box out and handed it to Isaiah to hold, and then opened all the jars and began to pour powder into the old box until it was nearly filled. He carefully replaced the lid by tapping lightly to re-nail the lid. "Put the box in the burlap bag," said Luc as he crawled up to the window.

He looked across the bridge, which was covered in fog, and began to see dark shadows darting about, and then his eyes grew large as he saw a dark hooded form beginning to ascend through the fog onto the bridge.

"Luuuuccccc...," came a gravelly, heavy breathing voice. "I have been looking for you. I want that box."

Isaiah grabbed Luc and spun him around and yelled into his face, "Don't listen, Luc, that is the very Prince of Darkness himself." Luc was now bewildered and confused at what was happening. *Who was this person or entity? How did they know his name? What did it want with the box?* Isaiah shook him again and got his attention and asked, "What was that powder you put in the box?"

Luc stuttered, "Black powder I found in the back," and this seemed to shake him back into reality. He turned to Isaiah and asked, "Do you still have that oil lamp I gave you earlier?" Isaiah nodded affirmatively.

"Come now, Luc, let me see that box. Why don't you join us? We can all look at the box. In fact, we can help you get it back where it belongs," came the voice from the dark, hooded figure.

Luc once again heard the voice of the dark figure on the bridge and was being drawn with every word. Isaiah shook him again and said, "What do you want me to do with the oil?"

Luc snapped out of his daze and quickly said, "Pour it on this strip of cotton cloth." Isaiah started to saturate the cloth with oil while he asked Luc over and over again, "What's next, what's next?"

Wolves now stood beside the hooded figure on the bridge, and Luc couldn't take his eyes off them. The wolves crept further toward the end of the bridge while growling and working themselves into a frenzy. Luc jumped up, threw open the front door, and shouted, "Ok, if you want the box here, it is and threw it onto the bridge, which caused the wolves to jump, but the hooded figure didn't even flinch. Isaiah jumped, too; he didn't know what Luc was doing.

"Good boy, you did the right thing. This will all soon be over," snarled the dark, hooded figure with utter disdain in his voice.

"Oh yeah, you might need this to help open it," and with that, Luc turned and pointed his bow with a burning arrow tip, and he fired a shot that landed squarely in the side of the box and buried the tip deep inside the wood. The flame was burning bright, and the box started to catch on fire. The wolves began to poke around the box when suddenly an explosion occurred, and wolves and parts of wolves flew everywhere.

Luc turned to Isaiah and smiled, "That's going to hurt in the morning."

Dead wolves were everywhere, scattered on the bridge and in front of the store, but then Luc looked up and saw the dark, hooded form unscathed and still standing in the middle of the bridge.

"You thought that could hurt me. You are so naïve...boy. You have no idea what you are dealing with or who you're dealing with. You are a fool. I give you one more chance. Join me or die. Now or never, Luc. Now...or...Never!"

Luc stood in the doorway and stared at the dark figure. He realized the explosion had no effect. Fear began to grip him. He had nothing else to do, no more tricks, no more deceptions. He felt powerless, and the hooded figure had come across the bridge and was headed directly toward him. The dark prince was within twenty feet when he heard a blood-curdling scream. "Noooooo, you will not have him," and from his right, someone wielding a sword jumped at the hooded figure and hit it in the side with their shoulder. The individual bounced off the dark prince and spun away but took a sweeping swing with their sword that just missed the figure. The dark figure, who was truly irritated, turned on the individual and said in a loud voice, "Pierre, you have no power here, leave us," and with a motion of its left arm, launched the man across the cobblestone plaza into a wall, where he crumpled in a heap.

Luc heard the name Pierre and jerked his head to see his father, Pierre Dubois, lying in a heap against the wall. Luc wanted to fight back as the hooded figure turned its attention back to him, but he had nothing. He closed his eyes and waited for a final blow from the hooded figure. He began to tremble and shake all over when suddenly he felt a presence, a calmness. He opened his eyes, and a hand came to his chest, and a calm voice said, "Step back, Luc, you are not alone, I am here."

Isaiah stepped in front of Luc with steely eyes focused directly on the hooded figure. Isaiah began to speak with authority and purpose, "You have no power here." He began walking directly at the hooded figure, and it seemed like each word got louder and stronger with every step.

"You will leave this place right now." As he said this, he pulled open his long coat, exposing the Sword of Integrity, which was feeling warm and getting hotter with each step. He took the hilt in his hand and gripped it tightly, and he felt power surge through him. He took more steps toward the hooded figure, and it retreated and became less adamant and threatening with every step Isaiah took.

He continued to move forward, and Luc's eyes were now wide open, and his jaw dropped as he witnessed the scene. "You will return to the pit of darkness that you crawled out of this night," demanded Isaiah.

"I am a Journeyman, who is a servant of the Prince of Light, and you will not pass!" Isaiah felt strength, faith, and courage surge through his being.

"Leave us, Journeyman. This is not your matter. This has nothing to do with you. Leave us now," screamed the dark hooded form.

Isaiah just kept advancing with the sword now out of the sheath and glowing. The hooded figure was now distraught and shrieked, "Go away, leave me alone." It spun around and was now stumbling backward with every step Isaiah took.

Just then, he heard a horse whinnying, a loud, almost threatening whinny, and he knew who it was, the rider of a white stallion. He continued to move forward, and Ohtara rode up hard and swung off Aranco while she pulled out both swords in the same motion and now stood beside Isaiah.

The dark hooded figure gave out a blood-curdling scream of pain when he saw Ohtara at the side of Isaiah. It went into complete spasms, spinning and grabbing its head while stumbling backwards.

"You ok?" Ohtara asked.

"I think I got it," and he smiled, "but it's still so good to see you."

The hooded figure was now on the other side of the bridge and soon completely disappeared into the fog, which itself completely lifted a few seconds later.

"Let's get out of here. Where did your friend go?" asked Ohtara, and they both looked around but didn't see Luc anywhere. They also noticed that his father, Pierre, was gone. Both gone along with the box, the real box.

CHAPTER 27

SENATE CHAOS

Isaiah grabbed a couple of hours' sleep and awoke early to make sure he got to the castle in time for the Ascension Day events. As he came down the stairs and walked into the breakfast room. Ohtara smiled and said, "Good morning, it was a short night," to which Isaiah just smiled back and nodded in agreement. "Oh, a friend of yours stopped by to see you. He's on the veranda."

"Really, it must be Luc," and Isaiah turned and headed toward the veranda door. He opened it and started to say, "Good morning..." but before he could finish, he heard another familiar voice.

"So, what did we learn last night?"

Standing with his back to him, viewing the magnificent orchards, he recognized the long black coat flowing in the breeze with the gray shoulder-length hair.

"Iswa," screamed Isaiah as he ran and threw his arms around him. They both began to laugh.

"And how is my young Journeyman today?"

"Very well now, yes very well. Did you come for Ascension Day?"

"Of course, wouldn't miss it. I have looked forward to it for years, as have they," and he gestured to his right behind Isaiah, who turned and found Hon, Esty, and Riddle all standing there smiling.

The reunion continued with hugs, and Isaiah tried to fill them in on his adventures, but Ohtara walked in and said, "It is time to go," and the mood became very serious.

As they all headed out the door, Iswa declared, "Just a bit more work to do."

* * *

At nine o'clock, the entire senate was present in the Grand Hall, and the public had filled the seating in the balcony. Those without a seat stood against the back walls of the balcony and the main floor. The proceedings began with a trumpeter fanfare as Regent Theron entered the room with a strong, determined look on his face, while the senators all took their places around the large oval table. Otto and Isaiah had arrived early and had gotten seats that would allow them to clearly see Erestor as well as Theron. Iswa had decided to stay on the main floor and stood in the back against the wall while Ohtara was somewhere else on the main floor; Isaiah could not see her. As for Hon, Esty, and Riddle, they were on the balcony with Otto and Isaiah.

Theron called the senate to order and started to speak, "Before we get on with the business of the day, I have an important piece of business I must relay to the senate. Last night, after midnight, a large frigate entered the bay of Gebil and anchored off the shore of Gebil. So far, we have no indication of its intentions toward us, but it is the largest such ship we have ever seen in these waters. It's over three hundred feet in length and approximately seven hundred tons with over fifty cannons. There was a notable gasp in the room as members of the public and the Senate reacted in shock.

Erestor stared straight ahead and watched how his fellow senators reacted. He noted which ones were shocked and which ones were not. A senator stood to his feet and said, "We must immediately suspend all our plans for today to deal with this threat!" Voices of support rang out, "Here, here." Another senator jumped to his feet and said, "How do we know if they are a threat at all? Perhaps we are being presumptuous." With this statement, there were also voices of support from senators.

Erestor looked at Theron, who stood behind the podium, smirking at the panic. Theron had played one of his last cards in the deck. He was now using the very presence of the frigate for intimidation to stop Ascension Day.

As a senior senator, Erestor had great influence, and he raised his hand to be recognized. He stood and began to speak, "My fellow senators and citizens of Endemar, we have reached a crucial day in Endemar's history and future. Nearly eighteen years ago, King Aran went home to his final rest, and in preparation during his last days, he established this day as Ascension Day. The very day his successor would be named and take their position as our ruling monarch. Much discussion and debate have taken place regarding this day, and much effort has been made to delay it. Now, we have a strange frigate show up in our harbor, and are we actually willing to undo months of discussion, debate, and decisions? Yes, we need to ask, whose ship is this and what is their intent, but not at the cost of seating our new king or queen." Several senators shouted "Here, Here," in support of his comments.

Erestor continued, "Perhaps that is the entire purpose of this ship. To delay our seating a new leader to rule. But that question would be better placed with Regent Theron, since I have it on good authority that he funded the building of this ship!" At these words, the senate floor erupted in chaos with shouts of "outrageous," and "nonsense." Theron scowled and leered at Erestor with absolute contempt. Theron finally used his gavel to restore order so Erestor could continue speaking.

Erestor went on, "I believe an audit of our treasury will find a substantial amount of funds missing. However, if you go to the far north shore, you will find the builders of this ship who now possess a large sum of our money!" Theron repeatedly pounded his gavel to stop Erestor and bring order to the senate floor, but this statement set off a brand-new chorus of shouting by senators, both supportive and outraged by Erestor's accusations.

Theron's face was blood red as he tried to control his own anger. Erestor was deliberately poking the bear, so to speak, to get a reaction. He wanted to push Theron to the edge. Get the cool long-term politician to make a mistake. Theron finally restored order.

Theron quickly covered his noticeable outrage and looked at Erestor and said with a smirk and wink to the other senators, "My dear senator, these are quite outrageous accusations, but what, if any evidence, do you have to support your wild claims, or are you simply so desperate that you have fabricated all this in your head."

Theron stared at Erestor, and for what seemed like minutes, their eyes were locked on one another. Theron had basically called Erestor's bluff. He had said, "Prove it or shut up." Failure to produce concrete evidence of his claims would destroy Erestor's credibility and most likely swing the upcoming vote on delaying Ascension Day in Theron's favor.

Erestor said a quiet prayer, "Please help me." Theron's call for evidence was exactly what Erestor wanted. The rules of the Senate dictated that you were not allowed to bring any other person to the floor during open senator debate unless the chair called for it. Erestor now saw an open door with Theron's call to produce evidence. Erestor now completely rolled the dice. He did not know if his evidence was even there, but now he had to produce, or all would be lost. Erestor turned to face the audience and looked intently for some sign of hope that his evidence had appeared. His heart sank as he saw no sign that his evidence was present and began to stall for time.

"Perhaps a recess for us to gather our composure would be good for everyone," suggested Erestor.

Theron sensed a weakness and seized upon it and moved in for the kill. "I think not, our composure is just fine. Produce your evidence, man, or sit down," he said emphatically.

Erestor responded, "I request a recess, so I can confer with my colleagues."

"Denied," yelled Theron, "produce now or sit down and shut up, senator."

Erestor looked around desperately but saw no sign of the evidence that he had hoped to find. He started to sit down when a voice came from the back wall under the balcony. "I am here," followed by the sound of footsteps moving toward the center of the room. The crowd under the balcony parted, and a distinguished, well-dressed man with graying hair stepped forward into the light. He wore a sling to support his right arm. Erestor's face lit up with a big smile, and he turned to face Theron and said, "I present my evidence, Monsieur Dubois."

The senators and crowd erupted with gasps and murmurs as Dubois walked forward. Monsieur Dubois' reputation was well-known, but he had rarely ever been seen in public. He was considered a very dangerous man that you never wanted to cross.

Theron's expression changed from arrogance to shock and, for the first time, a hint of fear. He immediately gaveled the senate back to order and said, "This is out of order; no speakers other than senators are allowed on the floor during open debate."

Erestor quickly came back, "Point of order, Regent Theron, you requested that I present evidence. I present Monsieur Pierre Dubois, your evidence." Theron plopped down in his chair, clearly irritated.

Monsieur Dubois came forward and sat in a chair in the center of the circle created by the enormous round senator's table. Theron suddenly did not look so well. His face became pale, and his hands began to tremble. He looked around nervously, trying to gauge the reaction of the senators. They all looked intently at Dubois, anxious to hear what this man, an enigma, had to say.

Erestor asked Dubois to state his name and business and then asked him to share what he knew about the ship in the harbor and certain business dealings involving Regent Theron.

Monsieur Dubois began to slowly speak, "I am here today to set the record straight regarding the large frigate currently in the harbor and the events surrounding its construction, as well as the chaos created recently by wolves and mercenaries."

The senators and audience all leaned forward to hear every word from this mysterious man. He continued, "Two years ago, Regent Theron approached one of my agents about building a very large ship and equipping it with cannons. At the time, we thought this was a job commissioned by the senate to provide protection for Endemar. However, we were wrong. Theron had demanded absolute secrecy regarding the ship's construction. He said that any failure to keep it a secret would result in swift and immediate death. As construction neared its completion, we began to see wolves and mercenaries coming to the ship and loading it with weapons and supplies. Theron even visited on one occasion to inspect the ship."

Theron jumped to his feet bellowing, "Liar, I have never been on board that ship."

Erestor held his hand up to silence Theron and said, "Please continue, Monsieur Dubois."

Dubois continued, "The mercenaries and wolves were part of an army assembled for one purpose...invasion. While the ship was being finished, there was a constant stream of smaller boats that left with wolves and mercenaries weekly. They came back empty, so I had my people investigate, and we found that the boats always unloaded on the shores of Endemar forest.

"So, what does this have to do with me?" shouted Theron.

"I had my men follow your agents, and they all came back to this very castle time and time again and met with you directly in the middle of the night. We also followed bags of gold that were used to pay for supplies and cannons. Gold that had come from the Endemar Treasury."

He then looked directly at Theron and said, "Regent Theron and I have been, shall we say, business rivals for a number of years. We have had numerous conflicts and disagreements, but this ship and the use of wolves and mercenaries reached an entirely new level and went to a place I choose not to go."

For the next forty-five minutes, Dubois shared additional facts and details about Theron's business dealings, corruption, and intimidation, along with additional information on the ship construction project and the stealing of Endemar funds. Theron continued to interrupt numerous times by shouting liar, nonsense, and complete fabrication. The senators sat and listened attentively until finally he finished.

Erestor looked at Monsieur Dubois and said, "I have one final question. Why did you come forward now?"

There was a long pause, and then Dubois spoke, "Recently, I met a young man, a Journeyman in fact, who reminded me of something that I had forgotten a long time ago. He reminded me that knowing the right thing to do and doing it is important, even if it comes with a high cost."

There was dead silence in the room, and finally Regent Theron spoke, "Well, thank you for your entertaining story of utter fiction, Monsieur Dubois. You may step down, and as you do, I would like to remind all of the senators regarding Monsieur Dubois's dubious reputation." He chuckled and continued, "Of course, nothing he says can be considered credible. Why, in fact, we should have him arrested right here and now!"

"Yes, we should do that. Guards, arrest that man."

The Grand Hall was dead silent, and no one moved, including the guards. Monsieur Dubois stood up from his chair and stared directly at Theron as the words came out of Theron's mouth. If looks could kill, Theron would have been dead on the spot. Dubois turned around and walked toward the exit. The crowd parted in complete silence, and he walked out of the Great Hall. Standing outside the door, looking straight at Monsieur Dubois was Iswa. Dubois approached him, and their eyes caught each other, and they both hesitated. Nothing was said initially, but they just stood there a minute and looked at each other, then Dubois continued to his carriage, and as he passed, Iswa said, "Well done, yes, well done...Journeyman."

Before Erestor or Theron could say another word, a senator leaped to his feet and proposed a special counsel be assigned to investigate these allegations. Another senator seconded the motion, and a third called for discussion and a vote. No one dared dispute the proposal, as an investigation was the logical and appropriate move for such allegations. The vote passed unanimously with all fifty votes.

After the vote, there was a lull in the room as senators let the events of the last hour and a half sink in. Theron sat in his chair, stunned, and suddenly was very alone and exposed as senators and people in the gallery looked on at him through new eyes. His options were about to run out, and Dark Storm looked like his only option left.

Finally, Erestor stood up and called for the vote on suspending Ascension Day. The clerk read the name of every senator, and they verbally gave their vote, "yeah" if they supported the delay and "nay," if they rejected the delay. As the clerk started to call the names, each senator responded one by one. He quickly began to realize that the vote would reject the delay. As each vote was read, Erestor got a bigger and bigger smile on his face. He looked at Ohtara, who stood on the floor against the wall, and then up in the gallery to Otto and Isaiah. When the vote was complete, it was unanimous: Ascension Day would proceed.

Erestor whispered, "Praise God."

CHAPTER 28

ASCENSION DAY

Isaiah and Otto had watched the events of the last two hours unfold in front of them and were totally amazed. It was now eleven in the morning, and by decree, the official Ascension Day process would begin at precisely noon. The senators adjourned for a much-needed break, and Erestor, Ohtara, Iswa, Otto, and Isaiah all gathered in Erestor's office during the break to regroup. Erestor's first words were, "Hallelujah, but we still have more work to do." We must keep track of Theron at all times. I have assigned several of my people to closely monitor his every movement and report anything unusual to me immediately. Otto and Isaiah stay in a place where I can see you, so if we need to react, you can be ready. Erestor and Iswa both looked at Ohtara and smiled, and Erestor said, "Today is the day."

Erestor headed out of the room to get something, and Isaiah turned to Otto and asked, "What happens now? What is the Ascension Day process?"

"Patience, Isaiah. You will see in short order," replied Otto, and with that, Erestor returned to the room carrying an ornate red and gold box that was approximately eighteen inches by twelve inches by five inches deep. Everyone looked at Erestor and smiled, and he left the office carefully, carrying the box in front of him. Isaiah, though, was stunned. He recognized the box. The previous night, he had actually held one of these in his lap in a plaza not far from here. Isaiah then noticed a group of guards waiting at the door that immediately escorted Erestor away from them to some unknown location.

Both Otto and Isaiah had returned to their seats to be able to see the events of Ascension Day unfold when Isaiah turned to Otto and blurted out, "We may have a problem." Otto looked at him quizzically and said, "What do you mean?" Isaiah looked at Otto and said, "Believe it or not, but last night I sat in a plaza with one of those boxes in my lap."

Otto's eyes grew wide under his wire-rimmed glasses, and all he could say was, "Oh my."

Suddenly, there was commotion at the back of the Great Hall. Isaiah and Otto leaned forward to see what was happening, but all they could see was a senator with his arms moving frantically about and guards running everywhere. Something was terribly wrong, and Isaiah had a good idea what had caused the commotion upon unlocking the vault and the safety deposit box for this senator's box. They found no box.

A senate page raced to the front where Regent Theron stood and whispered into his ear. Isaiah could see a small smirk appear on Theron's face, but he controlled it enough not to be too obvious. Otto and Isaiah looked at each other and realized that Theron still had a few cards up his sleeve. He was truly the master of plans and backup plans.

Regent Theron began to speak, "Ah, ahem, excuse me, senators, but we have a situation." All of the senators turned to look at Theron. "It appears that one of the boxes has come up missing." There was a gasp among the senators who began to look around and mumble to one another. "I suggest we take a one-hour delay to resolve this problem. Do we have agreement?" All agreed, and they adjourned to caucus and discuss the events. Few noticed that as Theron turned to sit down, a grin came across his face. He knew that the box would never be found since it had been reported to him that it had been blown up in the plaza the night before.

Isaiah turned to Otto and said, "We must find Luc, right now!" Otto and Isaiah ran out of the Great Hall, which was now in hysteria as word spread not only through the crowd but out into the large plaza filled with people. Isaiah and Otto split up but agreed to meet back in an hour with or without Luc to coordinate efforts.

Isaiah knew the last time he saw Luc was in the small plaza, but he had disappeared along with his father. *Was he still with him? Where had Monsieur Dubois gone?* He ran to the large gates that led out of the castle area and caught a glimpse of Dubois' carriage moving through the streets. He ran as fast as he could and weaved through streets with vendors and crowds. He came to an alley and decided to try to cut off the carriage by taking a shortcut. As he ran down the alley, some of Pilu's gang unexpectedly stepped out of the shadows and started to yell at him and then tried to block his path. In one motion, Isaiah slid to a knee, avoided a wild punch thrown at him, and took out the attacker's legs. He kept running, and another thug came at him from the left, swinging a club. Isaiah rolled on the ground and sprang to his feet with his sword pulled out, and the club was severed in the hands of the stunned would-be attacker. Isaiah then spun and punched a third attacker, which sent him sprawling into crates as he continued running out of the alley, right as the carriage was coming down the street. He yelled, "Whoa, whoa!" to stop the carriage.

Isaiah stood in front of the carriage, nearly out of breath, and the carriage guards started to come at him, but a voice from inside the carriage called out, "Let him be, let him come." It was the voice of Monsieur Dubois.

Isaiah climbed into the carriage and quickly explained to Monsieur Dubois the situation and asked if he had any idea where Luc might be. Dubois leaned back, "Yes, possibly I do. He pulled me out of that plaza last night but then left me when my people showed up. Said he needed to get away and think." He called up to the driver with new instructions, and the carriage lurched ahead, moving as fast as possible through the crowded streets.

They arrived at a familiar street on the east side of Endemar. Monsieur Dubois stopped the carriage and said, "I think you may find him here; he goes here when he is confused or needs to talk."

Isaiah was surprised. It was the same house that they had used to sneak into the castle. "Knock on that door and when an old woman answers, tell her you're here to see her grandson, Jean Luc." Isaiah's eyes got wide upon hearing this revelation, and he jumped down from the carriage and did just as Dubois had instructed. He was seated at the table in the small room when Luc came down the stairs.

He embraced Luc and asked, "Do you still have the box...the real box?"

Luc looked at Isaiah and didn't answer. He just stared for what seemed like minutes. Isaiah asked, "Are you ok?"

"Yes...I guess," responded a hesitant Luc, "but who are you? I cannot explain what took place last night. I have never experienced anything like that in my life. I was powerless in front of that thing, but you stood up to it, and it actually fled screaming. I repeat... who are you?"

Isaiah smiled and said calmly, "I am a Journeyman, called by the Great Prince of Light through the Voice to save the Kingdom of Endemar...and also...you."

He continued, "I know this is all new to you, but believe me when I tell you that there is much to learn, and I will help you, but can we return the box right now?"

"Isaiah, I am scared, I mean, really scared. My world has been turned upside down. My father went to the castle today and exposed himself and his entire organization in front of the whole senate. When I challenged him on why he was helping anyone, he said, knowing the right thing to do and doing it sometimes has a cost. You know what else he told me.... he mumbled something about finally completing a mission he started many years ago. None of it makes sense," cried Luc.

Isaiah smiled and said, "It will, but let's start by saving the Kingdom of Endemar."

"If I come waltzing in with that red box, they're going to lock me up and throw away the key, or worse."

"That could happen, but ask yourself this: is it the right thing to do? If you answer yes, then the next step is to do it despite the cost. Your father made that choice earlier today. Let's go." Isaiah held out his hand, and Luc hesitated, but then took it as Isaiah pulled him out of his chair, and they left the house and climbed into the carriage.

As the carriage raced up to the large gates in front of the castle, Monsieur Dubois urged them to hurry, for the hour was just about up. Luc and Isaiah fought their way to the doors of the Great Hall, and guards were not letting anyone else inside, but then he saw Iswa open the door and speak to a guard who waved them both inside.

People were packed once again into the Great Hall, and the atmosphere was filled with both tension and anticipation. Regent Theron called the session to order and asked if the box had been found. A sweating, upset senator who was responsible for the box began to stammer that, "No, they had not retrieved the box."

"Very well, then these proceedings are...," and just as he lifted the gavel to end the session and Ascension Day, a voice from the back called out, "Wait, wait."

The crowd parted, and this tall sixteen-year-old boy with brown hair and dark eyes walked forward with a burlap bag clutched to his chest. He walked cautiously and tenuously forward. "Who are you? Speak up! How dare you interrupt these proceedings?" demanded Theron.

"My, my name is Luc, and I believe I have something that belongs to you...or I mean the castle...or senate...or whoever." He was clearly intimidated by the thousands of eyes staring at him, and especially Regent Theron, who stood at the other end of the table, glaring at him. The very man whom he had heard days before plotting his assassination. Isaiah suddenly appeared at his side and whispered, "Go ahead, show them. It'll be all right. It's the right thing to do."

Upon seeing Isaiah, the look on Theron's face suddenly changed. A look of contempt and rage came in his eyes, and a snarl appeared on his face. "Guards get these two out of here before they waste any more of our time," demanded Theron.

The guards moved forward, and Luc looked around and reached into the burlap bag and pulled out the red and gold adorned box with the seven key holes and held it above his head.

"I believe this may be yours."

The crowd erupted in shouts and gasps as the guards grabbed the box and Luc and Isaiah, but they truly were more interested in the box than either Luc or Isaiah. The guards confirmed the authenticity of the box, and the senator announced that all boxes were present, and Ascension Day could proceed.

Theron slumped down in his seat, and the trumpeters played a fanfare that announced the beginning of Ascension Day activities. The senators paraded in together to the fanfare and stood behind their chairs at the round table. Isaiah noticed six other senators also carrying boxes like the one Erestor carried. They proceeded to their chairs, placed their boxes on the table in front of them, and continued to stand with the rest of the senators. Isaiah was amazed at the formal nature of every movement. Every action was done with precision and exactness.

Regent Theron, who was still fuming, called the session to order and turned to the senate secretary, who stood and read aloud a proclamation. The proclamation had been written eighteen years ago by King Aran and established this day in the future as Ascension Day for his throne. No one was to assume the throne before this date, and a Regent would act as chosen by the senate until this date.

Isaiah leaned over to Otto and asked, "Why did the king choose this date?"

Otto smiled and said, "It's simple. On this day, his heir becomes eighteen years old and has reached the age required to ascend to the throne."

"But who is the heir?" asked Isaiah.

Otto smiled again and said, "Ah… that is the question everyone is asking and the great mystery of Endemar."

Isaiah looked at him quizzically, "Nobody knows who the heir is?" he asked in an astonished voice.

Otto calmly looked at him and said, "That's right … almost."

The secretary continued to read the proclamation, which described the extensive process put in place to keep the heir's identity hidden to this day. It also described the process for revealing the heir to the throne, which created a complex maze of checks and balances to protect the heir's identity until this moment.

Isaiah turned to Otto and asked the obvious question, "Why was the king so secretive in revealing his heir?"

Otto replied, "The king and queen were deeply in love and had but one child because sadly the queen died in childbirth. The king was also gravely ill at the time of the baby's birth and knew he had little time left on this earth. The king knew that his child would be easy prey for his enemies, so he kept its identity secret and protected it from his enemies. He arranged for the child to be hidden and raised until they reached eighteen years old and could assume his throne. That brings us to this day.

The secretary completed the proclamation and sat down, followed by the senators. Theron's role was very scripted by protocol, so he simply was required to follow each step of the process, whether he liked it or not. He looked totally miserable. He stood and went into the center of the circle.

He stood in the center and said, "Let us begin the process of Ascension for the new monarch of Endemar."

The senators responded in unison, "So be it."

Theron reached down to the Endemar coat of arms inlayed in tile in the center of the Great Hall's floor and turned a knob to the right and then another to the left. Finally, he placed his hand on a specific tile and pushed. There was a rush of air as if pressure was released, and the floor began to move. From the center of the floor, a cylindrical column rose out of the floor and began to transform in front of everyone. It rose to a height of about four feet and stopped. The entire gallery was completely silent and mesmerized by what they were seeing.

Theron spoke again and said, "Let us unlock the boxes so the secret may be revealed."

The senators responded in unison, "So be it."

Each senator, who had carried an ornate box into the hall, stood and carried their box to the center and placed it on a ledge just below the top of the column.

Isaiah whispered to Otto, "I see that Erestor and only six other senators have the boxes. What is that all about?"

Otto explained, "The seven most senior senators were tasked with being the keepers of the boxes. They were to guard them with their lives and keep them hidden and sealed away until this day. This is the first time they have been seen in public in eighteen years."

Theron once again directed the next step of the process and said, "Let us all unlock the secret."

The senators responded in unison, "So be it."

Each box had been locked with seven locks, each of which had to be unlocked to open the box.

Otto leaned over to Isaiah and whispered, "Each senator was given a key when they became a senator and told to guard it with their life. Today they get the opportunity to use that key."

One by one, each senator pulled out their key and went forward to a box and tried to unlock it. If their key worked, they returned to their seat. If it did not work, they moved on to another box until their key worked.

Otto continued, "No senator ever knew which box his key worked on or who else held keys to the same box. This provided a very secure system."

Isaiah simply nodded and continued to be enthralled by the entire process.

After a considerable time, forty-nine of the fifty senators had gone forward and found the lock that fit their key. All seven boxes were unlocked. One final senator with a key walked up to the column and inserted his key in the lock mechanism and turned the key. The entire top of the column began to glow, and the top transformed with tiles moving, changing, and disappearing until an indented pattern approximately two inches deep appeared across the top of the column.

Theron declared, "Now let us open the boxes and put the pieces all together."

The senators responded in unison, "So be it."

The original seven senators all stepped up to the column and opened their boxes. Isaiah leaned forward to see what was in the boxes. It looked like pieces of various colored tiles, all in various shapes and dimensions. As he looked closer, he noticed that each box had seven pieces.

Otto whispered, "They now must put the pieces together."

Isaiah responded, "Like a puzzle?"

Otto smiled and said, "Yes, I guess you could say like a puzzle, a very important puzzle. This represents that the senators have the responsibility to pull the seven regions of Endemar together to be ruled by one monarch."

After several minutes, the senators all stepped back from the column. The pieces were all perfectly in place and fit exactly within the indented space on the top of the column. There was one small empty space in the exact center. There was complete silence in the room. Isaiah and the entire gallery held their breath. No one in the Great Hall moved or made a sound.

Finally, after a long pause, Theron stood and said, "There is but one piece still needed. Let the true heir to the throne of Aran come forth with the final piece to fulfil their destiny! No one moved, and there was a small hint of a smile that started to appear on Theron's face. Had he been so fortunate that no heir would come forward, and he would simply remain as Regent of Endemar.

Several seconds turned into a long minute and then two when suddenly there was movement in the crowd under the balcony. A murmur among people in the gallery began to grow as the crowd began to part like the Red Sea. Finally, the crowd parted, and all the senators and gallery turned and cast their eyes on the parted crowd. From the crowd stepped Ohtara.

Isaiah grabbed Otto's arm and gasped, and then looked at Otto, who simply smiled. Isaiah immediately noticed that he was not surprised and then thought to himself, "Of course not, he's Otto!"

Ohtara walked forward to the column and glanced at Erestor, who simply smiled and nodded. She stepped up to the column with the tiles set within the indented forms and reached behind her neck and undid the clasp on a necklace she had worn her entire life. Hanging from the necklace was a dark blue gem. She paused and looked at it carefully and then stepped closer to the column and placed the gem into the center space and said softly, "Thank you, Daddy."

The gem fit perfectly into the open space, and suddenly light began to come directly through the gem and project a star pattern throughout the Great Hall. The crowd and even senators gasped. The column began to transform once again, with several drawers spiraling out of the column.

The first drawer had a parchment document inside, and the senate secretary came over and removed it and began to read it aloud. "I, King Aran, do declare on this day that my daughter, Princess Ohtara, is to become Queen of Endemar and assume all the responsibilities and privileges of serving the people of Endemar. Let God bless her as Queen, and may she always let the Lord God in heaven give her wisdom and direction to lead the good people of Endemar. May she constantly strive to hear the Voice and live a life of integrity before all citizens, whether human or animal."

"Long live the Queen," shouted the Secretary, and the crowd erupted in cheers and applause.

Isaiah and Otto both applauded and cheered wildly.

The other drawers in the column contained a royal scepter, a royal blue robe, a copy of the Good Book, and the crown, all in separate drawers but all now open. All the senators immediately bowed to Ohtara, and she replied with a nod. The bells in the bell tower at the Great Hall began to ring out, and the pipe organ began to play a resounding celebration.

Erestor stepped forward with a huge smile on his face, bowed, and said, "This way, your majesty." Ohtara couldn't help but laugh at the sudden formality from Erestor.

Ohtara was ushered to the throne, and she ascended the steps slowly, turned, and took a seat on the throne. The crowd erupted again in applause, and the trumpeters began a fanfare of celebration and announcement that the Queen was on the throne.

At this very moment, Theron's rule as Regent ended. He was now completely irrelevant and powerless. For eighteen years, he had ruled in absentia of a monarch, and now he had no power whatsoever. Theron looked on, seething, and he whispered under his breath, "Replaced by a gardener, what an insult." All the senators lined up and went before Ohtara and introduced themselves and pledged their loyalty as was protocol, but there was a genuine excitement in the air, an anticipation that a new era had arrived for Endemar. The bells continued to chime above the city, and crowds that were packed in the streets began to cheer wildly as word passed quickly that Queen Ohtara had ascended the throne. The formal coronation would come days later, but as of this moment, Endemar had a queen, Queen Ohtara.

Isaiah exhaustedly looked at Otto and just laughed. He finally sat down and said to Otto, "I think you have much to tell me."

Erestor looked up at Otto and Isaiah and nodded for them to join him in his office. Erestor walked through his office door to a waiting Iswa, Otto, and Isaiah, who were all beaming. They embraced, and Erestor looked at the small band and said, "We still have much work to do, or this could be the shortest reign in history. Theron is more dangerous right now than ever, and we must keep track of him at all times. Dubois' people are working on securing the harbor, but they're not quite done yet, so we must keep Theron from giving any kind of signal to attack. I have people tracking him everywhere, and they will keep us informed of his every move."

CHAPTER 29

NOT BLUFFING

The rest of the afternoon was a blur as Ohtara appeared on the balcony of the Great Hall and waved to the huge crowds in the streets below. She knew that today was simply a beginning and there would be much hard work ahead. There would be days of joy and grief, but she also knew that she had been prepared for this day and what lay ahead. She thought of her father's love and his close friends, Erestor and Otto, who had hidden her and arranged for her protection and upbringing to prepare her for this day. It was all so amazing, but she realized there was still an imminent threat that could bring it all down, and she must be shrewd; she must think and act as a Queen.

As the day passed into evening, there was a great gala celebration at the castle in honor of the new Queen. Ohtara dressed and prepared for this with the help of many handmaidens who seemed to simply appear out of nowhere. She was dressed in a very regal blue gown with a diamond-filled crown that looked stunning and regal. Ohtara was the focus of a formal receiving line in which each senator or dignitary and their spouse would be formally announced to the queen, and then they would proceed to her with the men bowing and the women curtsying. Her education over the last eighteen years had been complete, and she was well prepared with the graciousness and proper etiquette for such an occasion. Her mentors had prepared her well.

As the receiving line proceeded, she looked around and noticed that Regent Theron was nowhere to be found. She caught Erestor's eye, and he also seemed concerned and on guard. Theron had been under surveillance the entire afternoon, but from all reports, had not left his office. He had chosen to be holed up in his office with a few remaining confidants.

Iswa, Otto, and Isaiah were at the event but not in formal attire. Instead, they watched from the shadows of the balconies. They kept their eyes open for anyone or anything that looked like a potential threat, which included Theron himself. The dinner and celebration proceeded with no disruptions, but the clock was closely approaching nine o'clock and the formal lighting of the signal towers.

Around eight thirty, Erestor looked up at Otto and Isaiah, very concerned. He signaled for them to meet him in a back hallway.

Erestor pulled them aside in the hallway and said, "Something just does not seem right with Theron hidden in his office all this time, and the fact that he has not shown himself even once. His ego and arrogance simply will not allow that. I need you to go to his office and make sure he is still there."

Otto and Isaiah sped off and practically ran toward Theron's office. When they arrived, there were two of Erestor's people outside Theron's office, and they quickly conferred with them, and they assured Otto and Isaiah that no one had come out the door all afternoon.

Otto paced back and forth, considering their options, and then uncharacteristically turned and kicked the office door with such ferocity that it flew open. He turned to Isaiah and said, "Oh look, Theron's office door is open, let's go check it out." Isaiah, Otto, and the two staff members ran into the inner office and found it completely empty.

"Nobody is here. Where are they?" asked Isaiah.

Isaiah turned to Otto, and they both said together, "Of course, the bookcase." They went to the case and pulled it open to the secret passageway. Otto looked at Isaiah and said, "You go up and I will go down, but we must be on that roof by nine o'clock, not a minute later."

Otto took off down the stairs, and Isaiah raced up the stairs and prayed that they were not too late. The stairs led to the top of the ramparts and the cool night air. Isaiah found himself staring down at a celebrating city where bonfires burned, and people filled the streets dancing and singing in celebration of Queen Ohtara. He looked toward the bay and could see the large frigate with its anchor dropped right in the middle of the bay in an almost defiant position that dared anyone to challenge her. As he looked more carefully, he could see a lot of activity on the decks. People were scrambling around, and small boats were being lowered into the water. It was obvious that they were planning to land troops as soon as they received the signal from Theron. He also noticed one other thing: fifty to sixty small boats were out in the harbor with partiers celebrating and partying. These boats were scattered but surrounded the frigate. He wondered if they were celebrating or simply wanted to get a closer look at the frigate.

The clock was now five minutes to nine, and Isaiah ran toward the fourth signal tower to see if Theron was there, but he was nowhere to be found. As he got closer to the tower, he noticed the door to the tower was open, and he ran inside. Isaiah heard footsteps coming from outside and turned to see Otto come through the door, panting and out of breath.

Otto was all bent over to catch his breath, and he looked at Isaiah and barely got out the words, "Gooooooo!" Isaiah raced up the steps to the signal tower platform, and just as he reached the platform, he heard Theron bellowing, "It's too late, you can't stop it now."

Isaiah stopped and urgently shouted, "Regent Theron, you can't do this!"

"I can and I will!" thundered Theron. "This kingdom is mine, all mine, not Queen Oh…tar…a's. I built it up, I made it all work, I should be king!" and he turned and grabbed the jars out of the small closet. By now, Otto had climbed the stairs and stood beside Isaiah.

Theron continued to rant, "In a few minutes, hundreds of troops will come off that ship in the harbor and finally create order in this kingdom. You and your kind will be eliminated forever. I will be king!" Theron stepped toward the signal pot in the middle of the platform and grabbed a burning torch from a wall sconce. He heard the nine o'clock chime begin to ring and looked toward the other towers, which were coming alive with fires. The other three towers were now shining with bright blue flames that were growing by the second.

Theron turned and screamed, "Now to signal the ship and begin this war!" He threw all three jars into the signal pot and took his burning torch and touched it to the chemicals in the pot.

Isaiah heard Otto say, "I wouldn't do that if I were you!" and there was a huge explosion and flash of blue light. The blast threw Otto and Isaiah back down the stairs, where they tumbled end-over-end.

Isaiah landed on Otto, and once he gathered his senses, he and Otto raced back up the stairs to find the entire platform consumed in a blue fire. The beams that supported the roof were burning, and they heard a scream. They both looked across the platform and saw Regent Theron's clothes on fire, and he was frantically trying to put them out.

This enraged Theron even further, and he screamed, "You are a sniveling little vermin. You have been nothing but trouble since the day you got here, and I'm going to kill you once and for all." He pulled a sword out from under his coat and took a wild swing at Isaiah, who jumped out of the way. Isaiah reached into his coat and pulled the Sword of Integrity out while also putting himself in front of Otto to protect him. The structure was on fire with a bright blue light burning brightly in the pot. They danced between burning timbers that fell from the ceiling. Theron lunged at Isaiah with his sword, and Isaiah sidestepped it and easily deflected his blade. Theron lunged again, and Isaiah again easily deflected and said, "Regent Theron, I don't want to fight you. Please come with us, and we can talk." Theron became more enraged by the moment and took another huge swing at Isaiah, who threw up Integrity, which broke Theron's sword in half. Theron stood with a broken sword, which he angrily threw at Isaiah and Otto while screaming obscenities. Isaiah and Otto tried to grab him, but suddenly he ran to the edge of the platform, climbed onto the stone wall, and jumped.

Isaiah looked at Otto, stunned and not quite sure what had just happened. They ran to the ledge and looked over just in time to see a huge dagger hawk carrying Theron away into the night sky.

On the frigate, the captain of the ship and the general of the mercenaries both looked intently at the fourth tower through spy glasses. They saw the signal tower come ablaze with blue light and looked at each other. They had both expected a crimson flame launching the attack. At the same moment, a lighthouse in Gebil began flashing its light on and off in a series of distinct patterns. The captain of the ship recognized it as a form of code for communication and called for his communication officer to interpret the message.

From the signal tower, Isaiah and Otto could also see the light house flashing, and their stomachs sank. They both thought, "Was this another back-up plan by Theron or had Monsieur Dubois double-crossed them all?"

The communication officer turned to the captain and handed him a piece of paper with the message. The captain read it carefully and then turned to his first officer and said, "Weigh anchor." He handed the message to the general. The message read,

This is Monsieur Dubois. We have no disagreement with you, but if you do not leave immediately, we will blow you out of the water. The small boats around your ship are filled with enough explosives to blow the hull completely off your ship and sink you to the bottom of the bay in fifteen seconds. The next move is yours.

The captain knew immediately that Monsieur Dubois was not bluffing. While everyone's attention was on the lighting of the signal fires, the small boats had come even closer to the frigate, and the operators had swum to a waiting boat to take them to shore. The next move was his, and he wasn't going to gamble, not with Monsieur Dubois. The frigate weighed anchor, and within minutes, sails were deployed, and the ship left the harbor.

Isaiah and Otto embraced and started to cheer as they watched the frigate leave the harbor.

CHAPTER 30

WAR

Ohtara was surrounded by her royal entourage, made up of her attendants and ladies in waiting. She looked stunningly beautiful in her royal gown but was beginning to show fatigue. Erestor noted this and suggested, "Your majesty, may I suggest I escort you to your royal quarters. I am sure you want everyone to be fresh for all the activities tomorrow." This also gave the guest the liberty to call it an evening and head home since nobody dared to leave until the queen left.

Ohtara took the cue and said, "Of course, let's call it an evening," and took his arm as he led her down the long hallway. She whispered to Erestor, "Any news on Theron?"

"Nothing new, he was last seen being carried away by a dagger hawk into the night sky."

"Interesting, was the dagger hawk trained or just a free bird, so to speak? If a free bird, I expect that's the last time we ever see Theron."

Erestor smiled at her free bird comment and said, "Here we are, your majesty, at your quarters."

Ohtara smiled, leaned over, gave him a hug, and said, "Thank you for everything, my friend. Can you and Iswa meet me here at seven tomorrow morning?"

* * *

At eight o'clock the next morning, a royal officer suddenly entered the breakfast room and asked, "Have you seen her majesty this morning. I have a critical message to deliver to her. I must see her now." Both Otto and Isaiah were a bit stunned by the sense of urgency of the soldier, but both indicated they had not seen her yet.

Just then, the door opened and Ohtara stepped inside dressed in her everyday clothing. She was followed by Erestor and Iswa. Isaiah smiled and thought to himself, she's now a queen but looks no different than any other day, but then he noticed something. She had both swords and an entire array of daggers in her belt. Her hair was pulled back, and one thing was clear: this was the Ohtara who was ready for business.

"What is it, Captain?" asked Ohtara.

He handed her a message and began to talk. "One of our scouts observed the frigate anchored off the shore in Corbin Cove last night, and they began to unload troops and equipment. Another scout indicated that troops of wolves and mercenaries who had been snuck into Endemar over the previous months were also headed toward the cove to link up."

Ohtara calmly turned to Erestor and Iswa and said, "It's like we thought, this is still far from over. Theron will not give up without a fight, and if he wants a fight, that is what we will give him. Captain, convene my war council, immediately."

An hour later, Ohtara and her army officers met in a large war room at the castle. Iswa, Erestor, Otto, and Isaiah were also present in the back of the room. Isaiah noted how mature and professional Ohtara handled herself. It was like she had been preparing her whole life for this moment. He looked over at Iswa, who had a small smile of satisfaction as he watched Ohtara lead her military staff through plans to defend the city and take the fight to the enemy. He had mentored her well in military tactics.

Ohtara put her finger down on a large map at the table and declared, "Here is where we will make our stand, Sador's Pass." Generals and colonels around the table nodded their heads in agreement that this would be the right place to mount a defense. Ohtara continued, "The pass is the only way to Endemar city from that direction. If we stop them there, we can keep them out of the city and push them back to the sea. Choruses of "I agree" rang out around the table, and she began to assign generals to take battalions of soldiers to various points along Sador's Pass. "We will make the old fortress at Sador's Pass, Taras, our command center. We fight and win from there," declared Ohtara, and they all hurried out of the room.

Ohtara turned to Erestor, Iswa, Otto, and Isaiah and smiled and asked, "My friends, you have already done so much to help me get to this point, but may I ask that you stand with me one more time?"

"Of course, your majesty. We wouldn't have it any other way," they all replied in unison.

Ohtara rode Aranco to Taras, followed by her friends, each on their own horses. Taras was an old fortress that had been abandoned years ago. Walls had cracks, and plants and trees had begun to take it back over, but it did have walls and gates and would provide some fortification and protection. Ohtara began to move up and down the battle lines, encouraging soldiers to be courageous and fight to save Endemar. Isaiah took note of the fear in the young soldiers' eyes, but he also saw the confidence that came every time Ohtara spoke. Her reputation was renowned far and wide, and soldiers trusted her not only as their commander but as their new queen. She rode Aranco up to a group of soldiers trying to build a barrier and jumped off her horse and joined in helping them lift heavy logs into position.

Before they realized it, she was back on Aranco and riding off to help another group. She was continually encouraging the troops and building confidence. Isaiah was amazed at her show of leadership.

A young soldier rode up to Ohtara and handed her a note, and she turned Aranco and raced off to the ramparts of Taras. Meanwhile, Isaiah had noticed that Otto had split off and was working feverishly with a group of soldiers building something. They had erected long poles with what looked like fine wire stretched across the ramparts in a crisscross pattern over and over again. It was rather odd-looking, and he had no idea what it had to do with the pending battle.

Ohtara raced up the rampart steps, and a general handed her a spyglass which she used to peer toward the woods some five hundred yards away and the cove beyond. The general began to speak, "Scouts have told us they are forming in those woods, and a large force could attack any moment." Suddenly, they all heard a distant cannon boom, and seconds later, a shell landed forty yards short of the fortress. "They have long-range cannons on that frigate and intend to soften us up before the infantry attack." A series of distant booms was followed by explosions much closer to the fortress.

Ohtara turned to the general and said, "We can't reach the frigate, but we can reach those woods. Give them a volley to drive them out of there." The general gave the signal, and twenty cannons behind them erupted, sending shells into the woods and beyond. This forced the troops hiding in the woods to advance or retreat, and they chose to advance across the field toward Taras. Isaiah was stunned at how the woods suddenly came alive with thousands of mercenary soldiers and wolves marching quickly across the field directly at them. The frigate's cannons increased their firing, and shells were landing even closer. The ramparts were hit, and soldiers were thrown injured in all directions. The smell of gunpowder and sweat filled the air. The crackling of musket fire from soldiers rang out as the enemy troops advanced. The Endemar cannons also continued firing and found their mark by landing in groups of enemy soldiers and wolves, with many killed or wounded. However, they continued to come across the field toward Taras, getting closer with each step. Isaiah scrambled behind a wall as a shell hit nearby, but Ohtara stood on the ramparts defiantly shouting orders to troops to return fire and move into new positions. Smoke drifted over the battlefield from gun and cannon fire, along with burning structures. The enemy troops were now partially covered in smoke, and Isaiah could see them marching through the smoke, getting ever closer to the ramparts of Taras. Suddenly, he saw a battering ram appear out of the cloud of smoke. The mercenary soldiers had brought up a ram to knock down the Taras' gates. Ohtara yelled, "Archers, aim for the battering ram, fire now!"

Isaiah looked over at the archers and was stunned to see Luc standing there with his bow alongside dozens of royal archers. They let a volley go directly at the ram carriers that killed many, but they were quickly replaced by others. Troops were now at the walls and trying to put ladders up when he heard the terrifying screech he had come to detest. Isaiah spun and looked up to see at least ten huge dagger hawks sweeping down toward the troops on the ramparts. He pulled Integrity out to defend himself and looked for some cover from the diving hawks. He suddenly heard Otto scream over the noise, "Get under the wires."

The project that Otto had been working on with soldiers had strung dozens of thin wires over the ramparts of Taras. The wire was fine and nearly invisible, but very strong. As the dagger hawks dove, they twisted to lead with their venom-filled talons, but just as they reached the ramparts and were about to grab soldiers and drag them away, they hit the nearly invisible wires and suddenly found themselves thrown off balance and, in some cases, came tumbling onto the ramparts now snagged in wire. The hawks screamed in terror as archers and swordsmen attacked and killed them. Isaiah looked around, and there were five hawks lying dead on the ramparts, entangled in wire, while others were quickly fleeing.

The remaining dagger hawks regathered above Taras and began another dive at the ramparts. Much of the wire had been taken down in the first attack, so they were now more vulnerable to the remaining dagger hawks. Isaiah heard the Voice say, "Attack, use Integrity." Isaiah looked up and grabbed the hilt of Integrity and began running on the ramparts toward where the lead hawk was diving. As he ran, he thrust Integrity high above his head toward the lead dagger hawk. The sword glowed with the intensity of a thousand suns and blinded the diving hawk, who became disoriented and crashed into the rampart instead of pulling up. The hawk tumbled down the rampart directly toward Isaiah. He jumped over the tumbling hawk and spun and buried Integrity directly under its wing into its heart. The hawk let out a squawk and died. The few remaining dagger hawks broke off their attack and flew away, apparently done with this fight. Isaiah took a deep breath and suddenly noticed Iswa on the rampart fighting off mercenaries trying to breach the ramparts on ladders. Iswa smiled and yelled, "Well done, Journeyman."

The strategy had been to weaken the Royal forces with the dagger hawks, but now they could turn their attention back to the troops still trying to ram the gates, as well as those climbing ladders to enter Taras. With the royal soldier's full attention now back on the invaders, they had gained ground in repelling them. Mercenaries were falling from ladders with screams and moaning.

While fighting continued, Ohtara stood back and looked at the battlefield, and suddenly turned toward Iswa and Erestor and said, "Something's wrong, that was too easy. Where is Theron?"

Erestor responded, "Hmm...that's a good question, I haven't seen him at all."

"Didn't you say he always has a backup plan?" asked Iswa. They both nodded in agreement, and he continued, "So, what would his backup plan be in this scenario?"

Otto had walked up and, over all the noise of the ongoing battle, yelled, "Feleg Cave, we forgot about Feleg Cave!" Ohtara looked at him, stunned, knowing he was right. Isaiah turned to Erestor and yelled to be heard, "What's Feleg Cave?"

Otto explained, "Feleg Cave is a series of old gold mines that were built into the mountain years ago. They are a maze of caves and tunnels that come out on this side of the mountain at several places. Once someone enters the other side, they come to branches that split and divide and run through the whole mountain. You can get lost in there if you don't know where you are going, but you could also transport a whole army. An army that could surprise us from behind and surround us."

Ohtara turned to Erestor, Iswa, Otto, and Isaiah and said, "Take some men with you and head to the caves. Work your way toward the other side of the mountain. We must stop any troops from getting down into the tunnels and the branches. Go quickly!"

Erestor, Iswa, and Isaiah grabbed forty men and followed Otto toward the nearest tunnel entrance. Otto hurriedly grabbed some materials they might need as they left and stuffed them in his backpack. They lit torches and started into the dark tunnels and moved as fast as they could. Isaiah couldn't help but think about his experience fleeing the wolves in the caves with Dwiddle and Edam. They worked their way quickly through the caves, and Isaiah realized the complexity of the system. Branches ran off everywhere with additional branches off the branches. It made the entire inside of the mountain seem honeycombed with passages everywhere. He now understood Ohtara's command to keep the enemy troops from getting to the branches. If they reached the branches, they could just disappear and come up from behind, very quickly.

Iswa, who was at the front of the group with a scout, raised his arm for the group to stop, and he signaled to get down low. Just in front of them was a small detachment of mercenary soldiers and wolves. One of the wolves stopped, raised its head, and sniffed the air. "I smell something, smells like trouble. Fan out and sniff around." A mercenary commander roared, "No, we don't have time for your games. We must clear this path and make sure canons can get through this passage. Get back to work, you flea bags." He cracked a whip to get the wolves' attention, and with grumbling, they all went back to clearing rocks.

Iswa and Erestor silently moved into position to deal with the fifteen enemy troops, and then, without any words, there was a sudden flash of blades. Iswa and Erestor killed all fifteen without a sound being made. As Isaiah and the other troops moved forward, their torches lit up the bodies of all fifteen mercenaries and wolves now dead where they once stood.

They pressed forward toward the far entrance to the tunnel system, and Iswa stopped the group again, but this time he came back and gathered with Erestor, Otto, and Isaiah, as well as the captain of the guard. "We are very close to where the branches begin, but just ahead of us are a large number of enemy troops that are about to enter this section. We must stop them, or they can go around us or even surround us. We must seal this tunnel so they cannot use it to get to the branches. No one gets past us. Do you understand?" Everyone nodded in agreement, and then he looked at Otto and asked, "My friend, do you have a way of sealing this tunnel?"

"Yes, but I need some time to mix the right batch of explosives. Can you buy me some time? It's critical I get the mixture right and we place it as close as we can to the tunnel entrance, so the explosion seals the whole opening."

"We'll give you the time," replied Erestor, pulling his sword out of its sheath.

The forty men spread out with Iswa, Erestor, and Isaiah leading the attack. Iswa turned to Isaiah and said, "Stay by my side, and you'll be fine. Remember, the mercenary armor is weak under their arms. We protect each other."

Erestor gave the order to attack on his signal, and when they had gotten into position. He dropped his hand, and they sprang out of hiding upon the enemy soldiers. Blades flew and penetrated wolves and mercenary soldiers before they knew what had happened, but there were so many of them that some had time to put up a fight. Iswa pulled his sword back over his head and leaped at a mercenary soldier who threw up his blade to block Iswa's blade, but Iswa used his other hand to land a dagger blade blow to the stomach, and then he finished him off. A wolf jumped at Iswa while he was fighting the mercenary, and Isaiah caught it in midair with Integrity. It crumpled dead to the cave floor. Erestor quickly took out the mercenary commander in a quick sword battle. The commotion of the battle caught the attention of the soldiers outside the tunnels, and enemy commanders immediately rushed troops into the tunnel to join the fight.

The balance was now changing, and the enemy troops had the advantage with overwhelming numbers of troops. Isaiah continued to stay at Iswa's side as they fought together, wildly repelling enemy soldiers and wolves one after another. Erestor was doing the same on the other side of Iswa, and the royal troops were holding their own, though they had taken some casualties. The clang of blades was deafening as swords rattled back and forth. Musket fire was heard echoing off the walls of the tunnel, and gun smoke filled the tunnel.

Dead enemy soldiers and wolves were piling up, but they just kept coming down the tunnel. Isaiah was landing blow after blow, and fatigue began to set in. He thought, *How long can we keep doing this?*

The royal force was slowly getting pushed back down the tunnel as enemy troops kept coming down the tunnel to fight. The enemy did not seem to care how many men or wolves they lost. They were determined to come down this tunnel. Iswa called out, in a loud shout, "Otto, how much longer?"

Otto, who was working feverishly to mix gunpowder and some nitrates back down the tunnel, yelled, "Just about there, give me a minute."

"We may not have a minute," came a response from Erestor. The royal force was now pushed back to just in front of where Otto was working, and fighting was going on all around him.

Otto yelled, "I got it ... it's ready, but it's got to go off in the entrance!" The group had been pushed twenty-five to thirty yards up into the cave, and just before the first branch. Time had run out.

Iswa turned to Erestor and shouted, "We've got to push them back to get this explosive planted right!"

"I know, but there are just too many of them," yelled back Erestor. Iswa and Erestor were now shoulder to shoulder, swinging their blades back and forth again and again, but even they were growing weak. Gun smoke, sweat, and blood filled the cave along with the wounded, dead, and dying.

Isaiah looked back at Otto, who was holding the backpack filled with explosives in front of him with two hands. He looked ahead at the carnage and the mass of enemy troops in front of him and took a deep breath, and said to himself, *Knowing the right thing to do and doing it sometimes has a high cost.* Confidence welled up inside him, and power surged through him. He grabbed Integrity's hilt a little tighter and turned and looked at Otto, who looked overwhelmed with fear in his eyes. Isaiah smiled and said, "I got this. Give me the backpack." Otto was frozen by the scene and didn't respond. Isaiah took a step closer to Otto and got right up in his face and said confidently, "Otto, I got this, give me the backpack!" Otto's eyes met Isaiah's, and he let go of the backpack. As Isaiah turned with the backpack, Otto yelled, "Isaiah, pull the cord and make sure you get as far away as possible; you only have ten seconds.

Isaiah nodded and took off running directly up the tunnel toward the entrance, carrying the bag of explosives directly through the oncoming enemy soldiers. He swung Integrity and landed blow after blow. He landed blows first on his right side and then his left, and then back to his right, and over and over again as he ran through the enemy soldiers as hard and fast as he could travel. Suddenly, there was a huge explosion.

CHAPTER 31

FINAL SHOWDOWN

Ohtara's troops had turned the tide on the advancing enemy forces. The mercenaries and wolves had pulled back to regroup and make another attempt with the battering ram when Ohtara heard new rounds of cannon fire. The cannon fire sounded quite different, though, than what she had heard earlier. She grabbed her spyglass and scanned the woods and cove beyond, where she saw three schooners now sailing around the frigate and unleashing cannon fire on the large ship. They were much smaller than the frigate, but in the cove, the frigate could not maneuver easily while the schooners were quick and responsive. Their cannons were no match for the frigates, but they were still able to inflict damage. Ohtara watched one of the large frigate masts and sails plummet to the deck. She also saw small fires burning on the deck. She scanned the decks of the schooners and could see the distinguished figure of Monsieur Dubois. He had chosen to join the fight on the lead schooner. She smiled and thought, *These last two days have been filled with surprises.*

With the frigate now occupied by the schooner attack, Ohtara saw an opportunity to order a counterattack. She immediately ordered her troops to charge the enemy lines. She climbed on Aranco and rode back and forth in front of the troops with her sword high above her head. She screamed, "Soldiers of Endemar, this day is your day, your day to take back your kingdom, your day to right wrongs done by Regent Theron, so fight! Fight for your freedom, fight for your families, fight for Endemar! Attack!" and she turned and led thousands of troops as they raced across the field with blood-curdling screams toward the enemy lines.

The mercenaries and wolves had not expected the counterattack and were stunned and intimidated by the voracious attack. All discipline broke down among the enemy troops, and some turned and ran as they tried to get away from the oncoming onslaught. Ohtara and her cavalry swept through the enemy troops with their swords, landing blow after blow on fleeing mercenaries and wolves. Those who decided to hold their ground were rapidly surrounded by royal troops who dispatched them quickly.

Ohtara reached the woods with her cavalry, who were soon followed by infantry. They pursued the enemy through the woods to the coast while completely devastating them, but just as Ohtara reached the woods, she heard a massive explosion to the north. She stopped Aranco in his tracks to assess what had just happened and said, "Aranco, we must hurry, run swiftly, my friend," and Aranco and Ohtara raced off in the direction of the explosion.

* * *

The explosion was massive and threw rocks in all directions. Mercenaries and wolves inside the cave were either knocked over by the blast or killed. The same occurred to enemy troops massed directly outside the cave entrance. The rocks hurled at them like missiles and wiped entire lines of soldiers away like an angry hand sweeping across a chess table. There was nothing left but the sound of tumbling rocks settling to the ground. The blast had been so large that there were no bodies. They were simply gone, vaporized, or blown away by the blast.

The ground began to shift and move, and a dust-covered arm reached up and pulled away rock, gravel, and dust. A head covered completely in dust began to appear, and the individual coughed to clear his lungs and slowly pulled himself up to his feet while he tried to brush some of the dust away. Isaiah stood, covered in white dust from head to toe, and tried to grasp the enormity of what had just happened. He had grabbed the explosives from Otto and run as hard as he could up the cave toward the entrance. As he fought his way there, he pulled the delayed fuse and threw the bag of explosives against an entrance wall and kept running straight ahead. He realized there was no use in going back, so he kept running as hard as he could. He immediately saw a crevice in the rocks to his left just outside the entrance. He remembered that he had escaped the dagger hawk when he used a similar crevice, so he dived headfirst into it just as the explosion went off. The blast went right over top of him, throwing rocks the size of boulders. He was miraculously unscathed and just covered in dust from the explosion. He looked around and saw nothing but debris and trees that were now damaged from the rock blast.

"You're a disgusting little brat. You have been a pain since the day you arrived in Endemar. Constantly sticking your nose in my business," screamed Theron as he pulled himself up over a pile of rocks. His once distinguished regent robes were now tattered and covered in dust. His gray hair was all over the place and made him look wild, unkept, maniacal, and unbalanced in appearance. "I am going to kill you once and for all," as he lifted his sword above his head.

"No, you're not, he's mine," shouted Temp, who came over another pile of rocks opposite Theron. "This day has been coming for a long time. Do you remember Isaiah? I always said, one day, yes, one day, you and I would have at it. Well, today's the day. Just you and me. Let's do this." Temp was coming toward Isaiah, growling with drool running out of his mouth. His eyes were a brilliant yellow with black pupils standing out like daggers. "I am going to enjoy killing you, and I am going to do it slowly."

"Easy boys, let's just take a moment and take this all in," came the voice of the Dark Prince, the hooded figure that Isaiah had dealt with the night before. He appeared standing between Theron and Temp, with Theron on his right and Temp on his left. "Perhaps, young Isaiah has reconsidered his situation and wants to join us, or maybe he has had enough and just wants to go home. Obviously, all your friends are dead and buried in that cave. My offer is still on the table, Isaiah. Join us or simply walk away right now, and all of this pain and suffering can end...right now. It will be like it never happened. Just walk away or better yet... join us and bask in the rewards that will ultimately be ours because you know, we will win, yes, that is inevitable."

Isaiah stood up tall and looked at the Dark Prince and said, "I am a Journeyman! I have been called on a mission by the Prince of Light to save Endemar. I will never join you, and I will never walk away. I am where I am supposed to be and doing the thing I should be doing, fighting the likes of you three."

The Prince of Darkness recoiled at the mention of the Prince of Light and angrily said, "Very well, then, boys, have at him. Just not quickly, I rather enjoy the pain and suffering part."

Both Theron and Temp started to step toward Isaiah, and he reached for Integrity, but it was no longer on his belt. In the course of the explosion, it had become detached and was lost somewhere, most likely under tons of rubble. He took a deep breath and said a prayer. If this was the way it was meant to be, then so be it. He would fight them both with his bare hands, and he took a defensive fight stance.

"How about we even this up a bit," came a voice from the top of a rubble pile. Silhouetted by the sun behind her stood Ohtara. She stood with her long coat and hair blowing in the breeze and a sword in each hand. She looked at Isaiah and asked, "Are you alright?" and he nodded at her, and Isaiah suddenly heard the Voice speak to him, "Remember the sword chooses those who are worthy, so extend your hand and receive it."

A smile came across Isaiah's face, and he reached back and opened the palm of his hand while not taking his eyes off Theron, Temp, or the Prince of Darkness. Suddenly, the rocks began to vibrate and move. They tumbled away and opened, and the Sword of Integrity flew out of the pile of rocks and landed hilt-first squarely in Isaiah's hand.

Ohtara smiled and returned her attention to the evil triad, "Theron, you have lied, cheated, stolen, killed, and nearly destroyed the kingdom of Endemar. That all ends today!"

Theron screamed and lunged toward Ohtara, swinging his sword. She easily side-stepped and threw up her sword to block his swing, and he fell forward into the dirt. He struggled to his feet and screamed, "I deserve to be king, not you, a wretched gardener. You are not worthy. I have led this group of misfits, cowards, and 'ne'er-do-wells' for years. It is I and I alone who built Endemar into what it is. It's mine, not yours," and he took another wild swing at Ohtara, who again blocked it easily, but this time the sword flew out of his hand and landed in the dirt six feet away.

"I am the daughter of King Aran, the rightful heir of the throne of Endemar. Led by the Prince of Light and guided by the Voice I have endured, I have prepared, I have fought evil and I... am the queen."

"Speaking of your father, King Aran. His death was a horrible way to die. It's amazing what concentrated dagger hawk venom can do to a person when they drink it in their ale. It was truly horrible, but I was rather proud of myself for the creativity and initiative," sneered Theron.

Ohtara's eyes became fixed on Theron as she contemplated how to react to the revelation that he had poisoned her father. Rage boiled up inside her, and through gritted teeth, she spoke, "I should kill you right here, but I choose not to begin my reign with your blood on my sword. Leave this place and never return. If you do, it will be your instant death. Now go!" Ohtara turned her back to look at Isaiah, and he screamed, "Look out!"

Theron had pulled out a dagger and was about to throw it directly into Ohtara's back, but out of nowhere, an arrow flew and buried itself in Theron's heart before he could release the dagger. Theron fell backward dead. Ohtara spun and looked up at a pile of rocks and saw Luc standing with his bow in his hand, still aimed at Theron.

Luc smiled and nodded at Ohtara, "Sorry, I'm still a work in progress. Just couldn't let him walk away after he tried throwing a dagger in your back."

Isaiah turned back to Temp and said, "Yes, our day has arrived, let's finish this." Temp lunged at Isaiah, who stepped aside, avoiding his fangs, which were snarling and snapping at Isaiah as he passed within inches of his throat. Temp quickly gathered himself and crept closer, being more measured in his attack this time. He lunged again, and a claw caught Isaiah's back as he dove to the ground and rolled under Temp. Blood began to trickle down Isaiah's back and could be seen through his torn shirt and coat.

"Ah...first blood, I love it. It's just a precursor to what is to come; more blood, more pain, then weakness and finally death." Temp lunged again, but Isaiah raised Integrity and slashed Temp across the face. Temp now had an ugly blade slash across his face that ran across his snout and over his left eye. Blood flowed readily from the wound.

"Yes, you were right, more blood, but not mine, but rather yours," taunted Isaiah.

Temp was now enraged and gathered himself for a final death blow to Isaiah. He had decided it was enough. It was time to kill this young boy. "Young man, this is your end. It all ends today. You are not worthy of me," and he lunged straight at Isaiah with his claws out and fangs open, ready to clamp down and snap Isaiah's neck in one motion.

Isaiah went to a knee, sliding under the lunging wolf and ramming Integrity into Temp's underbelly. There was an audible yelp by Temp and a sudden release of air as he tumbled onto the ground in a heap. As Temp lay there bleeding and gasping for air, he began to transform back into a man. The same tall thin man with shoulder-length black and gray hair and dark eyes. The man stumbled to his feet and immediately slipped off into the woods, leaving Ohtara, Isaiah, and the Prince of Darkness.

A noise behind Isaiah caused him to spin and look back at rocks being pushed out of the way. He recognized Iswa's gray hair as it popped out of the collapsed tunnel entrance. Iswa climbed out, followed by Erestor, Otto, and royal soldiers. They had survived the blast and dug their way out of the tunnel.

Isaiah turned his attention back to the Prince of Darkness, who stood there unmoved by the events that had transpired, and said, "You can't win. You do realize that, don't you? Man's heart is inherently evil and dark. Men will go on cheating one another, stealing from one another, hurting one another, and ultimately killing one another. It's inevitable."

Ohtara came alongside Isaiah, as did Erestor and Iswa on his other side. Isaiah looked at Erestor and said, "Good to see you," and Erestor simply nodded and, with a smile, replied, "It is good to be seen." Isaiah looked at the Prince of Darkness and said, "I know we have many faults, and we will continue to make mistakes, but I also know the Prince of Light and his Voice. He will continue to call men to take a stand against you and your kind. I know that light, even the smallest light, always repels darkness," and Isaiah lifted Integrity to his shoulder height, and it began glowing. "The more light that is shown forth, the harder it is for darkness to win. People begin to see the darkness for what it really is: empty lies and promises that lead to pain and suffering. To change the world, it takes men knowing the right thing to do and doing it, despite the cost." As he spoke, he lifted the Sword of Integrity over his head, and it was glowing brighter than a thousand suns.

The Prince of Darkness screeched in pain and revulsion at light and began to back up and get smaller and smaller until it disappeared. There was sudden quiet and peace over what had been a brutal battlefield.

CHAPTER 32

SIR ISAIAH

The next morning, Isaiah came down from his room to the breakfast area at what he now had learned was the Summer Palace. Otto walked in and sat down to drink a cup of hot tea and smiled and said, "Yesterday was quite a day."

Isaiah laughed and said, "Yes, it was, but perhaps you could fill in a few holes for me."

Otto smiled and said, "Of course, you deserve some explanations," and he continued,

"Ohtara's mother died in childbirth, and her father died shortly thereafter. Some say from a broken heart, but we now know he was poisoned. Ohtara's father, King Aran, Erestor, and I had been best friends from childhood, and when he found out that he was dying, he asked us to care for and protect Ohtara until she could become queen. He knew that his enemies would try to find her and kill her to take over the kingdom. We vowed to hide, protect, and make sure Ohtara was well prepared to become Queen of Endemar on her eighteenth birthday. We decided the best thing was to get her out of Endemar, so we took her to Tiree, to Purposeville, and to Riddle. We added Iswa, Hon, and Esty, and we became a brotherhood of protection."

Isaiah shifted closer to Otto and listened carefully to Otto's words. His eyes grew large as he realized the linkage of Ohtara to Riddle, as well as Iswa, Hon, and Esty.

Otto continued, "She lived there, was raised there, and was educated by the teachers and trained to be a watchman by Iswa, Hon, and Esty. All had a role in her upbringing until she was thirteen years old.

When she turned thirteen, she returned to Endemar and lived at the old Summer Palace as a gardener in the orchard where only Erestor and I knew her true identity. She daily interacted with the citizens of Endemar and learned about their lives and struggles. Her skills as a horsewoman and swordsman became legendary as she stood up for the oppressed and sought justice for the abused. Men of evil intent came to fear her, while everyday men and women saw her as their champion.

King Aran established her eighteenth birthday, two days ago, as Ascension Day. Regent Theron knew the date and that King Aran had once had an heir, but he had no idea who it was or if they were male or female. No one, except our small brotherhood, knew if an heir would even show up. We had watched Theron for years grow into a power-hungry despot who was obsessed with power, money, and fame. It became clear that he would not step down graciously. This all led us to the successful ascension to the throne of Queen Ohtara and the battle we engaged in yesterday."

Isaiah sat quietly and listened as Otto described the decisions and events of Ohtara's life. He could only smile and realize how his steps had been orchestrated by the Voice to be a part of all that had happened in the last few days. He felt humble, very humble.

Otto stopped and looked directly into Isaiah's eyes and said, "Thank you, my friend, my brother," and quickly wiped his eyes and added, "I must be off to the orchards, I have been neglecting them far too much lately." He stood up and headed out the back door toward the orchards.

Isaiah was left alone at the breakfast table, processing everything Otto had just told him, along with the events of the last few days. He decided to take a walk through the orchard to clear his head and determine his next step on his journey.

Isaiah walked a short distance and stopped at a grand vista view of the orchards. He heard a voice say. "Beautiful, isn't it?"

He recognized the voice of Ohtara and turned to see her and instantly threw his arms around her to hug her. He then stopped and said, "Ah…ah…excuse me, your majesty. It was inappropriate of me. I beg your forgiveness…please."

She looked at him, shook her head, and laughed. Ohtara smiled and stopped him before he said another word, "Isaiah, when we are together, you need not call me majesty, I am simply Ohtara, your very dear friend."

Isaiah returned the smile, and both turned once again to look at the view. "Oh, by the way, happy belated birthday. Did you do anything special?"

Ohtara laughed, shook her head, and put her arm around Isaiah, beginning a slow walk with him. "So, tell me, Journeyman, what have you learned?" she asked with a low voice like Iswa's, and then she giggled.

Isaiah also laughed but took a moment to gather his thoughts and then spoke, "I struggled with Theron's speeches and promises to everyone. He represented himself as one way, but then in reality he was someone completely different."

Ohtara listened intently and responded, "It is an ugly thing when a man sells his integrity. Theron sold his integrity a long time ago when he started lying to people and trying to manipulate people and situations, all for his own benefit. A man's word is incredibly important; it defines his character. When he says something, is it true? When he promises something, does he follow through and deliver, or at least try his best to fulfil the promise? Theron not only lied to people, but he also lied to himself by continually justifying his actions."

Ohtara paused and then continued, "When a man doesn't conduct his life with integrity, he destroys trust. He may get by with no integrity for a while, but once exposed, it destroys all his credibility, and it is very hard to rebuild."

She turned to Isaiah, grabbed his shoulders with both her hands, looked straight into his eyes, took a deep breath, and said, "A man's integrity cannot really be stolen; it can only be forfeited."

They walked a bit further, and Isaiah asked, "Were you surprised that Monsieur Dubois testified in front of the Senate?'

Ohtara smiled and nodded her head, "Yes, I was. I understand that you had a lot to do with that."

Isaiah looked at her, a bit confused.

"It turns out that what really impacted and convinced Monsieur Dubois was a certain young man who saved his son's life. He repaid that debt and realized Theron was behind trying to kill his son. He decided it was time to get involved."

Isaiah looked at Ohtara, who smiled, lowered her voice, and with another giggle said, "Well done, Journeyman, well done."

She suddenly stopped and said with surprise, "Oh, we're here, come with me," and Isaiah followed her up the steps into the beautiful cathedral in the orchard. Ohtara led him to the very front, where there was an altar with a huge cross hanging from the ceiling. The light filtered through the massive stained-glass window that created a rainbow of colors through the building, which reflected off marble floors, columns, and the altar itself. The scene was breathtaking.

Ohtara walked to the very front as Isaiah trailed behind her, and she suddenly stopped in front of the altar and turned to Isaiah and said, "Isaiah, please kneel."

Isaiah looked around, confused and somewhat self-conscious, but wanted to be obedient to Ohtara, so he kneeled in front of her. Ohtara reached into a wooden box that had been laid on the altar and turned to face a now kneeling Isaiah.

"Isaiah, it turns out that as Queen of Endemar, I have certain rights, privileges, and responsibilities. One of those responsibilities is to recognize those who have distinguished themselves with bravery, service, and integrity to the Kingdom of Endemar. You, my dear friend, have done all three, and as Queen, it is my privilege to recognize you. It turns out that as queen, I alone have the right to bestow knighthood. So, my dear friend Isaiah, as Queen of Endemar," and she reached in the box and pulled out a sword and placed it on his right shoulder and then his left, saying, "I do knight you as a Royal Knight of the Kingdom of Endemar with all associated privileges and responsibilities. From now on, you shall be known as…Sir Isaiah…you may now rise."

The stillness of the cathedral was broken by hands clapping and shouts of, "Here, here!" from behind Isaiah. He turned, and standing behind him were Erestor, Otto, Iswa, Hon, Esty, and Riddle, along with Dwiddle, Sarta, and their kids, all cheering. Isaiah could say nothing but, "Thank you," while tears streamed down his face.

Ohtara hugged Isaiah and said, "Sir Isaiah, walk with me and Iswa." The three of them walked out of the cathedral and into the orchard with no words being spoken.

Finally, Iswa spoke, "Isaiah, you have completed your mission; you helped save Endemar. You also saved Luc…multiple times and have helped set him on a new direction in his life." Isaiah looked at Iswa with a puzzled look. "Oh, you didn't hear? Luc is going to go back to Tiree with me and spend some time with all of us." A big grin appeared on Isaiah's face.

Ohtara chimed in, "Isaiah, it is amazing what happens when someone chooses to do the right thing. It can have a profound impact on many people's lives. Luc has been changed, the citizens of Endemar have been impacted, and even Monsieur Dubois appears to have been impacted."

"However, your mission is over, and it is time to go home," interjected Iswa.

Tears, once again, welled up in Isaiah's eyes. He didn't want to leave his friends, but deep inside, he knew it was time. Time to go home to his mother, father, and brothers.

* * *

The next morning, the brotherhood escorted Isaiah into the woods well beyond the palace grounds. They came to a clearing, and Isaiah hugged each one, and they all cried tears of joy. Ohtara and Iswa each put a hand on his shoulder and said, "Well done, Journeyman, well done."

Isaiah looked at Iswa and said, "Who can I ever talk to about what happened here, who will understand?"

Iswa paused and then looked Isaiah in the eyes and said, "I understand that Riddle told you about the two journeymen I trained before you. One of those was named Pierre, and the other was named Charles. I think you'll have someone on the other side who will not only be a good listener but understand."

Iswa smiled and put his hands on Isaiah's shoulders and looked deep into his eyes. "It is time for you to go home...Sir Isaiah."

The entire group hugged one last time, and Isaiah turned to Iswa and asked, "But how do I get home?"

Iswa responded, "The same way you came…across the river," and he gestured with his open hand over Isaiah's shoulder. Isaiah turned and saw the same swift-moving river he had crossed weeks before. There was a large tree lying across the river; however, this one looked much more stable than the first tree he used to cross the river.

Isaiah turned, smiled, and said, "Of course."

Isaiah went down to the tree and turned to wave goodbye, and Ohtara called out, "Oh, by the way, I believe you'll find your farmhouse just around the bend."

Isaiah took one last look at his friends, his brothers, and sisters, and walked across the tree to the other side. As he stepped off the tree to solid ground, he stopped hearing the rushing water and realized he was back in his world. He couldn't help but turn and look back, but all he saw was a dusty road and trees. He smiled and started to walk down the road but stopped and felt his belt; his sword was gone. He felt all around, but it was nowhere to be found. He then felt something fairly large in his pouch. He reached in and found a book and slowly pulled it out. It was a copy of the Good Book, a new kind of sword.

CHAPTER 33

HOME

Isaiah knew what he must do when he got home. He walked into the barnyard and looked immediately for his father, Charles. He ran to the barn, but he was not there, so he ran to the wood mill and found him sharpening blades. As he got to the door, his father looked up, and a big grin appeared on his face. He ran to Isaiah and threw his arms around him. They both stood there and held onto each other with no words spoken. Both understood the moment, and yet neither had words to adequately express their feelings.

Finally, Isaiah whispered, "I love you, Dad," and they cried together. After several minutes, Isaiah asked his dad to sit down. "Dad, I have much to tell you about my adventures, but first I need to talk to you about the fire that destroyed Granny Rose's store."

Isaiah explained everything that happened that night, including his being asked to be a lookout. He apologized and took responsibility for not coming forward and telling the truth about what had happened. He also talked about his fears of intimidation and bullying, and that he wanted to do the right thing but had been afraid. He asked his father to forgive him for not standing up and acting with integrity. Finally, he told his father he fully intended to confront Jason and Brian about their involvement.

Charles listened quietly and smiled with pride at his son's maturity and willingness to take ownership of his role in the fire. He was also pleased with his commitment to challenge the other two boys to come forward. After Isaiah had laid out the story, Charles asked, "Would you like me to come with you to talk to the sheriff?"

Isaiah looked grateful and said, "Thank you, Dad. That would help, but before I go to the sheriff, I want to give Brian and Jason a chance to come forward with me. Do you understand?"

Charles understood and nodded in agreement.

Isaiah stood up and said, "I am going now to find them. I'll meet you at the sheriff's office in an hour." Isaiah left the wood mill and headed directly into town to find Jason and Brian. He looked at the usual places, including behind the grist mill, where they often hung out shooting their slingshots, and downtown at Jason's family general store. They were nowhere to be found, but he decided to go over to Brian's family barn, where he finally found them.

Jason looked up when Isaiah walked in and said, "Hey, Owens, where have you been? We haven't seen you in a long time."

"Been on a journey."

Brian laughed and said, "What did you have to do, deliver some firewood or eggs?"

Isaiah didn't respond to the comment but stood in the center of the room, looking at the two older and larger boys. He stood tall and spoke with conviction and confidence in his voice, "We need to discuss what happened a few weeks ago in the alley."

The barn was suddenly very quiet, and Brian stood up from the bench he was sitting on and walked right up to Isaiah and looked down on him in an act of intimidation. "What do you mean we have to talk? We have nothing to talk about, and neither do you...punk." Jason laughed and walked up next to Brian.

"Nobody talks about anything. This is all in the past. You'll keep your mouth shut if you know what's good for you."

Isaiah stood his ground and didn't move and responded, "I want you both to know that I am going forward to the sheriff. I encourage you both to go with me. It's the right thing to do."

Jason tried to shove Isaiah backward, but when he hit him in the chest, Isaiah didn't move. Jason got right in Isaiah's face and screamed, "Don't tell me what to do, punk!" He then stepped back and took a swing at Isaiah, who quickly and easily ducked it, which caused Jason to lose his balance and fall to the ground. Brian lunged at Isaiah, who calmly stepped aside, causing Brian to also miss and fall over Jason.

"I am going to the sheriff to tell him the whole story. I encourage you both to join me and come clean on what happened."

Jason had gotten back on his feet and was now swinging wildly at Isaiah, who slipped each punch effortlessly. He started to curse Isaiah in an effort to intimidate him, but Isaiah simply smiled and asked, "Won't you join me at the sheriff's office. I am on my way there now."

Jason picked up an axe handle off the workbench and put it right under Isaiah's nose. "I am going to beat you senseless if you say a word...and then I am going after your brothers." Isaiah stepped backward and saw a broom leaning against the barn wall and quickly stomped on it, breaking the broom end off. He now had a makeshift wooden sword. He spun it in his hand and came down across Jason's axe handle, knocking it out of his hand. He then swiftly brought the broom handle up behind Jason's knees, taking his legs out from under him. Jason hit the floor hard and lay there gasping for air with his eyes wide open. Isaiah pointed the broken end of the broom handle right in Jason's face and said, "Don't ever threaten my family again, or I will be back...and I won't be so generous next time. For that matter, stop bullying everyone, including Peter."

Brian had scrambled back to his feet and screamed, "Why are you doing this? Why can't you just leave it alone?"

Isaiah looked at him and calmly said, "I am doing this because it's the right thing to do, the honest thing to do. Will you join me?"

Both Jason and Brian screamed additional threats at Isaiah, but his resolve simply grew, and he turned to leave. But, before he left, he stopped and pointed the broken end of the broom handle under Brian's chin and firmly demanded, "Brian, I also want Granny Rose's box...right now!"

"I don't know what you're talking about," screamed Brian.

"Yes, you do, it was the box you ran out of the store with under your arm," said Isaiah.

Brian looked stunned at Isaiah's recollection of the events, but still protested, "I said, I don't know what you're talking about."

"Ok, then the sheriff can add grand larceny to the charge of arson."

Brian looked stunned at the revelation and became very nervous, moved to a cabinet in the barn, and opened a door with shaking hands. "Here, take the stupid box. I could never get it open anyway." He threw the box at Isaiah and stormed out of the barn. Jason left behind him, cursing Isaiah.

Isaiah tossed the broom handle aside and walked out of the barn carrying Granny Rose's box under his arm. As he left, his eyes caught a glimpse of movement from the woods behind the barn. He turned his head and froze. In the distant woods, he saw the now familiar hue of narrow yellow eyes and white bared teeth. A low guttural growl came from the wolf, and Isaiah stood his ground and stared him down. Isaiah shook his head from side to side and calmly and firmly said, "No, not today, you don't scare me... now, get!" The wolf turned and ran off into the woods, and Isaiah turned back and saw his dad leaning against a large oak tree across the road. His dad smiled and said, "Well done, Journeyman, well done."

Isaiah and Charles went to the sheriff's office, where Isaiah told him the whole story about the night of the fire, which included his role as a lookout. He talked about hiding and then took responsibility for not coming forward. He wanted the sheriff to know that he accepted responsibility for his part in the events of that evening. The sheriff listened carefully and took notes.

The next day, the sheriff brought Brian and Jason into his office with their parents for a conversation that lasted for several hours. Jason and Brian would have to pay restitution for the damages they caused and do some community service. Isaiah willingly accepted discipline, including detentions and a loss of privileges for a while, but he accepted them all to bring closure. He reminded himself that knowing the right thing to do and doing it sometimes has a cost.

Two days later, on a fall afternoon with the leaves changing colors, Isaiah walked through the downtown area with a burlap bag hung over his shoulder. He saw Granny Rose sitting on the bench across from her store, which was nearly done with repairs. He walked up to the bench and sat down beside her and said, "Hello, Granny Rose."

Granny Rose smiled and said, "Oh my dear Isaiah, how are you? Please tell me about all your adventures, I want to hear everything and don't leave out a thing, not a single thing." She winked at Isaiah as she repeated, "Not a single thing."

Isaiah smiled back, "Of course, but before we get into that, I have something for you," and he reached into the burlap bag and pulled out Granny's box.

A broad smile lit up Granny's face and she became very excited, "Oh my, my box, my box. Where did you find it? I have so missed it. I thought I'd never see this again. It holds my most precious treasures."

Isaiah smiled and said, "Well, I'll get into that story in a minute, but first, I always wondered, what are the treasures that you have in this box?"

Pure joy came across Granny's face, and she said, "Oh, of course, these are my most precious possessions, and she proceeded to take her necklace off and fit the stone from the pendant into a section on the lid of the box. The lid popped open, and it was full of letters and two small jars. "These are more precious than gold to me," said Granny. "They are letters from my loved ones, and these jars hold locks of hair from my son and my granddaughter. I believe you have met her; she's the Queen of Endemar.

— The End —